CANARY GIRL

ABIGAIL C. EDWARDS
CANARY GIRL

Canary Girl by Abigail C. Edwards

acedwardsbooks.com

Copyright © 2024 Abigail C. Edwards. All rights reserved. No portion of this book may be reproduced in any form without permission from the publisher, except as permitted by U.S. copyright law. For permissions contact: acedwardsbooks@gmail.com

ISBN: 9798346633464 (print) First Edition

To Claudia,
who looked at me one night from across our bedroom
and said, with the utmost despair:
"What if no one ever knows about Harry Markus?"
Now they do.

-A.C.E.

AUTHOR'S NOTE

I've written and rewritten and trashed this forward more times than I can count. Memories twist and malform in retrospect. As with the writing process of this book itself, characters fall in and out of play, making this tale even more troublesome to tell with each passing year. I do not know how much to tell, nor how to tell it, yet I've mustered the audacity to make a bold attempt.

I often say the predecessor of *Canary Girl* was born on my 14th birthday, but it was actually several months prior. My sister and a couple of our friends began writing a story together over Gmail chat and emails—back and forth entries in the form of a diary, from my perspective. The resulting book was a jumbled mess of contradictions and violent deaths; people we perceived to have wronged us in some way made appearances as villains, and we were all involved in secret "world powers" trying to take over the universe. The story leapfrogged from kidnappings to attempted assassinations to air raids. And the character of Abby was a brash 14-year-old who wrote a prophecy that served as "the key to world domination": Incredibly Inspired Information. *The Triple I.*

On the morning of my 14th birthday, I woke to an email from an unknown address in my inbox. It contained a single line: *in the dirt we mumble.* I truly do not know what went through my mind when I read that, but as I recollect, I didn't give it much thought. I suppose I assumed it was spam. I simply deleted it and didn't think to tell anyone. Later in the day, when my friends and my sister Claudia sat down to read *The Triple I* aloud to me and that line made an appearance in the first diary entry, Claudia revealed that she'd created an email address simply to send that email.

They read the story aloud over the course of the afternoon. It was insane and nearly impossible to follow. At the time, I don't think any of us really believe it would go beyond that.

Over the course of the next year, we were proven wrong. For each person's birthday, the other three would team up and write a sequel. The stories grew progressively worse. The rules for the universe we'd created grew more tense and fights broke out. We wrote spinoff shorts that some of us embraced as canon and others hated. One of these was an origin story for the suave anti-hero Harry Markus, a creation birthed from the mind of Claudia, as Athena from the cranium of Zeus.

I remember the night we made the decision. Our family had moved to Monticello nearly a year before. Claudia and I held out hope that we'd construct DIY loft beds in our room, but we hadn't settled on a design, so we still slept on mattresses on the floor. We sat across our bedroom from each other.

"What if no one ever knows about Harry Markus?" Claudia said.

The next day we parked it on the front porch with a thick stack of our "fake books"—the badly-formatted, stapled tomes of fan-fiction and canon installments in what we'd titled "The Doomsday Chronicles". We began drafting up a plan. The idea was to integrate all the stories into a single book, to somehow make it palatable to a wider audience, to save every character and every scrap of a scene. We rearranged scenes and removed vital characters, we integrated 50-page info-dumps into climactic points in the novel, we changed names and ages and locations. In the days following, when Claudia admitted that she didn't have the time to continue the project and left it in my undeserving hands, I grappled on my own with the themes and tones and inspirations behind this train wreck of a novel. I didn't know what I was writing. I didn't understand the character of Veronica—was she still me? I was scared to remove vital scenes from the original series. My inspirations were Marvel films, Stephanie Meyer's *The Host,* Douglas Adams. I floundered.

In May of 2022 I visited Claudia in Glasgow. I was in my senior year at Florida State, and I escaped for spring break to the Kelvinbridge area, where I sat in the park and read Neil Gaiman, and wandered the Art

Gallery with Lana Del Rey in my earbuds, and I sat myself at a cafe and I finished writing what would become the final form of *Canary Girl*. I edited and I let it stew. I published *The Time Walker*, and still, I let it stew. In October of 2023, Claudia told me it was time to quit procrastinating: summer of 2024 would be the ten-year anniversary of *The Triple I*; if there was ever a time for *Canary Girl* to happen, it was now.

In a way, this was terrible news, as I was in the process of leaving a job and moving from Dunbar to Edinburgh. Since then, I've moved flats a second time.

I think I am constantly running from something. I don't know what it is, but sometimes I feel it breathing down my neck. Maybe I'm worried that if I stay still and silent for too long, I'll get a good look at myself and my life and there's no coming back from that. Perhaps I'm like those twigs I wrote about, in the stream—always racing, never stationary, tumultuous and fleeting. Whatever the case, I don't think I properly understood Veronica Lewis until now; I didn't know what *Canary Girl* needed to be when I was 14. Ten years and four-thousand miles works its magic in growing pains and tectonic fissures between the past and present.

Canary Girl is a story about trust broken and purely selfish motives. It's about how the inside of someone's head can be significantly scarier than anything playing out in reality. It's about backwater towns that cling to your skin like an oil film, slick and inescapable; and it's about escape. It's the fearful breakaway, freedom to fuck up your own life and claw it back again. It's about consequences. It's about loneliness; it's about aloneness; it's about how those aren't the same thing, but they can sting the same way.

In many ways, it's the book I needed when I was fourteen and felt unlovable. It's the book Claudia and I would have laughed and cried over if we'd discovered it in our teens. It's a book with ten years of my life caught between the words.

It's also the stupidest thing I've ever written.

Cheers,
    Abby

"All through my life I've had this strange unaccountable feeling that something was going on in the world, something big, even sinister, and no one would tell me what it was."

"No," said the old man, "that's just perfectly normal paranoia. Everyone in the Universe has that."

- Douglas Adams, *The Hitchhiker's Guide to the Galaxy*

The Canary (I)

Close your eyes.

You are not a man. You are a wisp of vapor, and you will be gone by morning. You are something that lives in the hills and gazes at the stars. It's photosynthesis without the light. You do not recall the last time you cried.

Cryptid. This is madness.

When dawn breaks and spills golden light across the mountainside, you'll dissipate with the mist. This is your last night on earth, and instead of praying and pleading to a god of your choice, emptying your head onto paper, holding your daughter in your arms, you stand in the mountains with the weight of inevitability crushing your chest.

Cryptid. You are not a man. Perhaps you never were.

A year ago, the sky broke open upon this same mountain range. Weather alerts could not be dispatched fast enough; the storm came without warning. Low clouds rolled through the mist-laden hills and emptied their contents in the form of hail and gargantuan raindrops, wind that bent the trees nearly in half, wind that whipped the dark lake below Main Street into a frenzy of foam. And like a switch flipped, you watched from your window as lightning split the sky in two and a blackout spilled across the mountainside.

The faint static of power lines fell silent. Bedside lamps and orange streetlights went dead. On the mud road to Main Street, a car veered into a ditch—there was no one to hear. There was nothing to see.

    A flicker. A pop.

    Behind you, the kitchen was dark. But there: the snap and crack of electricity. And there: a faint light from down the corridor.

    Her bedroom door was blown wide; the window was open, the curtains flapped like gauzy ghosts in the wind. The single naked lightbulb from the ceiling—swinging, swaying in the storm—flickered on, and off, and on, and off, staccato.

    The town was dark. Humanity had slowed to stillness. The lightbulb swayed, and popped, and the curtains snapped.

    The girl in her bed was sweat-stained and wildly awake. Her fingers fisted the sheets. She was ghostlike. She looked as though she was seeing ghosts.

    In this moment, you are nothing. You are the smallest man on earth. You are a drop in the bucket, and not even a consequential drop. You sat on the edge of the bed. You folded her into your chest. She didn't see you, you didn't know what she saw, you did not want to know, and you still do not.

    You are a coward.

    "It will be okay."

    You are a coward.

    "I won't tell."

    Coward.

    "It's a secret."

    The whispering, slithering threads of Fate are closely followed by the great black wings of Death. Somewhere, a canary sits at the bottom of a coal mine. Its yellow breast is bright in the dark. It sings until it cannot breathe, until the blackness closes in and the poison fumes curl through its feathers in evil tendrils.

    The song is cut short. The canary flies away.

    And the world sits in silence.

1

Here's a still scene of a morning in Dane's Chapel—post-rain, mud like a post-war trench lining the creek-bank, and footprints sucking their way through the muck to the West End of town, beating a path down the incline. The air is thick and silty. The sky turns gray through a dense canopy of treetops, gray to brown to dirty rust-red and finally to a mind-boggling purple in a series of indistinct costume changes. Cicadas in the bushes, sand gnats in clouds, and the regular old gnats nipping through the brush. A trickle of water slips sinuous over creek rocks, surprisingly clean for all the mud and general filth of the West End.

The lop-sided sucking of footfalls treading through mud. *Enter our hero.*

Veronica Lewis appears around a bend in the creek, head hung low, a mop of hair obscuring her face as she focuses on her feet. She's scrawny under her faded t-shirt and cargo shorts. Her hands are big and they dangle at her sides. She looks like one of the kids who lurk up by the Bartleby brothers' cabin on the East End, because they know that Donny and Jack know a guy who knows a low-quality guy who cooks up real low-quality meth in his garage.

She's hung out with them and she's lurked there with the rest, but she doesn't touch the stuff. She's got enough demons.

One of them trails her through the mud, his bare feet plodding through silty soil. He's scrawny too, but in the hopeful way a teenage boy is; you look at Grant and you know he's gonna grow into it.

You look at Veronica and you question whether she eats cigarettes for breakfast.

She's walking fast. She's got her head down and she's only watching her feet, but it's almost necessary along this treacherous bank, with all its slick sharp rocks and hidden tree roots. The mud is cool and clay between her toes.

"You can slow down," says the boy behind her.

She doesn't slow down. Her heart is beating out of her chest for no reason at all. She imagines Benedict sitting on the faded orange sofa, reading a book, his feet up on the coffee table. *There's a plate of saltine crumbs, Jim Croce crooning from the stereo. His socks are dusty and he's waiting for her. He glances up when she appears in the doorway.*

"Have you read this?" He holds up a book she's never seen and he knows very well she will never touch. It's about satellites. Alien dust.

"Not bad," he says.

"He won't be there."

Her feet are interesting; her hands are more interesting. The little crescent whites of her fingernails have turned dusty gray over the course of the day, and the lines of her knuckles are creased with dirt, though she can't quite recall why.

"Slow down," says Grant.

He has this way of jerking her back to reality. It's like he's hooked his fingers into her gills, like he's ripping her out of the water, like she's hanging there at his mercy for the instant before she remembers who's in charge. Some days she wishes he'd never learned to speak.

"Veronica. Watch."

At the change in tone, she slows. She follows his arm to where he's pointing upstream.

A fat little boy stands in galoshes on the bank and pees into the creek. He hasn't seen her yet.

Grant sighs. "Still want to walk in the water? Get some shoes.

"You'll end up with parasites."
"Urine is sterile."
"Glass in your foot," he says. "Big shard of glass. Beer bottle. Or a piece of metal, from a soda can. Fishing gear. Wear shoes."

She ignores the boy as she comes closer, but he startles, zips his fly, and takes several backwards steps up the bank so he's standing in the trees, where a fishing pole and a tackle box hide amongst shadowy roots and dangerous tendrils of poison ivy. He does this in a matter of seconds, frightened by the muddy apparition and fast-paced mud-sucking footfalls. His moon face watches her from the treeline as she passes.

He's seen her before. She's seen him, too, but this is how Dane's Chapel works: you know faces, you don't know names. You recognize those who belong and you can smell a stranger from miles away, but there are no friends. It's all about self-preservation. Veronica knows the moon-faced boy in the oversized tank top lives in the upper area of the West End, near downtown, in a yellow RV with a rainbow-paneled umbrella duct- taped to the back of a rusty folding chair beside the driveway, but she doesn't know his name, or his mother's name, or the name of the crackhead stepdad who sits in the folding chair with ginger scruff on his neck and a threadbare Tommy Bahama t-shirt on his back.

Likewise, the moon-faced boy knows Veronica. He knows to stay away from her, because his mother and his crackhead stepdad told him she's schizo and probably dangerous, even if she is skinny. And he doesn't look too hard at her face when she passes him by, because despite himself it sends a shiver up his spine—all hollows and lines, wry lips, dangerous eyebrows over soulless eyes. Kids at his school are split between demonic possession and schizophrenia, when it comes to the case of Veronica Lewis. He's in the schizo party, because it's what his mother and crackhead stepdad told him, but also because she's walking down the muddy creek bank—*suck suck suck*—and talking to herself.

"He's still looking," says Grant.
"Like I care."
"You look insane."
"Grant." She pauses, looks back at him. In the distance, the moon-faced boy watches from the trees, transfixed by the spectacle.

Before her, the blond boy smiles his easy grin and spreads his hands, like *What? I'm just trying to help.* "Grant, with all *due* respect, fuck off."

"You don't mean it."

She turns her back on both boys and goes on stomping through the mud, along the creek. By the time she scrambles up the incline —drags her feet through the bahiagrass to strip off the skin of mud —and walks the spotty gravel drive to her father's trailer, she is alone.

Dane's Chapel is unimpressed. This retired mining town clinging to the Blue Ridge has seen collapses and explosions, blood and guts and creeks dyed black and filthy. When winter strips the mountainside naked, thin-walled barns shudder under the impact of torrential storms. When summer digs its fingers into the soil and brings forth new life, the deep shadows of the woods and the long-winded dusks hide a number of felonies and slightly lesser sins. No one hates Dane's Chapel more than those who live within its borders. And no one else is allowed to speak badly about it unless they really want dental implants.

Dane's Chapel is generally unimpressed, but it makes an exception for the case of Benedict Lewis. The drug busts and elderly people found dead in their homes are old news. Benny Lewis has sold a record number of county newspapers in the past week. Trappers and hunters without anything better to do deviate from their usual forest routes in the darkly curious prospect of discovering something abnormal and grotesque. Teenagers opt out of after-school activities for the sake of traipsing around in the hills and trawling wooded ponds. Townspeople are unusually invested in the Missing Persons Case of their favorite eccentric disgraced physicist.

Despite all this, they only find his body after Benedict has been missing for a week.

A few hours before Veronica slops through the creek-bed, Sheriff McMahon receives a report about a submerged structure at Lake Tan down near the slums. A local fisherman reckons someone is trying to drown their garbage, except it looks like an entire dumpster from where he stands on the shore, fishing rod in hand, gutted and inconvenienced because his fishing spot is occupied.

McMahon parks the patrol car near a flock of decomposing picnic tables. He grabs a flashlight and marches down to the water's edge, where Cliff Deacon paces the shore.

"Morning."

Cliff doesn't bother with a greeting. "Someone's dumped their trash at my spot."

"We've been over this, Cliff. It ain't your spot. It's the county's spot." McMahon switches on his flashlight and peers into the water; he wonders how Cliff saw anything at all. "Yeah, you said somethin' in that vein."

Nothing—not so much as a ripple. He switches off the light and crosses his arms. It's been a long enough week with the manhunt and all; he should be in bed for a good hour yet.

"I need to get this sorted before dawn," Cliff mutters. "Best fishing's before dawn." He rubs the fishing pole between his leathery palms. Old men and their rituals, waking before dawn to stick a line in coal-polluted water for the hope of a bite. They're all the same. "Well, whatdya reckon?"

McMahon rubs his neck and gazes first into the pond, then into the nearby trees—dark, rustling—then sideways at Cliff, who shifts his weight from foot to foot in aggravation. "Look, I'll buy you a fish, Cliff. Get you a can of tuna from the IGA. You don't need to sit here in the dark like this. It's got to be thirty degrees out. Linda know you're out here?"

Lake Tan isn't even a lake, it's an old spring that was blown open during the mining days—a would-be granite quarry foiled by Mother Nature and a whole lot of unwanted water. The project was abandoned quickly and a spankin' new lake was added to the list of landmarks created by Tan Construction. The lake is fed daily by equal parts aquifer and erosion. Mud and coal dust make it entirely unfit for swimming, but that hasn't stopped the old men of Dane's Chapel from trying to introduce a fishy population to its waters.

McMahon just shakes his head and gestures vaguely at the black lake. "Where'd ya see it at?"

"Well I don't know, that's your job, ain't it? I just told ya what I saw, now you go and detect it." McMahon is not a detective, but

Cliff only cares that his tax-payer dollars entitle him to this man's undivided attention. "There was a light," he says, "but it blinked off right before you got here."

"Light?" McMahon switches the flashlight back on. He scans the shore. "Where?"

"In the water, way down deep."

McMahon works his jaw. "And you think it's a dumpster?"

"It was big. Can you move it?"

McMahon doesn't answer. He redirects the flashlight beam and trails it up through the mud, all the way to the patrol car and the tables. There are faint trails leading to the muddy bank, tire tracks all the way down, even though cars aren't allowed down here. Folks know that, from the West End to the East. Everyone in Dane's Chapel knows that Lake Tan is a no-tailgate zone.

"What ya thinkin'?" Cliff chews his lip, watches the sheriff inspect the terrain.

It hasn't rained in a few days, though it smells like rain just now; the tracks could be a week old or more. They'd better get someone down here before the sky breaks open.

McMahon reaches for his radio. "I'm thinking, they never found Ben Lewis' truck."

Veronica waits on the roof—waits for the sheriff to show up, waits for the end of the world, waits for Grant to disappear and leave her in peace. She passed the flashing lights and sirens on the way down past Lake Tan, and she knows what's coming next. She usually does.

"Watch this." She extends an arm and points out over the trailer roofs, through a tangle of electric lines, up the mud road slope toward downtown Dane's Chapel. Between bare-rooted pines and scrubby brush, a white patrol car winds down the hill. It spits a cloud of exhaust in its wake. "Here he comes."

Grant gazes at her warily. "You almost sound excited."

"Well." She's chewed off the end of her cigarette—Ben's cigarette, the last of them, cold and unlit on her tongue—and spits it over the edge of the roof. "Isn't it exciting?"

"Veronica—"

"It's exciting. I'm ecstatic. Look—" She lets go of the shingles and slides down the roof till her heels jam in the gutter. She throws herself down onto the gravel drive, stubs her toe and scrapes a knee. Her calves are streaked with mud. She cranes her neck to look back up at the roof, but the boy is gone. He sits on the front step with his chin on his fist and vague disapproval in his eyes.

She crouches. "Look," she says, and points straight-armed to the car as if casting divine judgment. "An omen of death."

Mud. The patrol car is dirty with it. This town is dirty with it. Sometimes she wakes up in the night and feels that she's sunk below sea level and she's choking and drowning on humidity, and there's mud caking her throat. Ben says it was more humid in Florida, but she hardly remembers and it hardly matters. When summer spills its dull sun-baked haze across the hills and new life erupts in the crooks and crags of the Blue Ridge, the breeze carries a mineral sweetness and the bitter scent of dark greens. When the world dries to a crunching brown and orange in October-time, clouds of smoke and the smell of bonfires fills the ravines between the peaks; the folks who give a shit about landscaping burn piles of fallen limbs and leaves, with or without burn permits—the idea being that the sheriff cannot catch them all. The world smells like end-times, like God's sent another flood to remake the world and this one is of flames. Veronica hates this turning-over time of February. She hates the lengthening days, eternal sunlight, hot midday sun burning over the cold dew into a disorienting mist among the trees. She wants to crawl into the cool shadows beneath the trailer and wake up in September. She wants to sleep without dreaming.

She rises to her feet. "It's an omen of death," she says again, as if he didn't understand her perfectly the first time.

"Do you listen to the words coming out of your mouth?" says the boy.

He's not angry, he's never angry. He's condescending and judgmental and Veronica wonders what that says about her subconsciousness. "*You're* not listening," she says. "I'm a goddamn canary in a coal mine."

She's got a song in her head that she can't beat, some acoustic guitar melody, something like a tinkling music box. Her skin itches and crawls. Her throat feels tight. She drops her arm, drops the rest of the cigarette and stomps it into the gravel and grimaces at her dirty feet. *If I had a box just for wishes....* That's the song. The CD skips on that track, so Ben listens to it over and over sometimes without noticing, like time trapped in a moment, like an hourglass tipping over again and again.

"Veronica."

Her feet are muddy and the trailer's dirty, the whole town is a mud pit and she's drowning on the humidity. She pushes back her hair and glances up at the slow-approaching vehicle. She takes a deep breath. Clears her throat. She turns her back to the road.

The boy stands close by. He watches as she mounts the steps and slams open the screen door. "Where are you going?"

"I'm gonna brush my hair," she says. "And my teeth. So they don't think I'm crazy and send me to a crazy-person home."

"They already think you're crazy."

Veronica pauses in the doorway. "Whatever they try to do," she says, "won't help. It'll make things worse for everyone." She gazes out to the woods beyond the yard, considers, nods to herself. "Everyone. So," and she turns her back to the boy, to the car, "they need to leave me alone."

From within the trailer, she shouts back at an empty yard. "And so should you!"

2

Benedict Lewis' funeral is a miserable affair to all but his daughter, who stands beside a halfhearted dessert table and eats grocery-store cookies until she feels ill. They aren't even good cookies—notes of plastic and burnt rubber, a texture like wet chalk—but there is something distinctly addicting about them, and she is content. Nostalgia is a depressant and a sedative.

Her stepmother is in town. Her former stepmother, she reminds anyone who dares broach the subject, before the inevitable divorce five years ago and Teresa's move to St. Louis. She's brought her daughter Margot, who is somewhere in her mid-twenties, twitchy and uncomfortable, avoiding eye contact like the plague. Veronica is neutral in regards to Margot, but she loathes Teresa's existence with a vengeance; this crazy manipulative bitch married Benedict for his money when he worked for NASA, and then divorced him once it became apparent that he was serious about settling in Dane's Chapel and teaching community college. At that point, she'd packed herself and her daughter up (though Margot was at college up north for most of this brief window of time) and gone back to St. Louis to advance her career as a concert pianist, and to distance herself from Benedict's disgrace.

She is back, dressed in black and weepy. Everyone comforts her, because the alternative is comforting Veronica, and no one is comfortable with that.

She's only here because she wants attention and sympathy.

"And money?" This is from Grant, who bounces his back against the brick of a nearby wall, arms crossed. He takes it in turns scanning the room for anything vaguely interesting, and pointedly staring from Veronica to the dwindling cookie platter.

If no one could see *her*, she'd be sitting under the table, treating the plastic dollar-store tablecloth like a tent, reaching up slowly to retrieve each dish from the dessert table until she'd amassed a banquet in the shadows.

"There is no money," she murmurs.

Although Grant is right, that's probably why Teresa's here. She'll be disappointed to hear that there's no wealth to speak of, though she's likely already ascertained that from the state of things: the cheap funeral and cheap attendees, not the least of which is Veronica herself, who's gone through the effort of digging out a hand-me-down dress from the back of her closet: a navy A-line number that comes just below her scratched knees, a "church-goin' dress" courtesy of Anne Elizabeth who used to live up the road. It's two sizes too large and the collar is smeared with foundation. The Lewises not being the church-goin' types themselves—Benedict has always considered himself cautiously Agnostic—Veronica's never had cause to wear it until now. She'd liked to have paired it with a dramatic lacy black headpiece, something like what witches or widows might wear, but shockingly couldn't find anything like it at the Goodwill nor the IGA.

"Ms. Lewis?"

Veronica looks up from her twenty-second cookie. She narrows her eyes at the men intruding into her personal bubble. They looked like out-of-towners, but they also don't look like the sort Ben would have associated with in recent years: suits and stoicism; one tall and military, the other small and slumped and ancient-looking. *NASA trash, maybe.*

It was the military man who spoke. He's shaped like a rectangle and wears transition glasses still dark from the outdoors. "You are

Miss Lewis, correct?"

Veronica dusts off her hands onto the floor. She discreetly kicks the crumbs under the table. "I'm Veronica."

"We're very sorry for your father's passing," says the smaller man, who, on closer inspection, isn't quite as old as she previously thought; his eyes are sharp behind rectangular lenses.

"Uh huh," says Veronica.

"Everyone liked Ben Lewis," says a voice from behind her. Sheriff McMahon joins the two suited men in her little bubble of personal space and cookies. He claps a hand on Veronica's shoulder. "He was an interesting man. Well-spoken man, real decent guy."

The military man looks like he'd rather the sheriff leave, but he holds out his hand. "Andre Billings."

"Jeremy McMahon. Ya'll knew Ben?"

Much to her own surprise, Veronica appreciates the sheriff's intrusion; it distracts the strangers' attention and gives her the opportunity to eat another cookie and watch the proceedings as a mere witness. There is something protective about McMahon's stance, the way he makes himself big.

"No," says Andre Billings. "We're here on business. My partner and I work for a private investigation agency. The case of Benedict Lewis happened to come to our attention, and we think there might be something to look into, here."

McMahon stiffens. He drops his hand from Veronica's shoulder and hooks his thumbs into his belt. "Well, I don't know about that. We had the crime scene investigators down from Raleigh. The case is closed, gentlemen."

"We don't think it is," says the smaller man. "Pardon me. But there are some strange details in the case, Sheriff, and with Ms. Lewis' permission, we'd like to investigate further. There may be signs of foul play."

Veronica almost chokes on her cookie. Three male gazes turn on her. She clears her throat, but her voice is strained. "You think someone offed him?"

"*No—*" McMahon starts, but Billings overrides him.

"We don't know. That's what we're here to find out."

The sheriff is distinctly uncomfortable at this point. "With all respect to Veronica—she can't give permission to investigate the case. She's only seventeen. And who's paying you to do any poking around, huh?" The underlying message is: *the Lewises are dirt poor and there's no way in hell they can afford private investigators.*

"This investigation is funded by a private government sector. We're following up on a string of similar cases that we believe might be connected. Benedict's fits the description." Andre Billings slips a hand inside his suit, withdraws a business card, and offers it to Veronica. "All we need is permission to search the property and ask a few questions. And you might have some of your own questions answered along the way."

Veronica sighs, switches cookie hands, and takes the card.

"No questions," says McMahon. "Ruled it as a suicide." He glances at Veronica like she might be bothered by this, but she's examining the business card and munching on her cookie, apparently unfazed.

"Maybe Ms. Lewis has some questions," says the small man. "Maybe Teresa Lewis does, as well."

"Teresa Montclar," Veronica says, quickly. She fixes her soulless eyes on the small bespectacled man. "Montclar. She isn't a Lewis. And she doesn't care."

"Well." Andre Billings straightens his coat. "Well then. You have our card. We'll be in town for a few days."

"Give it some thought," says the small man, who has yet to share his name. "We just need a simple yes, and we'll be quick. Then we'll be out of your hair."

"Uh huh," says Veronica.

The men leave. McMahon stays. Veronica does not engage, but still he stays.

"I think they're trying to take advantage of somethin'," says the sheriff.

Veronica is silent.

"Well," he says, "you seem to be doing alright."

"Yeah," she says, "well, I don't think he's dead."

McMahon blinks. He seems confused, and then fearful—perhaps he has just recalled that people think Veronica Lewis is schizo. Perhaps he's now wondering whether it's true. "Veronica," he says, slowly, as if speaking to a small child, "I can guarantee you that I oversaw the crime scene myself, and I spoke with the *real* investigators, and there is no doubt that..." Well, now it sounds harsh. "That is...well, he was a good man."

But McMahon barely knows Benedict. No one really does. And it's funny, but with these strangers in town trying to stir the pot, McMahon is standing his ground; he's less likely to explore alternative theories of Ben's death than ever.

Out of the corner of her eye, Grant watches as if exhausted from seeing her tarnish her already abysmal reputation. "That's twenty-four cookies," he says.

Yeehaw, she thinks. But to McMahon she says, "Yeah, you're probably right. I guess it's grief, huh?"

"Probably." This, he knows how to deal with. "The tears might come later, don't be hard on yourself about that. Who's your next of kin, Veronica? Huh? Your dad got siblings? Grandparents still around?"

"Nope," she says. "And nope."

"Where's, uh...where's your mom in all this? I don't recall ever seeing—that is, people don't say much—"

"She's not around," says Veronica. She sets down the rest of her cookie on the side of the platter. "I think I should go home. I don't feel great."

"Twenty-four cookies," Grant repeats, voice strained.

"Will you be alright?" says McMahon.

"Oh, yeah. Probably just gonna go...cry or something. Read the sympathy cards from the dollar-store. Make a slideshow. Something soothing."

"Something soothing," McMahon agrees. He doesn't pick up on the sarcasm, but people rarely do; they accept Veronica's weirdness and can no longer discern sincerity from an excellent fucking joke. "Well, you take care, Veronica. You need anything, you've got my number. And I'll be in touch with you about your living situation, we'll work somethin' out."

He is referring to the fact that she is a minor, and now an orphan. He'd spoken about it briefly the other day, but she gets the feeling he'll be more proactive following the funeral. How long before Child Services shows up to cart her off to a foster home? How long before—god forbid—someone tries to track down

her mom?
   It hardly matters. She'll be long gone by then.

3

When Harry Markus arrives in Dane's Chapel, it is already dark.

He used to love the night, used to wrap it around his shoulders like a hero's cape and run into the darkness with childlike abandon. But he is no longer a child and he knows that more dangerous people than himself use the night for their own purposes.

So he finds the lone streetlight on Main Street—a dirty orange beam flickering in the wind, swarmed by moths and hungry frogs. He stands to the side, sandwiched between the low brick post office and the IGA. Across the street and up the hill, behind a white picket fence and a flock of dead-eyed vehicles, the funeral home spills light across the lawn. A man and a woman stand on the front porch between white pillars; they lean close, resting against one another. Her forehead is on his shoulder, his cheek on her head.

He'd like to get closer to the building, take a look inside, but he's found that it's difficult being incognito when you're Harry Markus. There simply isn't a casual bone in his body. If he walked through those doors, everyone would see him and immediately question his presence. There is a phrase that Howard often quotes to him, which roughly translates as something like this: *a wolf in a nursery*. It doesn't belong there, and it's going to hurt someone, break something, and everyone knows it.

Wolf in a nursery.

Harry Markus stands in the flickering lamplight. Dane's Chapel stands still around him.

There's something close-walled and depressing about the little town, with its single street, its abandoned mills and mines, relics of a failed industry. Despite the sprawling wilderness around Dane's Chapel, it feels like the clogged drain where all the dregs and scraps get caught up with no escape, trapped between mountains and ravines.

He stands there for a long time beneath the streetlight, until the last traces of dusk disappear below the mountains and the sky deepens to starless black. He waits until two figures leave the funeral home and make their way up the hill: one tall and military, square shoulders, long strides; the other small and slower, head tilted to the side as if listening to voices in the night. Then Harry Markus peels away from the wall. He still feels the brick against his shoulders as he follows the men up Main Street to the motel with its lazy neon sign and potholed parking lot. When Andre Billings and the small man disappear into their rented room, Harry Markus picks the lock on the suite next door and slips inside. The carpet smells mildewy and damp. The room is cast in a gray film of light from the gauzy curtains looking out over the parking lot. As he passes, Harry Markus parts the curtains a sliver so he can see outside. He positions himself between a bare mattress and a nightstand. He rests his ear against the thin wall.

"I really believe—I do, Andre—I think it would be simpler if we waited for her to leave and took a look around the premises," says the small man, who has a name, but no one uses it in full—they call him X, and he likes it that way. That's the name Harry Markus knows him by. "They say she's mentally unstable. Living with someone like Benedict Lewis all these years, being raised by a man like that—it makes sense, I suppose. But I doubt she's sane enough to be terribly suspicious, even if she did find out. She might think she's hallucinating. And if she did tell anyone…well, who would she tell? Apparently the Lewises are recluses."

"We need explicit permission. She could tell the sheriff. Small town law enforcement can make problems for us. Word gets around fast in places like this, with nothing else to do."

"No one would believe her. As I said, they think she's insane."

"There are procedures," says Andre Billings, who nearly always has a stick up his ass and cannot for the life of him imagine deviating from set procedures.

"I think, Andre, you spent too many years in the field. This is not an ordinary mission by any means. The old procedures won't work here."

"They'll work well enough."

"Weren't you in charge of the Webber operation?"

"Yes. And as I recall, you were sitting behind a desk."

The silence is loaded. Harry Markus shifts his position, impatiently waits for them to continue. He didn't come all this way to listen to two old men argue like an unhappily married couple.

"I only mean—"

"I know what you meant. This is a unique mission. It's a rare crossover between departments, and I'm sure North Enterprises has its reasons for providing your assistance, but this subject is a BEESWAX matter." Oh, how important Andre sounds. He doesn't want X here at all.

"Might I suggest that it is neither?"

"I've done this before. I know what I'm doing. Why don't you sit down and rest?"

A smile flickers over Harry's lips.

"Oh, I'm doing alright," says X, his voice withering.

"Well, good. I'm going to take a shower." The bathroom door slams. A moment later, the water runs and the overhead fan roars to life.

Harry Markus exits the motel room and locks the door behind him.

He makes his way back down Main Street, clinging to the shadows. He resumes his place in the lamplight and watches the funeral home. Several cars have cleared out since he left, and the man and woman on the porch are gone. A lone figure stands in the doorway, staring into the night with crossed arms.

Harry Markus stays perfectly still as the figure climbs down from the porch and makes her way through the cars, down the dirt walk to the picket fence, and from there onto Main Street. She stomps down the sidewalk, west, towards the slums.

He follows.

"If you walk down by the creek now, you'll get mugged."

Veronica casts a glance over her shoulder. Grant pads along behind, bare feet pale in the night. He swings his arms and raises his eyebrows. He's ghostly and angelic, strange and fair in the weird angles of the streetlights.

She turns away. "No one will mug me."

"You seem so sure."

"I'm the scariest thing in this town." Grant laughs. "I'm serious. No one will mess with me. But I'm not gonna walk in the creek. It's too cold. I'm not stupid."

"Well, you're having stupid thoughts."

"Well, get out of my head, then, if you don't want to hear them." She crosses her arms tighter. The wind is biting and damp, knotting in her hair and stinging her eyes. She should have brought a coat. She hadn't even thought about it, hadn't even considered that the sun would set and the chill would cling to her bare arms. *Silly dress. Silly funeral.*

She *is* having stupid thoughts. Crazy thoughts. Thoughts her father would have understood yet probably would still have disapproved of; he was allowed to do extreme things, but Veronica wasn't.

Ben isn't around, though. He's gone a bit too far and he isn't around to stop her from reacting.

"Are you trying to play hero?"

Veronica scratches the back of her neck. Her nails are jagged from picking. "I'm not a hero."

"No." Grant is quiet for a moment. His footsteps sound so real, but she knows that if she searches for his prints in the muddy creek bank near her home, she'll find that they disappear as soon as he's passed. Like he was never there at all. *All in my head.* "No, but you're trying to act like one, aren't you?"

"I don't know. Maybe I am. Some hero I would be. Fuck if I care. I'm just doing what I want, and if that's hero shit, then call me a hero."

"Veronica—"

"What?"

"Remember January."

Veronica pauses on the sidewalk. She clenches her jaw and suppresses a shiver. She's cold as she looks at Grant in the silver moonlight.

January. Veronica recalls the night with a sense of unadulterated panic, followed by a dawning understanding of loss; something was irreparably damaged between herself and Benedict. She'd like to blame Grant. He'd pushed her too far, and now he uses the memory like a weapon.

"I haven't stopped singing," she says.

"I don't think you have much of a choice." Grant nods. "January. You didn't mean for it to happen, did you? You could do it again."

She points at him, points a thin pale finger at the thin pale boy and clenches her jaw. "I decide. I'm the canary and I decide when I stop singing."

"I think the universe decides."

"I think you can go to hell."

She marches down the hill, towards the West End. She doesn't look back.

Once, she asked Benedict what it would be like at the end of the world. His answer made no sense to her then, and she hardly recalls what he actually said, only that his response left her overwhelmed by a sense of smallness and inevitability. But she imagines, in the cold bite of the evening, the descending darkness, the cowboy-careless ease with which she wanders away from the lights and loudness of humanity and down the lonely road to a home she knows she'll find empty, that this is what it must feel like: gentle, suffocating implosion.

Harry Markus follows her to the trailer. He watches from the shadows as she converses with invisible beings, speaks under her breath, shakes her head and stomps up the front steps and slams the door. He waits and watches for a while after. He takes in the view: a sagging white trailer hemmed with caked mud and dead weeds, green-curtained windows, the bare bones of a basketball hoop hanging sadly at the end of the gravel drive. No car. A light flickers on in one window, but the trailer is quiet.

He agrees with X. Veronica Lewis is insane.

But she also lives with Benedict Lewis, who is not insane. Benedict knows things. Which means that Veronica Lewis knows things. Which means that, unlike X and Billings, Harry Markus cannot discount Benedict's daughter as a mere pawn in the game. In a way, she is the new objective. She is the strongest lead, especially since North Enterprises does not seem interested in whatever she knows. *She's the key.*

He waits outside the trailer for a long time. When he finally backtracks through the shadows to Main Street, it is late and the town is still. The funeral home is dark and empty.

He finds a place to rest his legs, but Harry Markus does not sleep. He has not really slept in a long time.

Harry Markus fears the dark, and this is why: because he once loved it terribly and it broke his heart.

Memories of countless nights spent feeling alive and free are overshadowed by the ringing in his ears: explosions, the thunderous sound of a building collapsing, screams and shots echoing through the darkness. A strange humming—a mumbling—a murmuring growing louder in the night. The taste of sweat, the stench of blood and bowels, his hearing muffled from the roar. A limp body in his arms, a deadweight. And the dark growing thicker around him, threatening to eat him alive as his vision swims and the nightmare scene plays out before him.

Harry Markus hates the dark.

He hates the Mumblers.

4

Veronica is twelve. Teresa has just left Benedict, and Veronica is glad; she never liked Teresa. She hardly knew Margot.

But when Benedict leaves Dane's Chapel, she is lonely. And it would be nice if she weren't.

She has no friends. The Bartleby boys up in the East End say she's too young to hang with them and the other junkie high-schoolers who smoke behind their cabin—that is, unless she has time to do their homework for them. Anne Elizabeth, who is sixteen and wears a push-up bra and uses drugstore perfume, has outgrown everyone but her shady character of a boyfriend. The nice middle-aged lady who makes pancakes at the IGA for the truckers is out on maternity leave. And when Benedict Lewis takes his truck to Atlanta and from Atlanta flies to New Mexico, Veronica is alone.

She wakes one morning and her dad is standing in the bedroom doorway. He has that deep-thinking look on his face—jaw working, gaze unfocused. He stands there for a long moment and they look at one another. When he finally speaks, his voice is dull and shell-shocked.

"Peter is gone."

"Where did he go?"

His eyes focus on her, searching. Wary. Like maybe she knows, and she might tell him. "Disappeared. They got him."

Even now, she knows who *they* are. Or, rather, she knows of *their* existence. She knows everything is sensitive and secret. She's had suspicions for some time that a great and terrible *they* are trying to track down her dad, and as her father has said nothing to dispel these suspicions, they have only grown more concrete with the passing years.

Someone is looking for them. Someone wants to know what her father and Peter Webber are working on. But as far as the rest of the world is concerned, Veronica knows nothing about it. Veronica Lewis is insane. That's all anyone ever needs to know.

Who is Peter Webber? A saint painted by an iconographer's golden brush. Veronica recalls him with a halo. She knows him from the grainy photograph in his books: narrow face, dimpled smile, pale hair blending into the desert sky behind him. She knows him better from Benedict's anecdotes: the missing link in her father's knowledge, the missing sliver of his soul; how his stories are told in sepia tones until Peter's appearance in his timeline, and from there on out, his adventures are regaled in glorious color. Peter Webber is electric, charismatic, boyish in his unabated enthusiasm. The two went gallivanting around Eastern Europe for a year to work alongside the loose web of international scholars their fields had in common. Peter Webber got them drunk in a Ukrainian village on a frigid November night, and they passed out in a field till dawn. When Benedict graduated, Peter was the only family to show up. Peter Webber stayed in Florida for a week when Veronica was born; he walked her on the beach while Benedict stole what little sleep he could.

And then the stories ceased. A shroud of mystery was draped over the form of Peter Webber, around the same time Benedict uprooted their life and brought Veronica to Dane's Chapel.

The night after Peter disappears, Benedict flies to New Mexico. He leaves Veronica a handgun and a bunch of microwave dinners. She practices loading and unloading the gun, switching off the safety, aiming it at an empty tomato sauce jar balanced on a rotting fence in the woods behind the trailer—just like she's seen in the Westerns. *Gunsmoke. Get outta Dodge.* But the sound scares the neighbors, and she stops after a while.

She goes inside and locks the door, almost hoping someone will intrude so she'll have an excuse to break the silence and defend their property.

Her dad will come home. "What happened while I was gone?" he'll ask.

"Oh, I was alright," she'll say, "I took care of myself."

"What do you mean?"

"Well, someone tried to bust into the house and steal your stuff, but I took care of it." She'll spin the handgun on one finger, and holster it. Like the Westerns. "I've been practicing."

And Benedict will be so impressed.

But that first night alone in the trailer at the West End of Dane's Chapel, Veronica is truly alone. Not even an intruder to defend against. Just silence and the faulty radiator humming through the cold linoleum floors. Just Veronica and the pale boy without a name, who sits against the wall nearby and watches her with polite curiosity as she obsessively checks every lightbulb in the house, replacing the flickering ones, which is one of the only maintenance activities she knows how to perform. She can also replace the air vent filters, but she did that last week.

The boy doesn't speak. He never has.

Veronica speaks to him anyway, because she's lonely. Because she's a little scared, even if she isn't willing to admit it. Because if they caught up to Peter Webber, who's to say they won't catch Benedict Lewis, too?

What if Ben never comes home?

"Say something." She sucks on a burnt taquito and sinks to the floor beside the pale boy. "It's too quiet."

She could turn on music, but she doesn't like the idea of not hearing if someone approached the trailer and rattled the knob. Right now she can hear every little sound beyond the thin walls—skittering gravel, creaking tree branches, echoing shouts as parents call their children indoors for the night, distant low-thumping bass from car speakers.

"I won't sleep tonight," she says, and it's more a declaration than a prediction.

He doesn't have body heat. Even sitting this close to him, it's as if he isn't here at all. But she can almost smell him, the scent of him, like a piece of summer: marmalade, sweat, sunscreen. Perhaps it's the smell she's attributed to his person. Perhaps that's all in her head, too.

I won't sleep, she thinks, and yet she does. Or perhaps it's something other than sleep, because she does not feel rested when she eventually wakes. She does not recall slipping down against the wall, her mind drifting away into some dark space.

She often dreams that she is a bird, but it feels very real this time —she can feel her heartbeat in the yellow breast, the wind in her feathers, the impenetrable darkness and the scent of smoke.

Maybe the trailer is burning down. The radiators are shit; maybe they've caught on the curtains behind the sofa and burned the trailer to the ground and she is dreaming amongst the flames. But Veronica knows that isn't right. The smoke is in this dark space. As are the screams.

She isn't afraid.

As she drifts through the darkness, she lights upon a shoulder. The world takes form around her: walls built from a darker dark, winding twists and turns. The mouth of an endless labyrinth, and somewhere within, voices call out to her.

The canary looks at the shoulder she sits upon. She looks at the pale boy, who smiles, more real than he has ever seemed before.

"Shall we?" He gestures to the maze.

"What's in there?" she asks, though she is not sure how the canary speaks and how the boy understands.

"Things to see," he says, and she feels that she has always known his voice. "Things to know."

Does she want to know them? Yes, she does. But the maze is dark and the unknown is even darker. "What if I can't get out?"

His smile widens. His eyes are gray like storm clouds. "I won't lose you," he says.

She trusts him. They descend into the labyrinth.

She sees things and she knows them. And when she emerges

from the darkness, back into the girl's body, the boy is where she left him—leaning against the wall, shoulder-to-shoulder with her.

She stares at him, dumbstruck. He grins.

"See?" he says. "I told you I wouldn't lose you."

5

The night before Benedict Lewis' funeral finds Veronica in the hills beyond the East End, high above Main Street and the Bartleby boys' cabin, cloaked in shadow from the pines populating the mountainside. She does not carry a flashlight because her footing is sure. She needs no map because she's walked this hidden trail many times before.

There were days and nights when Benedict would disappear. He'd vanish from beneath the gaze of Dane's Chapel, and when people asked where he went (they rarely did), Ben called it "stargazing".

"Going out to the country to do some stargazing," he'd say. No one questioned his motives because they assumed he was NASA nerd trash, and he sort of was, but Benedict Lewis was a lot more. And he most certainly was not stargazing.

There is a telescope in the old RV. There is a skylight in the low ceiling that Ben would prop open, and a younger version of Veronica would sit cross-legged on the carpeted floor for hours while her father worked. She'd map out stars on scrapped graphing paper that drifted from his table; she'd make up names and constellations until her father grew frustrated and joined her on the floor with his arms full of star charts and astronomy textbooks.

"They already have names," he'd say, and she'd memorize the lists and charts he gave her, until she grew older and filled her head with other things—chemistry, obscure biotechnology theories, lamenting her flat chest, thriving in a permanent hurricane of paranoia and total indifference towards her tumultuous life. Now she has to search her memory for the names of astronomical anomalies.

She can hardly see them tonight, hiking the treacherous leaf-strewn path to the RV. She grips tree roots to help herself up a slope, cranes her head back and searches between rustling black branches, wishing for some glimmer of Ben's stars and constellations.

He's been gone a week. At first people said he was just stargazing, but from the first day he'd disappeared, she'd known it wasn't the same. He wasn't going to come home early in the morning, hands smeared with graphite from his notes, leaves in his hair, a faraway look in his dark eyes. Nothing was ever as it seemed with Benedict Lewis. Even when McMahon found his truck in the lake, even when the authorities pronounced it a suicide—she knew the truth. She knows it now.

They found Peter Webber. It was only a matter of time before they found Benedict Lewis, too.

There was a burnt-out husk of a body in Ben's truck. Apparently the labs had found a DNA match for her dad, but Veronica's read enough of Peter Webber's books and heard enough stories from her dad to know about corruption of evidence and something he tactically referred to as "financial compensation". There was, indisputably a body—until it was further cremated and placed in an urn this evening. Veronica doesn't know who it was—she doesn't particularly care—but it certainly wasn't Ben. If her dad is dead, he certainly isn't dead anywhere near Dane's Chapel.

The night before the funeral, Veronica climbs to the ancient RV with its round windows and its blackout curtains. She would have come sooner, but this is the first night she hasn't felt observed. This is the first night she dares make her way around the edges of

Dane's Chapel to Ben's secret place. The part of her that still believes in fate and fairytales nurtures the fantasy that she'll open the door to the old RV and find Benedict waiting inside. *You found me. Well done. The game is over.*

Veronica pulls out the key hanging around her neck. She unlocks the door, checks behind her, and slips inside Benedict's lab.

She finds things, that night in the mountains. Notepaper scattered as though hunted through in a great hurry. The telescope, toppled from its tripod, half-hidden under the table. The lockbox, agape and tilted on its side at the base of the wall.

She kneels in the moonlight filtering through the overhead window, her knees pressing gently into cold carpet. She draws the lockbox closer. Nearly empty—all of Ben's important folders and notebooks, gone. Yet she's somehow sure that this chaotic scene is her father's own doing, not the result of a violent struggle or a forced search through his belongings.

What were you doing? What are you trying to tell me?

In the bottom of the box, there are photographs. Polaroids. She pulls them out and holds them in the pale light.

She knows Peter Webber's face from his author profile in the back of his books—narrow and smiling, eyes bright, nose a bit long and crooked. In this photo he is young, his hair sticking up and his cheeks stubbly. He has his arm around Benedict Lewis, who looks smug—one arched brow, hair flopped over his forehead, showing his teeth in a halfhearted yet charmingly sarcastic smile. They both wear lab coats. Grad school.

There's a third man behind them. Older, with stooped shoulders and glasses. His face is a little blurry, and he seems surprised at being caught on film in the college laboratory. Veronica commits that face to memory.

The other photo is of a boy. A pale boy with a lopsided grin, freckles, sweaty hair, and sunburnt arms sticking out of a Captain America t-shirt. He perches in the low branches of a tree. In the distance, desert dunes roll up against the horizon.

She takes both photos with her when she locks up the RV and heads back to Dane's Chapel. She sneaks down to the East End by the trail behind the Bartleby boys' cabin, and through downtown, past the lake and down the potholed road to the place she calls home.

She sits on the floor beside the radiator and looks at the photos again in the kitchen light. She holds them up for Grant to see. "Have anything to say?"

He looks, but it's like he doesn't really see the pictures, he just sees her. "What do you want me to say?"

"Say that he's leaving a breadcrumb trail." She throws the photos down and leans against the wall. "Say that he didn't want me to sit back and watch the world burn down around us."

He doesn't speak. But he holds out his hand.

She doesn't take it. "Not tonight." With the passing years, it's become harder and harder to pull herself back out of that mysterious space in her mind. Sometimes she struggles to remember that she's a girl and not a bird. The canary sticks around when she wakes, and her mind forgets that she doesn't have wings. Besides that, she rarely likes what she sees.

"You want to know," says Grant.

"I want to sleep," she snaps. "Really sleep. Not whatever it is you do to me."

"You do it to yourself. I'm a byproduct."

"Oh, fuck off, byproduct boy."

And he does, until the funeral the next day. He watches her eat cookies and pull McMahon's chain, walks home with her and watches while she paces the trailer. Veronica retrieves the polaroids from where she dropped them the night before and lines them up on the counter.

"Those men aren't PIs," she says.

"Oh, you puzzled that out?"

"Since when have you been sarcastic? They aren't PIs. They know about my dad and Peter." She thinks about it. "He left that photo on purpose. He knew they'd come back, and he knew I'd find it. They're back because they didn't get what they came for the first time."

Grant is silent. He lets her work it out.

Veronica turns and leans against the counter. "Which means I'm a step ahead of them. And if I can find my dad's research first, I can figure out how to get him back."

6

The night after Benedict Lewis' funeral, Andre Billings and the man called X sit in their motel room, paging through old files.

Though he would never admit it to anyone, Billings is beginning to feel a bit frustrated with the mission. Mostly frustrated with X. And a bit confused by the fact that there are no adults to consult in this particular mission. He cannot go to Veronica Lewis' next available guardian and ask for their permission to investigate the case—there doesn't appear to be one. The sheriff doesn't like them. And Billings is married to the idea of sticking to his normal procedures, because they have worked in the past, and he feels that diverting from these plans is last-resort.

So it comes as a great relief when the phone rings.

X moves to answer it, but Billings is quicker. "Hello?"

"Hi. It's Veronica Lewis. From earlier. Uh...I've been thinking about it, and I think it would be okay if you guys took a look around. I don't think my dad would mind."

Benedict Lewis would definitely mind, and it's testament to the girl's mental instability—or perhaps the tumultuous emotions Billings has been told accompany grief—that she professes otherwise. An easy target on all counts.

"I'm glad you've contacted us, Miss Lewis. This is good news." X's eyes widen. Billings refuses to look happy about it. "How soon can we begin? We don't want to intrude..." He very much wants to intrude. X is furiously trying to catch his eye. Billings rises from his seat on the edge of the sagging mattress. He paces to the opposite wall and inspects the framed newspapers serving as decor. They're from thirty years before, but Main Street looks very much the same, just grainier and in shades of black and gray.

"Actually, I've been taking a look around my dad's stuff, and there's some weird shit in here. I don't know what was going on, but...it's weird. Is it too late? Can you come out tonight?"

Billings allows himself the smallest smile. "That sounds fine. We'll be over within the hour. What's your address?"

He knows. But it tends to unnerve people when you already know their home address before they volunteer it.

She gives it. "I'm in the West End. I might be in the back when you arrive, and the doorbell doesn't work. So you can just come in when you get here. Just, like, yell from the living room. I don't startle easy."

Indeed, when Billings and X arrive at the Lewis' trailer barely an hour later, the windows are dark.

"She said she might not answer the door." Billings parks their rental car at the end of the driveway. Their dress shoes crunch on gravel as they make their way up to the front steps.

Billings straightens his coat. He never knew Benedict Lewis, but the man's reputation precedes him, and it is hard to imagine the Benedict of legend living in this town, on this street, in this dumpster of a home. He must have fallen hard.

Billings knocks once, then opens the door.

The trailer is dark. And quiet. It feels undisturbed by time—a man's coat tossed over an armchair, a film of dust on every windowsill. Billings steps into the center of the room and peers down the hallway. Everything is still.

"Miss Lewis," he says. Nothing. "Veronica."

"Well," says X, which is an invitation for Billings to express his feelings about the situation.

But Billings says nothing. He points down the hallway.

X sighs. "I'll check the back."

As the old man moves out of the living room, Billings steps into the kitchen and tries the back door. It's locked. As he turns to review the living room again, his gaze lands on the kitchen counter. A Polaroid sits in the dim stovetop light. He crosses to it and bends over the counter, reluctant to touch anything. His eyes adjust.

His heart skips a beat. "X." There's rustling from down the hall, the creak of a door, but the old man doesn't respond. "X!"

Leather shoes patter down the carpeted corridor. X reappears. "Is she here?"

"No." A shiver runs down Billings' spine. He places a finger on the Polaroid. "Look."

X moves to Billings' side and squints at the photograph. After a moment, his eyes widen behind his glasses. "Oh—"

"You said all the evidence had been destroyed." Billings' voice is stony. "You signed waivers. You gave up your identity and you swore you'd burned every bridge."

"I didn't know he had—I didn't—" X picks up the Polaroid. His fingers tremble.

Billings glances around the trailer. She's gone. Here is photographic evidence that the PI in Dane's Chapel is not who he says he is, but knows her father and Peter Webber. The doctor behind the two young men in the photo is blurry, but his features are unmistakable, and the gesture of leaving the Polaroid for them to find is obvious. *A warning?*

"They were so young," X murmurs.

"It's a trap," says Billings.

Outside, lights flash against the windows. As if on cue, a siren cuts through the night, wailing through the West End.

A megaphone blares to life in the yard: "This is Sheriff McMahon. You are trespassing on private property. Come out with your hands where I can see 'em, or I'll send the boys in after you."

High in the East End, far above the Bartleby cabin and far beyond the flickering lights of downtown Dane's Chapel, Veronica stands in her father's RV.

There's a flip phone snapped in half at her feet. There's a heavy plastic container with a lengthy warning label gripped in her white-knuckled fist. She has a backpack slung over her shoulder, cargo pants tucked into her old hiking boots, two layers of socks and two layers of sweaters, and a cap pulled low over her forehead, so that her hair curls out at the base of her neck.

She opens the container cap with her teeth, juggles a flashlight in her free hand, and shines its beam along the path of clear fluid she leaves in her wake. She walks up and down the dusty, paper-littered carpet until the container is empty. Then she tosses it aside into a pile of hand-drawn star charts.

Her father wrote those charts. They don't mean shit. None of it matters, it's all NASA trash and Benedict's casual obsessions, surface-level research disguising a deeper study of the universe. *Trash*.

She tells herself this as she kicks open the door and stands looking out into the night.

The RV reeks. The night smells sweet, like rotting leaves. She glances back at the heaps of her father's work.

A figure stands in the dark behind her.

Grant tilts his head, a ghost of a grin on his lips. "Careful, Veronica."

"When am I not?" She exits the RV, misses the steps, and lands hard in a patch of dirt. The heels of her hands skid against packed earth. She rights herself quickly and steps away from the door.

"You're playing with fire." He's behind her now. She didn't see him move, but that's kind of Grant's thing.

"Oh, so you're funny now?"

He raises his eyebrows. "I've always been funny."

"You're killing me, Webber." She swings her backpack off her shoulder, into the crook of her elbow, and digs around in the front pocket. Replaces the backpack and strikes a match. "One night only. Grant Webber is a fucking comedian. He drives Lewis up the wall—"

"—you're already up the wall—"

"—and then comes January. *Remember January* he says, like it's all her fault. He tells her he won't lose her in the dark labyrinth inside her mind, and then he goes and does just that. Loses her." The match is almost burned down to her fingers, but she doesn't move, just looks at him over her shoulder. Her jaw is clamped tight. The canary is still and tensed, hiding deep inside, yet somehow closer to the surface with every passing day.

Grant has the decency to lower his gaze. "It was an accident."

"Pretty big accident."

"Neither of us could have known."

"You should have known. You should have fucking known. You let me go, and here we are." The match sparks against her fingertips, a tiny orange flame dancing in the night. She drops it in the RV doorway. It catches the trail of lighter fluid and races across the carpet and Veronica takes a step back from the rapidly-growing inferno.

The last traces of Benedict Lewis go up in flames.

7

Veronica is thirteen. Her father has pulled her out of school.

It is necessary; even she can see that. And she doesn't miss it much, since they've only just moved to Dane's Chapel and she doesn't really know the other kids in her grade.

The blur of elementary school and Florida beaches and the dusty smell of cicada summers are distant to Veronica Lewis. These are childhood memories from someone else's life, a different version of Veronica without anxieties or disturbing dreams or the dreaded sense of awareness polluting her waking days. She didn't understand gas prices or taxes back then. She barely understands taxes now, but she knows money drains from her dad's bank account into little envelopes and online transfers that go into the government's pocket. And she knows most of Dane's Chapel is hiding income particulars from the US of A.

Yet she is vaguely aware that she once went to a school with gourmet lunches, and there had been a man with a flatbed who cut their grass for them. The timing of their move from Melbourne to Dane's Chapel corresponded perfectly with Veronica's blossoming into a self-aware entity.

Childhood is a blur. This is the home stretch, actions and their consequences for keeps. The world is great and terrible.

She hardly sleeps these days and her thoughts are scattered, so Benedict schools her at home. He teaches physics and an astronomy extracurricular at the county community college by day. In the evenings he teaches his daughter about numbers and sciences.

In the mornings, Veronica roams unsupervised. She reads the books Benedict leaves lying around—Tom Clancy, Verne, Michael Crichton (his guilty pleasure). She reads books by Peter Webber.

When left alone, Veronica walks barefoot through the world. She explores the West End—a slight, wild thing with unruly hair and bored eyes. She climbs up and down the creek bank, collects shiny rocks for a slingshot she is making, sits under a tree and reads Ray Bradbury until her eyes grow heavy and the words spin off the page. Downtown, she takes out the trash for the lady at the IGA, who in turn provides her with blueberry pancakes. Her friends are scattered and few—Anne Elizabeth, Donny and Jack Bartleby, a tubby boy named Chase, and a little Christian girl named Candy Joy.

Within the first few years of Veronica's existence in Dane's Chapel, Anne Elizabeth moves to Raleigh with her boyfriend; her grandparents who raised her refuse to provide contact details, since Anne Elizabeth actually eloped in the middle of the night—an un-Christian thing to do—and she is, essentially, dead to her family. Chase loses interest in Veronica when she finally admits she knows nothing about MacGyver. Candy Joy overhears the Bartleby boys say she has a stripper name, and she tells her parents, and she is henceforth homeschooled and kept far away from "their lot"— which, interestingly, seems to include Veronica.

Jack and Donny stick around for a bit. Donny likes her because every now and then she'll run an errand between him and their friend Beau Huskey (the guy who cooks up real low-quality meth). Jack likes her because he is briefly infatuated in the way a teenager is taken by the undeniably sexy and forbidden notion of a cigarette; he likes the strange and scrappy idea of her, but it turns out he can't handle the heat. She burns. He gets a taste and decides it isn't for him.

Veronica, for her part, likes them all well enough, but she likes the idea of having a pack more than she does their individual personalities. She finds Anne Elizabeth strangely immature for someone with big boobs and an in-the-flesh boyfriend. Chase only likes her as long as she pretends to like the things he likes.

She runs with the Bartleby boys a bit longer. She is their dark shadow. She laughs at their jokes and occasionally does their homework while they dream big dreams about fixing up the car carcasses in the backyard for street-racing, cooking up bad moonshine with their uncle's still and a car radiator, and tasting it in styrofoam cups on warm summer evenings. It tastes like rubbing alcohol.

They aren't nice boys. Their jokes are mean, but she laughs anyway. Beau Huskey pulls a gun on her the first time she shows up to run Donny's errand, and a switchblade on another occasion, and when she tells them, Donny calls her a sissy bitch. Somewhere along the downward slide of Jack's feelings towards Veronica—the transition between *funny little friend* to *creepy little bitch*—he grabs her ass and then pretends she made it up, until Veronica begins to question whether it really happened.

"Be careful," says the pale boy. He speaks more and more frequently these days, out of turn, unprompted. Sometimes he speaks before she even realizes he's there and gives her a jump-scare.

"I'm not doing anything dangerous," she says, sitting on the porch steps, waiting for Benedict to get home. She's brushed her teeth twice, but the moonshine is seared into the back of her throat. She thinks it's killed her taste buds. She thinks taste buds grow back, but she can't remember for sure.

"You're bored. An empty mind invites dangerous thoughts."

She looks at him sideways. He sits crosslegged in the dust. "Go away."

"You could destroy yourself."

He's being so dramatic. Since when has he been this serious, this unsmiling and moody? Maybe he's a reflection of her own inner thoughts. Or maybe he's just become dull. "Who cares?" she says. "At least it will be interesting."

The pale boy stays with her for the rest of the evening. She makes a point of not looking at him throughout dinner and her father's lessons, but sometimes he moves out of the corner of her eye and Veronica finds herself following the movement.

Benedict turns and looks, at one point. "What is it?"

She flips a page in her workbook. "Nothing."

"Do you see something?" Because occasionally her night terrors follow her into the day, and he knows this much at least.

Her father, who believes that anything is possible until staunchly proven impossible. But she cannot bear to become a specimen or liability rather than a peer in his covert studies. So she shrugs and turns from the pale boy. "Horsefly."

That night when she lies awake in bed, a book open on her stomach, squinting at dancing shadows on the ceiling from the tree branches beyond the curtains, the pale boy sits beside her pillow and watches over her.

"You can go away," she says. "I'm not doing anything stupid right now."

"You need to sleep."

"You can't help with that. You just do the...the other thing."

"You can't sleep," he says, "because it's all building up inside your head. If you open yourself up to it, your mind will be clear and you can actually find some rest."

She rolls over to face him. "Go away."

"Just trying to help."

"It isn't helping."

"It could."

He's right. Because sometime in the night, she grows tired of not sleeping, and she finally gives herself over to the other version of herself—the one with wings and feathers in its yellow breast.

She rolls over in bed and in the next moment the mattress is gone and she is gliding on a stale, smoke-tinged breeze, sailing through the darkness.

The world spreads out seamless and silent around her. This is how it feels to exist on the ocean floor. She travels the seam between wakefulness and nightmare.

The pale boy holds out his hand. She rests in his palm.

They stand in the middle of the labyrinth. It's been many nights since they first entered its sinister walls, and at this point Veronica doubts that there is an exit. In the end, it always rises up around her. There's also more to explore.

The boy walks in silence. The smoke drifts away; the air is scentless.

They come to an open space, a black hole, a break in the maze. It is damp and tastes of soil and metallic stone. A low hum emits from the impenetrable shadows, steadily rising, rising until she realizes that it is not a hum at all, but a multitude of voices carving words out of the drone.

"What are they saying?"

The pale boy steps farther into the black hole. She wishes he wouldn't. "Listen."

And the words emerge. *In the dirt we mumble.*

Her feathers ruffle. "Go," she says. "Get out."

"We have to walk through it."

"No, get out of here."

"We have to walk through," he insists, "to get to the other side."

So they do. He carries her through the perfect darkness until the labyrinth disappears behind them and she cannot see where it reappears on the other side. The voices grow louder. Shapes move around them—hunched shapes, scurrying like insects, cold and dark and wretched.

In the dirt we mumble.

In the dirt we mumble.

Until at last they reach the end of the black hole and the pale boy stands in the maze once again. The darkness seethes behind them, and the voices follow the canary long after they leave the creatures behind.

Sometimes she sees wonderful things in the labyrinth. Sometimes—more often—terrible things. And she would like to see something amazing after an experience like this, but neither the pale boy nor her mind offer up any relief.

When she resurfaces, the canary's heart still beats rapidly in her chest. The boy is gone. She is alone. Her room is quiet, and shadows dance on the ceiling.

Veronica does not sleep.

The next day, she leaves the trailer and makes her way up to the East End. She sits out behind the Bartleby boys' cabin and draws electron configurations for Jack's homework, but she can't focus on the figures.

"Do you hear that?" she asks Donny, who sits nearby, stoned, his hand resting in a box of Cheerios.

"Huh? What?"

"She speaks." Jack drops down from the roof where he and Jules Whaley were sucking face. "Hey, you done with that? It's due tomorrow. Morning. Done?"

"No." Veronica sets down her pen. "Do you hear that?"

"No. What? What the hell you yackin' about?"

The sun is setting. The woods stop just shy of the backyard line, and she sees something move in the shadows—something large, and hunched, like a giant insect. "There!"

"There ain't nothin' there."

He's probably right, she realizes, and a weight like a bowling ball sinks in her stomach, and the breeze hisses through the trees. *You're the only one who sees it. Crazy.* And goosebumps rise up on her arms.

"I see it," says a voice at her shoulder. The pale boy stares into the woods.

"Not you," she hisses.

"What?" says Jack.

"Do you ever think," says the pale boy, "that the things you see might be more real than you realize? Maybe the universe is warning you about something. Or someone."

Veronica swats him away. "Nothing," she says to Donny and Jack and Jules Whaley, who has descended from the roof.

"She on somethin'?" asks Donny, to no one in particular.

"Nah." Davis Boone–built like a tree-trunk, buff without trying, a big eagle tattooed on his calf–drags himself out of the DIY hot tub and shakes himself like a dog. Hair slings across his forehead and sticks to his face. "She's just cracked is all."

Jack looks at her like she's the scum of the earth. "What're you on, Veronica?"

"Nothing." She wishes he'd make a joke out of it, or smile even, so she could laugh and they could move on. But he doesn't smile.

"They say her old man's cracked," says Jules Whaley. "He believes in aliens and Mars colonies and shit. My daddy said that."

Veronica snarls. "Fuck off, Jules."

"Hey," Jack snaps. "Don't talk to her like that." Behind him, Jules smiles. He shakes his head. "What's wrong with you? Fucked up bitch."

Tears spring to Veronica's eyes. *You can take it.* She hates herself for it. She hates that they hate her and she hates that she can't be one of them and most of all she hates that if she says anything, she'll be cut loose, she won't have a pack anymore, as weak and dysfunctional as this one might be. *Just take it.*

"Aw, man," Donny sighs. "Maybe it's, like, genes and DNA and shit. Maybe she's a nutter."

"She's kinda weird," says Davis Boone, as if she isn't sitting right there.

"In...the dirt...."

Veronica looks at the pale boy. Her heart is in her throat.

The creatures can't be real—they can't be in the woods. If one of the things she's seen is real, that means all of them could be, and she has seen terrible, awful things in that labyrinth, unspeakable things. The shadows creep across the yard and she shivers.

The things in the woods are *watching her.*

"Veronica."

She flinches. The pale boy is at her other side now, leaning close, and she can almost feel his breath on her skin—but he isn't real, is he? Just as real as the things in the dark. *Not real at all.*

He feels real. So do they.

"Look, she's all twitchy."

"Hey, maybe you shouldn't be doin' my homework." Jack takes it away. "Don't give her anything, huh? Yeah? She's on something already."

"Or maybe she's just cracked like Ben Lewis. Sick in the head."

"I told you something was wrong, Jackie—"

She doesn't go back to the Bartleby boys' cabin. She makes her way home in the dark, jumping at small sounds, watching for hunched shapes in the alleyways. Benedict isn't home yet. She locks the door and sits in the living room with her back to the wall.

The pale boy sits beside her. The scent of sun and citrus envelopes her. "I saw them too," he says.

"I know," she says. "Is it real?"

He does not answer, and they sit in silence together. She thinks about it for a long time, for years following that night—whether a time will come when the visions become too real and she really does lose her mind, when she doesn't just appear to be insane but truly descends into madness.

As time goes on, she sees more. It happens more frequently. Almost nightly she walks the labyrinth with the pale boy and they see things together—wonderful things, terrible things. And sometimes in her waking hours she'll sense a flicker of something in the corner of her vision, something that doesn't fit right into the world.

A yellow feather drifting on the breeze. Shadows bending around a shapeless thing. Smoke where there is no fire.

The canary has not stopped singing. Sometimes, Veronica wishes that it would.

8

The fire has not been burning for long when Veronica hears something in the woods behind her. She turns away from the RV. The flames are hot on her cheek.

There is a man standing at the edge of the clearing. It is not Grant.

Veronica takes a step back towards the fire.

He doesn't move. He's big. Long dark coat, dark hair. His body bleeds into the treeline, but as a breeze trembles through the woods, he stands perfectly still. *Oh, he's dangerous.*

He's not from Dane's Chapel. He's in town for the funeral. He's here because of *her*. These thoughts trickle through Veronica skull in a disorganized stream, and while she retains none of the feelings associated with being cornered in the hills by an unknown man, she archives the bits of information.

"Well, this is awkward," she says.

Something pops in the inferno. He doesn't flinch. "Nice fire."

He's got an accent, maybe something British. Or Australian. She's never seen him before and her dad doesn't have any British colleagues she knows of.

"Thanks," she says. "Made it myself."

"Yes. I saw. I wonder what you're trying to burn."

"Oh." Veronica steps aside, as if he can't see around her. "It's an RV." He narrows his eyes. He hasn't moved, but this is America, so he's probably armed. With a gun. She has a gun too. She's been practicing. *Yeehaw.* What would it feel like to shoot a man?

"So," she says. "What are you up to, in the woods, in the mountains, in the middle of the night? I've burned the only RV up here. There can't be much else to do."

"Thought I should get out of town," he says.

The fire catches on the roof—old wooden beams and frayed blackout curtains—and in the light she gets a decent look: pale eyes and a face carved from stone, a backpack strapped across his chest, combat boots and military-looking cargo pants. Definitely armed. "Oh," she says, "is it really so bad?"

"This place isn't too welcoming to strangers. The cops just arrested a couple of PIs on the western edge of town."

"Wow, that's really messed up."

He takes his first step forward. "Your father is Benedict Lewis." It's a statement.

"Astute." Veronica stands her ground. "I noticed you said *is*, as in, the present tense, even though he's dead. Rude. That's rude."

He tilts his head, raises an eyebrow. "We both know your father isn't dead."

"I don't know what you're talking about. I'm grieving. Fuck off."

"Your recent actions suggest otherwise."

"Wow, look at you." She adjusts her backpack. The fire is hot on her back, and she's getting antsy. "Mr. Articulate. You know a lot of words, don't you? Not enough to explain why you're here."

"The PIs are agents for North Enterprises. Whatever your father left behind, they want it. And I'm here to stop that from happening."

Veronica sweeps a hand across the expanse of the bonfire. Blue flames lick in the crevices. "This is what he left behind."

The man continues as if she didn't speak. "For the same reason they are so desperate to find Benedict Lewis' work, I am determined to keep it out of their hands. Except it seems they have hit a dead end."

She isn't absorbing anything he's saying. She's still stuck on where he found the audacity to follow her into the mountains and intrude upon this very private, dramatic moment. "This is what he left behind." Veronica kicks a smoldering chunk backwards into the fire.

"He also left behind his daughter, who the agents seem to have discounted." His tone says, *I haven't*. "They think you're crazy." And this isn't a statement, this is something like a question.

"I am," she says, "fucking crazy."

"But you know more than you let on."

"Mmm, mmm." Veronica shakes her head, taps her temple. "I just told you I'm crazy. Don't question crazy people, especially when they've just committed arson. I'm feelin' reckless tonight."

The man's eyes sweep her, as if assessing the potential insanity. She imagines, backlit by a bonfire, that she must look at least a bit intimidating. "But you do," he says. "You know more than you let on, because if you didn't you wouldn't be up here burning evidence after setting a trap."

"So what if I did?"

It's the longest a stranger has held eye contact with Veronica in a very long time, and she is once again unnerved. But in the end, it is he who looks away first. A small victory.

There's a sound in the forest behind him, like a door slamming.

Veronica's head snaps around. "Who's with you?" Sound echoes strangely in these hills; it could have come from a mile away, or far below, or far above.

"No one." He steps away from the treeline and scans the darkness.

This is her chance to make a run for it, while his back is turned, but she doesn't. *Where is Grant?* She doesn't look for him. She doesn't turn away. "That's weird," she says. "Maybe you should leave."

"Maybe we both should." He looks at her over his shoulder, his face lit up gold by the firelight.

"Nah."

"They're coming for you. And I know who *they* are."

They took Peter Webber, *they* took her dad. They won't take her. "That's bullshit." Veronica senses eyes in the trees. Not Grant's—

she recognizes his presence, and this is different. This is something looming and ominous. She shifts on her feet and cuts her eyes at the shadows. "That's bullshit, because I don't know how you know about them. I don't know who you are or where you're from. You could be working with them."

"No. You and I want the same thing: to keep Benedict Lewis' secrets buried. I don't want them getting their hands on his research either. And anyway, if I were working with them, they'd already have you." She'll just let him think that. "I'm trying to help you escape."

"I'm actually doing alright. Don't need your help. But thanks."

"What about the Mumblers?"

She hesitates.

He sees her hesitate. "You know about them, don't you?"

"No."

"Right." He doesn't believe her. "Well, you're about to."

This is why they are called Mumblers: because as they climb through the hills above Dane's Chapel, hunched bodies cloaked in darkness, their voices travel before them. Their words reverberate across the slopes.

"*In the dirt we mumble. In the dirt we mumble...*"

And Harry Markus hears them first, because that sound is ingrained into his soul. Veronica hears them second, because the fire snaps behind her and she has to drag the memories from her subconsciousness: the dark twists and turns of a labyrinth in her mind; terrible echoing voices rising out of her nightmares. She recognizes them all the same.

"*In the dirt we mumble.*"

"Well." Veronica fumbles with her backpack and slings it over one shoulder. She fishes around inside and draws out a handgun. Checks the chamber, switches off the safety, racks the slide, replaces her bag. She flips the hair out of her face. Her heart is playing a staccato beat in her chest, like over-caffeination, like nerves. She won't let it show. "Well. Looks like you're on your own, man."

"You're just running off by yourself?" His voice is flat.

Veronica smiles. "I've always been by myself. And I'm thriving."

With that, she takes off into the woods—around the RV, leaving the raging fire far behind. She crashes through the brush, diving so her backpack doesn't snag on low-hanging branches, legs pedaling against a carpet of dead leaves. Over the next rise, there will be an oak tree. Down the hill from the oak tree will be a ravine, and on the opposite side is a trucking highway leading south, and then west, and then out of North Carolina. The highway is mostly unused since the mines were shut down and the trucks stopped coming, but Benedict Lewis knew about it. Veronica knows about it too.

"*In the dirt we mumble.*"

Her breath is short. She is not afraid of the dark, but as she nears the crest of the hill and the oak tree rises into her line of sight, the voices rise as well. The mumbling in the woods grows closer till it surrounds her, echoing in the darkness, slipping between the trees. The shadows grow close.

Veronica is not afraid of the dark. But she is suddenly afraid of the Mumblers.

She is nearly to the tree when a thick hand grasps her ankle.

She trips in the leaves and bashes her chin on the ground. A coiled root knocks the air from her chest. The hand tugs on her ankle, drawing her back down the hill.

She struggles to roll over. She twists around, gets a mouthful of loose soil, wrenches her handgun out from under her. Without looking too hard at the thing in the dark, she pulls the trigger.

Her shoulder kicks back against the roots. The thing screams. Her leg is free. A bulky shape tumbles back down the slope, slams into a tree trunk, and continues shrieking even as she scrambles to her feet and sprints up to the oak tree. Her lungs are on fire. Her ears are ringing.

The thought comes suddenly, with uncharacteristic urgency: *where is Grant?* Because he talks big, that ghostly boy with his snark and bold propositions, but when she needs him most she's reminded that he's all in her head and she is, truly, alone. *Thriving.*

But there are others on the hilltop. She cannot see them, but she knows. Their voices are loud. Their voices are inhuman. As she looks down towards the ravine she spots bodies in the darkness, making their way up towards the oak tree.

"*In the dirt we mumble.*"

This is a scene from her night terrors. This is real.

How many bullets does she have? She raises the gun above her head and points it at the sky. The trees are grave markers. The things in the shadows, hollow tumbling weeds. *Like a Western.* "Yeehaw."

She stumbles down the leaf-slick slope, on her feet and then sliding on her knees. She smashes painfully through thorny brush. The monsters rise to meet her—shapes bent and disfigured, shiny black insects—their hands pale in the dull moonlight, white like corpses.

The leaves are slick. She can't slow her decent. A shape looms in the dark, and before she can dig in her heels, Veronica slams into a tree. Her vision flickers and she momentarily forgets to breathe.

She tries to find her knees.

A hand grabs her face.

Veronica screams through the fingers. She bites down on thick cold flesh, bites as hard as her jaw can bite down, until she tastes blood and her chin is slick with it, but the hand won't budge. She is still holding the handgun. She aims it in a random direction, guesses, fires. Veronica can hear others approaching—*in the dirt we mumble, in the dirt we mumble—*

Then, a scream. A flare.

The hand falls away. Veronica gasps and scrambles to her knees, spitting, pointing the gun wildly. The Mumbler tumbles through the bushes and lands against a tree.

The man in the coat stands above Veronica. He holds something that looks like a black rolling pin, but likely is not. As she climbs to her feet, he turns and points his weapon back up the slope, at the creatures moving towards them. The pronged tip sparks to life—fire or electricity, something that spits and sparks bright in the dark. The Mumblers falter and hiss. She can't look at it directly; she turns her head away.

"Okay," she pants. "So…you're not useless."

He keeps his arm aloft; the light illuminates the treetops, casts the branches white and ghostly. "That's what I was trying to tell you."

Air floods in and out of her lungs. "You could have just *said* that. You could have just said 'I promise I'm not useless' and I would have given it a second thought maybe."

He doesn't looks at her, but his brow furrows. "Would you really?"

"No. Shithead." Veronica hooks her elbow around his and drags him along behind her as she skids to the bottom of the ravine. He checks behind them every few steps, his weapon still lit. "What is that?"

"A baton."

Veronica snarls. "A baton. That doesn't mean shit. *Baton* is French for *stick*. Police carry batons in old movies. Baguettes are just bread batons."

He follows her out of the ravine. He's staring at her like he's regretting this. "What?"

"What kind of baton has a shocker at the end, huh?"

"What? It's not a—where are we going?"

Veronica clambers over the edge of the ravine. The ground is more solid here, less threatening to ankles. "Escape route." Her chest is tight from the fall. She can still taste the rubbery flesh on her teeth. Blood is cooling on her face. Her stomach churns.

"Off the mountain?"

"Don't ask questions," says Veronica, "it makes you sound stupid. Just keep that thing lit and keep the beetles away from us." She pushes a branch aside, feels her way between the trees. She strains her eyes against the feeble light until she makes out a shape in the distance.

"In...the dirt...we mumble..."

A shudder runs down her spine. She hurries over.

The tarp is covered with fallen leaves and pine needles. By the light of the baton she drags it to the ground, revealing a pitiful gray sedan a bit older than she is. It does not wear its age well.

She finds the key in her bag from feel alone, wrestles it into the lock, and wrenches open the door. The air that slips out is mildewy, but somewhat less concerning than the monstrous insect people scurrying through the hills. She slides inside and slams the door behind her.

The man jams himself into the passenger seat. "Go."

"I decide when we go," she says. The key is already in the ignition. It takes her one—two—three terrifying attempts to get the engine to start. She switches on the dim headlights and steps on the gas.

The sedan lurches forward. Veronica steers around a tree that probably wasn't there when her father last parked the car. There is an overgrown path leading down an incline to an unfinished gravel drive from the old coal trucking days, and then—with a rush of relief—the sedan hops the road's shoulder and skids out onto the open, empty highway. A rooster tail of dust and gravel and exhaust decorates the crisp air.

They speed off into the night.

The man turns off his lightning baton.

Veronica's handgun is wedged under her thigh closest to the door, out of his reach but very much within her own. "Remind me why I shouldn't dump you on the side of the road and just put a bullet in your brain."

She doesn't know that she could really shoot him. She shot the Mumblers, of course, but they didn't really feel human. Even now the snapshots from the chase are fading away into surreal memory. Did that happen? To *her*?

"The Mumblers want to kill you," he says.

"Well, you don't know that. Maybe they want to kidnap me."

He looks at her. "Why would they do that?"

"Same reason someone kidnapped my dad."

He shakes his head. "You are not Benedict Lewis. They'd rather you dead, than living with knowledge they cannot claim."

The gun is uncomfortable under her leg, but she leaves it there. "You can't claim it, either."

"What? Your father's research? I don't want it." He sounds sincere, but so did those agents at the funeral, and so did Jack Bartleby when he said she was pretty in fifth grade and then he turned around and told all his friends she had gap teeth. Veronica has trust issues. The sincerity of a stranger means jack-shit. "I want to keep it out of North Enterprise's hands. It's personal vendetta. I don't want them finding it, which means I need to find it before they do. And you know where it is, don't you?"

Veronica shrugs. "Maybe." She gnaws on her lip. The car stinks of sweat and smoke and mold. The headlights are dim and the road is hopelessly potholed. "So, you'll find it first and then you'll do what? Sell it to the highest bidder?"

"Destroy it," he says. "Probably."

Veronica thinks about that. "Yeah," she says, evenly, "destroying it is probably the best way to go."

"So you do know where it is."

"Would I tell you?" Veronica smiles. She shows her teeth. *Gap teeth*. "Would I tell you so you can stick me with your lightning taser baton and leave me for dead and go find it for yourself? I'm not taking you at your word. I might be a little crazy, but I'm not stupid."

Up ahead, an old orange barricade is toppled on its side. Veronica slows, edges around it, and speeds up again.

"So," she says, "why shouldn't I kill you?"

"Because the Mumblers want to kill you," he says impatiently. "I can keep them from doing that. And I can keep North Enterprises off your back."

"North *Enterprises*," she echoes. "That's where they're from? What a boring name. Well. I'm not too worried. I took care of the agents." Veronica is actually pretty proud of that maneuver. "And I don't know about this whole killing thing. The only person who's allowed to destroy me is me."

"Tell the Mumblers that. If you were smart, you'd be scared of them."

She can tell he's starting to get fed-up. She feels she's getting closer to winning some sort of prize. "What does that make you, Mister Not Scared? Hmm?" *A real dumb-ass*, she thinks.

"I am not scared of them," he says, with all the self-importance of pure-bred royalty, "because they're scared of *me*."

Veronica laughs. "Maybe they don't know me well enough yet. Give them some time to get scared."

No, she won't keep him around for long. Long enough to get the Mumblers off her tail and make sure she's left the agents far behind, long enough to throw them off her scent. Then she'll get rid of him. She'll lose him in some very effective way. If she can take down two secret agents from some secret organization, she can deal with an overconfident Englishman who thinks he's got her number.

"What's your name, baton man?" She looks at him, and in the car lights she realizes he isn't actually that much older than she is. Early twenties at the latest. "Baton boy," she amends.

If he's offended, he doesn't show it. He looks straight ahead. Face of stone, eyes pale and cold. "Harry Markus."

In the backseat of the sedan, Grant gazes out the grime-smeared window at the passing shadows. His gaze follows the shape of a mountain ridge. He catches Veronica's eye in the rearview mirror. He smiles.

The Boy (II)

In the hush of pre-dawn darkness, a man stands in an observatory and gazes out at the shifting desert.

People disappear in the desert. Souls get lost amongst the dunes.

The observatory sits high atop his lab, an ugly concrete structure recovered from a missile-testing outpost. It's solid; the foundations have their knuckles dug deep into the earth; yet the floor seems to shift and buckle beneath his feet, and it's only adrenaline that keeps him upright at his post.

There's a syringe clasped in his fist. He holds it so tightly his hand trembles.

When they come for him—when headlights appear over the dunes and great tires spit sand and the men break open the fence—he'll stand there, unmoving, unshaken. He's looking for something, in the desert. He's watching for a boy.

My boy. My rock-solid boy.

He prays the boy is fast. He prays the boy won't look back, won't stop for a second. He's never prayed before. He doesn't know who he's praying to. But while he's at it sending up aimless, desperate prayers, he prays something in the desert is listening this night.

When the men break into the lab downstairs, the man does not move. It's too late, he thinks. As they kick in the door and seize him, the syringe tumbles from his fingers. It clatters. It shatters. Bits of glass like dewdrops shine in the moonlight, but the syringe is empty.

It's too late.

A boy is running.

He won't stop, not till his feet catch on something solid and invisible, and he trips and falls into deeper shadow, and his head collides with something more solid than his skull. He'll lay there while blood blossoms in his hair and slivers of moonlight play strange shapes across the dunes.

He wants to believe that there is still a fight to be had. He wants to believe that it matters if he keeps moving. But it's too late, he thinks, as his visions shudders and shatters like a syringe of glass. The heavens erupt into starbursts and chittering laughter, like sand on the wind.

People disappear, in the desert. This is where secrets come to die.

9

When dawn breaks and paints the first hazy shades of pastel pink across Appalachia, the world is apocalyptically still. Veronica is behind the wheel of a dying vehicle hurtling down the empty motorway. There's gas in the tank and gold on the horizon and she feels like Armageddon; terrible and inevitable.

The windows are cracked because they won't stay rolled up. As she speeds along winding mountain roads and sheer stone cliffs and her ears pop and her skull sings she breathes in air that smells of sweet sunrise. The wind fills a cavity in her chest. The mountains shrink to hills and from hills to rolling fields and Amish-built barns and Mennonite farms. They blow through little towns with steepled chapels.

The gray sedan has just putted and squealed across the Tennessee-Kentucky border when the gas light flicks on, but Veronica doesn't want to stop. The Mumblers are behind. The open road is ahead.

Just past Scottsville, something buzzes in Harry Markus' backpack, and he bends—slowly, as if he might startle her with sudden movements—and peers into the bag before straightening again. He resumes the position he's maintained for the past five hours. He does not look at her.

"Whatcha doin'?" she says.

"Nothing important."

"Oh, well, in that case." She doesn't bother with a turn signal—she swerves into the next lane and screeches off the highway onto a sun-bleached side street.

Harry Markus grips the armrests. "What are you—?"

"Nothing important."

She lets him worry for a second before executing another sharp turn and peeling into the FiveStar parking lot. She stomps the brakes at the first pump and throws the car into park. The station windows are lit. There's a scrappy little pickup parked around the side of the building. Beyond, the parking lot sprawls and bleeds into a truck stop featuring a luminous Huddle House.

She throws open the door. "I need fuel." She retrieves a roll of bills from her backpack. "So. Go pay for a full tank at Pump One, and a bag of Fritos."

"A what?"

"Corn chips."

He looks faintly disgusted, but he takes the money and gets out of the car. "And what will keep you from driving off while I'm inside?"

"Mumbling bug men, that's what. I am frightened of the bug men, and you're a big strong man with a lightning baton." She laughs. "Go get my Fritos."

He goes and gets the Fritos.

Veronica checks the ad-plastered station windows before diving back into the car. She crawls over the center console and grabs at Harry Markus' backpack. The pager is at the top of the bag's contents.

Mumblers on the move. They followed you. They might know who you are. Come back and we'll figure out a plan. HM2

She sits back in the driver's seat and props up her knee against the wheel. She reads the message again. "What do you make of that?" she asks Grant.

He lounges in the back seat, head against one window and feet flat against the other. He glances at her over his arm. "He's dangerous."

"Well, yeah. Obviously. I knew that much." She throws the pager back in his bag. "He's a liar, too."

She digs around a bit more in there—a few packs of ammo, something that looks like an MRE. It's frustratingly empty. He seems like he probably has knives and stuff hidden on his body, though. She shuts the backpack and sits back in the driver's seat. "He told me the Mumblers were after me. But they're following *him*. Which means he's making up reasons why I should keep him around. Which means he doesn't have a real reason."

"So you'll get rid of him?"

She climbs out of the car again. She watches Harry Markus approach the station doors. "I'll get rid of him," she says. "At the right time."

Veronica Lewis eats her Fritos. She is probably insane.

Harry finds it disturbing how intensely she drives—jaw set, eyes narrowed, one foot resting in the door and one hand draped lazily in her lap. Her attention does not waver from the road. He thinks about her walking home from the funeral reception, walking down dark gravel roads and talking to herself as she went. He wonders if she's talking to herself right now.

Come back and we'll figure out a plan. HM2

HM2 is Howard. *Come back.* He can't, not until he's fixed this. Harry does everything for a reason, and in his mind, the end justifies the means in most every circumstance. This ethos is made simpler by his brothers' existence: it's a reminder of everything he has to lose, and at the same time, how little he has to lose before he has nothing at all. Sometimes he overreacts, sure. His personal standard of reasonable force is somewhat distorted. When his brothers *aren't* around, Harry struggles to maintain his balance. He understands that there's a job to be done and he can't let anything get in his way, but the tangibility of the situation gets away from him. He spirals. He turns into something that is distinctly not *Harry* and is a lot more *Markus.*

He has what is commonly known as *daddy issues.*

Veronica eats her Fritos. Harry Markus sits in silence and

pretends not to watch, but there's a lazy smile sewn into her face, stitched with malice and amusement, and he finds it unsettling at best. About an hour more into the drive, he finally speaks.

"Are you still not telling me where we're going?"

"That is correct," she says. "You're really quite clever."

And the strange thing is, he's starting to think that maybe she's clever, too. Insane, yes. But there's something calculating behind her devilish eyes, something that whispers *you don't have all the pieces in this puzzle.*

He's been to Hell and back. He's seen his share of demons.

Surely Veronica Lewis can't be any worse.

Veronica has a couple plans. None of them are particularly good, nor are they particularly idiot-proof. Plan A is flashy, and has a certain irony to it which Veronica enjoys. That's the one she's going with. She doesn't feel the need to explore further options.

"That's silly," says Grant, who sprawls in the middle of the back seat, legs hooked over the headrest, head dangling upside-down over the floor. If he was real and she hit the brakes, he would be in trouble.

Well, I'm a silly girl. If she hits the breaks, will he fly across the car, or simply disappear? It's tempting.

Harry Markus stares out the window, arms crossed. Bored and boring. She wishes she'd ended up with a more quippy hitchhiker, someone with banter and intrigue. Although the intense silence is intriguing in its own way, like the shiver of low-hanging clouds before thunder rolls through the sky, like pressure building in a bottle. She's in control. She could shatter him in an instant.

She tests the waters and switches on the radio. Staticky snatches of garbled dialogue drift from the dust-caked speakers.

"You're putting yourself in danger," Grant says, "and for what? Take some time. Think it through." She assumes he isn't talking about the radio.

I don't have time, she thinks. *There's not enough time, you're on the Veronica train now, there's no getting off. It's my way or the highway.... Do you have any better ideas?*

He doesn't respond, because of course, since when does the pale boy have original thoughts? His hair flops stupidly to the floor. "Don't cry to me when it fails," he mumbles.

"Oh, fuck off."

Harry Markus turns. His beak of a nose casts a weird shadow across his face, and in the sunlight his eyes have darkened to the color of restless water. "I didn't say anything," he says.

"Hmm?" Veronica reaches over and cranks up the radio volume. She fights the urge to glare at the backseat. "Voices."

After a moment of tense silence and static, he speaks again. "Are you really schizophrenic?"

"Shhh." She turns up the radio even louder, and between static breaks, strains of electric guitar cut through. She turns it up so she can't hear Harry Markus, can't hear Grant in the backseat.

"What are you doing?" She doesn't respond. Harry Markus is still staring at her. "Turn it down."

She cranks up the radio to its full, insufficient volume, and in her periphery Harry Markus winces. Now Veronica can never turn it down. "Do you know what this is?" she yells. "I can't turn it down. It's the law."

"What?"

"Huh?" A gust of wind sneaks through the cracked windows. Veronica smells rain. She turns her head so he can't see her smile; she lets Avril and the oncoming storm drown out both boys, the real and the imaginary. She lets the relief of doing something and flying down an open road and running away from Dane's Chapel fill her skull.

"Harry Markus," she shouts. "Listen to this masterpiece, this is art, this is a ballad, this is where pop-punk *peaked. He was a skater boy.*"

10

In the northwestern area of a country called the United States of America, in a hidden compound discreetly nestled between mountains and woods and situated above a dense maze of tunnels, there sits a non-confrontational young man named Howard. He sits in a pretentious office lobby and waits to be seen by a pretentious man with a bad mustache.

There is a large black-and-white canvas print of a pelican skimming the water's surface. He's been staring at it for the past hour. He taps his foot. He bobs his head to imaginary music. He kicks out his legs and slumps in his chair, gnaws his lip and glowers at the pelican.

"Markus." Cage's personal security detail, a brick of a man with tattoos on his knuckles, stands in the office door. "He'll see you."

"Well, took long enough." Howard leaps to his feet. He is channeling his most overconfident version of Harry. This makes him an asshole. He squeezes past the monstrous man and steps into Cage's office. "I've been trying to get a meeting for two days," he says.

Lawrence Cage barely looks up from his computer. The screen

light paints his face blue-white, and his stupid blond mustache hangs onto his thin upper lip with all the desperation of a scrawny caterpillar on death's brink. His lips barely move when he speaks, as if he can't be bothered to exercise the necessary muscles. "Sit down."

Howard doesn't think Harry would have sat, so he doesn't either. He stands behind the squeaky leather chair and looks down at Cage from across the desk. "You've been putting us off."

"Hmm." A few more taps on the keyboard, and Cage swivels his chair to face Howard. He has quite a bit of downy blond hair, but his hairline is rapidly receding. He sits back and grips the armrests with ringed fingers. "Your brother is a problem."

Howard can't count the number of times he's heard that line. "I've been telling him that for years, but you know older brothers. Think they know best." He shrugs it off, but the mere suggestion by this man that Harry might have erred makes Howard want to punch Cage's punchable face. *Fool.*

"Yes." Cage again becomes distracted by something on the computer. He leans over, taps the mouse, begrudgingly drags his attention back to Howard. "I don't care that you are brothers. I do not care about your chain of command, aside from the fact that apparently the whims of any one of you influences the others, more so than the commands of your superiors. Do you follow?"

"Hmm. This isn't about my brothers, actually. I mean, it's about something Henry found—"

"I don't want to talk about your brother in IT—"

"He's in Intel!"

"—I called you in because of your older brother."

Howard taps the back of the chair. He stares hard at Cage, trying to decide whether the man is purposefully messing with him, trying to determine whether Cage is clever enough to mess with a Markus brother. "You didn't call me in. I had to fight for this meeting."

"Sit."

Howard sits. The moment he does, he wishes he'd stayed standing; his foot jiggles and he doesn't like being at the same level as Lawrence Cage.

"Stop wasting my time. What do you want?"

Howard's fingers dance on his knees. "North Enterprises is stirring up something it doesn't want to mess with."

Cage blinks. "And?"

"And." Howard sits forward. "*And*. My brother's intel is picking up...activity. In an area where it should not be picking up any activity at all. In an area where activity should be dead and buried, and where, if activity should occur...we should definitely cease agitating said activity. Are *you* following?"

"Stop speaking in circles. Get to the point, or get out of my office."

Howard stands. "The Mumblers are on the move." Cage is still. He holds Howard's gaze but betrays nothing. "Mumblers. The *Mumblers*. The Bloody Mumblers. Does that name mean anything to you?" Because it means everything to him. Everything. And Harry—his life is consumed by that word. *Mumblers. The Mumblers. We should have killed them when we had the chance.*

Cage's voice is cold. "Do you have something of consequence to report? Or are you wasting my time?"

Howard's jaw clicks. What would Harry do? He puts back his shoulders. "I'm warning you. North Enterprises is stirring up a dangerous rival."

"You sound deranged."

Howard slams both hands down on the desk, fingers splayed, palms stinging. Cage flinches, then looks annoyed. "I know North Enterprises is working with BEESWAX," says Howard. "I know that whatever they are investigating, it's highly confidential and volatile. I know that the instant you began this operation, Henry started picking up activity in known Mumbler territory. He has aerial footage. Rare energy signatures. Records of departures from the area. North Enterprises has never seen this level of activity, and Henry has been trying for weeks to get it through to the operation commanders, and he is ignored over and over and over again. To the detriment of this entire mission, and possibly the world."

Cage knits his fingers together. "Are you quite finished?"

When it comes down to it, Howard doesn't really care whether North Enterprises comes crashing down in flames. But he does care about his brothers, more than he cares about life itself. And while Harry frequently—unwittingly, perhaps—puts them in danger,

Howard knows that his brother feels the same.

"No. I'm not finished." Howard stands upright. He crosses his arms. "I want my helicopter back."

"The way I heard it, you were performing...what was it...'wildly dangerous maneuvers that made your fellow pilots question whether you were suicidal'. So, no. You cannot *have your helicopter back*."

"Not dangerous," says Howard. "Unorthodox. And effective."

"If these Mumblers were a problem, we would already be concerned. We would have documented history of agitation. And we would know about any impending threat long before your brother managed to pick up anything of consequence." Cage wheels over to his computer, taps the keyboard and brings it back to life. "No, I'm not concerned about your brother in IT, nor your personal rivals. I'm more concerned about your other brother."

"What about him?"

"As we've just established, he is problematic."

"Problematic is a strong word."

"Not really," says Cage. "I could use stronger." He scrolls across a screen Howard cannot see. "It appears that he was meant to depart for an international raid with a hand-picked team. They left last night. They are in Nepal now. Tango's commander says your brother never reported."

Howard convinces himself that he knows nothing about it. "That doesn't sound like Harry."

"Actually, that sounds exactly like your brother." Cage grimaces. "From what I gather, he was quite insistent that he be included in the recent BEESWAX business, and when his request to join the mission was rejected, he failed to report for a raid—which, according to his records, he has never done before—and instead disappeared from the compound." Cage looks up from the screen. His pupils are pinpricks. "So. My question is: where is your brother?"

Howard thinks about it. Harry is very good at getting things done, but very bad at subtlety, which so often leaves Howard in this awkward position of coming up with clever excuses for his behavior. It's a small price to pay for not being in charge. "Reconnaissance."

"Reconnaissance."

"Yeah. Reconnaissance. I assume. Loves a good reconnaissance mission."

The computer screen flickers dark. Cage tilts his head. "Tell your brother in IT to stop chasing phantoms. And when Harry Markus gets back from his unscheduled, unapproved reconnaissance mission, tell him to report to me directly. Immediately."

"I'm sure he'll love that," says Howard.

"I don't care," says Cage. "Now get out of my office."

11

Veronica buys a soggy pizza with undercooked mushrooms at a hole-in-the-wall spot on the outskirts of St. Louis. She rolls down the windows in the parking lot, leans back her seat, sticks her feet up on the dash, and leisurely opens the box. Sunset sneaks between the buildings and paints gold panels across the cracked and busted parking lot.

"We need to keep moving," says Harry Markus.

"Relax, Action Man. We lost them." She offers the box, though she has no interest in sharing. "Do people like you eat pizza?"

He just watches with mild distaste as she drops the box back into her lap. Watches like she's an odd specimen indeed. "People like me?"

"Renegades in trenchcoats," she says. "Matrix people. Do you wear sunglasses?"

"No."

"You should. It really does something"—she waves a slice of pizza—"for the overall look." When he doesn't respond, she slides the box onto the center console and licks grease off her fingers. "How do you get into this line of work? Whatever it is you do. I think I'd be good at it. Did they recruit you out of the military?"

"What it is you think I do?"

The smell of yeast and weed drifts out the open pizzeria doors. The night brings biting cold with it, but Veronica likes the fresh air, and she likes that she isn't moving for the first time in what feels like days, and she likes that she's far away from Dane's Chapel and the hulking hills and the shadowy crawling things. She likes that she makes Harry Markus nervous.

"Well." She takes another slice, folds it to keep the cheese from sliding off. "You say you don't work for the fake PIs, but the mumbling insect men are apparently scared of you, which means you're somebody. If you really don't work for North Enterprises, then my guess is you work for BEESWAX."

Harry Markus merely blinks, but she knows it's a flinch. Veronica smiles. She burns her tongue on hot cheese.

He shifts in his seat but he doesn't look away once. "What...do you know about BEESWAX?"

She snorts, sets her half-eaten slice atop the box. She's forgotten that she's lactose intolerant, and the cheese is starting to give her bad feelings. "Ben Lewis is my dad, dumbass. You think I don't know about BEESWAX?"

He had. Because for his grandiose speech about how he isn't going to underestimate her like the PIs did, he has no fucking clue what kind of animal he's messing with. This animal has teeth. And its dad taught it to read.

Harry Markus eyes the pizza. He chooses his next words carefully. "What else do you know?"

"Lots of things. Just assume I know everything. Do you work for them?" She dusts crumbs off her hands, into her lap, and then onto the floor. "Not that you'd tell me."

"I don't work for BEESWAX."

"Hmm." Shadow spills across the parking lot. She cranks up her window a bit and shrugs on her jacket, but she doesn't turn on the car. "I don't believe you."

"We should keep moving."

"You don't even know where we're going."

"Your stepmother—"

"Teresa isn't my stepmother." Veronica hasn't even thought

about Teresa, but it's an excellent point—she and Margot live in St. Louis. "Teresa's just...a dumb bimbo who screws guys with money and leaves when they lose it. She didn't love him, and he knew it." She looks sideways at Harry. "I'm not running to Teresa Montclar."

In the rearview mirror, Grant watches her, quiet and cautious.

She sits in an ancient sedan with a dangerous stranger and a hallucination. She sits and bides her time while the pizza grows cold and the cheese gums up. "What about you, *Harry Markus*? Where are *your* parents? Are you a criminal? Ex-military? Watched too many action movies? You come off like a rich kid with expensive gadgets and a god complex."

(She couldn't possibly know it at this time, but that's more or less the whole truth.)

"What makes you think I'm going to answer that?"

"Because you're trying to earn my trust, jackass." She needs to move her legs. Veronica wrestles open the door and climbs out. She tucks her gun into the curve of the door. She plants her feet on asphalt.

"I don't need to earn your trust," says Harry Markus.

Veronica puts her hands on her hips and ducks her head to look at him. "You do. And you're doin' real badly."

She grits her teeth and leans back her head to look at the sky, which is royal blue turning to black in the east, fiery pink in the west. Sometimes, when she was a bit younger and Benedict Lewis was a bit less *gone*, they'd sit on the roof together and watch the sun go down behind the mountains. She recalls the scene in vivid detail: how the stars appeared early in the evening on a clear night, and shone brighter as the sunlight died. The sacred hush of moonlight and crickets in the brush, rustling wind and a few whispered voices on the breeze, how everyone slowed down and she sped up. It was tangible, and with Ben, it was beautiful. She remembers how once she laid on her back with the tin digging into her spine and she thought she saw a ribbon of lightning tear across the night sky, only it wasn't storming, it wasn't heat lightning either. It was a pure bolt of black destruction split across the heavens, and it lingered in her vision until her father spoke and she blinked and the moment passed on to another and another—

And she stands in a St. Louis parking lot with garlic on her breath and a lot of misgivings.

Where is he?

"You're on the wrong path," says Grant from somewhere behind her, but when Veronica turns, she can't find him. Just a disembodied voice.

Harry Markus hears them first. He's out of the car with his rucksack on before his mind catches up to his body.

She looks at him with those dark dead eyes and a bored, slack jaw. "What?"

For an instant, he considers the appealing prospect of simply leaving her here and following the next big lead. But the Mumblers would like a bartering chip, wouldn't they? It's less Veronica Lewis' welfare, and more Harry's own personal brand of spite, that propels him to act.

He rounds the hood and grabs her arm. "Run if you don't want to die."

She yanks her arm back. She grabs her handgun, her backpack, and slams the door. "Lead the way, hero."

He hurries down a side street; their footfalls echo off the close brick walls. He knows The Mumblers within her earshot when Veronica Lewis' pace quickens behind him. Then he breaks into a run.

Where are you going, Harry? He doesn't know this city. But he knows what the Mumbler's know: that there is one place where Harry Markus would never flee.

His steps falter. He pauses in the mouth of an alley, stares out across the street to where neon lights paint green and red splotches on the sidewalk. A car engine roars to life down the block, and somewhere a door slams, but otherwise the street is quiet. Veronica catches up to him, panting loudly.

"In the dirt we mumble."

It comes from behind. And around. They're everywhere, they're closing in, and he can't outrun them forever, can he? His breath catches in his throat. He exhales—he empties himself. And when he inhales again, the anxiety is anger, and heat rolls through his body. His mind quiets. He moves to the center of the street.

"What are you doing?" Veronica Lewis stands over him. "Are

you doing...what I think you're doing? Are you being serious right now?"

Harry blocks out the voices closing in. *Move.* He reaches into a zippered compartment at the bottom of his rucksack and retrieves a set a pliers. He flips them open and inserts one half of the handle and plier nose into the manhole grips—leans back on his heels, gets one hand under the rising lid, drags it aside. It hits the asphalt with a sharp clang.

She's silhouetted against the neon shopfronts. "I'm not crawling into a sewer."

Harry rises and finds a torch under his coat. He isn't anymore thrilled than she is, but he can't say that. It's too much like fear. Right now he can't think about fear or he'll lose his focus, he'll stumble. Fear gets people killed. Harry sniffs and shines the torch into the manhole. "You first."

"Nah," she says.

"I have to close the cover."

"I'll do it." He looks at her wiry arms. "I'll do it," she insists.

Maybe she thinks it's a power move, but he doesn't have time to fight about it. "Fine. Be quick."

In this moment, Veronica has a choice to make. Harry Markus is already down in the sewer below, shining his flashlight around, the *drip drip* of damp walls and distant running water drifting up to her. She stands with her back against a cement cylinder, one hand clinging to rusty ladder rungs. The manhole cover rests on the edge of the opening. If she moves fast, she can climb out before Harry Markus realizes what's going on. She can throw the cover on and take off through the streets of St. Louis. Alone.

The voices are nearby now. How far would she get? Yes, the Mumblers are after him, but they sure seemed interested when they chased her through the hills. She isn't sure that she wants to repeat that in an unfamiliar city.

"Lewis." Harry Markus shines the light into her face.

She blinks down at him. "Fuck off."

"Hurry."

Where is Grant? She wishes she could will him into existence. *Help me. Give me an idea. Tell me I'm not about to make everything worse.*

But as usual, he's ducked out when he's needed most. Granted, he'd warned her. Standing in the hole-in-a-wall pizzeria with smoke-stained Italian movie posters clinging to the wallpaper and a mustachioed teenager manning the register, smells of garlic and grass wafting from the kitchen, Grant had leaned against a plastic-covered booth and watched as she placed her order.

"They can all track you," he'd said. "Think about it, Veronica—you know this. If the Mumblers can find you, what about the PIs? Or any number of other people."

"The Mumblers would find us first."

The mustache boy looked up from the register. "Huh?"

"Huh?" she said.

He blinked. "It's twelve ninety-nine."

"Veronica—"

"They'll find us first," she said.

The boy was staring directly at her that time. "Are you talking to me?"

"Don't worry about it." Veronica ignored Grant's gaze drilling into her neck, ignored the furtive glances the cashier casts towards the kitchen, ignored the part of her that knew Benedict Lewis would hate to see where she is now, the things she's doing, the things she has planned for the near future.

"Don't worry about it," Veronica said again. She paid with her dad's credit card and snatched the receipt. "It's just that the Mumblers are coming."

12

It isn't a sewer, it's a cellar. Through a low-hanging archway, the space opens up into a narrow brick tunnel striated with filthy pipes. The good inch of murky water on the floor is already soaking through her socks.

She takes out her own flashlight and follows Harry Markus. From behind, he looks like a hulking giant in a cape, with that ridiculous trench coat majestically swooshing out behind him. She bets he's a lot smaller and dumber-looking under that coat. He's probably insecure about his shoulders or something.

She runs her light over the walls. Mold grows in the grout. There's a film of moisture over everything. The cold leeches into her bones. "Why're you so sure this'll work?" Her voice echoes. "Because it feels like you've trapped us down here."

"It's the last place they'll look."

"Howd'ya figure?"

"What?"

She considers just boinking him over the head with her flashlight and being done with it. "Dude, where are you from? You don't talk like normal people. People don't use words like baton and—and like, say ominous things in the middle of the woods like 'the cops aren't welcoming to strangers in this town'. What are you, from a movie set? Get out of Dodge?"

His boots leave a wake of tiny ripples. "Where do you think I'm from?"

"You sound like someone from *Doctor Who*."

"From what?"

"See, how come you don't know about *Doctor Who*? Do you live under a rock? Are you British or what?"

He pauses, looks back at her. "I'm...not British."

"You sound real British. Where do people like you come from? You never answered my question. Are you discharged military or something? Did you commit unspeakable war crimes in the service of the monarchy's legions? Where were you born?"

His pace slows. He cocks his head. He looks like he's thinking about it, which doesn't make what comes next super convincing. "Russia."

"Russia. How come you sound like the Queen of England, huh?"

He shrugs. "It's how I learned English."

"Say something in Russian, then."

"No."

"Come on. A cuss word. Prove it." She doesn't normally mind the dark, but this is different. This feels an awful lot like something that would only happen in her mind; it feels like a prophecy coming to fruition. She sticks close behind. "How come you know them? The Mumblers? What's their deal?"

"If I tell you, will you tell me where we're going?"

"No, but it would make nice conversation. And it might give me a really good reason to keep you around." A draft brushes past her neck; Veronica swats at it. The scent of metal and mold mingles with something else—smoke. She swallows and redirects her flashlight beam, catches up to Harry Markus. "Well? What's their deal, huh? Why do they mumble in the dirt?"

"Because they're insane. " His voice is guttural. "They dug themselves into caves. They've been hiding for hundreds of years —maybe a thousand. Hiding. Slowly evolving. Losing their bloody minds until they're..."

"Insect people?"

"They're not people. Not anymore. They're something else."

"But they're still human."

"Are they?" Harry Markus pauses and Veronica nearly slams into him. His flashlight beam hovers over the water, follows silver ripples. He turns and looks at her, his face ghostly pale in the dark. "Every few years, they crawl out from their holes in the ground." His voice is dreadful and hollow. "They move in the dark because they can no longer bear the light. When they return to their caves, they bring secrets from the outside world, and they bring people unfortunate enough to fall into their hands. People who have valuable information. They keep these people in the dark. They treat them as Mumblers are treated. But humans aren't meant to breathe so little, aren't meant to survive in the dark and cold, aren't meant to neither eat nor drink for as long as the Mumblers can survive without sustenance. If they don't die on their own time, slowly suffocating under a mile of caverns and stone, they die at the Mumblers' hands. Their eyes are cut from their head. Their lungs are removed from their bodies. They die listening to their own screams. Sometimes we find bodies."

His voice hovers in the silence. Veronica is frozen. Harry Markus looks down into her face, as if gauging her reaction, as if checking to make sure his words have landed. Then he turns and walks away. "Their lips are blue."

His footsteps retreat deeper into the shadow but she cannot will herself to follow just yet. "So they're not human," she says. "So they're not human, they're something else. That's what you're saying."

He does not respond.

"Are they aliens?" she calls after him.

Harry Markus pauses again. She sees the pale sliver of his face emerge from the darkness as he glances back over his shoulder. "Do you believe in aliens?"

"Duh. My dad's Ben Lewis." The subtext being that he was practically forced out of NASA for saying he found an alien wormhole, among other things. "Are they? Aliens?"

He continues walking. Still, Veronica does not follow.

"Perhaps," he says.

Her spine tingles and crawls. A shudder runs through her.

Veronica looks back over her shoulder.

The pale boy stands behind her.

She jumps. "Fuck. Grant." She blinks—he's gone. Blood pounds in her skull. She rushes forward to catch up to Harry Markus. "You've been there? To their caves?"

"Yes."

"Where?"

"North."

"Why?" When Veronica risks another glance behind, she catches a glimpse of Grant far back in the shadows. There is something about his face—no smirk, no worried tilt of his brows. He is unnaturally still, eyes glazed. There is something empty about him.

She blinks. He's gone.

Never has Veronica felt haunted by Grant. Never before. In her chest, the canary flutters its wings. She's walking the labyrinth.

The tunnel ends in another low archway. This one opens up into a large channel—a narrow walkway on either side, slow dark water drifting down a gentle slope into the distance. It's like an opening out of the maze in her mind, an opening into a place dark and populated by whispers and shifting figures. *In the dirt we mumble.*

"They live underground," says Veronica. She's terribly chilled, and pulls her arms tight to her body. "So why are we underground? Feels like their forte, doesn't it?"

Harry Markus steps onto the walkway. His shoulder hugs the wall. "It's the last place they'd expect us to be."

"You're staking a lot on how you think they think." She follows him, gripping the wet crumbling grout between the bricks to keep her balance.

"They know…"

"What?"

He glances back at her—briefly—and she barely sees his face before it's once again hidden by his upturned coat collar. "They know I wouldn't come down here."

"So this is a personal relationship you have with the Mumblers." They are leading up to it. *Fall into my trap.*

But whatever he says next, Veronica doesn't hear it. All she hears is the steady tapping of insect legs. It begins to her right. When she turns and looks and thinks she's pinpointed the source, it shifts and spreads, like a beetle skittering across glass, like drumming fingernails on a metal pipe. From all directions.

She comes to a stumbling halt. She nearly loses her balance against the wall. Her sneakers shriek on wet stone. The shadows detach from the walls. They condense into bodies—curved backs—

"What are you doing?"

The world snaps back into focus. The tunnel is silent. Harry Markus stares at her.

"What? What are you looking at?" Her flashlight has flickered out; it must have cast weird shadows on the walls. She taps it against the wall, twists the top a bit until it clicks back to life. She is suddenly, desperately cold. "Is there a breeze?"

"Yes."

"How come?"

He sighs. He resumes walking. "I don't know."

"Wow, you're useless."

"I got us away from the Mumblers."

"Did you?" She follows. Again with the tapping. This time, Veronica refuses to look around, just focuses on the center of Harry Markus' back and keeping her balance. She focuses on the stuff she knows is real: the sound the water makes against the channel wall, the dust and slick black mold she catches in the flashlight beam, the wet squelching of her socks and the way her sneakers rub her ankles raw.

This time Harry Markus stops first. She nearly runs into him again; she recoils. "Hey, a warning?"

"You don't hear that?"

The insect sounds echo in her skull, but she refuses to humor them this time. "No."

The tapping grows louder. Perhaps it is not in her head after all. Perhaps there really are monsters in the shadows of this underground tunnel, perfect for pale reaching hands and large hollow eyes.

"They're coming," says Grant's voice, disembodied in the darkness behind her.

For the first time, Veronica sees a flash of something like fear in Harry Markus' eyes. "They're here."

* * *

Shapes detach from the shadows. Behind them, from the upper end of the tunnel, crawling along the narrow ledge with frightening speed, the Mumblers arrive in droves. Whatever their armor or equipment, it rattles on the stone, clicking, scraping.

They're on the other side of the channel too. Veronica nearly drops her flashlight—the beam ricochets of sewer-slick walls, the gaping open faces of the Mumblers growing ever-closer. They wear something like gas masks. She catches her flashlight before it bounces off the ledge into the water.

"You said they wouldn't follow us," Veronica seethes through her teeth. "You said—"

"Yes, okay, I said that. Gun?" Harry Markus has pulled his own firearm.

"Yeah, I've got it—hey, move!" She kicks the back of his legs.

"Jump." Harry Markus squats, lowers himself over the ledge and lands knee-deep in the black water. "Hurry."

"You said they wouldn't follow us down here!" She follows him into the water—cold, sour-smelling water. The Mumblers are above them now and approaching fast. She doesn't see how this is any better. "How do we get out? You have a plan. Right?"

In the dirt we mumble. In the dirt—

He wades through the water at a brisk pace Veronica struggles to match. The water is halfway up her thighs. "This is a service tunnel," he says. His voice is nearly drowned out by the cacophony of echoing chants.

"Okay, so"—she bites the flashlight and uses both hands to check the magazine in her gun, then spits it out and continues slogging through the water—"what?"

Don't look behind you. Keep moving. She's already had this nightmare, lived it. Do the Mumblers recognize her?

No. The canary isn't real. Her heart flutters. "Hey! How do we get out?"

He rifles through his backpack as he goes, flashlight under his arm. She moves to avoid the spray he kicks up. "This is a service tunnel, there will be an exit somewhere nearby. Look for a ladder."

"How did they find us?"

"I don't know." Is that panic in his voice? He palms something from his bag and re-zips it. "Run."

The object he throws against the top of the tunnel looks like a grenade, and Veronica once again marvels at his immense stupidity. But as it collides with the arched ceiling, it shatters into an explosion of brilliant light. Sparks dance before her eyes.

Screams echo through the tunnel. The Mumblers scramble and cower against the walls. Veronica is still half-blind when she takes off running, stumbling through the black water after Harry Markus. She picks up her knees with each step, but it's still a terrible dream where she cannot run fast enough.

Remember January.

A shiver shoots through her. Veronica surges forward, scans the walls for a glint of metal, a hint of rusted steel leading to an escape.

"January," said Grant, the night of Benedict Lewis' funeral. "You didn't mean for it to happen, did you? You could do it again."

"There!" Buried in the wall up on the ledge, the lower rungs of a ladder.

Up ahead, Harry Markus slows.

Something slams into Veronica. She twists around, loses her balance. A huge body crashes down on her. Her head goes under and the world plummets into darkness.

She breaks through the water's surface for an instant to bring up her elbow, but she's blind, and she can't breathe, and she doesn't know where the head is, all she sees is shifting darkness and something huge, smelling like stone and sewage and death. Veronica gags and scrambles back, but a thick hand closes over her throat. It pushes her back under. Her arms flail.

Veronica is cold. Images snap through her head—gouged eyes, blue lips, the dripping of cavern walls.

She blindly aims the gun, presses it against flesh. She pulls the trigger.

The hand loosens. Veronica resurfaces, spitting foul water. She pushes the limp body off her chest. She scrambles to her feet, chest heaving.

January. January. She's buried under blankets in her sweat-soaked bed, she's buried in a crypt beneath a burning city, she's buried in a shallow stream and crawling through the mud to a burning mountaintop, she's a bird spiraling through a windstorm with broken wings.

She can't stop to search for her flashlight. Harry Markus' is flickering and weaving, locked between his teeth as he fires into the darkness behind her.

She swipes water out her eyes and searches for the ladder. She wades towards it.

Over the rattle of gunfire—staccato, ear-ringing in the closed space—the chant grates in her eardrums. *In the dirt we mumble. In the dirt we mumble.*

Her fingers lock on the concrete ledge above the channel. She jumps, hooks one elbow over the edge. Her feet scramble for purchase. The ladder is just above her.

"Lewis—!"

The flashlight flickers. It goes dark for an instant, and Veronica feels the draft, and something rushes in her ears. *January.*

When the light comes back—flickering, sporadic, frantic—a Mumbler looms on the ledge above her. A foot comes down on the gun.

She yells, but doesn't let go. Her fingers are crushed against the concrete. Her hand is numb. She grabs the Mumbler's leg and tries to pull it down into the channel. It might as well be bolted to the ledge.

The light goes out.

When it flickers back to life, it's shining into Veronica's face. Harry Markus slams the butt of the flashlight against the Mumbler's head. Bones crunch. Before the creature can react, a knife glints in the light. Harry Markus drives it into a break in the armor, under the Mumbler's chin. He twists the blade and slides it down the creature's front.

The Mumbler gurgles. Heat splatters across Veronica's face. Blood, fluids, something Veronica thinks might be guts, spill out onto the ledge and slip down into the channel. The body follows.

Harry Markus grabs Veronica's arms and pulls her up. His hands are sticky.

Veronica jams the gun into her waistband. She grips the lowest ladder rung and hauls herself up—her shoulders scream. She lunges for the next rung, and the next, fast before she can register the pain, fast before anyone or anything can stop her.

She pauses halfway.

In the dirt we mumble.

A breeze presses into her wet back. Her neck prickles. Harry Markus has one hand on the ladder, both feet on the ledge, firing at Mumblers wading through the channel.

At the top of the ladder, the ceiling opens into a cylindrical space. Veronica braces her legs against the concrete wall and uses her forearms to press and slowly, slowly lift the manhole cover from its place. She scrapes her elbows to the side, creating a narrow opening where she can fit her fingers and drag the cover the rest of the way. She pushes it open just enough to wriggle through.

She's on the sidewalk. The street is quiet, peaceful, unbelievable. Hell seethes below.

Harry Markus is halfway up the ladder. She can barely make out the mass of Mumblers assembling at its base. Can they climb? They're trying.

The flashlight flickers between his teeth. Harry Markus' eyes glint bright in the darkness, his face slick with sweat. He pauses, twists around, fires below. When he continues to climb, his eyes lock on Veronica's.

An instant before the light goes out.

An instant before she drags the cover back over the manhole.

And she turns, wind pressing into her shoulder blades. She turns and races, alone, into the streets of St. Louis.

13

Veronica runs until she can no longer feel the draft, until the night eases its edges around her and softens to faint neon and puddled sidewalks. There is trash in the gutter where she sits outside a dark-windowed nail salon. Her foot flattens a chip bag.

Her boots are wet. If she keeps moving she can keep her brain shut off, but the adrenaline has subsided and her muscles have stopped engaging. Everything clings to her. Ankles, raw from running in wet socks. Her clothes—her only clothes—are foul and chaffing. She shivers. She checks her gun and sticks it in her backpack, which is likewise soaked; she can't remember if there's anything important in there. Most of it is probably ruined.

In the neon green light from the cafe across the street—*coffee*, it reads, insistent, *coffee*—her hands are red and grimy. The nail of her index finger is split. The fingers of her right hand are already swelling, sore, probably sprained. Streaks of wet red extend to her forearms where Harry Markus pulled her over the ledge.

She closes her eyes and she sees his face: blue-green eyes unnaturally bright against the darkness, the flash of panic the moment he realizes what she intends to do. And then, less sympathetically: the way he so casually stabbed the Mumbler and dragged his blade through its belly, as if he'd practiced the motion before, as if splitting a crawdad shell. Like it meant nothing to him.

She thinks she shot one of them in the head. She can still feel the cold water closing around her ears, the thick rubbery hand tightening over her throat.

Her palms find the curb. She wonders if her neck is red.

And the wind.

The wind.

Her breath slows and she shivers, but it has little to do with the cold. She puts her head on her knees. Her cargos are gritty. The world tilts and sways around her.

I can't do this. Why did I think I could do this? Maybe he didn't leave me a breadcrumb trail, maybe he really wants me to sit and wait for him to come home. He wouldn't want me to risk it if he knew these things existed. He wouldn't.

But does she really know Benedict Lewis? He didn't tell her enough. If he really wanted her on the case, he would have told her lots more. She doesn't know enough about BEESWAX. Or North Enterprises. Or the Mumblers. Or Harry Markus.

She replays the moment again: dragging the manhole cover over the exit, watching the moonlight fade across Harry Markus' face like an eclipse of the sun. And then—nothing. Silence. A rush in her ears, a brief stab of guilt, or shame, or regret. And then her feet slapping the pavement. And nothing else.

A hand rests on her shoulder. "Veronica."

She doesn't react, because she knows it's coming a moment before it happens. That seems to happen quite often these days. "What am I doing wrong?" she says.

She opens her eyes and raises her head. The hand is gone. Grant sits on the curb beside her. His wide feet rest in the gutter grime, his hands are clasped on his knees. His narrow face is grave.

A spark of annoyance blossoms in her chest. "What?" she snaps. "What's wrong with you? What happened to you down there? Are you going to say 'I told you so'? Because maybe I'd do something different if you were any help at all. But it's just me, right?" She grimaces at him. "Who are you? What are you?"

He blinks, confused.

"You're a projection of my conscience. You're my subconsciousness. You're *Inception*, *Matrix*, sci-fi psychological shit. Bullshit."

"Veronica—"

"Don't." She leans away from him. "What are you?" And then, in a lower voice, her anger ebbing away into throat-clenching desperation: "What am *I*?"

He reaches out; she doesn't flinch. He smells like marmalade, he smells like home. She hates him. She can't trust him. He's the only constant thing in her life, growing as she grows, becoming just as frightening with every passing year as Veronica herself.

He plucks a feather from her hair. Even in the shadows, she can see that it's yellow. The canary heart flutters in her chest.

Grant holds out his hand.

"No." She snatches up her damp backpack and forces herself to her feet. Her knees shake. "No. I'm in control. It's *my* fucking life."

Grant watches her from the curb as she shoulders her bag and limps off into the night. The unsaid question hangs between them: *Where are you going?* And: *why?*

Towards the end of her thirteenth year, Veronica sits on the trailer roof and watches the dust clouds descending from the East End of Dane's Chapel. A car weaves down the hill, hits Main Street, and is lost amongst the buildings. The sun bakes into her skin. She lays on her back, tin grooves carving into her spine.

She hears her father through the grimy skylight beside her head. He's on the phone. "Okay. Okay. When did he leave? Did he say anything?"

It's the voice he uses when they sit on the floor of his lab together, as he scribbles formulas and draws connections too quickly for her to understand the mechanics of the final equation. Frustrated, uptight. *Pay attention*, it seems to say. *Do you see what's going on?*

More often than not, the answer is *no*.

"Okay. Last night. Where's Theodore? Has he called the police? No...of course not...right...."

Veronica raises her head. On the other side of the skylight, the pale boy watches her with mild interest.

"What's happening?" she murmurs.

He shrugs one tanned shoulder. Lays back with his pointed nose to the sky. His hair is so blonde in the sunlight, it's nearly white.

Veronica sits up on an elbow and peers through the skylight. Behind the scratches and splotches of lichen, her dad paces the living room. His hair is damp and messy from the shower, his shirt creased from living under a heap of clean laundry for a week. His head is low. He rubs his neck as he walks—sofa to kitchen counter and back, his feet tracing the same path over and over. She can't see his face, but she imagines his brows pinched together and his mouth a hard line.

"Okay," Ben says. "Stay calm. Stay where you are." A moment later he hangs up the phone and drops it on the coffee table. He sits on the edge of the sofa and stares at the wall.

Veronica lays back down. She scoots herself away from the skylight and glances at the pale boy, who is very still, as if sleeping —as if he can actually feel the sun on his skin, and is actually capable of sleep.

For a moment, she would like to pretend that something terrible hasn't happened. She'd like to pause this scene.

"Peter's son is gone."

She sits on the front steps. Ben stands above her.

"Grant." She knows his name.

"He disappeared in the night. They don't know where he went, but..."

"You have to go out there." *There* is New Mexico, where Peter and his lab live.

"I have to go."

She kicks at the dust with her heels. Scrubby weeds and dandelion greens grow around the base of the steps. "When will you be back?"

"I don't know. Soon. I won't stay away for too long. Will you be alright?"

"Yeah. Sure."

"Veronica." She looks up at him. His eyes are lighter than hers— gray or hazel or green, she's never been sure. "Will you be okay?"

Behind him, wandering around the yard by the corner of the

trailer, kicking at unshifting gravel with his hands deep in his pockets, the pale boy glances up and smiles. She doesn't smile back. "I'll be fine," she says. "I'm just gonna finish my book."

Benedict is gone by evening. Veronica wanders the woods barefoot, seeking shade where her toes find cool mud instead of burning-hot packed dirt from the trails four-wheelers and hikers make through the trees. She leaves the paths behind and walks until the sun sinks below the hills and the sky is painted pink and gold. Sometimes the pale boy walks beside her. There are squirrels, but she doesn't have her dad's gun, and she doesn't feel like disrupting the silence.

Halfway back to the West End, she grows tired and sits by the creek. It's a dry season, and the water is low—just a trickle skimming over smooth rocks and silty mud. A lot of the water around here is still polluted from the old coal mines, but in the evening light it looks pure enough. It slips cold over her toes.

The night is warm. In the distance, traffic hums through the downtown.

What if he doesn't come back?

"He'll be back."

The pale boy speaks more and more often these days, but it feels natural, not alarming; she thinks, in the back of her mind, that she should perhaps be more alarmed. "Yeah. I guess."

"He will."

She kicks a piece of mud at him. It flickers and falls through his leg. "You seem pretty sure. For being...not real."

He glances at the place where the mud fell, unfazed. "It can't start yet," he says. "You know that."

She shifts. A tree root digs into her tailbone. "It doesn't make sense. The canary. It sings until it dies, right?" He doesn't answer. "Well, I'm not gonna die."

"Will you live forever?"

She looks at him suspiciously, but he's grinning. Veronica lays back on the bank, arms flung wide—flexing her toes in the mud, wrapping sun-baked grass around her fingers. "Maybe. I just think...if I die, I want it to be because I'm doing something, not because something was done to me. Like"—she tilts her head to look at him— "fuck destiny. Right?"

He closes his eyes. "It's not like that, you know. The canary in the coal mine. It's more about...anticipation. Sensing it before it happens, before anyone else knows."

"Anticipating what?"

"The end."

"Of what?"

The dim evening light paints his face gray-blue. He smiles.

Later, back at the trailer, she follows him down into the labyrinth within her mind. The air smells like dust. The canary flutters on the pale boy's shoulder, and he takes her in his hand, gentle with her wings. The dark walls rise up around them. They wander for a time in silence.

Then the maze opens into a stretch of darkness. Nestled in the shadows, oblivious to their presence, a small girl and a boy play checkers.

They move closer. The boy is tanned and freckled, his cheeks sunburnt and still round with baby fat. His blonde hair is cut like a mushroom, fluffy and nearly white around his face. He wears an oversized Batman shirt. When the girl reaches for a checkers piece that is not her own, his eyes widen. "No!"

He swats at her, but she closes her chubby fingers over the disc and yanks her hand back. "Yes!" There is a devilish smile on her face. She is smaller, a few years younger, with a denim bucket hat over her tangle of dark hair.

"No!" The boy's face reddens. He grits his teeth. Trembling, overcome with rage, he grabs up another disc. He wheels back and slams it into her shoulder.

There is a moment of charged silence. The redness drains from his face.

"Oh," he whispers.

The girl lets out an ear-piercing shriek. It echoes through the darkness, it fills the void. The canary's feathers ruffle; the pale boy's fingers flex.

"Grant! No. Nooo." A man rushes out of the darkness, and even as the canary, Veronica recognizes him. Peter Webber is young here, like the pictures in the back of his books. He kneels beside the little boy and pries the checkers piece from his fat hand. "No. We don't hit girls." He reaches out and squeezes the girl's arm. "Hey, Nica.

You okay? You're alright. Grant, say you're sorry."

But the little boy is too traumatized to speak.

"We don't hit girls, Grant. We protect them."

The girl is done screaming, but her chest heaves with emotion. Footsteps echo in the distance behind her.

"What's this?" Benedict Lewis—easy and relaxed, his face unlined and hair without silver—squats back on his heels. He wraps his arms around the girl. "Crying won't help. You're alright."

"Grant brutally attacked her." Peter lifts the boy by his armpits, raises him to his feet. "Superheroes don't hurt girls, son. Say sorry to Nica."

"Sorry," he whispers. He cringes away from the little girl. His eyes are frightened.

"I think Veronica forgives him." Benedict gathers the scattered pieces and resets the checkers board.

Peter laughs. "I wouldn't be so sure. There's murder in her eyes."

"She's got her mother's eyes."

"Nah, those are yours."

They both laugh, but Grant is solemn, watching young Veronica's fists clench and unclench. There is something he needs to do, and he's gathering the courage to do just that.

Abruptly, he goes in for a hug.

She punches him in the mouth.

The image shatters. The scene is replaced by a bed of sand, a beam of silver-blue moonlight, a night wind whispering around a crop of rocks.

A body in the desert. Thin limbs at odd angles. A pool of blood collects in the sand below his temple, stark against the white and gray of the scene. His veins are dark in the starlight.

The canary's heart skips a beat. She has seen something that she should not have. She's seen too much.

The pale boy cups her in his hands and skirts around the scene, through the shadows, and back into the maze. "That's enough," he murmurs.

When Veronica opens her eyes, she can still hear the skittering of sand across the desert floor. She hears a high-pitched scream. She blinks, and the silver moonlight fades to dull orange—the nightlight in the outlet by her bedroom door.

She's curled up in the middle of her bed. On one side, nestled in the tattered quilt, is her dad's gun. On the other, the pale boy lies on his back with his hands resting on his stomach.

Veronica sits up. "I remember that."

"Do you?"

"I remember. We ate strawberry ice cream and it was really bad and the boy puked in the car."

He turns his head. He raises his eyebrows.

Veronica frowns. "You. The boy is you. I remember." She crosses her legs. "You're Grant Webber. You're Peter's son." And then the events of the day click into place. "You're gone."

"Disappeared," he says.

"You're not a ghost."

"I'm not?"

No, he isn't. She isn't sure what he is, but it links back to the fact that she knew him once, long ago. *Grant Webber.* They'd played checkers and she'd punched him. Had they met after that, or had Ben and Peter kept them separated for fear of associating their families, just as Ben had erased all public traces of their relationship? Maybe she remembers him from when she was young and has simply given this specter his face.

Only, he'd been in the desert. Older. Beaten. He'd looked the same as he does now, idly watching her puzzle it out.

"Are you really him?" she asks. He shrugs. "You're useless."

She wanders the trailer and gathers up all the Peter Webber books she can find. She flips to the back covers and inside sleeves, reads the bios. *Peter Webber. PhD of biotechnology, researcher at the University of New Mexico*—that was before he'd left, or been asked to leave, just as Benedict had gracefully departed from NASA.

There isn't much more information to be found online. After an hour-long search on the slow, overheating computer in her dad's bedroom, all she finds is an article with Peter Webber's name in a photo caption. Veronica scrolls through a low-budget website for a small-town newspaper until she finds it: Peter and Waverley Webber, pictured at the grand opening of Johnny Jim's Hog, Dog, and Bagel Breakfast Joint in New Mexico.

"That's questionable," says the pale boy—Grant—over her shoulder. "Hogs, dogs, *and* bagels?"

She abandons the whirring computer and lays back on her dad's bed. She gazes down the length of her body at the badly-pixelated screen. "Waverley." The woman in the photo is young, hugely pregnant, and leaning against a grinning Peter Webber. His smile is Grant's smile. "Well. This is enormously weird. Is that your mom?"

He shrugs. She wonders if he'll always do that when she asks him personal questions. She wonders if it will ever make an ounce of real sense.

"She's pretty," says Veronica. Her dad never mentioned Peter's wife. She wonders if Waverley Webber is still around, but only briefly—she doesn't have a mother of her own, and therefore has little interest in the concept of mothers in general.

"Are you going to tell him?" asks Grant.

"What? About you?" She hasn't thought about it. Benedict Lewis doesn't know about the pale boy, or the mumbling hallucinations, at least not as far as she knows. She's told him about some of the dreams, but not how they occasionally extend into the daylight hours. Into reality. "Am I gonna tattle? I don't think so," she says.

"Because you'll look crazy?"

She cracks a smile, but she doesn't feel it. She's tired now. "I already look crazy."

Now, four years later, Veronica Lewis is exhausted. She unzips her backpack in the echoey corridor of a bus station. The floors are cold, and it smells like people who haven't bathed in a while. Kind of like her.

After a moment of awkward rummaging, she slaps a handful of damp, crumpled cash on the counter. The lady on the other side of the bulletproof glass eyes her distastefully.

"New Mexico," says Veronica.

Deep in the labyrinth within her mind, the canary's song stutters. And it carries on.

14

The moment the cover closes over the manhole, Harry's life flashes before his eyes.

A much different time and place, navigating tunnels not unlike these, with blood in his mouth and desperation inflating his chest. And those damned voices filling his head: *in the dirt we mumble, in the dirt we mumble.* The realization that this might be it: this might be his last stand, and it is neither as victorious nor as heroically selfless as he had hoped it might be.

No. He can't die like this. *Howard. Henry.* They're waiting for him.

What would his parents think?

Harry releases the ladder. He drops with the flashlight between his teeth. He lands on a Mumbler's shoulders and snaps its neck. The creature collapses beneath him.

He pulls his knife and takes out the two Mumblers on the ledge; their bodies sway and teeter and crash into the black water below in perfect synchrony. From the channel, a pale hand grasps his ankle. In two quick movements, he saws off its fingers.

Kill them all. He'll kill them all. And maybe, standing in this river of blood, that cavity in his chest will finally fill, and he can stop running, and fighting, and hating.

The tunnel is full of inhuman screams. They aren't even chanting anymore.

He sees a burning city. He sees an ocean of rubble. He hears the dying breaths of everyone he loves.

He reaches for his baton and hesitates. Electricity and water don't mix. He might be able to withstand a brief electrical pulse, but can the Mumblers? He doesn't want to test that.

He grabs his gun instead, clicks the flashlight into place. Standing at the base of the ladder, he fills the tunnel with the roar of gunfire. Bodies splash into the water, screams ricochet in his skull, the river fills with countless shelled bodies. But they keep coming, an endless flood seething from the shadows. Always more.

There has to be an end to them. He has to find it. He needs to end it.

A hand grips his leg. He doesn't move fast enough this time—it draws him down into the channel. He lands on his feet in the cold water and he shoots up under the mask and busts a hole through the Mumbler's head. Prickles of heat sting his face. He knocks the body aside and lets off a round of gunfire into the encroaching horde.

The Mumblers have crawled across the opposite edge. They're approaching from both sides. He picks them off as they wade towards him.

The flashlight beam is narrow. It's stopped flickering but he still cannot see them all at once. He doesn't have time to climb the ledge. There is no break in the rush. He'll run out of ammo soon. His backup is in the bottom of his bag. He thinks again of the baton.

He thinks of his brothers.

Harry pulls the baton before he can think too hard about it. He pulls the trigger and the tip sparks to life, crackling white electricity.

The Mumblers hesitate. A worried sound echoes through the tunnel, a pained groan. They press forward, and Harry sweeps the baton out before him. If he can ward them off for long enough, he can make it up the ladder. He'll search for Veronica Lewis. He can make it.

A Mumbler crashes into him from behind, sending Harry to his knees. His arms plunge into the sour water, elbows-deep.

The baton shimmers and shocks. It radiates up his body. It curls in the edges of his vision. A howl resounds through the tunnel. He does not know if it is the Mumblers', or his own.

The city is burning. There is dust and blood in the air, detritus speckled through the familiar streets, smoke drifting slowly on the wind. In some places, eerie quiet grips the night. In others, the sound of the dying and their comrades rings in his ears.

He sees two men sitting against a wall. One is missing half his head. The other sits blinking beside the body, as if waiting his turn. Waiting to join the steady stream of souls departing the city tonight.

Would he do that?

There are nights where he imagines himself as that man in the alley, leaning against a caving stone wall. His breaths are shallow and slow, ever-slowing, trying to match the dead sets of lungs on either side of him: Henry, with his eyes carved out of his skull; Howard, with his chest blown to bits, shattered bone flecked through his raven hair.

Would he sit there and wait for death? Or would some cursed thing propel him forward, into a future without his brothers? He'd like to think he'd simply die there. But survival runs deep in his bones.

When he becomes aware, Harry is no longer in the water. Electricity still buzzes in his skull, but as it spirals into a peaceful hum, he hears other things: water rushing through pipes, the steady plink of droplets on stone. Someone breathing nearby.

He shifts. His neck feels as if it was broken and badly glued back in place. His wrists are shackled behind him, hugging a rusty pole– a pipe, hot against his wrists, gently throbbing with the force of water flowing through it.

He has tools for picking locks, one set in his right boot, another tucked into a pocket in his waistband.

His eyelids are heavy. His legs are spread out long in front of him. Where his bleary boots end, a shiny brown leather shoe taps impatiently.

Harry tilts his head to look the man in the eye. "X." His tongue feel clumsy in his mouth.

The old man adjusts his spectacles. His eyes are bright, for such a withered face. He has a camping lamp, and is gracious enough to direct the beam away from Harry's face.

"Now," the old man says, carefully, "how long were you watching us?"

Harry sniffs. He feels like he's just inhaled nails. "Who?" His voice grates.

They're in one of the tunnels. Maybe the same one he and Veronica Lewis came through before. There's no sign of the Mumblers. *She left me there.* He recalls the pale sliver of her face disappearing as the manhole cover was shoved back into place.

"I know you were in North Carolina," says X, "watching me and Andre do our job. Now, Agent Markus—yes, I'll be courteous and refer to you by your occupation and title. I'm a gentleman. Perhaps we can be civil and professional, despite your current unfortunate position. Agent Markus, we are both on the same team. I thought we were, that is. Would you care to tell me where everything went wrong?"

Harry leans forward as far as he can with his hands shackled. He looks down the length of the tunnel, strains his ears. "Where are they?"

"Well," says X, sensitively, "you killed quite a lot of them." He waits. If he expects an apology or any reaction at all, he is sorely disappointed, and sighs to show it. "If you think I'm working for the Myrmen, you are mistaken. We have an agreement, nothing more."

Myrmen. Harry hasn't heard that name in years. It crawls under his skin; he stiffens. He sits back hard against the pipe.

"Perhaps you should be thanking me. They were about to kill you when I arrived. I stopped them and sent them on their way. Not without effort." X tilts his head and regards Harry thoughtfully. "They hate you very much."

"You made a deal with them?" His skull buzzes. "You can't—

you can't make *deals* with the Mumblers. Does Cage know?"

"Of course not," says X, the picture of reason. "He doesn't understand the players in this game, and I plan to keep it that way." He puts his hands in his pockets and sighs, shrugs. "I know who you are. We don't have to speak in circles around this matter. I'm sorry for what happened to you, but I work for a greater cause than whatever petty grudges you hold. Greater than Cage and the whole of North Enterprises, believe it or not."

Harry cannot breathe. There's a blade pressing into his chest. The pipe is burning into his spine and his face feels hot. If he blinks, he'll be back on that endless dark road out of Hell, dodging sinkholes and cascades of rubble, dragging two bodies behind him, the eyes of the dead clinging to him from the alleyways. *This isn't real. Just another nightmare.*

And then X says the words that drive the blade home: "I have the other two at North Enterprises. I have them right where I want them, and by extension, I have you."

Harry doesn't trust himself to speak. Is the old man bluffing? Harry left Howard and Henry at the North Enterprises compound. He *left* them. If X wants to lock them down, it is within his power.

I know who you are.

The old man smiles in a way that could only be described as warm, as if truly sympathetic to Harry's situation. "Well, alright. You can keep playing the game if you wish, but it really doesn't matter. Your current position makes this quite simple: you need me, and I daresay I need your assistance. I suggest a collaboration. A new arrangement, since your loyalty to North Enterprises is clearly not binding enough."

"I don't deal with traitors." The words are clipped.

"Yes, very noble. Listen, Agent Markus—this is simpler than you're making it out to be. It's an easy choice. I'll say it again: I know who you are. Not everyone does. I might be the only one, aside from the Myrmen–"

Harry's voice crawls up his throat. "Don't say their name."

X continues, unheeding. "Call it blackmail if you will—"

"It's certainly blackmail, but that shouldn't stop you."

"Well, thank you."

Harry will kill him. He will. Perhaps not now, but the old man has guaranteed that he will not live long. If he's telling the truth, if he does know about Harry and his brothers, then he should have an inkling that his days are numbered.

X has Howard. He has Henry. Maybe Howard could escape and defend himself, but Henry? Harry thinks again of the man in the street, waiting for death beside his fallen comrade—waiting, perhaps wishing.

He cannot live like that. X will die. He puts up his chin. "What do you want?"

"Veronica Lewis."

"You found her once before. Why not again? You don't need me. You have BEESWAX."

X sets his lantern on the floor. He removes his glasses and wipes them clean on the hem of his shirt. "I appreciate the vote of confidence. We only found her in the same way the Myrmen did; by tracing her purchase. One mushroom pizza. She made it on her father's credit card. A silly mistake, and it led us straight to her."

He remembers the look on her face as she slid the manhole cover into place: grim determination. No, it wasn't a mistake—she'd *wanted* to be followed. She'd been planning to leave him behind the whole time. North Enterprises and BEESWAX might still be underestimating her, but Harry has spent one too many hours alone with Veronica.

"It's unfortunate that the Myrmen found you both first, and it's only with a great deal of luck that I arrived when I did to keep them from killing you. They weren't supposed to do that. There was to be no killing involved."

Harry can't believe what he's hearing. "You can't make a deal with the Bloody Mumblers. They have no honor."

"And you have a great deal?"

"I didn't say that," said Harry. "They'll betray you."

"Maybe. You did, despite your contract with North Enterprises. But they *are* useful. And it is fortunate for you that they possess a certain...duplicitous nature. Here is what I want, Agent Markus: I want to find Veronica Lewis. The Myrmen have uses, but they will likely tear her apart—their worth is in numbers and the element of surprise, not so much strategy and stealth. BEESWAX comes with resources, but unfortunately it also come with Andre Billings and a certain lack of creativity. You have some cunning. Find her for me."

"And?"

"Follow her. Benedict Lewis will not surrender the location of his research. It's nowhere to be found in Dane's Chapel. Clearly Benedict left her with some instruction, and Miss Lewis is trying to locate her father's work before we do."

"Why do you need it?"

X just smiles. "Is that so important? Just find her. Find *it*. And deliver it to me. Your brothers' lives are on the line. If you fail to complete this task...I might lose control of the Myrmen."

You don't have control over them. They cannot be controlled. X will realize this too late. The Mumblers obey no one but their own hive mind. "How do I know they're safe?"

"Your brothers? You don't. But we'll have a fair trade when you have secured the research and Benedict's daughter both—you'll see that they are alive and well. In the meantime, I suppose you'll have to trust me." The old man reaches down and plucks the lantern from the floor. "Can you do that? Do you remember how?" Shadows dance on the walls. X appears ghostly pale, flickering in and out of the wavering light. "I'd hurry, Agent Markus. As you've said, the Myrmen are difficult to control, and they've had a bit of an early start in Little Miss Lewis' pursuit. If she dies, so do your brothers. If you fail, you will truly be the last of your line."

Harry's blood runs cold. He watches with bated breath as X turns on his heel and heads off down the length of the tunnel. At the bend in the hall, he pauses to glance back at Harry. *The last of your line.*

"You have three days," says the old man.

He is gone. He leaves Harry Markus chained in the dark, with the thunder of his heartbeat loud in his skull, and fingers of fear closing over his throat.

15

"They're looking for us," says Howard. His voice is grainy through the radio, staticky on the S's.

Henry sits back in his chair, turns a circuit board over and over in his fingers. He runs his thumb along a ridge. Tilts back his face to the ceiling. "I know." Howard can be dramatic. Overreactive. "I know, Howard, I was the one who told you that. I know."

"No, not the Bloody Mumblers. Hey, are you there? Can you hear me?"

"I can hear you." But reception isn't great from this location.

"Where—where the hell are you, Henry?"

"The basement." His voice echoes.

The radio pops and crackles. "The—what?"

"Basement." Henry calmly sets the circuitboard aside and adjusts the radio. "Can you hear me now?"

"Look, where are you?"

"Fucking *basement*, Howard. Bottom floor."

"What are you doing down there?"

"My job." He sighs. He comes to the North Enterprises basement for silence and intense concentration, yet still people find a means to bother him. "What do you want? What's the problem? They haven't found Harry yet."

"No. I mean, *we* haven't. Cage hasn't. But the Mumblers are still tailing him. But that isn't the point. Listen, they're also on ours. Not the Mumblers, I mean, but BEESWAX. And North Enterprises. Where are you again?"

"Howard, I'm in the—"

"It doesn't matter, come find me. Or I'll find you. Look, I've got a rather bad feeling about this, Henry. I think Lawrence Cage and his posse are rounding us up. Big scary Scandinavian guys. Bigger than Harry."

Henry hesitates, his fingers on the volume knob. He turns the radio down slightly. "Who is *us?*" he murmurs.

"I can't hear you!"

"Who is *us*, Howard? Who are they rounding up?"

"Us! You! Me! Harry bloody Markus! It's us three again, and they can't leave us alone. Cage was decidedly sketchy the other day, and now Harry's gone rogue, I've got an awful feeling about what they intend for us. Oh! Also, the Mumblers are here."

Henry's hands are numb.

"Yeah, I don't think they know we're here, but Cage is definitely looking for us. I've been running all over, and every corner I turn, people are looking at me funny, and I swear I saw someone radio in when they saw me coming."

Henry leans forward. He's dizzy, the wheels of his chair feel a bit unstable. "Howard. The Mumblers? Are here?" His ears ring.

"Yes, they just breached the north entrance. I'm not too worried, though. We can escape with my chopper. I've only got to hunt down that French bloke with my access card to the hangar, then we'll be out of here. We can go find Harry."

Delusional. "Where are you now?"

"In a closet."

"Why?"

"Because there's an enormous blond man following me, and I'd like to make it halfway across the compound without Cage accosting me. He can't keep off the Mumblers, I certainly don't want to be stuck in a cell when they overtake this place."

"Just fight him off." It isn't often Henry speaks those words, not nowadays. He's halfway out of his chair. "Lose him, kill him, I don't care. We need to go now."

"Hey, don't worry." Howard is breaking down; Henry can hear it over the static. When he's caught off-guard, he becomes dangerously optimistic. "It'll be fine. I'll shake this guy and grab the chopper and circle around to—where did you say you were?"

They've taken the north entrance. They're on their way. People can be so stupid. Henry had warned Cage about the Mumblers, he'd warned Howard that the tyrant wouldn't take it too seriously, he'd warned Harry about being an idiot.

He's driven the image of the Mumblers from his mind, but he can still feel their hands—cold and hard like ice-slicked stone, inhuman strength in those joints, the terrible rustle and groan of their approach. It's those small sounds, he thinks, that make their presence so abominable. The murmurs, the whispers, the tapping of armor against armor. If they bellowed a deafening war cry they would be less ominous.

"—enry? You—me?"

"You're breaking up, Howard."

"I can't hear you. Say it—"

"Howard." But the basement is terrible for radio reception. He only has it down here because he's listening to a tape while he works, a collection of old classical pieces recorded live from an orchestra in Belgium. He found it in a cabinet somewhere. "Howard."

His brother is gone.

Henry is cold. He turns the volume down low, rises to his feet. His hand knocks the circuit board—he pushes it farther up the workbench and makes his way to the door. A current of stale conditioned air flows through the maze of maintenance halls below the North Enterprises compound. He shuts the door gently and cuts it off.

He throws the bolt. He finds the heaviest shelf in the room and pushes it in front of the entrance.

He settles himself again at the workbench. The radio is all static. Henry hopes that means his brother is out of the compound and on his way to the hangar. Some ridiculous part of his brain hopes that maybe Howard will find him in time and they'll escape together before the Mumblers arrive, but he knows how unrealistic that is; he will not remember where Henry is hidden, and he wouldn't be able to make it all the way down to the basement anyway, and Henry certainly won't be able to make his way out to the helicopter, even if Howard does retrieve his beloved chopper.

If Harry were here....

No. Harry is a fool. Harry got them into this mess. It's true that Harry would get him out of here, it's true that Howard sort of loses his head when their oldest brother isn't around, it's true that they rely on him too much and Henry can tell even from his voice that Harry Markus carries the weight of the world and so much more on his shoulders—

There is no *but*. He'll wait.

He'll wait while the Mumblers take North Enterprises. Then he'll wait for Harry to find him. He'll wait for his brothers.

There is a tremor in his hand. He reaches out and presses the tape back into the radio. It clicks and whirs. Then the second movement begins: slow, building.

Henry will wait.

16

Veronica Lewis doesn't look for Grant. Once on the bus, she slumps against a fogged window, backpack under her arm, and shuts her eyes.

She scrubbed the blood from her face with paper towels in a public restroom until her skin was pink and stinging. She threw her outermost sweater—blood-splattered and torn—in a dumpster somewhere between the manhole and the bus station, and now she's cold. The rest of her clothes aren't in much better condition, and she can't get the dried blood out of her hair, but if she sticks to the shadows and keeps the hood of her second-layer sweater on, she might pass for a teenage bum. She managed to salvage some first-aid supplies from her backpack and has wrapped the horrifically-bruised fingers of her right hand together with gauze, leaving just her thumb free, hoping that if there's a fracture she won't somehow make it worse. What she really wants right now is painkillers and a long, uninterrupted sleep.

The bus is half-empty. It's exhausted, soundless bodies swaying in their seats. It smells like shit. The driver sips loudly from a giant styrofoam cup. No one pays attention to the dirty girl with the devil eyes.

She dozes, head rattling against the window. Half-asleep, Veronica imagines the boy and girl hunched over their checkers board. She struggles to expand the image: where are they? A floor? A front yard? Where do their fathers come from? What was she doing in New Mexico, all those years ago?

Or maybe they'd come to Florida. Either way, her dad never mentioned her meeting Grant. Was he keeping it a secret? Why would he hide that from her?

January, she thinks. The air conditioning in the back of the bus sends a chill across her neck. She shrugs deeper into her sweater.

"Damn, they make these buses cold, huh?"

Veronica opens one eye. Then the other. She glances at the man seated a row behind, his elbows resting on the back of the seat beside her. Sleazy-looking guy in a leather jacket. Small teeth behind thin lips. His nose is, unfortunately, his most defining feature.

"I said it's cold, huh?" He smiles like maybe she's simple and didn't understand him the first time he opened his stupid fucking face. "You bundled up for the long haul, huh? It's *cold*."

If she doesn't say something, he'll keep talking. So she musters a "yup." She turns back to the window, but he isn't done.

"Where you headed, sweetheart?"

"Hmm."

"I said, where you headed? Huh? You can talk to me, I don't bite."

No, but I do.

"Where ya goin'?"

"Hell, probably," she says.

He laughs. "Yeah, me too. Hey, life is short, right? What's your name, sweetheart?"

He smells bad, and she smells remarkably horrible right now. She looks tries to communicate through sheer power of will how disinterested she is in his existence on the planet.

"I'm Del," he says, and holds out a ringed hand to shake. The sleeve of his jacket slides up, and he's got tattoos on his wrist.

"I...don't care."

"Aww, man." He smiles. Stupid teeth. "You got spunk, huh?

What's your name?"

The promise of sleep slips away. Veronica sits up straight. "Is this one of those sex trafficking things?"

A few passengers stir. Several rows up, a teenager in a beanie takes out his earbuds and looks back at her. Veronica raises her eyebrows. *Can you believe this guy?*

Del's smile disappears. "Uh, what? Where'd you get that idea?"

"Oh, you know. A sleazy older guy harassing an underage girl."

More passengers swivel in their seats. Del's eyes become panicked. "Nah, it's not—it's not like that. Uh, you don't look like a kid. And it's not like that, I just thought..." His voice dulls to a mumble, and he slumps back into the shadows.

Veronica moves up a few rows and slides in next to the hipster kid. He moves his legs to let her pass, and he takes out his earbuds again as she drops into the window seat.

"Don't talk to me," she says. "I just don't wanna get kidnapped."

She falls asleep against the window. She sees Harry Markus' eyes, green like neon in the dark. They fall away, sinking into the abyss, where she refuses to follow. She doesn't want to see him. She doesn't want to see the Mumblers. She won't go down into the labyrinth, not now, not without Grant.

Veronica wakes to a breeze on her cheek. She starts.

The bus is stopped. The doors are cranked open, allowing night air to slip in. People are grabbing their things and disembarking.

"Where are we?" Veronica tugs her hood up.

The hipster stands and takes out his earbuds. "Tulsa."

She has to change buses. It's early morning now, just after four. *The witching hours,* she thinks. She doesn't know where Tulsa is.

Veronica wanders into the station. Her next bus is due in two hours, so she hunts out the bathroom and sticks her head under the faucet in a bad attempt to get the blood out of her hair. It's in her scalp, dried to a gummy crust, and there's no way she can reach it like this. She eventually just twists the entire mess into a knot and hides it under her hood again. The water drips cold and rust-colored down the back of her neck.

"You're disgusting," she tells her reflection. The self-awareness helps a bit.

She buys Fritos and water from a vending machine. She catches sight of Del in his leather jacket lurking around the ticket counter, so she moves outside. She reclines on a twisty metal bench with interspersed armrests that won't allow her to lie down properly. It's cold, and the white floodlights don't offer any heat, but it stinks less outdoors, and the wind carries away her own stench.

She eats the chips. They're tasteless. She drinks the water and it scrapes down her throat. She has always liked the night, but she will be glad when dawn breaks.

"What's the real plan, Veronica?" Grant lounges at the other end of the bench, his legs sprawled over the armrests. If she reaches out, she could touch his bare calloused foot. Or she could try to.

"The real plan," she murmurs.

"You do have one."

"You know I have one. I always have plans. And look, they've all worked so far. Harry Markus is gone. I've lost the Mumblers. I'm on my way." She crumples the Frito bag in her fist. "The plan. Why don't you tell me, Mr. Webber?" She crosses her arms and rests her cheek on the back of the cold metal bench.

How old is he now? He's aged along with her. She didn't notice him getting older, she didn't even notice herself getting older, thinning, growing hard and haunted. His face looks a lot like his dad's. If she hadn't found out years ago that this specter was Peter Webber's son, she'd likely have guessed by now.

"Fine," she says at last. "I'm gonna find Dad's research."

"And?"

"And." Her jaw flexes against the metal. "That's what he wanted, right?"

"Is it?"

She sits up. "Shut up, Grant."

He doesn't move. His eyes are silver in the light.

Veronica wants to hit him. "That's what he wanted." She throws the balled Frito bag at him.

It bounces off his chest, but he doesn't flinch. "Then why did he hide it?"

"He didn't hide it. Not from me. He knew I would find it. He knew I know enough to find it, even if no one else can."

"And what will you do once you have it?" He knows. He lives

inside her head, of course he knows. "He *hid* it, Veronica."

"I'm really fucking aware." She wants him to leave. But then she'll be alone, and she doesn't want to be left alone. She's cold. "I don't know what he'd want me to do," she murmurs. "I feel like I need to find it. That's all I know. I need him back."

"He let them take him. He sent his research far away. How will he feel when—?"

"I don't know. I don't care. I don't know what to do without him, he didn't tell me what to do, I just need him back, and honestly, at this point—" Her throat is tight. She wipes her nose on her sleeve. "I want him back. I don't care about the research. But I can trade it to get him back."

She senses his disapproval. Is that her own subconscious disapproval? Probably. It's the voice of Benedict Lewis in the back of her mind: *Veronica, that's too dangerous. Please don't shoot the neighbor's cat, that will be expensive. That doesn't make sense, that isn't logical, why would you do that? Why would you do it like this?* "I don't know."

"And what if you get to New Mexico and there's nothing waiting for you?"

"I'll figure it out. I'll set a trap and I'll kidnap one of those fake PIs and I'll make a trade for my dad." It sounds ridiculous. "Leave me alone, huh?"

But when she closes her eyes, he follows her into the darkness. She doesn't recall giving him permission, accepting an invitation or a proffered hand, but the girl makes a seamless transition into the canary, and she is frightened.

It didn't used to be like this. It didn't always happen so quickly.

"Watch," says Grant. The pale boy takes her in his hand and walks the winding labyrinth—not wandering as they usually do, but with purpose. The canary's wings flutter, uncomfortable. *Stop.*

"Watch," he says again. His hand presses on her body, his thin fingers caging the bird. The walls fall away around them. The maze disappears. They are swallowed by darkness—the pale boy and the canary soul, hearts beating fast, the shadows swallowing their breath and body until there is nothing but dense, pulsating nothing.

Does she exist?

Does the world exist?
What have you done? What are you?
She is alone in the darkness when the universe splits open.

It begins as a hairline crack. A terrible seam emerges out of the shadows, a ripple in the fabric of reality. It grows before her eyes, wide enough to swallow the bird, the girl.

Nebulae. Nothing. Language and light. All these gold and silver strings, streaming across an infinite space. The moment she grasps onto one concept, it twists and becomes something new. Whatever is beyond the tear is beautiful in the way a tsunami is beautiful.

It makes no sound, but she feels the vibrations in her bones.

Where is the pale boy? Where is her body? She can no longer find her body.

The seam is growing. The darkness cracks around it, spiderwebs of light breaking through the walls of her world. It swims before her eyes. There are voices—in the shadows or in her head, she cannot tell.

Crying won't help, Nica.
Remember January.
In the dirt we mumble...
Do you ever think that the things you see might be more real than you realize?
My rock-solid kid. Rock solid.
Maybe the universe is warning you about something. Or someone.

It's too much. Her chest explodes. The canary flings out its wings and screams.

She stands in the light. Fluorescent light, blinding her. Her body is cold, hands numb, arms flung out from her sides like she still has feathers in her flesh. The tsunami towers in her vision, hovering, hesitating before a deafening crash.

In the dirt we mumble.

The wind is fierce. It's cold on her neck. She likes it.

The light comes and goes. When the wave comes crashing down, everything flashes before her eyes, and something tears loose inside Veronica.

She lands on her back. Her lungs empty.

★ ★ ★

Harry Markus watches from atop a dead-eyed bus on the edge of the parking lot. The cool metal roof presses into his chest. His cheek rests against his gun as he sets up the sights.

When the first Mumbler creeps into the floodlit lot, he takes aim. His finger tightens on the trigger.

When the rest of the horde emerges from the darkness, he isn't looking at the Mumblers anymore. He's lost his target; he's focused on the front of the bus station where Veronica Lewis is no longer sitting on the bench, slouched against her bag, but standing. She's standing, arms flung out from her sides, as the night breeze gathers strength into an unnatural wind.

A chill runs down his spine. Harry's gaze wanders to the floodlights, flickering, spasmodic. Across the property, they flash in unison. The wind tosses his hair into his eyes. The wind roars in his ears. He blinks away tears.

The Mumblers approach the station. They are black blurs in his vision. Harry refocuses on the sights, he tries to pick out Veronica Lewis in the windstorm.

An electrical charge rips through the night.

Lightning tears through the sky.

By the time Harry blinks the white specks from his vision, the Mumblers are dead.

He's on his feet. He slings the gun across his back and stands on the bus roof, surveying the scene. Veronica Lewis is on the ground. The Mumblers are on the ground, prone, spread out in a perfect circle around the girl. The wind quiets as quickly as it started. The night tastes of ozone.

Harry lowers himself over the side of the bus. The crack of his boots on the pavement echoes across the silent parking lot. The lights flicker once—twice—and then return to normal.

In the sudden silence, he approaches the scene. The stench of post-battle bowels drifts across the carport. Harry nudges the closest Mumbler with the toe of his boot. He swallows and moves on to the next, kicks it in the head, watches the neck loll limply to the side.

The station door creaks open. "Hey sweetheart, weather looks bad, you wanna—?"

A man in a leather jacket stands in the doorway. His jaw drops, revealing small yellow teeth and silver fillings. His gaze sweeps the Mumblers, the girl on her back, and then Harry Markus, who raises his gun and shoots the man between the eyes.

After a moment's reflection, Harry goes ahead and puts a bullet in each of the Mumblers bodies. If there's anyone else inside the station, they've surely realized something is wrong by now. He quickly kneels beside Veronica Lewis. Snaps his fingers under her nose. "They're dead."

Her eyelids flutter. He wonders if she hit her head on the way down. He holds out his hand and yanks her to her feet.

She stumbles. He releases her and lets her catch her balance. "We have to go."

"What the—" Veronica Lewis blinks, turns around dizzily a few times, takes in the scene. She stops and stares at him. "What did you do?"

"They're dead. Let's go."

"How the fuck are you here?"

"You mean how am I not dead after you left me to the Mumblers?" He grabs her rucksack from the bench. She catches it against her stomach. "Not to be fucking arrogant, but I'm Harry Markus."

"But—"

"Look, these are dead. But there are more. I followed them here. They won't stop until they get what they want. So your best chance is to keep me around and just let me save your life, alright?"

Her eyes fix on the man in the leather jacket. A pool of blood puddles under his head. Her nose wrinkles. "Did you kill him too?"

"No, he grabbed my gun and did it himself. Does it matter?"

She barks a laugh from the back of her throat. Her brow furrows. She blinks hard and frowns at him. "I'll just get rid of you again."

"I'm sure you'll try."

"You bet your ass I will." She pulls up her hood. "Stop lying to me. At least pretend to have ulterior motives."

Three days. "Fine. What are yours?"

Veronica gazes at him uncertainly. She surprises him by actually answering. "I'm getting my dad back."

Which means she'll trade any information to North Enterprises or BEESWAX. She'll find her father's research and hand it over in exchange for Benedict Lewis. "They have my brothers."

That gets her attention. "What?"

"North Enterprises," he says, "has my brothers."

"You have brothers?"

"Yes."

"Are they assholes too?"

He sighs. She smiles. "Look." Harry nods at the glass doors; there are figures moving in the bus station, curious faces peering out at the carpark. "We need to go."

She doesn't budge. "You want to trade my dad's research for your brothers?"

"Yes, close enough. And you want your father back. We both want near the same thing, I'm sure we can come to a reasonable agreement when the time is right, but that isn't this moment. Now, we run."

She's staring at her hands. Her gaze drifts to the closest Mumbler, and her eyes narrow, as if she's trying to remember something. Harry thinks about that flash of light. He remembers the wind. Where he comes from, the nights are cold and the wind is fierce, more like the unnatural gusts of this evening than anything else. He almost wishes it would happen again.

Concentrate. "Now, Lewis."

For an instant, when she looks at him, her eyes seem all black, pools of ink in her sockets. But she turns her head and it must have been a trick of the light, because her face is normal—as normal as it's ever been.

Wrongness hangs in the air.

She knows it, too. Harry hot-wires a car that smells like feet, and she lets him drive because if the console with its exposed wires explodes in someone's face, she wants it to be his.

"Follow the highway," Veronica says. She watches out the window as the gray sky lightens to gold on the horizon. She runs a hand through her hair.

A yellow feather comes away between her fingers.

17

January.

    The sky splits open in torrents of rain on a town nestled in the craggy Blue Ridge of North Carolina. Rainwater avalanches down the slopes and spits into rivulets and creeks, dousing the countryside with hail and mud. Electricity buzzes along ill-maintained power lines. Severe weather warnings have been issued, and the residents of Dane's Chapel hide within their homes like frightened rabbits. They watch plastic chairs and lawn ornaments waver and topple in the wind. Lake Tan lashes against the shore. The creek is swollen; the bank turns to mud and washes away, twists through the West End and disappears into the woods.

    Veronica is sixteen. It is a January night.

    They walk the maze of her mind. Familiar passages, over and over again. She will grow weary of this as the years go on, she knows it. Perhaps she will go mad. Everything looks the same, and there's never any end to it. Occasionally, a break in the darkness—a scene, a glimmer of something beautiful or terrible—and then more of the same winding labyrinth.

    She is reminded of Sisyphus from the myths, always pushing his rock uphill, always watching it roll back to the bottom again. Eternal punishment. She grows weary. She wants to leave. She cannot. The canary flutters its wings. *Let me go.*

"Just a bit farther," the pale boy murmurs.

No. Now.

"There's more to see."

I don't want to see it. Not anymore. I can't do this forever. She's tired. She's tired of seeing things other people do not, she's tired of hiding it from her dad, she's tired of not understanding.

Let me go. She pecks the boy's wrist. He cannot feel pain, but he jerks with surprise.

Weightlessness. He's gone. The canary reels. *He's gone.*

Grant is gone. She is alone.

And whatever has been grounding her to the concept of three dimensions and concrete space disappears in a broken breath of wind. As she spins in the darkness, golden wings flapping against the smoke-tinged air, hurtling through nothing, into nothing—

—a seam in the darkness—

—a spiderweb of light—

—a flash of electricity breaks through the sky above Dane's Chapel.

The night cracks open in a white bolt of light. Wind tears across the mountain—topples trees, screams through the woods, tangles in power lines. It is the angriest wind these hills have ever seen. It is frightened and furious.

It is unnatural.

A blackout spills darkness along the mountain's slope. Dane's Chapel plunges into silence.

Her eyes fly open to see the flickering lightbulb above her bed, the darkness playing dancing shadows across the ceiling, a scream frozen in her throat. She does not know what it is she saw. She does not want to see it again.

The wind is a cool caress on her neck. Loose papers and dust spinning in a gentle cyclone around her now drift back to the floor. She cannot speak. Her chest heaves. Her fingers knot around her sheets, because the world is spinning—she is a small canary body tossed in a violent wind.

Her door sways, creaks in the breeze. The light flickers—*on, off,* on.

He's here. He holds her against his chest, but she doesn't hear a heartbeat—she hears wind, and screaming, and wind. He smells like smoke. Her stomach heaves. "It will be okay." Benedict Lewis' voice is low. If his eyes betray emotion, his tone and words do not. They are an anchor. "It will be okay, you're safe. But we can't tell anyone. Hey? It's a secret. We'll figure it out, but no one can know."

They've always known something was wrong. He knew she had dreams. He knew she sometimes saw things that weren't there. He knew her better than any other living person, he knew her so well that he could tell her she'd be safe and she believed him. *He knows me. He knows. He knows what to do.*

Flickering lightbulb: dark, light, dark. In the darkness, the night is complete and she could almost pretend that she is dreaming. In the light, she sees the worry in her father's eyes. She sees the pale boy standing across the room, caution scrawled across his face.

The canary in her soul shrinks back into the shadows. In a distant, dream-state way, she feels the pale boy's long fingers close around the bird—gentle this time, almost apologetic. With her father holding Veronica's hand and the boy cradling the bird, her heart rate slows. The breeze dissipates.

Across Dane's Chapel, electricity hums back to life.

Veronica finds Grant again in the corner of her room, arms behind him, back pressed to the wall. He nods.

Benedict Lewis knows her best; Grant knows her better.

Just a bit farther.

"I won't tell," she says, as electricity buzzes and the lights flicker back to life along the mountainside. She speaks to her father, but she looks at the boy with the gray eyes. "It's a secret."

18

Snapshots, if you will. Glimpses of a universe where time and space blur together into a seamless film strip of face, and face, and poor intention, and ill consequence.

First up: a tired man with a confused soul and perhaps not the purest of intentions. But isn't that human? Buried deep beneath a base desire to do good is the knowledge that if you don't, eternal torment awaits you. He does his best. He thinks that's not good enough. He isn't sure that he *is* good. He becomes less sure every day.

Benedict's nights are full of tormenting quiet. His days are full of a different breed of torment: psychological horrors, threats and lies, and above all, the knowledge that his concept of day and night has irredeemably deteriorated.

He's a man with very specific routines and habits best known only to him. He has been this way since highschool–early mornings and rigorous research and physical training for the most personal and mundane of reasons, carefully orchestrating his diet and sleep schedule. Even throughout college and postgrad work he maintained firm control over his time and how he chose to spend it. Even after Veronica.

Seemingly impromptu walks into the hills were premeditated hours–if not days–in advance. He guarded his consistent six hours of sleep as he guarded few fixtures in his life. Every time he dared sneak up to his lab in the East End of Dane's Chapel, he had a mentally curated agenda of what exactly he would be doing, and for how long.

The neurotic tendencies gnaw at him throughout the hours. He does not know day from night, his meals are delivered according to no consistent schedule, and his grip on the life he's always fought to maintain is loosening. His tight fists slacken; his knuckles ruddy from clenched white bone to a chapped red.

He tried to keep track of time for a while. But the lines scratched into the floor of his cell stop somewhere around the fifth day. The idea of time slipping away from him, forgetting minutes and hours, slowly losing track, is too much. Now he simply pretends that he isn't bothered. It takes all his strength of will to keep his mind from shattering into a million pieces. It takes everything in him to pretend that he doesn't care.

"He won't talk," says Billings. "I've been here for two days overseeing the interrogation. He is unusually resistant."

X walks beside him down the corridors of ARC, a distorted honeycomb of cells and cryochambers and lounges where guards and doctors drink coffee and play Scrabble, as if they work desk jobs in a skyscraper instead of a top-secret prison system buried off the coast of Maine. The old man is uncomfortably aware of the pressure weighing down on this place, of the freezing black waves lapping against the rocky shore high above. What if the ceiling breaks open? They will all drown. All of them. He doesn't understand how Billings breathes so easily.

"I've heard you aren't having any better luck."

X starts. "Sorry?"

A vein in Billings' temple twitches. "You haven't found his daughter."

"Not yet. No."

"And when will you?"

X considers reminding Andre that the two of them were

outwitted once by Veronica Lewis; he is not alone in this struggle. But the polaroid on the trailer's kitchen counter silences him. Nothing of his past was supposed to have survived, so he is at least partially responsible for what happened in Dane's Chapel. "I'm working on it," he says. "I have a lead."

And that is all Andre Billings needs to know. X believes that's all he can handle; of course Billings doesn't know about the Myrmen, or that Harry Markus has been sent on their trail. This is X's area of expertise, much more than it is that of anyone at BEESWAX or North Enterprises. This is his game, and he knows the rules. Too many players would muddy the strategy of the board.

"So you'll have her soon?"

"Her, and Benedict's work. If all goes according to plan." Small victories like digging his hook into Harry Markus' throat lend him a confidence boost; for the first time in quite a while, he feels faintly optimistic that he's finally got the right man on the case.

Billings swipes his access card at the end of the hallway. A door slides open to reveal a dimmer corridor, all cold cinderblocks and heavy mechanized doors. "Yes," he says blandly, "having world events play out according to your preconceived plans is certainly the most challenging part of the job."

X smiles pleasantly at the military man, who holds open the door, and X steps into the concrete corridor. The door snicks shut behind them. "And *you* are having lots of luck?"

"He won't talk," Billings says again. "He's reached the pinnacle. I've seen it before— they hold themselves together, power through to the breaking point without betraying anything. They seem stable. But when it becomes clear that there is no end in sight and we won't give up, they waver. And break."

"Is that what happened with Webber?" X saw what happened to Peter Webber.

Billings ignores the jab. He pauses in the corridor, taps his access card against a doorframe, but doesn't unlock it. "He's through here."

X doesn't move.

"Do you want to see him?"

Suddenly, he doesn't. Memories are resurfacing; it was too hard to watch what they did to Peter, and he doesn't think he can stand seeing the collapse of Benedict Lewis as well. Even if it is for a greater cause. Even if he is but a speck in the cosmos of this unfathomable plan. He remembers Ben and Peter in his classes. They were unstoppable, electric. They were the brightest students he ever taught.

"No." X steps back from the door. "I believe I've seen enough."

"Do you want to view the cryochambers? Halleck can bring you there." Andre's gaze is level, brutally intelligent. "But I am busy."

What an excellent way to remind X that he's not a priority. "No." X wanders back down the hall, and Billings follows. "No, I have things to do. I need to check up on mission progress. Can't do that down here."

"No, I suppose you can't." Billings locks the door behind them. A smile flickers at the corner of his lips. "I hope you've come up with a nice story for that fiasco in St. Louis."

"What about it? I didn't do that."

"I assume you had a hand in it. No—don't bother. You forget that BEESWAX has a strong hand in North Enterprises operations; I know more about your job than you think you do mine. Hence, here I am in an entirely separate division. Still in a superior position." Back in a well-lit area of the honeycomb, Billings snaps his fingers at a break room as they pass the door. "Mander. Go find Halleck to escort our visitor back to the surface."

A woman leaps to attention and rushes from the room.

X is tired of power play. He does not speak as they navigate to the exit; he is simply ready to ascend out of this freakish underwater Hell. He feels the cold in his bones.

Halleck rounds the corner ahead of them—a slight, pale man with a shock of brown hair. His uniform is loose around his shoulders. He looks like he lives under a rock. He technically does.

"Commander Billings, sir. There's news from North Enterprises."

X slows his stride. *He should be receiving news from Cage and North Enterprises; Billings doesn't even work for them. Did he set this up? Overkill.*

"What news?" Billings' voice is low.

"They've been compromised, sir. The compound has been overtaken. Those who escaped have been airlifted from the area and will be arriving here shortly. Agent X." Halleck turns to him, as if just noticing the older man's presence for the first time. His jaw is tight, eyes wide. "Sir. You are not to return."

19

It is noon in St. Louis, and a construction crew is busy standing above an old sewage line on the city's outskirts.

Howard Markus slouches against a stop sign nearby, a cap pulled low over his eyes, legs crossed languidly at the ankle as he views the scene over the lip of his steaming paper cup. To the casual observer, he might be a local who just stepped out from the coffeeshop to view the commotion. He left his uniform in the helicopter where he landed it this morning, in some overgrown farmland well outside the city; he's inconspicuous in khaki cargos and a weathered brown bomber jacket. Just a *guy*, just a civilian. Sometimes it's thrilling to play pretend. Admittedly less thrilling when his brothers' lives are on the line.

Cage's men are good; he wouldn't be able to tell them apart from the common road maintenance crew if he didn't already know they were from North Enterprises. He tapped into their radios as he flew through the night, dropped in and out of the line before they could detect an eavesdropper.

He tucks a stray curl into his cap and watches as the taped-off area grows in population. He doesn't recognize anyone here. But then, he only runs with the pilots really. If he spent less time in the hangar and more time in the compound itself, perhaps he'd know where Henry works. He wishes he did.

An ache settles in the pit of his stomach. He drinks his tea so quickly that it burns his tongue; he feels the heat in the back of his throat.

Harry would have gotten Henry out. If he thinks about it too much, his mind races. He's bombarded with images of a different time and place where the Mumblers have them cornered and helpless; he's dragging Henry's body through crumbling streets, fear as thick in the air as any other stench. He's doomed Henry to that again. He's left him behind.

If you hadn't left, they'd have gotten you, too.

Harry wouldn't have left. He'd have gotten them all out. But Harry hadn't been there, had he? He'd run off on some crazy adventure, once again leaving his brothers behind.

He gulps more tea. He doesn't taste it. *Find Harry. He'll fix everything.*

What if the Mumblers discover Henry before Howard can find help? What if they discover who he is?

Find. Harry.

He has a starting point. Harry was here, he's sure of it. A fair bit of destruction, mysterious circumstances, and people cleaning up after him is a Harry Markus trademark move.

"What does X want?"

"He's in touch with Cage. He says to regroup at ARC."

The voices come from a nearby alleyway. Howard doesn't move, doesn't look, but he hones in on the conversation.

"We aren't finished here."

"You have an hour. Cover it up. Priority is to get the bodies through the tunnel. I'm sending Delaney up the way with a van and we'll retrieve them at a more discreet location. No witnesses. Tell Natalia's crew: clear the water. We'll let the city do the rest, just get the bodies out."

"Okay. Okay, I'll tell her. But an hour—"

"Do the best you can. We can't deal with these things, right? We don't know how to deal with them. But there are dozens dead down there, and more in Tulsa—"

"What, Tulsa? When? When did that happen? Why didn't I know?"

"Early morning. I just got the call. Bodies are hours old. Locals are losing their minds, witnesses won't keep their mouths shut. I mean, someone knows how to kill 'em apparently, but we don't. I don't like that. X doesn't like that. Bullets in all of them, piled up at a Greyhound station in Tulsa. We need to lock down until the other guys figure out what's going on."

"The other—?"

"BEESWAX. Cage is down, but BEESWAX is still intact. Let them clean up this mess, this is their business. We're clearing out."

"Two hours, man."

"You've got an hour thirty."

By the time the two men exit the alley and duck back under the ribbons of yellow tape, Howard is gone.

20

Lush farmland gives way to arid plains and dust-blown interstates. Sagging billboards warn her that she'll burn in Hell, and there's a casino at the upcoming truck stop, and there won't be another gas station for a good long while. She hadn't realized there could be so much flat nothingness; the endless sprawl of sun-baked midwest, so far from the mountains and the Atlantic, seems hopeless and desolate. Suffocating. Dead-eyed warehouses, long and low barns, retired bars—all hunch roadside as if readying to spring at passing cars. Power lines and a dry shade of brown follow them for miles out of Oklahoma and chase them into Texas.

As the sun climbs and Veronica dozes out of sleep, she glances across to Harry Markus. His gaze is alert and singularly focused on the operation of the vehicle. Unguarded, he looks tired. In the sporadic beams of sunlight it's difficult to tell apart shadows from bruises, but he holds himself with a stiffness that suggests he did not escape the Mumblers unscathed. He doesn't really move, doesn't shift in his seat at all, but from time to time he works his jaw, and his eyes scan the road so that his pupils periodically disappear from Veronica's view, and he looks like something that's died but Satan's coughed back up.

'The Devil Went Down to Georgia' gets stuck in her head in an irritating loop as she continues to play dead and watches him drive in silence. *He was in a bind the way behind and willing to make a deal.* She isn't sure if Harry Markus is the Devil, or Johnny with his fiddle.

"I didn't know you have brothers."

He flinches. He glances at Veronica, apparently disturbed to find her awake. A slow smile spills across her face. He blinks once—twice—then faces the road again. His throat bobs as he swallows. "I didn't tell you," he says. The subtext being: *so shut up about it.*

"I had a step-sister," says Veronica.

"I know."

"How do you know? You have files on me?" When he doesn't respond, Veronica straightens. "Do you?"

"I don't. But they exist."

"Who has them?"

"If they have files on Benedict Lewis they certainly have files on you, too."

"I can't imagine they have much." Benedict has always kept a low profile for Veronica. She sometimes felt, growing up, that she had a big red *confidential* stamp on her forehead. "Who's *they*? Who knows about me?"

"Anyone who knows about Benedict Lewis, I imagine."

"You don't have to imagine. You know. Who else?" He hesitates. Veronica's smile slips away and she gazes at him through her eyebrows, chin tucked to her chest. She's like those barns beside the motorway, waiting to spring and bite and sting. What will he do if she reaches over and pinches him? Or tries to grab the wheel? "Who?"

Harry Markus exhales. "North Enterprises. BEESWAX, probably. They're working together on this operation. I assume they're pooling resources."

"Cool." She reclines again in her seat and watches the sunlight play golden patterns on the felt ceiling. "What's the difference? Which one's more dangerous?"

"That depends on what sort of threat you pose."

"Threat!" She laughs. "Am I a threat?"

He doesn't dignify that with a response. "BEESWAX addresses biohazards and biotechnology, North Enterprises is more interested in security and tech." He adjusts his coat collar. "I really don't know much about them."

She thinks she might be a biohazard. Veronica tilts her head against the seat. "You seem to know plenty. What about Peter Webber?"

Now that he knows she's watching, he doesn't react to the name. Still, he takes long enough to answer that she knows she's messing with his head.

"What about him?" says Harry Markus.

"What do you know about him?"

"He worked with Benedict Lewis. He's gone."

Oh, he knows. He knows lots more. "Do you know who took him?"

Harry Markus' eyes flick to her briefly. "Probably BEESWAX."

"Was Peter Webber a biohazard?" Veronica asks, partly to herself. She crosses her arms and presses her cheek against the headrest. "So, is he dead?"

"Who?"

"Peter Webber, dumb-ass."

"I don't know."

She wonders if Grant Webber knew. She wonders at the possibility of them both being alive somewhere, father and son, shut up and hidden away for years on end. At least BEESWAX, or whoever had taken Benedict, had bothered to stage a suicide; the case of the Webbers carries a shroud of mystery and incompleteness. How could they have gotten away with it? How could anyone keep up the charade for so long? And how many years could BEESWAX afford to keep Benedict Lewis hidden away?

Veronica sees red behind her eyelids, sunlight filtering through the windshield. She doesn't find the labyrinth, the canary, the pale boy; she smells unwashed bodies and an evergreen air freshener instead of smoke on a breeze. Lightning does not split through her mind.

There is a pit carved into her gut in the shape of her dad. Inside, something ugly rears its head and bares its fangs and threatens violence. Veronica thinks of that moment of release, the labyrinth breaking open into a splintering seam of blinding light, and how it felt like a weight off her chest, a fresh breath of air. In that moment she hadn't thought of Benedict at all, just rage and vengeance and power. Simmering menace is preferable to the distress of abandonment.

Without opening her eyes she says, "What happened with the mumbly people?"

"They're dead."

"Yeah, I got that. I mean back in St. Louis."

"They're dead, too."

She opens her eyes. "All of them?" He's lying. That makes her smile. "Wow, there were a lot of them. That's super impressive and almost unbelievable. You must be really fast and strong."

His knuckles are white. He reminds her of that young Grant from her labyrinth: fists tight, teeth clenched, struggling to control the violence seething through him. She's finally gotten under his skin.

"So. What are your brothers' names?" she says.

"Why do you need to know that?"

"I'm a curious little critter."

For a moment, she thinks he won't respond. Then he sighs, a muscle in his cheek twitches, and he says, "Howard. And Henry."

"Seriously?"

"*Yes.*"

"Your names are Harry, Howard, and Henry?" She laughs—a harsh, barking sound that cuts through the closed space. He flinches again. She tilts her seat all the way back, deeply satisfied. "What are you, triplets?"

His scowl deepens. "Yes."

"Oh my god. Those are the most British names ever."

"We aren't British."

"You sound pretty British."

"We aren't British." Then he seems to realize she's goading him, and he cuts his eyes at her—pretty blue-green eyes like translucent sea glass in the sunrise. She remembers how they looked when she closed the manhole cover over his face.

She holds his gaze. *I know I killed them,* she wants to say. *I know I did something and the Mumblers died and you're pretending it didn't happen like that.*

The dust settles. Silence fills the car, and Veronica puts words to the stiffness of Harry Markus' shoulders and his furrowed brow, the clipped cut of his words, his furtive glances.

He's scared.

The City (III)

Images from the past. Count them, spread throughout time yet knotted together with the golden yarns of Fate.

A boy stands on a ledge above a burning city. The flames reflect in his eyes, the explosions and avalanches of rubble pulse in the stone beneath his feet, vibrating his bones, puncturing his lungs with every collapsed building, every dying breath.

"We have to go," says his brother. "They're coming. They know where we are, they saw us."

What if he stopped? The city, in flames. One brother on the brink of death, the other with a question in his eyes: What now?

I don't know. I don't know. The adrenaline trickles away, and his body wants to lie down and die. I don't know. His whole life has been a cycle of not knowing and still acting. If he's honest with himself, he knows that falling and getting back up again is the only way he knows how to live.

When they continue up the mountainside—two stumbling gaits carrying a deadweight between them—it feels like the ascent out of Hell.

21

There is a speck of a town nestled between reservations and sprawling desert in the southwest of New Mexico. This town is called Harley.

Harley is mostly built up around a poorly-funded public school, home to the Harley Gharials, county pickleball champions. There's an overpriced gas station on one corner, a bar & doughnut shop across the street from that, and somewhere amongst the scattered collection of post office, police department, newspaper, and gitchy thriftstore, Harley also manages to house a population of approximately two-hundred sun-baked ruffians. Half have roots in the place and don't plan on leaving. The other half is too poor to even consider moving away.

You're born in Harley. You die in Harley. Or the desert claims you.

That's what happened to the Webber family. Desert claimed Peter, who was out at his lab in the middle of the night. Here one day, gone the next, never seen again. *Coyotes,* some said at the time, but coyotes don't drive eighteen-wheelers, and there were some massive trails left when the sun rose over the desert.

Grant Webber disappeared a couple years later. The town didn't know Grant too well, but the folks at the local diner did; the slight blond kid would come in at least three times a week for a massive milkshake in a vain attempt to bulk up. He was tragically lactose intolerant and usually ended up puking in a nearby garbage can. After a while, they stopped serving him dairy and suggested he start liking sorbet.

He enjoyed the movie theater, which is dingy and smells like burnt butter most of the time. He tried playing sports and almost died, so he built model rockets instead. He had one friend at the public school: Jasper, the town's pride and joy; the freckled redhead escaped Harley two years ago to enlist in the U.S. Marine Corps.

With every year that passes, more of the Webbers slips away, as if eroded by each sandstorm that passes through town. Their story, one of neighborhood peculiarities and firsthand accounts, fades to lore; the account gets scooped up by conspiracy theorist groups and paraded as proof of extraterrestrials and lizard people. Life resumes its odd ticking rhythm in the wake of tragedy. The weirdness of the ordeal might disappear entirely from local memory if not for the continual weirdness of one Theodore Webber.

It is Sunday. The post office is closed and no one is getting mail today, because Hector Diaz has parked his dinged Jeep with its "U.S. Post" stickers outside Johnny Jim's Hog, Dog, and Bagel Breakfast Joint. He will not move it until he has consumed all three and probably a few beers.

"Tell Johnny what happened yesterday," says McGee, who slouches a few stools down from Hector at the bar. His elbows are on the counter, and he picks his crooked overlapping teeth with a butter knife.

Johnny—heavy and perpetually tired in a grease-stained apron—clatters a dish on the bar before Hector. "That's hot."

Hector knows it's hot. The bacon-wrapped burger is still sizzling. "You wanna know what happened yesterday on my route?"

"You'll tell me anyway," says Johnny. He's big and brusque, but his eyes are kind. He's got his dad's eyes, the Bear, big fella who left him the funds for the Joint when he had an aneurism nineteen years back. Johnny's done his old man proud.

"Yeah, he'll tell you anyway," says McGee. "Tell 'im, Hector."

"Out on Sunshine Boulevard—"

"Behind the dump," says McGee.

"Yeah, back a ways behind the dump, down Sunshine. All the boxes are right there at the corner. Got out to drop the mail, doing my thing, minding my own business—"

"And guess who showed up?" says McGee, overexcited.

Hector cuts his burger in half. The juice runs out. He looks from Johnny to McGee. "Who's telling the story? Me? Or you?"

McGee points his butter knife. "Yeah, you. Go on. Get to the good part."

"I hear this static like a radio, but my radio's off in the car. Turns out there's like this walkie-talkie shit rigged up on the back of one mailbox. Starts saying stuff about me being on camera, 'put my hands up'—well, I was scared. Thought it was some of that alien shit again—you remember way back with Arizona Tom?"

"I remember Arizona Tom," says Johnny. "Told everyone an alien pod done crashed his trailer."

"Thought it was that kind of thing. So I see the cameras rigged up a distance away along that chicken-wire down the road, but it was kinda hidden back there. And once the camera saw my uniform, the radio stopped squawking. And I moved on."

He bites into his burger. The fat is still hot. It instantly fries his tastebuds.

"That ain't legal," says McGee.

"Sure as hell ain't legal," Johnny turns back to the flat top. "You wanted a bagel, Michael?"

"Yeah, sure," says McGee.

The noon service down the street has just let out. The diner door bangs open and a crowd of Sunday brunch ladies enters. Johnny waves from behind the counter.

"You know who it was, don't you?" McGee sits forward.

"Sure," says Hector. "Sure I do. It was that crazy Ted Webber."

Johnny looks up from his bagel construction. "Ted?"

"Yeah," says McGee, "Ted Webber, he's gone nuts."

"He's been nuts a long time," says Hector. "Not the first time I've had to dodge around his crazy on my route, but this is a new one. Gonna have to report it."

Johnny's scratching the back of his big bald head. His gaze is distant. "I remember when Ted moved out here, way back when. From Nebraska or thereabouts. Moved in with Peter and the kids awhile after Waverley passed."

McGee looks uncomfortable. Hector pushes his fries around.

Johnny shakes his head. "But ya'll don't like talkin' about all that."

"Nah, it's not like that, Johnny, it's just..." Hector glances over his shoulder. "Makes people nervous, is all. Like them ghost and alien stories. People 'round here get nervous 'bout that shit. They just remember Arizona Tom."

"Ted's a madman," says McGee, "and that's about all there is to say about that. Got that place locked down like a fortress, got half the population of Harley worried he'll go postal. Feel sorry for that girl."

"Oh, she's alright," says Johnny. "Here's your bagel, Michael. Stop picking your teeth with my silverware."

Veronica's fingers catch the yellow sunlight and hold it. She holds rippling sunbeams on her fingertips as the car rips through the desert and her forehead grows hot against the window. *This is simple and explainable.* Heat from the sun soaks into her skin and she photosynthesizes. She might grow sleepy if she weren't humming with anticipation. Her pulse is steady and heavy.

So close. She could catch it and hold it. *So fucking close.*

They pull into Harley in the late afternoon. The sun is already setting in shades of orange across the dusty-toned town. In some ways, it reminds Veronica of Dane's Chapel. But the air is dead-dry. North Carolina smells like Christmas trees and minerals and water; Harley smells like sun-baked sand and bacon grease. Or perhaps that's just the diner parking lot.

There's only one Hog, Dog, and Bagel Breakfast Joint in the whole world, and that's in Harley.

"Stay here." Veronica checks the passenger-side mirror, decides that there's nothing she can do to make herself even moderately presentable, and jumps out of the passenger's seat. Her boots land with a snap, echoing across the pavement.

Harry Markus lolls his head at her. "Are you going to disappear?"

The parking lot is mostly empty; she spots a few pickup trucks and a battered Jeep parked around the side of the building beside the dumpsters. The stolen car looks conspicuous in the dusky lot.

She smiles at him with her teeth and no emotion. She slams the door in his face and flips him off for good measure.

Inside, the breakfast joint is dimly lit. Sunset filters through the dust-fogged windows. There are a couple guys hanging around the bar, a few teenagers playing the arcade machine beside the ice cream cooler. Two old ladies with globes of blue-gray hair glance up from their table near the door.

Veronica pulls up her hood. At the bar, a large-bellied man with a heavy face turns to meet her. There's mustard on his apron and a spatula in each hand. "Yup?" he drawls.

The men at the counter eye her closely. *Conspicuous.*

She didn't plan this far ahead. She'd be quicker on her feet if she weren't exhausted and the smell of fried food wasn't so prominent; when was the last time she'd had bacon? She'd kill for bacon. She's had pizza and Fritos and not much else. She wants coffee and waffles and bacon, and if it means Harry Markus sitting in the car for two hours, so be it.

The chalkboard behind the man says the breakfast menu finishes at noon. Something inside Veronica shrivels up and dies.

"Honey, you alright?"

So close, so far. So wildly confident that everything will turn out just the way she expects it to, no consequences, all fabulously according to plan. She doesn't know how to ask for what she needs like a normal person. She doesn't even know if the Webbers are still around.

Harry Markus is sitting out there in the car with his bored wolf eyes turned towards the building, waiting for her to slip up, because when a venomous snake enters your foyer you don't fuck with catch-and-release—you take it out with a BB gun and toss the carcass in the woods. He was scared in the tunnels with the

Mumblers, and she remembers all too well how he dealt with *them*.

Veronica slides onto a stool and rests her elbows on the bar. She knits her fingers together. Her legs dangle. "I don't think there's a not-weird way to say this," she says, "but I'm lookin' for the Webbers."

The two men at the bar share a glance. The fat man sets down the spatulas and wipes his hands on his apron. His eyebrows pinch together. "Well, now, I've gotta ask: what do you want with the Webbers?"

"It's a long story."

He gives her an appraising look, and she prays he sees more desperation than danger. "Maybe you should tell me a part of it, then," he says. "Most folks don't come 'round here asking for the Webber folks, not in a long time anyway. And if they do, I reckon' they're lookin' for a spot of trouble. We don't need any more of that 'round here."

"You don't want to go there, lil' missy," says one of the men slumped at the bar. He picks his nails with a butter knife. "Ask Hector. Hector went down there just yesterday, almost walked into a bear trap."

"Nah, that was last month," says Hector.

Veronica looks back at Johnny Jim. Something in her chest decompresses. "So they're still in town?"

Behind him, the coffee machine beeps. The endless black stream slows to a drip, and Veronica watches the line on the coffee pot rise and waver and still. Johnny Jim follows her gaze. He switches off the machine and turns back to her. He wipes his hands down his aproned belly again and sighs. "The ones still around are."

"I'm just in a tough spot. My mom was friends with Waverley, she said to go to them for help if I ever needed it."

Johnny Jim raises a single eyebrow. "Waverley."

"Yeah, Waverley Webber."

Johnny thinks about it. "Knew Waverley. Sweet woman." His gaze softens.

"You in trouble?" says Hector. "You need to talk to the sheriff? My brother's the sheriff."

Ah, shit. "No, that's alright. But if you could tell me where I can find the Webbers, that would be great."

"Well." The man behind the bar scratches his big bald head. "Like Michael said, it isn't like it used to be when Peter and Waverley had the place. I've heard it's locked down like a little fort. Don't know that you'll get much help out of Ted."

"They're all the way down Sunshine Boulevard," says Hector, his voice low. "Barbed wire, loads of cameras. I don't go 'round there much, just drop the mail and get out real fast. Isn't like it used to be."

"Did you know Peter?" Veronica asks.

Hector drags a finger along a hairline crack on the linoleum counter; it used to be white probably but the coffee stains and rings from mugs have tie-dyed it with splotty brown. "Sure," he says, head down. "Everyone knew Peter."

"Did you go out there?" she says. "To the desert? When he went missing?"

"Sure," says McGee, "everyone went out there. Biggest thing to happen to Harley since Arizona Tom. 'Course everyone went out there. Weirdest thing. They said aliens done it, but everyone says *aliens* when things happen out here, or Native spirits or somethin'. Mexican voodoo."

"You live in Harley long enough," says Johnny Jim, turning back to the counter with a paper cup of coffee, "and you'll believe most anything." He presses on a lid and slides it over to Veronica. "Don't listen to these fools."

"Johnny was there," says McGee. "He was with them when they found the boy."

Veronica pauses midway through climbing down from the stool; she stands with one foot on the floor. She looks from McGee to Johnny Jim. "The boy?" The hair on her neck prickles.

Johnny Jim lowers his gaze. "I say, what the desert takes we let to rest. No good digging 'round in tragedy. Waverley's passing was sad enough."

The boy. "You knew Grant Webber?"

The kids by the arcade glance their way. McGee's finger-picking slows.

Hector crosses himself. "Amen to what Johnny said. Let it rest."

Johnny Jim scoots the to-go cup closer to the edge of the counter in what Veronica takes to be gentle dismissal. "I'll say it again," he intones, "just so you know, most times people wander into Harley lookin' for the Webbers, things don't turn out too good for any of 'em. Webbers and strangers both. You best not bring trouble into town for that poor family, God knows they've seen enough of it. But if they can help you somehow I'm happy for it. And if they can't, you come on back here and Hector will sort you out."

Hector offers a two-fingered salute. McGee runs his tongue along his teeth and jigs his foot.

"I'll do that," says Veronica. She takes the coffee. "Thanks."

And as she leaves the diner and steps back into the dry golden evening, the bell on the door clatters and the arcade machine pops and pings, and the kids say something to the men at the bar. Veronica only catches one word: *Grant.*

22

Harley stands in shades of gray and darkening blue. The stolen car weaves down a narrow dirt road. Scrubby vines line the fences on either side and brush the car windows as they roll on past. Through the foliage, Veronica can make out glimpses of mobile homes, abandoned farm equipment, stripped-down trucks.

They creep along in silence for a half mile as the sky deepens and the shadows thicken, until at last the road ends in a circular dirt lot hedged by more chain link and dark brush. A padlocked gate looms before them, festooned with a fantastic assortment of security cameras and a festive garland of barbed wire.

Harry Markus throws the car into park. He sits back. "Who lives here?"

"I'm not sure. Someone named Ted."

She gets out of the car. He follows. It's then that she notices the signs lining the edge of the lot, hand-drawn in fat marker strokes on the backs of old political campaign signs. There's a dense cluster around the gate, like an absurd garden patch.

I KNOW MY SECOND AMENDMENT RIGHTS.

"Good to know," says Veronica. Harry Markus' hand slides

under his trench coat and rests at his hip. "Hey. No guns, cowboy. I didn't come all this way to murder my only hope."

"But you don't mind the idea of your only hope murdering you?" he says.

Veronica smiles. "What makes you think he's hostile?"

OUR HOME SECURITY IS PROTECTED BY MY M16. BACK OFF!!

DO NOT APPROACH IF YOU ARE: LIBERAL EXTREMIST, ISIS, MORMON, REPTILIAN, ILLEGAL ALIEN! NO!

GIRL SCOUTS = GOVERNMENT SCOUTS! STAY AWAY!

BEWARE OF MAN WITH GUN!!!

Veronica laughs. "Look, you've just gotta have a healthy fear of rednecks. You learn that from living in the South. They don't have rednecks in Russia or England or whatever?"

He doesn't answer, and he also doesn't take his hand off his gun. "Healthy fear," he murmurs.

"Like swimming and fire and shit."

"There is no healthy fear."

Veronica approaches the gate, but keeps him in her periphery. "Were you raised in, like...a brainwashed soldier bootcamp or something?"

His voice is grave. "Fear is a deadly tide. You let it in and it grows until you can't control it, and it controls you. There is no healthy fear."

Veronica's teeth flash. "You're not afraid of anything? Not even crocodiles?"

He frowns.

"Oh, that's right." She stands before the gate and peers through the wire, squinting against the growing dark. A green farmhouse crouches in the distance, over a low rise and down what looks like a gravel drive. It's a subdued landscape painting. "That's right, everything's scared of *you*, right? Bug men. Crocodiles. All tremble in fear. They just...quiver in their boots, don't they? But I bet I know who doesn't." She points at the signs. "That guy."

As if in response, a gunshot rings out across the yard.

Veronica drops into a crouch. "Shit."

Harry Markus stands to the side. His gun is out.

Veronica scoots behind a patch of ivy. She waves at him. "That won't help. Put that away. Get down." She leans around to get another look at the house. A tiny figure now stands on the porch. Veronica cups her hands around her lips and takes a deep breath. "We're not gonna hurt you!"

From way across the yard, a cracked voice responds: "The big 'un's got a gun! You think I can't see it, but I've got cameras! I see everything! Can't pull a fast one on me! What are you, Mormons?"

Veronica wonders briefly what sorts of Mormons they have out here. She glances at Harry Markus. "Drop the gun."

He sighs. "No."

"Drop the motherfucking gun, cowboy. You want to stick around and see what happens? I'm in charge. He sees you've got a gun, drop the gun." She's never felt more like a cowboy in a Western.

He holds her gaze.

The voice rings out again. "I can see you! Two of you! You Mormons? Girl scouts?"

"No!" Veronica shouts back. Then, through her teeth: "Throw the gun. Put it somewhere he can see it."

Slowly, maintaining eye contact the whole time, Harry Markus aims and tosses his gun back towards the car. It lands in a cloud of dirt and dust. He's just opened his mouth to speak when another sound echoes from the house over the hill—a door slamming.

Veronica carefully rises out of her crouch. An upstairs window has been thrown open, and a figure leans out to shout down at the man on the porch. A girl's voice says, "Ted, what the heck? It's probably the UPS guy."

"It ain't the UPS man! I don't order from the UPS man because he's been casin' us for the IRS."

Veronica cups her hands to her mouth. "I'm Veronica Lewis! My dad is Benedict Lewis! He knows Peter!"

The wind whistles through dry leaves, and Harry Markus not-so-subtly glances at his gun. Veronica straightens and risks a step into the open, hands held away from her sides, palms exposed.

The girl's next words are lost on the wind. The man is shaking his gun as if cursing the gods above. Finally, he turns and reenters the house. When he emerges a moment later, he stands on the porch and wrestles his skinny legs into a pair of cowboy boots. He stomps down the steps, along the gravel drive, and down towards the gate. He appears to be muttering to himself, shaking his head as he approaches.

"I reckon he made the signs," says Veronica.

"That seems correct," says Harry Markus.

She suddenly recalls, with a shiver, a scene from years gone by: sprawled on a warm tin roof, watching Grant from across a smudged skylight, her father pacing the trailer below, rubbing his hair with one hand, a phone in the other: "Where's Theodore? Has he called the police?" The day Grant disappeared. She hasn't seen the pale boy since Tulsa.

"This is Peter Webber's house," says Harry Markus.

"Oh, you figured that out. Only took two days. Gold star."

His eyes narrow as if he's trying to puzzle something out, trying to unravel the method behind her madness. She stares back and his posture immediately becomes disinterested. He turns away.

Ted appears over the rise—a wiry man with tattered jeans, his mouth a displaced slash on his stubbly face. Theres a gun strapped across his back. He looks like the hardened survivor of a plane crash who has returned to society with a lot of disturbing coping mechanisms.

"He seems pleasant," says Veronica.

He pauses before the gate and scowls deeply. She's aware that she looks abominable most of the time, so she can only imagine how truly horrendous she seems in her current state. He takes her in: the blood-splattered cargos, the set of her jaw, the strands of dirty hair escaping her hood.

"Goddamn it," Ted seethes. "You really are his. Goddamn Benny Lewis."

23

It's barely six o'clock, but Creed Webber is already in her pajamas. Her bare toes curl against the soft wood stoop as she stands against a porch banister and gazes out across the yard.

She knows the people in town say she's locked up in Ted's little prepper fortress, but the Webber property has never felt that way to her. They used to called it "the farm", even though they've never had anything but a rabbit. It does look like a farm in a way: there is a great barn in the back, painted the same green as the house, and Ted has a bit of a caterpillar tunnel where he messes with hydroponics. The five acres of shorn lawn used to sport little potted plants and raised garden beds, but these have since been decimated by the summer heat.

She thinks her dad called it a farm because she and Grant were wild little animals, which very much makes this property hers, and therefore she can never feel trapped by the silly little fences Ted favors. No, more often than not, when that gate squeals open as it does now, she feels like the survivor in a post-apocalyptic film, anxious that some plague or beast might infect the tranquility of the life she's carefully curated for herself out of ruins and rubble.

Creed crosses her arms. Her hands are numb, but it isn't even chilly out—it's been a warm winter in Harley, hasn't gotten below fifty since the beginning of February. She hugs her body tighter as, with a metallic screech, Ted shuts the gate behind the two interlopers.

The taller one towers over Ted. As she watches, her uncle forces him to disarm—pulling weapons from his long overcoat, his belt, his boots. This goes on for a full minute until her uncle is satisfied and moves on to the girl.

Veronica Lewis is only a dark smudge at this distance. She wonders if there will be something familiar there, something like answers. Another part of her hopes dearly that this wave will crest and pass by harmlessly, just a ripple, hardly a disturbance to the still waters.

She shivers. *Benedict Lewis. Benny Lewis.* She can still hear her dad's voice, speaking to Grant in whispers: *Ben this, Ben that. Back in school, Ben and I—*

She shuts her eyes and exhales. She wants this to wash over her. She wants to keep her feet.

It's over. Over and done.

Five years ago, when she was eleven and Ted was new to Harley, they'd driven together to Las Cruces to pick up Grant from the hospital. She waited in the cold lobby in flip-flops and pink cotton shorts. She was ready for her big brother to be home, even if he was an annoying little nerd. She was ready for things to go back to normal.

But when Grant careened into the waiting room in tennis shoes two sizes too big, tripping over himself, backpack sagging between his narrow shoulders, and straightened—it was in that moment that Creed felt that something had irreparably shifted in their lives. It's difficult at the age of eleven to get a sense for the enormity of one's lifetime, but even then she sensed that her childhood had come to an abrupt end.

Back at the house, she and Grant and his best friend Jasper sat cross-legged on the kitchen floor and ate mint chocolate ice cream out of a communal tub set between them. She remembers the heat, the dryness of the day, and the sheen of sweat that stood out on

Grant's pink forehead. She remembers crossing and uncrossing her legs because the backs of her knees were sweaty.

"Ted, this is absurd," Grant said at last. "We've gotta turn on the AC. Look as Jasper! He's all sweaty."

"I *am* all sweaty," said Jasper.

"Grant's sick," said Creed, "turn on the AC."

Ted, at that time, had still been moving his doomsday materials into the barn out back, and he found it necessary to inspect every cardboard box he hoarded away and label it according to what sort of apocalyptic help guides it contained. He sat on the back porch step, paging through magazines and newspapers with a degree of speed and attention that suggested imminent danger. Through the web of the screen door, his shoulder blades jerked and he shook his sandy head. "You know what's absurd?" he growled. He always had a bit of a drunken slur to his raspy voice. "That we can be so dependent on something like air conditioning. That's how they get you. Get over it. Grant isn't sick, that's why the hospital let him out."

"I've still got a concussion."

"And a scar," said Jasper, rather jealously. "How many stitches? Fifteen?"

"Twenty," Grant said through a mouthful of ice cream.

Creed hated the stitches and what would become the horrific scar. It ran down the side of his stupid pointy sun-freckled face. She loved that face. She had a sneaking suspicion that her brother's body had been peeled open and some alien imposter had taken his place.

"When's Dad coming back?" she asked, watching as Ted chucked a stack of magazines into a sagging banker box.

"Oh, soon, probably," said Grant. He dug his spoon back into the ice cream. His grin was wide and easy, but it still didn't look right; it was crooked now because of the stitches. "You know how he is."

"How is he?" said Jasper.

"Busy. Doing stuff."

"You're lying," said Creed. Once she'd had a dream that Grant was a dark wizard who'd turned Harley evil; she'd been wary of her brother for the rest of the day. That was how she felt now. She took another spoonful of ice cream and watched his face closely as he selected his next words.

"I'm not," said Grant. "That's not very nice. Jasper, am I lying?"

"Grant doesn't lie."

"You guys lied to me about the lion you caught behind the barn."

"That wasn't a lie," said Jasper, "that was a joke."

Creed rested the cold spoon on the back of her neck. "Where's Dad?"

"He'll be back," said Grant.

"When? I'm not stupid. I'm smart. Smarter than you, probably."

Jasper laughed. "You do read a lot of books."

Grant finally set down his spoon. He'd reached his limit with the lactose and it was beginning to show on his face. He unfolded his legs and propped his elbows on his knees and rubbed his eyes—gently, careful around the stitches—and glanced at his hands as if expecting them to come away bloody. But it was just sweat staining everything. It was a dry summer. Creed cannot recall a hotter one since.

He smiled at her. His eyes were tired. "I know you're smart. So trust me, huh?"

Creed is in the kitchen making tea when the strangers enter, followed closely by Ted. Her uncle is all but foaming at the mouth with excitement.

The radio mutters from its spot atop the fridge, always flooding the room with weird little ideas for her uncle to obsess over. Creed pushes a pile of MRIs and protein powders aside and plugs in the kettle.

Ted doesn't like the electric kettle. He says it's a gateway to depending on the government for beverages, and he'd rather die than depend on the government for anything. That's why he's got a wind turbine hooked up in the backyard and its electrical output is shit.

She perches on a barstool by the stove and watches them enter.

The big guy enters first. *Something is wrong with this one*, she thinks. It's like he exists in a different dimension—the shapes, the colors, the lines of his face and body and his sheer size speak of wrongness in a way Creed cannot quite describe. His movements are all casual prowess and power. *Dangerous*. His eyes are pale, his hair pitch black, the contrast unnerving. His gaze is measured and shifty. He's like something pretending to be human.

And Veronica Lewis. If the man in the trench coat is *wrong*, Creed is not sure how to evaluate the levels of wrongness surrounding Ben's daughter. It's the set of her brow, the tilt of her chin, the narrow twisted lips. The shadows of the room seem a bit darker around her.

Creed cannot hold the girl's gaze. She looks away.

"Don't sit down!" Ted barks at them, though neither has made a move towards the kitchen table or barstools.

Creed turns back to the kettle. "Let them sit, Ted."

"I gotta frisk 'em!"

"You've already frisked them, let them sit down."

For a moment it seems that Ted might argue, but he has very little energy to put towards arguing with Creed these days; it's a futile exercise. "I ain't got no rights in this house," he mutters.

No, he doesn't. Because it isn't his house.

Veronica Lewis drags out a chair from the table and sits. She glances at the tabletop, at the scattered packets of instant oatmeal and seed-saving supplies, measured scoops of white protein powder. Creed has grown accustomed to the chaos and can only imagine what it looks like to an outsider.

The man in the coat stands against the doorjamb, ankles crossed, hands in the pockets of his coat, giving off distinctly bad vibes. Ted side-eyes him as he shuffles into the kitchen and switches off the radio.

The kettle clicks. Creed fetches a mug and teabag. "What do you want?"

"I already asked them–!"

She speaks over him. "What do you want *to drink?*"

"Nothing, thanks," says Veronica. Her voice is low, husky, smooth with a Southern twang. It doesn't match her face. Creed can't recall whether Benedict had an accent.

Ted stands at the kitchen counter and furiously shuffles his scattered caffeine pills into their box. Creed fixes her tea and sits across from Ben's daughter. She wraps her hands around the mug and inhales peppermint. "What do you want?" she says again.

Veronica's eyes flick to the side, indicating the young man in the coat.

She doesn't trust him either. How odd. Creed nods. "Who's the unhappy guy in the unseasonable coat?"

In her periphery, said unhappy guy stiffens, as if objecting to having his feelings discussed. Creed raises the mug to her lips but does not drink, only raises her eyebrows.

Veronica traces a crack in the tabletop with her finger. Her other hand taps against her thigh. Her face is still. "Harry Markus fights the monsters and I keep him around because I tried to get rid of him once and it didn't stick."

"How did you and Harry Markus find us?"

"I looked up your dad in some newspaper bit from like twenty years ago. Johnny Jim's, Peter and Waverley at the diner." Veronica licks her chapped lips. "I didn't know he had a daughter."

"He did. He does. I'm Creed."

"My dad was friends with Peter."

"I know."

"My dad's gone."

Creed lowers her mug back to the table. "I know. Does Harry Markus want to sit down?" she asks Veronica.

"He doesn't," says Harry Markus.

Creed raises her eyebrows. "You're foreign."

"He's a Soviet or something." Only now does Creed notice that Veronica's fingers are bandaged, and the gauze is is splotched the rusty color of old blood. There's brown in her hairline. There's blood on her sleeves. Veronica catches Creed's eye and tilts her head like a curious bird. "How did you know about my dad?"

"Saw it in the news."

Something clatters in the kitchen sink. Ted whirls around. "We don't have TV! We don't pay the cable people!"

"I saw it at the gym, Ted. Take a chill pill." Creed's hands are still numb, wrapped around the mug. She takes a sip and burns her lips.

"It was in the news?" Veronica looks impressed. "What'd they say? Did they say he was unstable? 'Disgraced NASA scientist sets himself on fire and drives his truck into a pond'?"

"Something along those lines. They said you were missing, too."

"Well, I'm glad they noticed. I'm a pivotal part of that community. Local cryptid and all." She sits back and crosses her arms. "Why didn't they fake a suicide for your dad?"

The question catches Creed off-guard. "I guess...no one would have believed it."

"The folks at Johnny Jim's seem to think he was absorbed by the desert."

Creed has to smile at that. "Aliens is a popular theory. I guess, out here, you don't really have to explain too much. People make up stories themselves and everything fades to fiction."

"So what really happened?"

Creed shrugs. "I don't know. I was only eleven when Dad left, and Grant didn't tell me a lot. He was fourteen, he thought he could carry the world and he didn't want help. I think he knew too much and he didn't know what to do with all the information. Dad handed him too much."

"I don't need to hear this," Ted mutters. He chucks something into the sink and stalks out of the room.

Creed doesn't even flinch, just waits till he's gone before continuing. "The night Dad took Grant to the observatory—it was his lab, he worked out in the desert a ways, just south of White Sands. I don't know what happened that night. Grant wouldn't talk about it. We didn't hear from them for a full day, and when a search party finally went out to look for them, they found Grant pretty far off from the lab with a concussion and a big gash in his face from face-planting on a rock. Dad was gone. Grant got stitches in his face and he was sick awhile, but he claimed he didn't remember anything from before."

"Do you believe that?"

"Of course not. And he knew I knew he was lying, but he did it anyway because he thought he was a hero." Creed taps her fingers on the mug. She inspects Veronica from across the table. "My dad did too. He thought he was a hero. As I recall, so did yours."

Veronica blinks, and the shadows seem to solidify around her. Her eyes are soulless things. "You know my dad."

"We saw him from time to time. Haven't seen much of him since Grant left. He was Grant's godfather, did you know that?"

Veronica didn't. She shifts in her seat, restless, impatient. "My dad...never played hero. Just mad scientist. Occasionally."

"Exactly," says Creed. "They knew they were messing with things they shouldn't have, and they knew they'd put everyone in danger, but they did it anyway."

Veronica frowns. "It wasn't about us, it was their work."

"It *should* have been about us. It should have been about their families, but their research was a higher calling, wasn't it?" She stands and takes her mug with her. "They were supposed to be dads. Not superheroes. Not mad scientists."

Veronica's chin juts out. "My dad's brilliant. I'm gonna find him."

Creed walks into the kitchen and sets her mug in the sink. The sound echoes through the room. "That's what Grant said."

"And?"

Creed turns and leans against the counter. "He said he was gonna bring Dad home. He left. He never came back."

"And did you try? To find him?"

Creed stares at her. "Why?" she asks.

Veronica looks down at her hands.

She's saved from a response by Ted rushing back into the room, nearly tripping over Harry Markus in the doorway, catching himself, then whirling around and waving a rolled-up newspaper at Harry as if he's a bad dog. "Ya'll ain't talkin' 'bout this," he says. He shakes his head at Creed, then at Veronica, then he fixes Harry Markus with a remarkably nasty scowl. "We don't talk about this crazy shit, Peter's weird friends, we don't talk about all that shit."

"His weird friend's daughter is sitting at the dinner table," says Creed, "so I guess we do."

Veronica watches, terribly amused, as Ted barrels ahead. "Benny Lewis was nothin' but trouble. I told Peter, I said 'that boy has got too many sci-fi ideas' and then I said 'and those NASA folks are bad news, they're stealin' our tax dollars to send monkeys to space and open wormholes for aliens'."

"That's exactly what my dad did at NASA," Veronica says.

Creed snorts. "You don't have to get all riled up about it, Ted. It's too late in the day for drama." Before her uncle can fire back, she faces Veronica again. "We'll discuss this later. It's dinnertime, I'm tired. I want a glass of wine." She is sixteen and she does what she wants. She used to be a barnyard creature but this is her farm now; she traded childhood for agency. Sometimes, she thinks she'd give anything to be eleven and wild again. Creed turns back to the sink and runs the tap for no reason at all.

"They aren't stayin' the night," says Ted.

"I can fix up the upstairs room for you," Creed says over the running water, "and trench coat dude can take the futon."

Creed shows Harry Markus the downstairs shower, which has been converted into something like a hoarder's closet, stocked with too many cotton balls and bottles of rubbing alcohol. "For the apocalypse," she explains, before shutting Harry inside and leading Veronica upstairs. "I get some hot water in my bathroom, but Ted shut off the big water heater a few years ago because he doesn't want us going soft and relying on the government for...I don't know. Heated water, I guess."

She hands Veronica a stack of towels and flicks on the bathroom light. She points across the hall to a door with a Batman symbol carved into the wood, at about eye-level for a little boy. "That's Grant's room. I use it for a home office, but I'll clean some stuff off the bed."

"Thanks."

"Is that blood?"

Veronica glances down at her cargo pants. "Yeah."

"Yours?"

"I dunno." They stand in silence for a moment, considering that response. Veronica looks up. She smiles. "Life is shit, right?"

Creed shrugs. "Sometimes."

"Do you ever...like...see him?"

"Who?"

"You know. Grant."

But it's always been like she's waking from a bad dream, that lingering feeling that her brother actually died on the day they brought him home from the hospital with the stitches in his face, that whoever replaced him did a fabulous job with the deception. That churning in her stomach when she thinks she hears his voice. The tightness in her chest, sorrow turned so quickly to anger after he left, determination to remain unruffled by the saga of abandonment.

Ted constructs fences to keep out the Feds. She's built some walls of her own.

"I used to," she says, "when I closed my eyes. But not anymore."

24

Harry Markus stands in the shower for a long time, long after the water runs clear. He enjoys the senselessness of drowning as much as he enjoys anything; the way the water fills his ears and and eyes, the blur and darkness, almost like sleeping. Almost like rest.

He cannot rest in this place. Harry Markus does not believe in ghosts, but there is something whispered and secretive hidden within the farmhouse walls. Something waiting to pounce and bite. *Get in and out. Do your job.* He only has one job, and that's his brothers. Never mind ghosts, he's got the living to contend with.

When his mind quiets and well-leashed thoughts edge into the forefront of his consciousness, he switches off the water and steps out of the shower. He crushes the heels of his hands against his eye sockets. He inhales the shower steam and exhales in a huff.

Do what needs to be done. Be who you need to be.

Veronica sits on the floor of the shower for a long time, long after the water runs cold.

She watches dirt and rusty blood spiral down the drain. She closes her eyes and finds herself in the tunnels beneath St. Louis:

slow-moving water against brick, mumbling voices, a river of blood pulsing beneath the skin of a city.

A sense of smallness hits her like a truck. She wants to sleep in her own bed with the moaning trees outside her window and the shitty plumbing glugging through the walls. Instead, she's brought herself to the other side of the country and she's covered in monster blood. She can't scrub it off her skin. Some filth runs too deep.

Creed's left a pile of clothes outside the bathroom door: yoga pants and an oversized Harley Gharials Fun-Run shirt. Veronica finds a comb in the cabinet under the sink and spends several minutes taming her hair into its part. There's a tender spot on the back of her scalp, a bruise where she hit her head at some point.

She unwinds the gauze from her fingers like she's peeling open a chrysalis. The skin beneath is raw and bruised. She blows out her cheeks and rubs her eyes as if she can smudge out the dark circles. When she can't stand to look at herself in the mirror any longer, she makes finger-guns at herself through the haze of condensation. She forces a wild smile. "Crazy bitch."

There's someone behind her.

Veronica pivots, but Grant is gone.

"*Fuck* you." Has she pushed him too far? Is this some sort of punishment? A haunting. An absence of something that had always been there before, whether she liked it or not, and has become her default existence. *Fuck him.* This is a haunted house.

Veronica gathers her dirty clothes and carts them across the hall.

There's a busy desk in the corner of Grant's bedroom, covered in stacks of newspaper and notebooks. The walls are plastered with dusty superhero posters and model rocket diagrams. Shelves are crowded with framed photos and interesting rocks, Lego in dust-filmed plastic tubs. There's a plaid quilt folded on the bed, which has been freshly made-up with Captain America sheets and a Spiderman pillowcase. Disused dumbbells and something that looks like a shinguard stick out from under the bed.

It is as if, in the four years since his disappearance, Grant Webber's memory is still clinging to this place. Creed has done nothing to dislodge it.

She's still waiting for him to come back. Veronica sits on the edge of the bed, her spine tingling unpleasantly.

Is this who she will become? Seventy years from now, a gummy toothless Veronica wandering around a dilapidated trailer, talking to her imaginary phantom friends, making dinners and doing laundry for a Ben Lewis who will never return to Dane's Chapel. She can't imagine waiting that long. She can't imagine staying and sitting and doing nothing but waiting for him to come back to her. He wouldn't expect her to. *How does Creed stand it?*

She explores the room. Model planes and stale expired stashes of Halloween candy, graphic novels and National Geographic and a framed photo of Grant with a lopsided grin, an ugly scar running down from his temple, his tanned arm looped around the neck of a taller freckly boy with a shock of red hair.

There are three smaller photos lined up one beside the other on the edge of a shelf, frameless, small like yearbook photos, equally spaced; she can imagine Grant casually straightening them, his attention to detail betraying their importance. The first depicts a young Peter Webber in his doctoral regalia, his wide smile showing teeth like he's sharing a joke with the photographer. Then there's Creed, small and determined with big eyes and blond braids. The third photo is sun-bleached and faded: a blonde woman standing before a zoo exhibit, windswept, distracted by the big cats behind the bars. Her profile is familiar.

Veronica looks up at the ceiling, where glow-in-the-dark star stickers cling to flaking paint. The memories smell like summer. The room smells like marmalade.

She wants to scream. She wants to leap out the window and stab something and scream. She won't sit here. She won't wait. She won't turn old and bitter and wait for Ben to come home, she won't wait, she won't stop. She'll kill Harry Markus and sneak off in the night. She'll go out into the desert and find Peter's old observatory and she'll hunt for her father's work, for anything that'll get him back.

She'll do anything. But not this.

January.

That lightning crack in the universe, the pulsating dance of everything and nothing in the labyrinth of her mind.

January.

Without turning, Veronica murmurs, "Grant?"

Knuckles rap on wood.

Creed stands in the doorway. Veronica swallows and holds up the photo of the blonde woman. "That's your mom?" Creed nods. "She's pretty."

"Yeah. I don't remember her. She died just after I was born." Creed glances around the room as if perhaps there have been new developments since it was abandoned four years ago. Her eyes return to the photo. "Where's your mom?"

Veronica shrugs. "Gone."

"Sorry."

"Well, she's not dead. Not as far as I know." She replaces the photo beside the other two, fitting it into the dust-free space where Grant left it.

Grant Webber, cursed and divine. The prodigal son, the sacrificial lamb, anecdotes and lore stacked so high to obscure who he might actually be. If Veronica breathes too deeply she'll suffocate on that smell—summer and sun and marmalade—and she'll forget where she is, she'll forget he isn't actually here. *Sometimes*, she thinks as she places a hand on the shelf, to ground herself, *I'm not sure what's real anymore.*

Creed gazes at her with Grant's eyes. Two secret daughters in their fathers' homes.

Something snaps and cracks in Veronica's chest—a loosening tether. "It's here."

Creed takes a deep breath. She nods.

"In the house?"

"In the barn. It showed up in the mail a couple weeks ago and I figured Ted would burn it or something if he got his hands on it. Seeing as it was from Benedict Lewis. That much was obvious. That's never done us much good." She considers. "Maybe *I* should have burned it."

Veronica forces her hands to be still. She contains herself from leaping across the room and shaking Creed—*give it to me!* "Do you know what it is?"

"Do *you*?"

She thought she did. But the longer she's on this chase, the more questions crop up. She isn't sure of anything, least of all Benedict's intentions. *What does he want me to do? What was he hiding?* She's standing in the bedroom of a boy who ran after his dad and was absorbed by the desert, and the longer she clicks around these chess pieces, the more she feels she's ankles-deep in sand.

Her eyes drift to the door. She thinks of Harry Markus' eyes, too bright in the dark tunnels, hearing the Mumblers too soon in the pizzeria parking lot. "Can we go outside?"

The radio chirps atop the refrigerator. Ted Webber sits at the kitchen table working his way through a bowl of porridge. His spoon clinks on the bowl. There's a stack of magazines to his right and a book to his left, but he touches neither; all his attention rests on the young man in the living room.

Harry Markus reclines on the sofa, flipping through a firearms catalogue. He isn't paying any mind to the reading materials either; he's more focused on Ted's undivided attention and on how to sway it. The man moves like a spider; he's twitchy. His eyes haven't left Harry Markus for at least a half hour. *Wolf in a nursery.*

Ted goes in for more porridge. Harry risks a glance, and their eyes meet across the room.

The tension is palpable. Harry's lips twitch. Ted narrows his eyes and sets down his spoon.

The stairs creak in the hall. Two sets of bare feet pad down the corridor. Harry Markus slowly sets down the catalogue and watches the doorway. The front door opens and creaks shut, and after a moment, voices drift in through the kitchen screen door. Ted's frown deepens.

Harry Markus waits a moment before rising to his feet.

"Where are *you* goin'?"

Harry raises his eyebrows. "Toilet."

"Hmm."

Oh, what a silly little man. His eyes follow Harry out of the room and down the corridor until he's out of sight. Harry goes into the bathroom and switches on the light. He switches on the fan. He twists the lock on the doorknob, steps back into the hallway, and shuts the door so that Ted can hear it.

He sticks close to the side of the steps to avoid the creaky points. He stops at the top of the stairs and crouches in the shadows, listening.

The fan hums in the bathroom. Ted's chair scrapes back in the kitchen and his shadow appears in the corridor. Harry listens to the man tread to the bathroom; he imagines Ted pressing his ear to the door, trying the knob. After a minute, his shuffling footsteps resume, and he returns to the kitchen. Once his chair creaks and his spoon starts clinking around the bowl again, Harry rises from his crouch.

The shifting shadows from the window at the end of the hall paint dappled blue and gray light across the floorboards. He didn't notice it before, but here in the dusty farmhouse, far from the open road and confines of the stolen car, Veronica Lewis has got a scent to her: something freshly charred and smokey, a strange yet deeply familiar smell. It unsettles him that he can identify it as hers.

He wants to be done with her. He wants her to fade from memory once the job is done. Anyone he's known who has held on to memories too tightly has been the worse for it, and he thinks if he reflects on his life too long and remembers every life he's taken, he'll devolve into something less hardwired for survival.

At the end of the day, he's still a Markus. There will be no escaping from that.

Harry stands in the doorway and surveys the bedroom. Cluttered, dusty. He finds her rucksack beneath the edge of the bed. Everything within smells of damp, and rusty water. He searches the side table for anything remotely interesting, but finds only tissues and Lactaid tablets.

He retrieves a small stoppered bottle from his pocket and dribbles a bit of clear fluid onto the pillows. He switches on the ceiling fan for a moment to dissipate the odor.

Then he leaves the room as he left it, and descends the stairs in silence. He picks the bathroom lock, flushes the toilet, and shuts off the roaring ventilation fan in the shower. He retraces his steps back down the hallway. He resumes his position on the futon.

Ted stands at the kitchen sink and stares at him and gnaws his lip.

"Did you wash your hands?" he says.

Bare feet hiss through the grass. Veronica and Creed beat a path around the farmhouse. Whenever they pass through a pane of golden light, Veronica glances indoors to find a new angle of the kitchen or living room view: Ted at the table, Ted at the kitchen counter; Harry Markus reclined on the sofa, reading a magazine of all things.

"Grant knew," Creed whispers, though Veronica is sure even Harry Markus cannot hear them out here; an arid breeze whistles through the yard and there's a choir of insects screaming under cover of darkness.

"Knew what?"

"What Dad was working on. He knew too much. Whatever happened that night in the desert, Dad told him something he shouldn't have, and Grant wasn't the same after it. It wasn't just because Dad was gone that he started acting weird. There was other stuff."

"What kind of stuff?"

Creed crosses her arms. She hangs her head low as she walks, brow furrowed. "My dad was a biotechnologist."

"I know. I read his books."

"What, all of them?"

"My dad has them."

"Of course he does." Creed sighs. "Well, I haven't read them. I never got that stuff, but Grant loved it. He read those books and he reread them and he begged Dad to let him get involved in the lab stuff and Dad loved that Grant loved it."

"He was experimenting with manipulating genetic codes and DNA sequences to force physical mutations," says Veronica. "Anatomical mutations and shit. He had this bit on bioluminescent amphibians—"

"No. Veronica. Listen."

Veronica pauses. She looks at Creed. Her heartbeat is weird. Her pulse is doing strange things. "Do you think he did something to Grant?" The moment she says it, she knows the answer.

Creed looks pale in the moonlight. She shrugs, but her eyes say *I've had years to think about this.* She'd made up her mind about what happened, a long time ago. "What you need to understand," she says, slowly, "is that my dad's research was twofold. At the least. It's what you said. But it's also…other stuff. He investigated isolated anomalies."

"Like hydras and shit."

"No."

"No?"

"No. Not genetic. Anomalies. Random, unexplainable. This stuff wasn't peer-reviewed because no one would take him seriously, no one but Benedict Lewis. I'm not talking about genetic mutations, this is about freakish events worldwide. Kids are born with altered brain function, altered...physicality."

"Like, tails?"

Creed hesitates. "Like...there was a girl who walked through walls."

Veronica stops again. She stares across the yard. "Okay," she says.

"And," says Creed, "a boy who blew up the power lines in his town. Just...snapped his fingers and everything sparked up, the electricity died."

Veronica rubs her temple. "How?"

"I don't know. That's how he found them—it was just weird cases that stood out. He paid attention to freak events and he traced them back to their sources. There's a girl who set her school gym on fire. Just...spontaneously combusted, but didn't burn up. She started the fire without matches or anything, and she was perfectly fine. There are tons of stories like that. He found them all."

Veronica eyes the dated superhero posters. "Like...X-Men and shit."

"No, just kids. More kids than older people. He saw they were becoming more common, more people were being born with these...altered...I don't even know. Just *different*. But they weren't superheroes or anything, they were just people living their lives and pretending like they were normal. Then BEESWAX started picking them off. Grant called them 'the BEESWAX freaks'."

"What does BEESWAX do with them?" Harry Markus knows at least that BEESWAX handles biohazards; how far does his knowledge extend?

"I don't know. I don't think Dad knew either. People started disappearing and no one talked about it, which was when Dad started getting weird visits from weird people, and I remember he started spending more time at the lab. He talked about your dad a lot more. It was *their* lab, of course—they renovated it together, they put an observatory up top for your dad. Grant said Benedict used to spend a lot more time out here before he left NASA." She tilts her head at Veronica. "I don't understand what your dad did."

"He thought there was a rip. In space."

"A what?"

She hears Benedict in her voice—explaining the concept to a younger Veronica, seated together on the floor of his lab in the hills. Stargazing. Pointing out constellations sprinkled across a diagram. *This and this. These go together. But here...there is nothing.* "Like, if reality is a knit of time and space and other threads mixed in— things we don't even understand yet, volatile unknown variables— and gravity is a bend in that fabric...but if it bends too much, the knit weakens and a hole opens."

"In space? Like a black hole?"

"No, not a black hole. That's different. It's just...I don't know how to say it. That's how he explained it to me. It's just a big weakening rip in the fabric, and you can see it in astronomical geography. Orbits, heavenly bodies, everything realigned to accommodate." They pass the kitchen door and fall silent. She can't see Harry Markus from this angle, only Ted's back and the mess of rations on the counter. They move on and Veronica whispers, "He thought it might cause trouble for the knit of reality."

"In what way?"

Veronica glances up at Grant's bedroom window. "Mutations, maybe."

They walk on. "When you think about it," says Creed, "there's so little proof for any of it. We only know this and we only believe it because it's been fed to us."

"I believe it."

"Of course you do. You were raised by Benedict Lewis. And I believe it because both my dad and my brother were crazy nerds."

"They weren't crazy." *I've seen monsters.* But she'd be hard-pressed to testify against her own madness.

"*Folie à deux,*" says Creed.

Benedict Lewis didn't mold his whole life around protecting his daughter and his research just to obsess over a delusion for fifteen-some years. Either he is a genius, or insane. There is no median ground as far as Veronica is concerned.

Veronica stops in front of the old farmhouse. She sits on the porch steps. Creed stands before her, familiar and distant, a foil and a phantom in pink pajamas. A moth flickers through the night.

"I'm not gonna stop," says Veronica. "This is all I have. Nothing much to lose."

"Your life," Creed points out.

"What life?" Veronica spreads her hands. She smiles, but the look is tired and resentful without any of its usual malice. What is life without Ben? What is life as a solo player? Even Grant is not who he once was. Her father is the only real person who's ever tried to love and understand her. He may have been bad at it, but he cared enough to try.

Creed gazes at her for a long moment, drinking in the sight of Benny Lewis' disaster of a daughter. "I hid it for a reason. I thought I might burn it. Maybe I should have."

"No."

"It changed my dad. It changed Grant. It made Benny Lewis drive a truck into a lake. It might turn you into something unnatural."

Unnatural. Rogue. Batshit crazy. Veronica tilts her head. "Might be too late for that."

25

There was a time not long ago when Veronica sat on the floor of her dad's lab in the hills above the East End, wrapped in blankets, reading Verne with a flashlight in hand. Benedict had his eye to a telescope. He preferred working in darkness.

Her eyes peel away from the page and she watches him for a moment, his profile painted in silver moonlight. She gets the feeling that her solar system orbits around this man, and one day she'll be a carbon copy. What a privilege. What a burden. An ache fills her chest and she dog-ears her page. She does not understand love, but she's terribly familiar with adoration.

Ben speaks before she gets the chance. "You dreamt last night."

Veronica sets her book aside. Her fingertips are numb. "Yeah. I did." There's a question there.

"I heard you."

Even if she doesn't tell him, he knows. He knows her that well. "What did I say?"

"Nothing." He is still glued to the telescope. Part of her wishes he'd look at her when he spoke. Sometimes it seems as though it isn't just his mind in the heavenly cosmos, but his whole person.

"You were crying," he says. "You didn't used to do that."

She glances down the trailer's length, where Grant sits against the opposite wall with his knees pulled to his chest, long arms wrapped around his legs. He smiles and gives her a thumbs-up. She doesn't smile back. Maybe she didn't used to cry in her sleep, but she also didn't see the pale boy so frequently, and she didn't always know his name, and he didn't always speak to her. He didn't always wait in her room every night and hold out his hand and lead her down into the labyrinth in her mind, where she nestled in his shoulder beside his sharp chin or in the palm of his hand. It wasn't always like this.

Things are changing. She isn't sure her father knows how rapidly. She isn't sure she wants to tell him. She pulls the blankets tighter around her. "Do you ever talk to yourself?"

"Sure."

"Does your brain ever talk back?"

His lips twist into a smile. "Imaginary conversations? Fake arguments in the shower?"

She smiles. "Sure." This feels like rapport; she could do it forever.

"Sometimes, Veronica. Why?"

She glances at Grant again. He raises his pale eyebrows, and she feels that ache inside—the pulsing empty feeling, the fear that she'll never be able to fully explain what goes on in her head. She's the only one who sees Grant Webber. She's the only one who wanders that same dark maze, because it's in her mind, and only in her mind. And that's the missing piece in her relationship with her dad; he'll never truly know her.

Her smile fades slowly. Grant sways as if to music. "Sometimes I just feel kind of crazy," she says.

"Crazy or different?" says Ben. He finally turns away from the telescope. His eyes are darker than hazel in the moonlight, more like hers. "The world could use more of both."

"I'm not sure they need this kind of crazy. Especially not Dane's Chapel."

"Dane's Chapel isn't the world," he says. "It's just a place. We grow out of places, but we don't grow out of ourselves. It doesn't matter where you go, whether you stay in Dane's Chapel forever or leave, you'll always be you." He squints up at the window, starlight painting silver in his hair. "Concentrate on growing into your skin. Not growing into a place."

Maybe my mind is a place, she thinks. *Maybe I'll never grow into myself because I'm too many layers of a person. Maybe I can't grow into myself because I'm part girl and part canary, and sometimes I cannot tell the difference.*

"Don't grow into a place," says Benedict Lewis. He caresses his fingers over a chart by his knee. He turns once more to his telescope, as if he simply cannot keep away from what he sees there. "Let the world grow into you."

The night is still. The silence is punctuated by crickets and tittering insects, hunting around the scrubby brush and crawling through the dry ivy clinging to the sides of the farmhouse. There is no air conditioning, but drafts creak and warp the floorboards along the staircase, as if a shadowy creature is creeping up the corridor.

Veronica shuts her eyes and feels the world surrounding her, stretched around her shape like she's a black hole in space: dust and wind and whispers of an old house, hushed and waiting. A calm before the inevitable storm.

She is the storm.

She senses Grant in this place. She stands against the door of his old room and she can smell him: sunscreen and sweat, glue from his model rockets, the dry dustiness of the desert clinging to his skin. Sun-baked summer. A living, breathing boy.

What am I? she asked him. *What are you?*

He is gone and she cannot reach him. Will he be back? Does she want him to come back, if he is becoming more real with every passing day? She does. And she doesn't. And her life long ago stopped being about what makes her uncomfortable and what makes her feel stable, it hasn't been about that sort of thing in a long time. Her default is instability. Watch her army-crawl her way across the finishing line to insanity.

"I know you're here," she says to the empty room. "I know you can hear me."

January.

"This isn't about me. This is about you. This is about Dad."

January.

It isn't about her. Yet she feels wrong in her skin as she crosses over to the bed, places her hands palms-down on the thick shipping envelope. *This has nothing to do with me.* Grant said it before: the canary is about anticipation. The canary knows the poisoned fumes as they descend. The canary does not kill the miners.

Yet she feels there's truth to what Creed said. This moment *is* about her. It's about what she does with her dad's work, the choices she makes, the cool paper and the way it feels beneath her palms. It's about how people change when they learn forbidden things. It's about how she's already changed beyond repair and this can only make her worse.

She imagines Benedict wrapping his notebook, sliding it into the envelope. He'd shipped it from outside of town so it couldn't be traced back to Dane's Chapel—no name, no return address. He'd known he would be taken. Peter probably had as well, right before it happened, but Ben knew because of his daughter. He knew because he watched the way the dreams became worse, watched as she became paranoid and the universe contracted around their small world, watched on that January night when everything held its breath and came crashing down. He'd watched, and when Veronica thinks back to that night, she imagines there was fear in his eyes like there was in Harry Markus' when the Mumblers dropped dead in a circle around her.

That was the moment he knew for certain. And he was afraid. He sent his research far away, back to the source, back to the last place anyone would think to look—anyone but her.

He wanted her to be here. He wanted her to find this.

I'm not doing anything wrong.

But as she opens the envelope and unfolds the brown paper wrapping, wrongness wraps tendrils around her chest and squeezes her lungs.

I won't tell. It's a secret.

The notebook comes out stuffed with mismatched papers. The black cover is scratched and scribbled with old pen-marks and dents from being tossed around the trailer. This is the book she remembers Ben putting his most important notes in, the one he kept in the lockbox in his lab. Heavier paper slips out from the front pages: folded charts and sheets of equations, years and years of multicolored ink, increasingly urgent handwriting. Notepaper and sticky notes and random scraps of thought: napkins with formulae and names, a sheet of paper from that notepad Ben keeps on his bedside table.

Veronica flips through the pages, faster, faster. The handwriting changes to a scrawl she doesn't recognize: slanting and spiky, almost indiscernible columns of organic compounds bridging into chemical reactions and a mess of names and article titles and hurried notes wedged into the bottom corners of pages: *check this, double-check that, exponential growth—check with BL.*

BL. Benedict Lewis. She holds the holy grail: Peter and Ben's research, all the answers, all the unfinished puzzles coming together into this one ominous image.

Her hands are numb as she turns the pages. She cuts her fingertips on the paper. Her jaw grows tight and tighter.

It could be for hours that she stands there. It feels like seconds.

There are charts she doesn't understand. There are diagrams she recognizes from the walls of her father's lab. There are mind-maps and printouts of scholarly papers marked with red pen. There are letters from Peter to Ben and Ben to Peter, pages with both their handwriting, as if they collaborated on bits and pieces.

Anomalies, Creed called them.

A tear in the fabric of the universe, said Benedict Lewis.

"What happens, in the end?" Like a child flipping to the end of a storybook, desperate for consolation. She cannot recall if she actually asked her father the question. She only knows that he told her once, and that his answer is lost to the endless knotted maze of her memory. She finds it anyway, within these pages, whether she asked it now or later: past and future are nonlinear; once put to paper, words are circular and infinite.

"There will be signs." She imagines crossed legs, a dusty carpet, eyes always glued to that telescope as if there was nothing more important in this world. Not even his daughter.

She understands more than she realizes. The papers are a blur before her eyes, a fan of turning pages and streams of data, as the room around her is taken by shadow.

"What signs?"

"It's all theoretical."

Her entire life is theoretical. She knows nothing for sure.

"A tear in space. A tear in reality. We'll see things we shouldn't, glimpses into parallel dimensions, and past, and future. A timeline is delicate. I think our perception of what is real, in this time, and isn't—that would be the first to go. Reality quite literally unraveling one thread at a time."

"And then?"

"Physical events. Natural disasters, genetic anomalies, concrete phenomena without readily apparent explanation."

"Can we stop it?"

"We? I certainly cannot. And I don't know."

Darkness creeps from the corners of the bedroom and clings to the walls, spreading to the edges of her vision, until she is just a girl with a canary soul standing in a world of night and the sound of snapping pages, paper scratching paper, the creaking of night along the floorboards of an old house.

"And then...what? Nothing?"

"I don't know about *nothing*. But I think...there would be a spell of silence."

Silence. "Before what?"

Benedict considers. He looks up through the skylight. He's stargazing again. "Before it falls apart."

The darkness is more real than the room. Is she a girl? Or is she a bird? The pages sound like furious wings. Her heart feels like the canary's heart, small and rapid, beating against the delicate bones of her chest.

Above her, a crack breaks through the darkness. She hears it, like thunder. Like a mountain splitting in half. She feels it in her chest.

A seam of white light.

She's a girl kneeling in the bottom of a well. She's beating the ground with her fists and beating canyons into the earth and beating splintering cracks into the porcelain black surrounding her. She's a girl choking on her own tears. She's screaming; her screams sound like mountains splitting. She's screaming. She's a daughter. She wants her father.

A slow splinter. It widens and spreads with spiderweb cracks, and her heart beats louder, and the pages turn faster.

The crack spreads to her skin. A seam of light traces its way up the veins of her forearms, crawls around her shoulders, nestles in the hollow of her throat. She feels every splinter and tremor of the universe.

The light settles behind her eyes. Darkness oozes through her skull.

She's screaming. She's screaming.

The pages stop turning. Her heart stops beating.

The girl—the canary—whatever she is—leans forward and studies the open page. She cannot tell if it is writing or a drawing or something stranger, a combination, something new, pure information. She cannot see. She can only feel. She can only hear feathers and wind.

The final puzzle piece fits into place with a gentle whisper.

Veronica.

There is a rip in the universe, in the shape of a girl. She's screaming.

Veronica.

Reality is splitting, and its strands are strangling around the form of a canary. Its vocal cords are tight. Its song is almost done.

Canary in a coal mine. Harbinger of doomsday.

Benedict was right. There is a rip in the fabric of the universe. Every year it grows, and every year, anomalies are reported throughout the world. Reality is splintering, and it is intrinsically linked to a human form.

It's a secret.

"Veronica."

Cool hands circle her body, ruffling the golden feathers. His touch calms her heartbeat. Sound and sense and thought slip back into place. *Summer and citrus.*

She is alive. The notebook lies still, a crack in the spine, but she cannot look at it anymore.

Grant holds her tight. He backs out of the shadows. He carries her into the labyrinth.

When Veronica opens her eyes, she is crumpled beside the bed.

Loose pages scatter the floor, fluttering in a dying breeze. Outside the open window, wind screams through the night. Inside, the lights flicker and threaten absolute darkness. She's reminded of a night like this one. *January.*

Veronica blinks and straightens. The flickering stops.

"I'm the connection."

Grant sits up in his old bed. Her throat tightens when the light falls on his face; a pale jagged scar runs down from his temple, along his jaw, tapering to a point at his chin. "Time passes," he says, his voice low, almost lyrical, "and you see more. The tear widens. The universe splinters. It's about anticipation, and you see the end coming. You feel it."

The notebook isn't wrong. The scattered pages aren't wrong. *She is wrong.* The room spins. "Why me? I'm...I'm losing it. I can't—" *Can't what?*

"You've never been insane, Veronica. It has always been this."

No. "Tell it to get its weird light out of my veins." She scratches her forearms with ragged fingernails, as if she can tear the splinters of light from her flesh. Her eyes are playing tricks on her—her veins are dark, black in her wrists, gray spiderwebbing up her arms. "Tell it to fuck off." Her breath gets stuck in her throat. She grips her neck.

"You want me to tell the universe to fuck off?"

"Who decided this?"

Grant smiles. She wants to hurt him. "Reality. God. The universe. Or maybe Fates bind the world with golden threads and clacking needles. No one ever asks us to shoulder the weight of our forebears. The choice is in how we choose to carry out these trials."

Veronica is too numb to argue. She cannot breathe. The wind is laughing at her. Everything is hopeless and soulless and inevitable. Her fate was spelled out by birth and carried out by her father. *Unnatural.*

She brushes yellow feathers from her hair. She crawls across the floor and gathers up Ben's notes.

26

Harry Markus sits on the edge of the sofa as the wind shakes the farmhouse and energy hums through the walls. He sits in the dark, hands clasped on his knees. The bulb over the stove flickers, irregular as lightning. This is a warzone of elements, this is a storm in short form.

Harry Markus' eyes pierce through the darkness, pale in the flickering light.

When the wind quiets, his mind fills with noise—mumbles and chattering voices and screams echoing against his skull. A headache pulses at his temple. The stove light is too bright. He bows his head and removes his boots.

One minute passes, then two, then five, and finally he rises and moves to the corridor. He leaves his coat on the futon. He stands at the base of the stairs.

He does not count the minutes. Strangeness stays in the air. He waits for the house to settle itself, waits for sounds of wakeful movement. The pale body of a moth throws itself against the front door. Insects hum in the night.

What are you waiting for? He inhales, forces away echoes of X's voice—*three days, three days*—three days to get Veronica Lewis and her father's research to North Enterprises. Three days to save his brothers. North Enterprises does not make empty threats. *One day more.*

He takes the steps one at a time, leaning into the creaks and groans of the wood, the natural sounds of the house. He stands outside the bedroom.

Three days. What are you so afraid of?

He turns the knob and opens the door a crack. He presses his cheek to the doorframe, peers inside, finds the still figure of Veronica Lewis half-tucked beneath a quilt, a giant white t-shirt swallowing her body. Any scent of chloroform has disappeared, stolen away by the uncanny wind.

Harry steps inside. His eyes adjust to the darkness. There's a thick shipping envelope beside her rucksack.

She seems unconscious enough, but he doesn't trust the chloroform against whatever unnatural current runs beneath her skin. His eyes do not leave her face as he crouches, conscious of every stretch in the fabric of his trousers, the shift of the floorboards beneath him. His fingertips skim the top of the envelope.

Her eyelids twitch.

Harry freezes, inches from her face—her face, hollowed and ghostly pale in the night. Her eyes slide half-open, and they are all black without any white. Her eyebrows pinch in her sleep, but her breaths are even and deep. Harry hovers in his crouch, barely breathing.

He smells smoke. He smells cities burning.

Her eyes drift closed.

Harry takes the envelope and steps back into the hallway.

He flips through the notebook as quickly and quietly as possible. If Veronica's revelation was a storm of knowledge, his is mere flickers of understanding. Science and magic, Peter Webber's DNA charts and chemical equations, lengthy formulae. Meaningless numbers trailing from page to page to page—

—and then a star chart.

Harry pauses. He inspects the lines and constellations with their scribbled names and numbers. He licks his lips, unsure. *What is this?*

A chill creeps up the back of his neck. *This is Benedict Lewis.* This is the NASA scientist whose suicide was faked and whose research will pay for the lives of Howard and Henry.

Harry wasn't lying when he told Veronica Lewis he wanted to keep the research out of North Enterprise's hands. He did, initially. If it is something Cage or the Mumblers want, Harry has an instant distrust and strong urge to destroy that thing, or else use it to his own advantage. He's an asshole like that.

Harry flicks through the pages, anticipation building in his gut, cold fingers trailing up the skin of his back.

Star charts are the least of his worries: here are satellite scans. Here are space-time diagrams.

The notes return to chemistry and convoluted anatomical sketches. Harry slides the scans and space-time data from the notebook, folds the stiff paper between his fingers, and tucks it into the waistband of his trousers.

He feels as if he's moving outside his body: his hands are too big, his pulse is loud in his skull, and the dusty house is confining. Too small, too tight. He wants to be outside, he wants the wind to blow and rip his soul outside of his body, to peel him apart, he is so close to staggering and breaking down. If he indulges in introspection, he is a soldier staggering across the battlefield, moments from collapse.

Howard, he thinks. *Henry. And Howard.* His hands steady. *Three days.*

Back in the bedroom, he stands above Veronica Lewis. He hesitates. Harry does not hesitate often; apprehension is a killing force, much like fear. Yet he pauses here at the crossroads, because he has not made up his mind about Veronica Lewis, whose father hid her from the world, who killed a pack of Mumblers without visibly yielding a weapon, who knows her father's research and consequently knows too much—who he cannot possibly deliver to North Enterprises, because to hand her over is to give them information they can never know. X wants both: the girl and the research. This is handing over *everything.* She's as bad as Benedict Lewis. She's a missing piece in a puzzle he doesn't want X to complete.

He should kill her.

Three days.

I should kill her.

He retrieves his things from downstairs and removes his weapons from the lockbox where the gun-man secured them.

He leaves Veronica Lewis and the green farmhouse behind. He escapes into the night, where the darkness melds into his edges and hides him in its embrace, where something about the smells of the desert and the lingering scent of smoke remind him of a home that no longer belongs to him, and yearning and rage entangle in his chest.

The last trace of an otherworldly wind snaps his coat behind him. He is gone.

In years gone by, there was another night when Harry turned his back and left everything behind. His motive was the same then as it is now: his brothers; his blood. Perhaps it is something like pride that fuels him, as if they are extensions of himself. Or perhaps they are really so strong a brethren. Even Harry is not sure. He becomes less sure with every passing year.

There was a time when a city fell in stone and screams around the three of them, and they had a choice to make. They offered this choice to their eldest brother, who did his best. They poured their lives into his hands, and Harry is locked in an eternal juggling act, striving to keep them whole and unbroken. There is sand running between his gapping fingers.

There was a time when a city fell in stone and screams and the Myrmen peeled away from the shadows to descend upon everything Harry ever loved: a city where the wind ruled the night and day, a brutal wind, a wind he loved and hated as he does nothing else; a city that slept in the day and came alive at night—*at night*—at night when the Myrmen opened their eyes and crawled from their crevices; a man with dark eyes and a voice like mountains, soothing Harry's rage, staunching his blood, until his skull was crushed by the bloody Mumblers and his brains rested on his shoulders in gentle tendrils and his voice was quiet forevermore. A night when Harry Markus stood on a cliffside and made a choice he will never be able to take back, a choice that will haunt him forever:

Stay or leave?

It was his brothers who provided the answer to their own question: Henry, with his face covered in blood, his life leaking out through his ears; Howard, his eyes glassy with pain and grief.

Harry Markus made a choice. He has hated himself ever since.

27

"He took the car."

Veronica kicks the fence. She kicks the gate. She stomps up and down the car tracks carved into Sunshine Boulevard, drags her heels in the dust. The notebook is gone, the car is gone, Harry Markus and his stupid trench coat have flown the coop and he isn't coming back. He isn't. He's far away and he took the only hope she had.

I should have killed him, she realizes. She could have, probably. Maybe not on purpose, but perhaps on accident. Collateral damage.

He's taken it, the bright neon sign saying *Veronica Lewis is the answer to all your questions*. He's taken the only leverage she had.

She tilts back her face to the sky, exposing her pale throat to the sun, squeezes her eyes shut and bares her teeth. She inhales through the pain in her chest. Then she bows her head and she spits in the dust. "Fuck."

Creed is waiting on the porch. Her feet are bare and she has a bathrobe pulled tight around her waist. Her eyes are glazed as she watches Veronica mount the creaking paint-peeled steps. "I shouldn't have shown you."

"I came all this way to see it," Veronica says. "To get it. I wasn't going to leave without it. You had to show me. I would have found it either way." She sits on the top step, plants her elbows on her knees, but almost immediately stands again. She can't stay still. "What now?"

She looks around, almost expecting to find Grant leaning against the railing nearby, a cryptic suggestion on his wry lips, disappointment in his stormy gray eyes. But it's only his sister on the porch, watching her with those same eyes, something lost and confused flickering across her face.

"What do you think he'll do with it?" Creed's voice is dull.

"Oh, some bullshit about trading it for his brothers. Because someone's kidnapped them and he needs them back. But that was probably a lie. He just lies. Mother*fucker*."

Creed's eyes clear. "What were *you* going to do with it?"

Veronica looks at her.

"You were going to bargain it away, weren't you? You weren't going to destroy it."

"I don't know." After last night, after realizing her entire existence is written into this nightmare of a group project, she very much wants to burn the whole notebook and scatter the ashes on the wind. But the notebook isn't here, is it? And destroying it won't help Benedict anyway. "I just want him back." Veronica kicks at the railing. "I hardly give a shit at this point, what I do to make it happen. I want my dad back and they want the goddamn notebook. What difference does it make? We're all fucked either way, we were fucked from the start. He made sure of that. Now it's just…now I just want him back. If they're going to fuck everything, I just want my dad back." Veronica looks at Creed out of the corner of her eye. "You wouldn't do the same?"

"No," says Creed. "But you sound like Grant did when he came back from the lab with stitches in his face. That's something he would have said."

"You don't have to say it." Veronica kicks the railing again. She can't stop kicking things—she wants to break something, she wants to scream. "You don't have to say 'and look where he is now'."

The breeze carries with it the distant clattering of leaves. Neither of them has anything left to say. Creed goes back into the house. Veronica stands on the porch and glares down the gravel drive, feet cold, temple pounding. She wills the world to crumble around her. She wills Harry Markus to go to hell.

She is still standing there when helicopter blades cut through the silence.

Ted is already on the roof with a bazooka.

Veronica doesn't bother asking where he got it or what he thinks he's doing. She rifles around in the foyer lockbox, already wide open thanks to a helpful Harry Markus. She finds her handgun to stick in her pocket, then remembers she doesn't have pockets—she's wearing yoga pants—so she sticks it in her waistband instead and digs around a bit more till she finds Ted's rifle. She shuffles through the cardboard boxes of ammo and loads it as the helicopter grows louder and the farmhouse starts to tremble beneath her feet.

Creed is in the kitchen, mouth agape, watching dust cyclone in the backyard through the screen door.

Veronica doesn't look at Creed as she brushes past and kicks open the screen. She steps onto the back porch and lets the door clatter behind her. Through the glare of morning light, she watches the helicopter descend.

It's smaller than she initially thought, and it isn't visibly armed. There can't be too many people aboard. Between Ted's bazooka and the rifle, they should be able to take care of this.

The thought is startling. *Okay, you heartless fuck.*

She shields her eyes from the tornado of dry earth, holds her breath, one-handedly slings the rifle off her back and braces herself for the first figure to appear. *Like a Western,* she thinks, and imagines a glass bottle shattering into a million pieces on a rotting fencepost. *Yeehaw.*

But the doors don't fly open, and no one opens fire upon the house. The helicopter touches down between the porch and garden shed, and the blades slow, and through the thunder of slowly-dying thwapping, one door cracks open and a voice roars through the yard: "If that man on the roof blows up my chopper, I will be very upset!"

Despite herself, Veronica lowers the rifle. The door opens the rest of the way. And Harry Markus steps out.

No. The world flips around and reorganizes itself.

It's Harry fucking Markus in a blue flight suit, his black hair buzzed into a military crewcut, a very un-Harry expression on his face: bemusement, worry, something without its usual edge of stone-cold sociopathic intensity. Veronica can only stare as he places his hands behind his head and slowly moves out of the chopper's vicinity, as he approaches with a gait somewhat like Harry's yet with less of a stomp and more of an unconscious swagger.

She is stupid with shock.

He scratches his neck and quickly returns his hands to their position over his head. "Tell him not to blow up the chopper, please." Same accent, different voice, coming out of Harry Markus' mouth.

"I...Creed!" Veronica shouts without turning. She subtly shifts the rifle against her hip; she aims at the man's legs from her spot on the porch. "Ask your uncle to wait."

A pause. Then footsteps creak through the house as Creed leaves the kitchen and heads for the stairs.

The man exhales. He opens his mouth to speak, but Veronica beats him to it. "You're Harry's brother."

Genuine fear flashes across his face. "Uh. Yes. Howard. Yes, but —" He offers a tight-lipped smile. "I really don't any trouble. Of course you know Harry, that would explain why you kind of look like you're debating killing me. The charming personality didn't quite settle right in my eldest brother. Sorry." "

Veronica's jaw clenches. "He said his brothers got kidnapped."

"Well." Howard's brow furrows. "One of them. Sort of. More like *locked down*, but definitely being held against his will, sure. How does he know that? Could I speak to Harry? I'd sort of like to hurt him."

Veronica slowly raises the rifle a bit higher.

Howard's eyes follow the barrel. His lips twitch. "Are you trying to intimidate me?"

"I want to see you flinch," she says.

"Okay, I get it, really—we look a lot alike, but Harry's an arse and I really try to not be one. I'm not trying to trick you, I really don't want anything to do with you, I just need to see my brother. It's urgent. Henry's in trouble."

Veronica watches over his shoulder as the helicopter blades spin to a slow stop. "Harry isn't here."

"What?"

"How did you know we were here? Did he tell you? You were the one paging him, weren't you?"

"No, he—I mean, yes, but—" Howard knits his fingers together on the crown of his head and turns in a full circle, surveying the yard for any sign of his brother. As if Harry might miraculously appear and save the day. When he faces her again, there's a deep line between his brows. "He *was* here, right? Where is he now? Where did he go?"

She speaks through her teeth. "How did you find us?"

Howard swallows. "I—I tapped into the North Enterprises radios. Not really tapped, I guess. I mean, I'm still on the channel. I reckon I'm just ahead of them. They've been following the Mumblers and I suppose they deduced where you were heading."

Veronica's mouth is suddenly quite dry. She runs her tongue along her gums. She gnaws the inside of her cheek. "So…."

Howard shifts on his feet. He splays his fingers like *what can you do?* "Harry shouldn't have left such an identifiable trail. Honestly. The pile of Mumblers in Tulsa? Messy."

"That was me," says Veronica, "and it wasn't *that* messy."

He looks at her, politely curious; it is astonishing to see the expression on Harry Markus' face. "You're Veronica Lewis."

"So I've been told."

"Oh. I suppose I thought you'd be a bit…bigger. Or scarier. Or something." She huffs and hefts the gun. Howard shrugs an apology. "Look, under any other circumstances I'd be more inclined to keep up the banter, but really, I need to find Harry. It's an emergency. It really is."

"Well, he's not here. He robbed me blind and took off in the night."

The screen door creaks behind Veronica; Creed slips onto the porch.

"Ted wants to know if he's with the IRS."

Veronica shakes her head.

Creed gazes down at Howard. "He also wants to know if he's an alien, and if so, has he ever frequented a certain trailer park in Arizona?"

"That's very specific." Howard squints against the morning light. "No. You wouldn't know where he's gone, would you? Harry?"

Veronica feels a door of opportunity open—she gives it a nudge. "You'll follow him?"

"If I can."

She tilts her head. "He said North Enterprises was holding his brothers hostage. He said he needed to get them my dad's research before they killed you. So my guess is, he's booking it to North Enterprises, wherever that is."

The canyon between his eyebrows deepens. "Where'd he hear *that*? I'm not—that's not how it happened. Look, the Mumblers took the compound. They locked it down, Henry got trapped inside, I made it out. I've been trying to find Harry since. But North Enterprises is scattered, there's no one there." Howard squats in the dust, deep in thought. He rocks back on his heels. "I think...this is bad. Bad. He doesn't know about the Mumblers? At the compound?"

"Not that I'm aware."

"Well, damn." Howard rises to his feet. Veronica raises the gun, and he holds out his palms. "Don't, don't. Just..." Howard rubs the heel of his hand into his temple. "If you're right, he thinks he's heading to North Enterprises to strike a deal with Lawrence Cage. But he's not. He's running into a den of Mumblers. Cage isn't even *there* anymore. The Mumblers might not even know who Henry is, not at this point, not until Harry shows up to save the day." He is distinctly blanched by now.

Who is Henry to them? Who are any of these men, to the Mumblers? "Sounds like you need to stop him."

"I might be too late. Is he flying?"

"Like Superman?" Veronica finally lowers the rifle and leans it against the porch railing. "He stole the car."

Howard exhales. "I can catch him."

"Okay," says Veronica. "I'll come with you."

"Uh—"

"I can give you three reasons why, just off the tip-top of my head." She reaches under her billowing shirt and draws the handgun from her waistband. "That's one. Two, I can fight the Mumblers if it comes to that." Although the tunnels in St. Louis prove that she isn't as adept at killing the bug-men as she'd like. "And three, your brother is a fucking idiot and he doesn't know what he's doing."

"Harry usually knows what he's doing," says Howard.

"I assure you, this one time, he certainly does not. The research he stole is dangerous." *To me.* Bile churns in her throat. "If he loses the notebook, if the Mumblers take it"—*I won't be able to get my dad back*—"they could do some really fucked-up shit with that information."

Howard's pale eyes flick from Veronica to Creed and then back again. He gazes at the handgun dangling at Veronica's side. "What sort of information?"

Veronica glances at Creed, whose face is neutral. She can imagine Grant standing at her other shoulder, staring her down reproachfully, but she hasn't seen him since last night, since the wind and the girl-shaped hole in the universe and the light tracing its way through her veins.

She grimaces. She looks back at Howard Markus. "There's a huge rip in the universe. There are mutant crazies running around lighting stuff on fire with their bare hands and walking through walls. It's all linked together and highly sensitive, and if someone tried tampering with it..." How would it be tampered with? She feels like she's constantly tampering. And then what? *It falls apart.* And she'll see all of it, every step of the way, and her brain will melt. "Shit goes down," she concludes. "So no one can know. Not North Enterprises or BEESWAX or the Mumblers."

Howard fishes for words. "Rip...in the universe, you say? Does Harry know?"

"No. Unless he's a lot more literate than he looks, and he read an entire notebook full of complicated research before hopping in the car. Then no."

"Alright." He nods slowly. "If you're right...that's quite bad."

"Quite," says Veronica.

"You...you can come with me, and we'll find Harry, and you

need to tell him that—all of it, the rip and the link thing, okay?"

It's an odd request, but Howard's more pleasant than his brother, and much easier to manipulate. Veronica loves easily-manipulated people; it makes her life a lot simpler.

This isn't over. She can catch up to Harry Markus, she can stop him, she can take the research and remove the really important parts and use it to barter for Benedict Lewis. She can kick in Harry's head. *This isn't over.*

The hoodie she digs out of the back of Grant's dusty closet has a Batman symbol on the front. *Always be yourself,* reads the back, *unless you can be Batman! Then be Batman.*

She yanks on her hiking boots and shoves everything else into her backpack before stomping downstairs. Ted is nowhere in sight, but she hears rummaging and muttered curses from down the corridor.

Creed waits inside the back door. Her arms are crossed. "They're coming, aren't they?"

Veronica glances out at Howard, waiting beside the helicopter. She looks back at Creed, who seems both terribly young and desperately old for her age. "Yeah, they are."

Creed stares out the screen door at the chopper. "I think Ted's secretly pleased," she says joylessly. "He's been training for this for years. His friends have a camp in the mountains. Weird prepper guys with a doomsday bunker. He'll have the van packed and we'll be gone in an hour." She faces Veronica. "I have a job. I'm supposed to graduate early. I got into a college writing program. I thought, I might even move away. From the desert. Maybe."

Everything inside Veronica revolts; she isn't chemically designed for guilt and shame. She thinks: *I've never gotten close enough to another person to ruin their life.* "I think," she says, in a small voice that does not sound like her own, "I've ruined your life."

Creed blinks. "I think you probably have. But so did my dad. And Grant. And your dad. And it doesn't really surprise me anymore. I think I always knew this was coming."

"I'm sorry." It sounds hollow.

Creed shrugs. "Whatever comes of this, I hope it was worth it, Veronica."

She brushes past. Veronica stands still, staring at the spot where she'd stood, seeing only Howard pacing before his helicopter. *Oh, if only Ben could see you now.*

Creed's footsteps are soft across the living room, hesitant, as if she can hold on to this moment and this place and never have to flee from Harley. Her childhood home, where she lost both her father and her brother, where their ghosts cling so tightly to every bedroom and small reminders lurk in the shadows.

"Creed." The blonde girl looks back at her. "I'm gonna get my dad. And your dad. I'll find them both. I'll bring them home, I swear."

A draft slips through the room. The walls groan. Veronica's pulse hammers in her skull.

After a beat, Creed turns away and continues into the corridor. "You know," she says from the staircase, "you sound exactly like Grant."

Outside, Ted has disappeared from his rooftop perch. He's taken the bazooka with him. Veronica scans the farmhouse windows as she swings her backpack into the helicopter, but neither Creed nor Ted watches her leave. In fact, the place already seems deserted. A haunted house on the edge of a desert waste.

The helicopter roars to life, and Howard hands her hearing protection. She slams the door and puts it on.

"I'm going to follow along the route to the compound," he says through the speaker. "There's only one road he could take. When we get closer I'll fly low and we'll scan for the car."

Veronica watches the blades pick up speed until they disappear into a gray blur. She anticipates the sudden drop, the feeling of weightlessness as they take to the air in the little spinning death contraption. She's never flown before. She doesn't think she'll like it very much. "How did you get this, anyway? The helicopter."

"I took it from the hangar on my way out of the compound. They seized my access card a while back because...well, they're stupid, and they didn't like how I was flying. I'm a very good pilot," he reassures her. "The best. But I had to hunt down a fellow to get the card back, and then I ran to the hangar. Barely got out in time." His face is grave, as if reliving the scene: leaving his brother behind, running for his life. Then he breaks out into an uneasy smile and slaps the console. "The *Medusa* and I have been through a lot together."

"So you're a pilot," Veronica says. "Does Harry fly for North Enterprises too?"

"Oh, no. He's good, but he's much better at the whole hands-on espionage and strategy bit. He's an agent. Gets the flashy jobs. But doesn't get a chopper."

"Right." Veronica sits back as the helicopter lifts off. She focuses her gaze on the sky above, not the ground dropping away, not her impending doom. "That's funny," she says through her teeth, "because he told me he didn't work for North Enterprises."

Howard is silent for a long moment. Static pops in Veronica's ears, and something like sinister satisfaction twitches at her lips. Then a nervous laugh breaks through the speakers.

"You know Harry," says Howard. "He'll say whatever he needs, to get what he wants."

28

X takes a stuttering breath. He wills his pulse to quiet. He wills his hand on the styrofoam cup to still and sturdy itself. Halleck, who does not drink coffee but has fully emptied two cartons of chocolate milk in quick succession, works a stress ball in one hand and makes a full-time job of averting his gaze from the old man. His lip visibly quivers. He periodically kneads the bridge of his nose between thumb and forefinger, sniffs, and glances around the break room as if it might have changed. But no one else enters into the bare-bones officers' lounge. The coffee machine switched off an hour ago and the room has been silent ever since. Outside, around and above and below in the dreadful honeycomb of ARC's many-layered corridors, the hive hums and screeches and bleeps.

Incoming refugees from North Enterprises are packed into rooms where they will be held and halfheartedly questioned. Prisoners are pushed lower and lower into the compound's recesses, packed into close-walled cells and packed away into cryochambers to make room for the newcomers. Cage's dispatched squads will be redirected to return to ARC instead of the North Enterprises compound in Wyoming. And once numbers are accounted for and Westmore signs off, X reckons it's a matter of hours before North Enterprises is, for lack of a better word, fumigated.

"Cage's records are so out of date," says Halleck. He taps the stress ball on the tabletop, still looking anywhere but to X. "No accountability. No way to account for everyone. North Enterprises staff will be lost out there and we won't even know their names." He shakes his head. "Their families."

Oh, he's young. If he hasn't already figured out that having a family in this line of work is a tragic liability, this might be the moment he rethinks his future.

X raises the cup to his lips. It smells like melting plastic. He takes a sip.

Harry Markus.

He inhales and chokes.

"Alright?" says Halleck.

X sets his cup on the table; coffee sloshed over the side. He pounds his chest and coughs it out and feels like he might have a small heart attack as his mind races and the awful truth catches up to him: he's sent Harry Markus straight into the Myrmen's waiting arms. How can the young agent know the Myrmen are at the compound? He thinks his brothers are held captive there; X told him as much. Even if Howard and Henry managed to escape before the attack, how will they find their brother in time to stop him from returning to North Enterprises? And if Harry Markus finds himself in the compound with Benedict Lewis' daughter and his research, X might very well lose all three at once: Markus, Veronica, and the key to everything. *Everything. In the hands of the Myrmen.*

"I think I have to leave," X manages, with coffee in his sinuses.

Halleck frowns. He sets down the stress ball. "You can't leave. We're locking the place down."

"People are arriving," says X. "Therefore, I can leave."

"No," says Halleck. "No, I can't—we're not allowed to let anyone out."

"Well, at the risk of sounding insurrectionary..." X rises to his feet. "I think I'm above that particular rule. This is a matter of security." *World security*, he thinks.

Halleck stands slowly, hands out, as if the old man might make a run for it. "You'll...have to speak with Westmore. Westmore gave the order. I can't go against that."

"I don't have time to battle with the bureaucracy, Anthony."

"You're not going back out there, are you?" Halleck reads it on his face, which is surely pallid. "You can't. That's suicide. You can't stop them, the place is swarming. Westmore is assembling a BEESWAX force to go in, but that's Billings' territory. You could be stepping into a minefield. You can't leave."

"Well," says X, "at the risk of sounding suicidal, that is exactly what I intend to do."

He's likely the only person in the world with even a bit of leverage with the Myrmen; there's a chance something remains in their expansive hive mind of the deal they made with X and what he's promised in return: vengeance. *Oh, Xander. What a dangerous game you play.*

He drops his cup in the bin and steps into the corridor. "I'll need a pilot."

Halleck follows. "I can't do this. I can't allow you to leave. And I certainly can't assign you a pilot."

He trails a few steps behind X down the winding hallways, past break rooms and sealed steel doors and infirmaries crowded with Cage's refugees and armed ARC personnel tasked with quelling inevitable disturbances amongst the disturbed. The place has, in a matter of days, turned from a state-of-the-art containment facility to a clumsy refugee camp.

"What's the threat?" says Halleck. "What could possibly be so important? How serious is this?"

X considers. "Catastrophic. I sent a man on an undercover mission and he doesn't know what he's returning to. He's off the radar. Couldn't know what's happened."

"Send someone else," says Halleck. "Look—slow down—listen. We'll try to get word to him, or I'm sure he'll figure it out. But we can't send *you*."

"Why not? Because I'm old?"

"Because you're too *important*. If we're going to send someone to rendezvous—and we can talk about it, certainly, but I'm making no promises—it really can't be you. Cage needs you here."

Cage! What a laugh. X turns to the young man and heaves a theatrical sigh. "Anthony, I don't know how else to explain this. This isn't Cage's mission. He doesn't know about this. This isn't North Enterprises at all. This is directly from the top, and I am personally responsible."

"From the top?"

"The top."

"From Westmore?"

He inflates a bit. "Indeed."

"But—"

"I'll need a pilot."

They continue through the compound. Halleck doesn't argue, but ducks into the next break room, packed full of ARC and North Enterprises pilots. He pauses in the doorway; he raps his knuckles on the jamb. The room falls silent.

"I need a volunteer pilot," he says "Someone to go back in."

"Ask for the Raccoon," someone says from the back of the room. "Two doors down."

Two doors down there's a card game going on in the center of the break room. A crowd of pilots and spec ops gather 'round the players.

"Where's the Raccoon?" says Halleck.

The cards slow. A dark-haired man seated at the table raises his head and then raises his coffee cup in acknowledgement. He wears the solid gray flight suit of an ARC pilot.

"We need a volunteer."

"Is it dangerous?" His tone says he hopes it is.

"Most definitely," says X.

Halleck steps to one side. "Agent X from North Enterprises. He needs to go back in. I need someone to fly him and then get him out again in one piece."

The Raccoon lobs his styrofoam cup across the room; it lands with a *snick* in the bin. He stands and pulls his flight suit up over his shoulders. He zips it to his chin. "Overtime?"

X is sure he's joking, but Halleck shrugs. "If you get him back alive, this could mean a hefty bonus."

Get him back alive stirs the room, but the Raccoon only smiles, and X wonders about the man's psych eval.

"Merry Christmas," says the Raccoon. "You've got a pilot."

29

Benedict Lewis's notebook sits on the passenger's seat. The loose pages twitch in the air con. The black leather cover reflects sunlight into Harry's eyes as he barrels down open desert roads at a breakneck speed.

And then there's the silence. The silence forces him to think, and he falls back into his old thoughts, and they are dark. He never thought he'd miss having Veronica Lewis in the other seat, but her disturbing conversation was noise at least.

He switches on the radio after an hour. The skater boy song shrieks through the car. He quickly turns it off again and rolls down the windows; the roaring wind fills his eardrums.

His knuckles are white on the wheel.

X can't afford to kill his brothers, not with Harry on the loose. *Oh, but he can hurt them.*

The thought dredges up images. The images distract him from maintaining his speed, getting out from behind vehicles driving at the legal limit, keeping an eye out for highway patrol. He exhales and his foot lowers on the gas pedal. He inhales and holds the breath for as long as he can stand, until his head swims and his chest burns. When he breathes again he relaxes his whole body—he unclenches his jaw and lowers his shoulders—he settles into the cold, languid undercurrent that cuts through his ever-present clouds of fury. The storms quiet to a dull roar.

So what if he doesn't have Veronica Lewis? X will have to be satisfied with the notebook. He'll tell the old man Benedict Lewis' daughter is dead, then he'll go back and kill her. She knows too much. He should have killed her before. Why hadn't he? She'd have done the same to him, he's sure.

Could you kill her if you tried? A cold hand grips his heart as he recalls the night at the bus station, the chill metal of the bus pressing into his chest as he prepared to kill the Mumblers, and the flash of light, her strange unconscious form, the creatures in their broken bodies. She's too dangerous to live, definitely too dangerous to hand over to X. She'll have to go.

He glances at the notebook, the flickering pages. He'll hand North Enterprises the world for his brothers—he doesn't care for the world much—but there are particular slivers of information he'll die before relinquishing. Pages he hand-picked like flower. This morning feels like a nightmare: the hush of the corridor, the scent of smoke, the black of her eyes. Unnatural and unholy. The darkness of a night bracing for dawn. The scuff of his boots on gravel. He can still smell the house on himself, all dust and desert and citrus.

He puts a hand to his waistband, where the stolen pages rest against his abdomen.

They are not there.

He nearly slams on the brakes, but he's going too fast for that. His breath hitches in his throat. He continues speeding down the highway as he feels frantically along his trousers and trench coat pockets.

He might have absentmindedly moved the pages. He might have put them in his rucksack.

He checks the floorboard, the back seat, almost going off the road in the process. A car blares its horn behind him. He stomps on the gas and faces front again, he swerves around slower traffic, he puts miles between himself and Harley and Veronica Lewis, and his fate feels held by trembling fingers.

His eyes burn. He inhales and coughs on clouds on dust. He rolls up the windows and his ears pop. He stews in the silence.

He hopes they've been snatched by the wind, hopes they find a place scattered throughout the desert. He sends up a desperate prayer to some distant strange deity who has, to date, taken no notice of Harry Markus' life or misfortunes—hopes and prays that those pages do not fall into the wrong hands.

Ironically, these all-important pages are in the hands of Veronica Lewis. More accurately, they're buried within the grubby confines of her backpack. She found them at the end of the driveway this morning, while inspecting the tire tracks Harry left when he stole the car and disappeared into the pre-morning stillness of New Mexico desert.

Harry Markus is correct: she knows too much. But she always has.

"I've got a question," she says, adjusting the mic on her headset. "How old are you?"

"Oh." The question catches him by surprise—it's such a small thing, age. Unimportant, really. "Twenty-something, I think. Maybe twenty."

"You don't know?"

He laughs, but it's an uncomfortable sound. "I've lost track of the years, I suppose. Henry, he might know. Harry and I...live too fast, I guess. Lose track of things."

"What year were you born?"

Howard doesn't respond.

"I don't think you're from Russia. Or the UK."

"Well...we're not," says Howard. He clears his throat. "We, uh...I do speak Russian, and a few Slavic dialects, but—"

"So where are you from?"

There's a long pause. Howard licks his lips, frowns, and finally says, "I'm not going to answer that. Sorry."

Delicious. She basks in his discomfort. She digs in her claws and drags the truth closer. "Why is it so important?"

He flushes. "You should stop asking. It's better if we don't discuss this. It's better if you don't know. Sometimes people acquire too much information and things happen to them."

"Is that a threat?"

"No, it's a fact. It's just how things are. I'm not going to get rid of you, but I can't make promises for Harry. He'll do what he thinks is right, with the force he considers to be reasonable, and sometimes people get hurt."

Veronica thinks about those pages again, the delicate figures worked out in her father's deliberate scrawl. And she thinks of the Mumblers, the way they don't seem too interested in her, but rather in her connection to Harry Markus. "Do you want to hear my theory?"

Howard's mouth is a hard line. His free hand drums out a nervous beat on his leg. "I'd rather not," he says.

In the heart of the western Wyoming mountains, in the bowels of the North Enterprises compound, buried beneath levels of concrete and basement, Henry Markus is cold.

He is not used to being so cold. Or rather, he is usually unaffected by it. He remembers a home left behind, which was much colder than this, if only superficially. This is a chill he cannot shake, and he is not sure how much of it is mental and how much has really settled into his bones.

He found some old rations in the back of a cabinet, a few days ago. Those are gone now. His water bottle is empty. The barricaded room smells of piss and fear, and something else, something distinctive to the Mumblers' presence: a scent like bloody soil, metallic and unholy.

Henry breathes evenly. When he is very quiet—when he holds his breath and concentrates on the world around him—he can hear them. He hears their skittering footsteps on the levels above, the occasional slamming of doors and, once, the horrible rise and fall of their droning voices: *in the dirt we mumble.*

And he thinks, unbidden, that Harry wouldn't let him die like this, Harry hadn't let him die before. Harry and Howard had carried him out of that burning blood-soaked city stinking of the Myrmen, and Harry had tried to put him back together, and Harry hadn't done well enough, and Henry will always be broken because of it.

Harry is a fool. But there is some relief in knowing that this particular fool stands shoulder-to-shoulder with him, an extra layer of strength and protection. There has always been comfort in knowing Harry will come running to save him.

Henry isn't so sure anymore. If Harry was going to save him, surely he would have done so by now. Perhaps he simply will not come. Perhaps Henry will die like this, locked up in a basement chamber, frozen and starved.

The thought propels him to his unsteady feet. He finds his way to the desk. He switches on the radio.

Faint strains of classical music drift from the speakers, filling the room with their soothing hum. Henry takes a deep breath and hunts around the drawers for the things he found yesterday: a bit of rusty pipe, about the length of his forearm, scavenged from behind a filing cabinet; a bolt on which he'd almost impaled his foot; the handle from a cabinet with the screws still attached, sharp enough to skin his knuckles when he'd discovered it.

He puts these things in his pockets. He rests the pipe on his shoulder and moves toward the door.

He can't die like this. And he can't wait for his brothers any longer.

30

Andre Billings is unhappy.

Outwardly, he is just as stoic as usual—always the professional, an emotionless lump of human flesh and muscle with merciless protocol chiseled into his brain. The only telling signs of his simmering rage are a jaw slightly more clenched than usual, the heavy footsteps verging on *stomp* territory, and flames smoldering in his eye sockets.

Andre marches out of his makeshift office at ARC and walks right into Halleck. "Did X leave?"

Halleck's eyes widen. He steps back and takes a moment to process the question. "He...he did." He composes himself, clasps his hands behind his back, tucks his chin. "He did."

"No one is supposed to leave." Billings' voice is calm.

"His mission was sanctioned by Westmore, sir. We had a volunteer pilot take him, and he should return within the day. Good pilot."

"I am not concerned about the pilot." He is more worried about X meddling where he shouldn't. Truth be told—and he would never admit this—the fact that X might never come back doesn't bother him too much. The old man is a nuisance. But people going over his head, especially during this cataclysmic stage of events, infuriates him. "He shouldn't be in there."

Halleck's throat bobs. "But. Orders from Westmore...."

"Did he have orders? Did he show you?"

"He said he had them."

"But you didn't see them."

"He is senior—"

"He is *old*. The older you get in this organization, the more risks you take. Watch: senior officers go on suicide missions, they take more risks with their own lives. X is old and he knows his chances." Billings nods. "He likely won't come back. Hawk is sending the force in now, and we can't guarantee that anyone will come out alive. You might have signed that man's death warrant."

Halleck's lips are pale. They struggle to form the next few words. "This is…a BEESWAX team?"

The first. But Halleck doesn't need to know that. Neither does Cage, though X is about to find out. Billings was always the kid in school who found group projects endlessly frustrating, and here he is managing a top-secret organization with a crew of inept overgrown toddlers. He wants them removed, every last one. Disappointment is exhausting.

He turns away from Halleck and steps back into his office, where the radio set on the table chirps and buzzes, and the last two meals brought to him remain uneaten. He pinches the bridge of his nose between thumb and forefinger. He shuts his eyes briefly. Then he drops his hand to his side and glances over his shoulder at Halleck. "Your people need to clear out more space for refugees and prisoners. They'll bring the surviving creatures here."

"We're trying to consolidate cells—"

"Do it faster."

He slams the door. He waits for Halleck's footsteps to fade away before he returns to the table and lowers himself into the chair and sits facing the radio and its blinking channels and the many voices awaiting his direction.

He prays BEESWAX works quickly. He prays X does not meddle.

"Are you sure you don't want to hear my theories?" Veronica

glances back in the helicopter, almost expects Grant in the empty space behind the seats: the pale boy waiting for her to turn, waiting for a brief moment of eye contact. And then he'd smile, a light in his gray eyes. He'd smile like it's their secret, and maybe he'd hold out his hand.

"I really don't," says Howard, "and as I said, I think you should stop talking about it."

"Maybe I'll tell you anyway." She turns in her seat to look at him, this second Markus brother, so similar to the first and yet so different in his manner. "You do look a little Russian, if we're going by stereotypes. You've got that Eastern European look. Kind of washed-out and cold. Your eyes look like ice."

Those eyes flick to her. A muscle spasms in his cheek. "Poetic."

"Thanks. But you don't sound Russian," she says. "No accent. Your brother said you learned English in Britain."

His eyebrow twitches.

"Which is obviously a lie. Not a good one, and definitely not the biggest. Liars can always spot other liars, you know." A deep sense of calm settles over her, with the sunlight streaming in the windows, and the hum in the headset; she settles back against the seat. She's about to drop into a den of Mumblers and her killer lightning is unreliable. She's going to get Ben's research back and she'll remove the bits that have anything to do with her—just like Harry Markus did, so obvious and crude, incriminating in his selection of pages to tear from the notebook—and she'll trade the rest for Benedict Lewis and then they'll disappear into the desert together. Hide in the hills. Find their way back to someplace green and piney. They'll forget and forgive and her forewarnings will keep coming like a rising tide until her chest splits open and her ears bleeds and her eyes see nothing but the endless twisting walls of her labyrinth—

She blinks. She's forgotten to breathe.

No, it won't end.

It won't end when she gets Ben back.

"Does anyone else know?" she murmurs, and Howard flinches. She smiles. She knows it's uncanny; her smile is too wide, her lips too narrow, she shows too many teeth and they are shaped sharply. She knows she has a smile like a wolf. "Has anyone told you that

I'm crazy?"

"Are you trying to upset me?" Howard looks ready to pop from the nerves. A vein pulses in his temple. His eyes scan the windscreen, careful not to stray towards her. "To be honest," he says, "I know very little about you or your father. Let's just...concentrate on finding Harry. Look, keep an eye out down there. What does the car look like?"

Veronica forms her hand into an O. She peers through it at Howard's profile. "Do you think he actually knew what it meant, that hole in the universe, the way it's widening?"

He opens his mouth to speak. She beats him to it.

"The weird blips on satellites, from five years ago." She tilts her head, gazes out the windscreen through her telescoped hand. She stares at the sky, the piercing blue without a cloud in sight. The staggering void beyond. "Maybe he just saw the stage set for it. Maybe I'm the first to actually put it into words. You know?"

She lolls her head at Howard and inspects his angular profile, the lines of his nose and the frosty sea-glass green of his eyes. She raises the telescope again.

"You certainly look human," she says.

Nightfall is the best time for espionage.

When Harry Markus used to love the dark, he did his best work by moonlight—in and out, merely a shadow in the periphery of a guard's vision, gone just as quickly and quietly as he'd arrived. He still works by night, but it carries an uncanny stillness with it. Something that was once comforting is now foreboding.

Crouching in a bank of trees above the North Enterprises complex, staring down into that innocent valley with its hulking concrete blight, Harry wishes it were dark. It is only afternoon, and sunset is still hours away, but he is reminded of a day that was quiet like this one. Quiet and unassuming. Until it wasn't.

He shifts on his feet and peers through the fence. The lights are dead, from the big floodlights near the hangar to the smaller ones lining the footpaths. He can't recall if they're usually on during the day. The fact that he notices suggests that something is different.

The notebook is secured in an inner pocket of his trench coat. He needs to get in, find X, grab his brothers, and disappear again. He

breaks it up into steps to minimize the impossibility of the task.
You never used to hesitate this much.
But the compound is so still. And something is wrong.

Henry's footsteps are delicate on the concrete floor, soft, mimicking the hush and drip of the plumbing in the walls.

The Mumblers have evolved across the eons; as their bodies adapted to their underground way of life, their eyesight became more suited for darkness and dust. And so their other senses slowly evolved: keen hearing, a sense of smell overstimulated by the aboveground world, sensitive to vibrations and shifts in temperature.

Henry pays painful attention to his pace and the small unnatural sounds he makes along the corridor. He holds the pipe steady on his shoulder. He does not trail his fingers along the wall to guide himself through the darkness.

He's wandered these basement tunnels almost daily for the past few years; it's the only place in the entire compound where he finds the quiet to focus on his work without being distracted by the madness above. He's had terrible migraines since the accident, stabbing pain in his skull from loud noises, overlapping voices, and the gentle ambient hum of the basement corridors quiets the screams in his head.

He knows this place. He knows the Mumblers. He does not know what he will find on the levels above.

He reaches the first flight of stairs.

If Henry believed in a god, he would consider this a test of faith. As it is, he's simply been dealt a shit hand in life, and the best he can do is deal it hell in return.

Don't be stupid, Harry says.

Wait, let's talk about this, let's see what Harry thinks, says Howard.

Every fight is a good fight, says Henry, in a voice like a general declaring war.

He mounts the stairs to the upper levels.

"There. You missed it, dipshit."

"Excuse me?"

"Sorry, I said *you missed it, dipshit*. The car. Circle back a ways, he drove it off-road back there."

Howard does circle back, a frown carved into his face. He drops down on a relatively-flat clearing between two slopes, above the pale bit of road snaking through the mountains. Veronica points it out as he lands the monstrous flying death contraption: a solid bit of shadow on the roadside below, dented charcoal-black and dirty chrome.

"How did you spot that?" The blades slow. Howard rips off his headset and throws some switches on the console.

"I used my eyes," says Veronica, removing her own headset. "I was paying attention while I was grilling you. It's called multitasking."

They abandon the *Medusa* and navigate down the hillside in silence until they hit the road, which is more dirt-filled pothole than asphalt. Beyond the road is an overgrown lookout point, and beyond the lookout is another treacherously sheer drop through the trees. The car is nestled into the shade of the lookout. It is empty.

Howard slams the door shut and rubs his hands through his hair. He grimaces down the road to where it curves around the mountain and disappears. He sighs. "Well, that would have been too simple."

"Where's he gone?"

He points down the mountainside. "He's gone ahead on foot. To the compound."

"Okay. That sounds exhausting." Veronica pulls up her hood. She squints at the sun climbing lower in the sky. They stand a chance if they can penetrate the compound by daylight, before the Mumblers come alive at night. "Let's go."

They continue down the mountainside, using branches and roots to anchor themselves. Howard moves like an athlete, sure of his movements and his own strength. Veronica feels more like a spider scrambling in her own collapsing web. Her backpack catches on a branch, and she tugs it loose. Her hair gets caught and she tucks it back under her hood.

Howard pauses at one point, perched on an outcropping of rock, waiting for her to catch up. He's rolled up the sleeve of his jumpsuit. His right forearm is discolored with splotchy scars. He watches her like she's some exotic animal approaching.

"Why do you care so much?" he says.

Veronica struggles out off her hoodie. She ties it around her waist. "About what?"

"This. Your father's research. Harry. You're so young, and you're...alone."

Jesus. "You're young too," she says irritably.

"But I've always had Harry. Always."

"And I've always had my dad," she says. "Always. And I want him back. So I guess that answers your question."

Howard considers. He shrugs and slides down off the rocks and continues through the trees. He's clearly still bothered; he can't pinpoint exactly what's wrong with her.

"So what about your other brother?" she calls after him.

"What about him?"

"Is he an asshole?"

"I'm not an asshole," says Howard.

"I didn't ask," says Veronica.

He pauses. He tilts his head at her. "You're not very nice."

"Life hasn't been very nice to me."

His expression is inscrutable. "My brothers and I haven't enjoyed a privileged life, either. Especially not me and Harry. Our home was destroyed and our family is likely dead."

Oh. She schools her features into careful indifference. Something twists in her gut, something caresses her ribcage. Feathers and fear. The breeze, she thinks, smells faintly of smoke. And her ears...ring. They ring, and something far away is screaming. Did she see this? Did she perhaps see a city falling in blood and flames? And a boy—three boys—

Howard looks up. The boughs tremble in the sudden breeze; dancing sunlight plays across the hillside. He looks back down at Veronica.

The wind dies. Veronica smiles. "Harry Markus strikes me as less tragic and more of a rich kid with too much military training and a god complex and expensive weapons and delusions of immortality."

Howard's eyebrows shoot up. "He might be all of that, too."

They continue the descent. Howard seems sobered by his own

words, like she pulled the reaction out of him and he's uncomfortable with it. He doesn't meet her gaze, but when her heels slip on a patch of wet leaves, his arm shoots out as if to catch her.

"So what about Henry?" she says.

"Henry's alright," says Howard. His words are careful. "He's become more like Harry, over the years. He's a bit jaded. Doesn't like that we try to take care of him, which makes it difficult. He's bitter."

"Why? Is he the baby? Youngest child complex?"

Howard looks at her sideways. "No. Because he's blind."

31

Sometimes, Henry Markus imagines that the Mumblers cut his eyes from his head.

It would certainly have been cleaner that way—easier to cope with, easier to heal. In his perpetual darkness he sees their shadowy forms leaning over him, steel glinting in the firelight. He feels them pry open his flesh and pull his eyes from their sockets, feels the warm wet of his own blood pooling down his cheeks. His skull splits with the pain.

And that's just it: it's the pain that reminds him. It wasn't knives and deliberate slices that severed him from his vision, it was a knock on the head—a crumbling building, a near-deathly blow, and days and nights without treatment. So the trouble expanded within his skull. Blackouts. Sickness. And, finally, the dark creeping corners of his vision contracting until all he saw was black.

He hadn't known he would lose his sight. Perhaps his brothers had known. Maybe they'd discussed it behind his back: *Henry will go blind, what should we do? Should we tell him? No, let's not—it will be harder that way, knowing it's coming and that he can't do anything about it. He can't handle the knowing.*

But he would have liked to have known. He could have stood the torment of slow-encroaching darkness if he might have drunk in the world a bit more, a bit longer, paid more attention to the way the light filled with dust and the shadows carved curving lines into the floor. He would have looked at his brothers and memorized their faces a bit better. The color of their eyes. The color of *his* eyes.

Five years to stumble through relearning life. He taught himself to navigate. He focuses on the way the air brushes over his skin, the direction of the current, to locate entryways and vents. His migraines have become less frequent. He learns to trust his fingertips, the paths they draw, variations in energy. He works with plugs and circuits, works on displays that can read to him, memorizes the pitches and sequences that a machine sings to him. His senses have always been good, and this is the ultimate test.

He knows his way around the compound. He is not sure he knows his way around the Mumblers.

And what will you do if you make it out? What will you do then? He hasn't gotten that far. He hasn't gotten so far as escaping the highest basement level.

Harry would laugh at him. *"What, you haven't made a plan? Where's your strategy?"*

"Think about it," Howard would say, *"maybe you should listen to Harry. He's never led us wrong, after all!"*

And Henry would say something that would make them both, almost audibly, roll their eyes at one another. Something witty like "fuck you, Harry".

He stands at the base of the last flight of stairs. There's a door above, and it creaks loudly when opened. Then there's a cold, sterile corridor of nameless chambers and mudrooms and storage space. If the Mumblers are here for Cage, they shouldn't be on this level, at least not in great numbers—if they are, it probably has something to do with the quiet. The stillness. It probably reminds them of their caverns.

If they're here for another reason, Henry is likely to be killed on sight. Or tortured. Or used as bait for his brothers.

The Mumblers do hate his brothers.

He takes the stairs slowly. He shifts the pipe on his shoulder, arranges it so that it doesn't tap the door when he leans against the handle and pushes it open. The hinges squeal, but only softly. He holds his breath and pauses in the doorway. He listens for approaching footsteps.

The corridor is silent. Their stench is stronger up here, mingling with the chemical strength of bleach and lemon-scented sprays. Blood and soil and citrus. His nose wrinkles. He lets the door shut behind him, but does not move for a long moment.

They could be standing still. Would he know? Would he feel their presence?

He's waiting for something. A bang. A shock and stuttering gasp. For the world to crumble away beneath his feet, for the world to erupt in thunderous crashing and a cacophony of screams. He waits with bated breath until the moment passes, and still the discovery does not come.

He is alone.

There is an elevator at the end of the corridor. Do Mumblers use elevators? The stairs will probably still be his best escape, because there's nothing like a loud dinging to announce your arrival on the ground floor. He makes his way to the stairwell, cracks open the door, listens.

He climbs slowly. Carefully. Every muscle is tensed. He hardly dares breathe. It isn't a question of whether he'll be caught, but when.

The steps quake beneath him.

He stumbles on the landing, falls to his knees. Somewhere high above, metal screeches. The pipe is shaken loose from his shoulder, falls clattering out of reach. He gropes for it.

The building is collapsing.

His pulse is rapid. The stairs have stopped shaking, but he is still unsteady when he regains his feet. His heartbeat skips and pounds. He smells dust and something burning. He hunts for the pipe with mounting panic in his chest.

He has to get out of here. He's made too much sound.

Something is wrong.

The wrongness sources from Harry Markus, whose rucksack full of random gadgets houses all the parts to throw together a simple explosive. Though the weapon was manufactured by North

Enterprises for more structurally traumatizing maneuvers, Harry simply does not care, and will gladly use expensive and sophisticated gear to rig a detonation for personal reasons.

He needs to get to the upstairs offices, where Cage and X keep themselves. He needs to do it without being caught.

When the bomb goes off near the south entrance—buried on the edge of the fence, a few yards from the outdoor armory and range—Harry is already stalking the west entrance. He hears the bang, sees the windows rattle, the curling tail of smoke.

He runs.

He hurls himself up the side of the fence, lays his coat down over the barbed wire, and drops to the packed earth on the other side. He sprints across concrete and dodges around the guard's post. The whole sequence of events takes place in a matter of twenty seconds. He whips out his keycard and slams his shoulder into the western doors.

They don't budge.

He stumbles back, breathing heavily. He tries his card against the scanner again, but there's no electric beep, no flash of light. Inside, the lobby is dark.

He glances over his shoulder. The guard still hasn't emerged from his post. In fact, the whole compound is eerily silent. A flock of startled birds rises up from the trees near the south of the grounds.

Probably some weird lock-down procedure from the deluded mind of X himself, something that will make it infinitely easier for Harry to climb the levels and find the old man and shove Benedict Lewis' manuscripts down his scrawny throat.

Get his brothers. Get a chopper. *Get out of here.*

Easy. Easy when he breaks it into simple steps. He's gotten them out of worse situations. *Easy.*

He pulls his gun and activates the muffler. He shoots the keypad, which doesn't even spark. The electricity is dead. *Stupid.*

He takes a knife from his boot and jams the blade between the doors, finds a sliver of space, fits in his fingers and draws the crack wider. The door squeals on its track. He slips inside, leaves it gaping open behind him.

The reception chamber is silent and perfectly empty.

They can't be locked down because of the explosion. Even North Enterprises doesn't react that fast. A drill?

It doesn't matter. Get in and out.

Dull late-afternoon light bathes the lobby, but fades in the mouths of the winding corridors beyond. He stands still for a brief moment, drinking in the silence, the darkness laid out before him, the eerie still. *It's the calm before the storm*, he thinks, but he does not sense any storm on the horizon. Perhaps it just hasn't arrived yet. Perhaps he's become paranoid. Perhaps his whole life has been a series of *survive* and *almost die* and *somehow live* and *always be prepared to die*, so that he cannot fathom this stillness and he feels like a wolf in a nursery again—something incomprehensibly dangerous that simply doesn't belong. Something that will bring bloodshed upon this peacetime.

This is not peace. They have his brothers.

A sense of calm purpose descends over his body. He knows his role. Harry Markus blinks slowly, adjusts the knife in his grip, and walks into the belly of the beast.

"Is that normal?" Veronica watches the spiral of acrid gray rise up south of the complex. A flock of birds swarms from the trees nearby; their flapping wings mingle with the smoke before they disappear into the mountains.

"No." Howard's eyes are distracted. "This is...the western entrance. I think Henry's down in the north basements somewhere, he likes it down there because it's quiet. But the Mumblers are probably also down there because they don't like the light."

"The power's out," says Veronica.

"What?"

"The power. Is. Out." She points to the windows, the dead floodlights. "Unless everything's tinted and North Enterprises never turns on the lights. So the whole place is dark and the Mumblers can go anywhere they want."

"Oh. You're perceptive."

"And you're distracted." She rises from the bushes where they crouch, yards from the fenceline. The Mumblers won't be out during the day, but she reckons they're aware of the explosion near the compound, and they're probably scrambling around inside the confines of this concrete coffin. "That was Harry, wasn't it?"

"Probably."

"He's already inside. Are you scared of them?" Howard's features are unsure, unsettled; determined, yes, but less confident than his brother. Somehow that annoys Veronica. "You're scared."

"You would be too, if you'd seen what they can do."

"One of them stepped on my hand, like, really hard, and that hurt pretty bad. So I guess I do know." He can't tell if she's kidding. She doesn't wait for him to figure it out. "You find your blind brother wandering around the basement. I'll stop Harry."

Howard barks a laugh. "Stop Harry? Will you stop the tides, too?"

Veronica heaves a sigh. "The way you said that was archaic and annoying. I'll ignore it, considering your situation. Where will he go?"

"Harry? If he wants Cage, he'll go to the top floor. But I don't know that he'll make it that far, not if he doesn't know—"

"I reckon he'll figure it out soon enough." She reaches into her rucksack and squats beside the fence.

Howard slowly rises from the bushes. "You carry wire cutters with you?"

Veronica looks up from her work. "Well, yeah. Why not?"

32

X does not speak to the Raccoon, whose real name he has not bothered to learn. A pilot is a pilot. He does not have the energy for small-talk. But he points out the approaching mountains, the valley nestled between them like a robin's nest. "There."

The Raccoon's voice crackles in his headset, amused. "I know, man. I've got a GPS." And when X doesn't comment: "I know, they rigged these babies out. The newest gen. We've even got floaties under the seats."

X shifts and cranes his neck to see better. Through the hills and trees he catches sight of the fast-approaching concrete cube. It has always reminded him of a hideous parking garage—all glass and cinderblock, barbed wire jungles and dark floodlights towering over the grounds. And a cloud of ominous smoke climbing up the south side of the compound.

"What happened there?" X murmurs, forgetting the headset.

"Isolated detonation, looks like. Right off the armory. Are you going in alone?" X doesn't answer, but the Raccoon keeps going. "Did they tell you it's a suicide mission? Because from what I've heard, it's pretty gnarly inside. Real apocalyptic mutant alien shit."

"Emergency landing pad is there." X points.

But the Raccoon is already slowing, gently dropping to the cleared area hidden in the hills above the compound. "Did you see that other chopper back there?"

"There's a hangar."

"The one left by the side of the road."

Someone else came back. Harry Markus has a chopper. He is already here.

"Should I keep it running?" The Raccoon leans back in his seat, folds his arms behind his head. He looks at X sidelong.

He doesn't expect me to make it back. H has an understanding with the Mumblers, but part of that understanding was that the Mumblers weren't supposed to interfere with North Enterprises or the other divisions. Now that they've forsaken one agreement, what's to say they haven't scrapped the rest?

"Yes. Keep it running."

He thinks of Harry Markus, carrying with him the heavy weight of Ben and Peter's research, carrying Veronica Lewis right into the arms of destiny. There are some causes greater than one man's life. Ben and Peter both understood that, even if they were misguided in their choice of causes. X understands it too.

"Good luck," says the Raccoon.

But there is no luck, X thinks. *Only fate.*

When Veronica was young, she would sit on the floor of her father's trailer and stare at the stars through the skylight. She'd cross her legs and lean forward, elbows planted in the dense dusty carpet, and let the moonlight bathe her face. The pale silver light filling her bedroom, the gentle haze of gray over the black treetops.

She loved the moonlight until it meant other things: Benedict leaving in the middle of the night to go stargazing again, disappearing for days at a time, forbidding her from following, coming back and asking her—asking her *has she seen anything? Has she had any odd dreams? No? Did they stop? Oh, they just haven't been very odd? Well, why not?*

He might as well have grabbed her by the shoulders and shaken her.

She loved the moonlight until she preferred the darkness,

because in that sacred silence—in the dark twisting labyrinth of her mind—Veronica Lewis is alone with the pale boy.

"I won't lose you," he says. And she believes him.

The corridors are dark, and she is terribly alone. The darkness smells of smoke.

She is walking that labyrinth now, but it feels very real. The canary's wings beat in her chest. Veronica holds her gun in one hand, the crumpled dirt-stained pages of her father's writing in the other. Harry Markus didn't want those pages before, or didn't want them read. Well, she's read them. And she reckons he'd like them back now.

Howard disappeared into the depths of the western stairwell, with whispered warnings of Mumblers and no guarantees for her survival if she should meet them. Alone, Veronica ascends.

So dark. She fumbles for the handrails and makes as little noise as possible. She wants to hear if the Mumblers approach. She doesn't know what she did in Tulsa, and she does not know if she can do it again. *January. Tulsa.* The list is growing. She feels her soul splinter with each name.

What am I?

"Do you know where you're going?"

She jumps. Even in the perfect dark she can make him out distinctly, as if he is illuminated by some hidden spotlight: lounging against the handrail on the landing below her. "Sure I do," she breathes.

Grant grins up at her, his stupid crooked smile. "Are you lost, Veronica?"

She shakes her head. She turns her back to him and faces the glaring darkness of the stairwell.

He is beside her. He offers his hand—long pale fingers, the back of his hand sprinkled with freckles. A ropey scar twists its way down his jaw. His voice is close to her ear. "Don't you trust me?"

Doesn't she? This doesn't feel quite like the Grant she knows. *Everything is wrong.*

She shakes her head again and keeps climbing. She won't talk to him. She won't acknowledge the slight release of pressure, the brief moment of relief when she first heard his voice. She doesn't need him. *Just Ben. I need my dad. I need Benedict Lewis back and he'll fix*

everything.
   Veronica would sit on the floor of his lab in a beam of moonlight. "What are you looking at?" he would ask. Her dad, from his seat at the table, from his mural of notepaper and ink.
   "It looks really close," she'd say.
   "The moon?"
   "No." And she'd point, though she'd realize later she was the only one to see it. "No. That one. The darker planet, between the stars."

   They're moving him. Ben's body is slow, but his thoughts are quick, coming faster than he can react, assaulting him: *they're moving me, are they killing me? Did they find Veronica? Where are we going?*
   His hands are not even bound. They know he doesn't have the energy to escape. His mind is tumultuous as they shuffle him along, a guard on either side. He hears their words as if from inside a dream.
   "James said to put them down by the cryochambers."
   "We're putting them under?"
   "No, no. There are more rooms down there."
   "What? We're putting them all together?"
   "Moving as many as possible. Make room up top. We need to empty the chambers, though—talk to Anthony about that, huh?"
   "Oh, I'm not talking to Halleck. That guy…."
   "Scared?"
   "Something's wrong with him, the way he talks. Makes me uncomfortable."
   "Welcome to ARC. Get comfortable with discomfort. We need to empty the cryochambers soon. Something tells me we're gonna be putting a lot of people under, in the next few days. Talk about uncomfortable. Hey, get that door."
   "We're bringing the monsters here?"
   "Don't call them that."
   "Well, what are we calling them?" Something beeps, a door squeals open.
   "You want to know what Anthony Halleck's calling them? He told James, he said 'we've got extraterrestrials and no one's about

to say it, but I am'. Halleck himself called them aliens. How about that?"

"I think I prefer monsters."

"Yeah, me too. Get the lift, would ya?"

Henry is just below ground level when he hears the screams. He presses his ear to the door, but the sound comes from above, in the northern area of the compound. His heartbeat drums against his ribcage. In the perpetual darkness, in his head, he is back in a burning city. These are not the screams of the dying. These are the screams of those who wish they were dead.

The door squeals. It shuts against the voices.

The corridor is cool and stagnant. Henry holds his breath has he moves along, keeping close to one side, letting his fingertips skip over doorways before reattaching to the wall. When he thinks he's gone far enough, he starts reading the braille beside the doorframes.

When he finds the southern stairwell and slips inside, it's quiet. He allows himself to breathe. He ascends.

The ground level is quiet. There's a draft, the first scent of evergreen and fresh air in days, and Henry gulps it down. He keeps one hand on the wall, clutches his rusty pipe with aching fingers, and slowly moves down the corridor in the direction of the draft. His steps are soft yet sound so loud to his delicate hearing.

He waits for the sound of footfalls. Waits for the rise of mumbling voices. The tapping, the clacking. A door to open and the screams to flood back out.

Instead, he hears the unmistakable sound of a hammer cocking.

Henry freezes.

X levels his gun at the Markus boy, a serene sense of calm settling over his body.

"Henry Markus," he croons. "Do not move."

33

Harry Markus hears the screams, and he walks towards them. He has learned to block out fear and horror, to cordon himself off into a field of cold stoicism. He hears the screams, but he does not feel them in his blood. He knows they do not come from his brothers. He wanders the northern halls of the upper floors until the screams are loud in his ears, echoing in his skull.

Then they find him.

He senses them before he sees them, and he wonders afterwards why he didn't smell the Mumblers first. But the scent of smoke is still thick in his nose, and the darkness presses inward. He only sees the shapes when they come close.

Too close. They are silent.

Harry lurches back as the first Mumbler grabs at him with clammy cold hands. A flash of disgust, and then rage—he slices through the body and it falls away with a gurgle, but there are more, pressing in at his sides, crowding the hall around him.

The Myrmen are here. They are not supposed to be here.

He grits his teeth. He presses forward.

Light—there's light around the corner, he needs to reach the light.

Where are his brothers? He needs them like he needs air.

He fights his way through, stabbing and slicing, kicking them aside and cutting off the fingers that grip him. The stink of smoke is gone and all he can smell is blood, bloody soil, metallic on the tongue.

It is so dark.

At last he presses through and he runs, runs towards the screams. Here, around the corner: a window at the end of the hall, the slatted blinds hanging loose and letting cracks of light break through. Here, at the end of the hall. Here, to his right: a wide open doorway. A window into Hell.

Veronica recognizes the screams. The smoke is a familiar scent. And the feeling of Grant pacing beside her through the winding dark corridors—well, all she needs now is a pair of wings.

She opens the stairwell door a crack, leans into the hallway. A thin beam of dusty afternoon sunlight creeps in from a window. It illuminates a ghastly scene.

The Mumblers are hunched on the floor like horrible boils growing out of the building itself. Their curved backs shiny with strange metal armor. Over the sporadic screams, the corridor rings with the eerie keen of their whispery voices, moans and death-rattles.

The stink of blood hits her like a truck. Veronica gags.

They are moving. They are creeping down the hall, away from her. They leave their dead and wounded in pools of spreading death.

Harry Markus is here. They cannot have him yet.

Veronica slips out of the stairwell. She pulls her hoodie over her nose to block the stench. Her eyes water. She stumbles over the twitching bodies.

Something hot and liquid splashes her ankle. She moves along the wall, steps over the dead. She keeps her eyes fixed on where the Mumblers have gathered at the end of the corridor.

The screams are frantic and broken, growing louder. Her skin crawls. *Run. Run. Run!*

But the notebook. But Harry Markus. But Benedict.

A cluster of wounded Mumblers has gathered around the doorway, but they do not enter; they mumble and hiss, they grow in number, they ignore her as she gazes out over their heads and into the room.

There are people. Not Mumblers—people. Humans, in rags of business casual and various stages of deterioration. Veronica can hardly make out whether they are male or female, or whether they have faces at all at this point, because they are strewn about the room, shackled to walls and desks and something that might once have been a swamp cooler under a boarded-up window. They are screaming, and their voices are raw. The smell of blood is thick. They have been screaming for a long time. There are tools scattered around the room—knives and pokers and masks, things Veronica can't identify, things she doesn't want to imagine in use. Her stomach turns over and she retches where she stands.

Grant is gone. There are only devils here.

And there is Harry Markus, standing amongst them, gripping a Mumbler by the throat. His voice is loud enough to almost drown out the screams. "Where are they? What did you do with them? Where are they?"

The Mumbler gurgles and spits, and Veronica realizes he's driving a knife deep into its belly. His arm twists and the creature lets out a piercing shriek, then falls silent.

He drops the body and spins to face the Mumblers in the doorway. "Where are they?" His voice cracks. His eyes are pale and wild in the dark.

They latch onto Veronica.

She raises her gun and fires into the Mumblers.

Hell unfolds. The screams are lost in scrambling footfalls and a surge of groans. They scatter and fall away from the doorway, they turn to face her. Even as Veronica shoots again, and again, and the creatures inch closer, and Veronica takes a step back, she recognizes this moment. She heard it once before. She saw it inside her labyrinth, and now it's real.

A pale hand reaches for her—she knocks it aside, steps back, fires again and takes another step backwards until her shoulders press into a wall. And she doesn't know how many bullets she has left, but it is dark and the voices are loud and overlapping, drawing out the screams, drowning out the sound of gunfire.

In the dirt we mumble. In the dirt we mumble.

She thinks of that flash of light, the splintering crack breaking through the darkness and shattering the Mumblers around her. She thinks of something beautiful and ghastly and looming just outside her vision. It thrums in her veins. Her body trembles.

Harry Markus is there, cutting a gap through the Mumblers. He is huge and horrible, splattered with blood, face like stone as he reaches out with both hands and snaps a Mumbler's neck, kicks it aside, drags his knife across another's throat.

Veronica is out of ammunition, but it doesn't matter. The monsters are dead. Harry Markus stands before her, a look of horror and confusion and disgust twisting his face. "How the hell did you get here?" He breathes heavily.

"I flew," says Veronica.

She vomits on his shoes. Her knees buckle and she collapses against him.

"No," says Harry. "No." He takes a step back from her and turns away. "No, you can't be here."

She can't be here. She knows too much. She has to go.

He faces the room where the human bodies still twitch and cry on the floor. None of them are his brothers and they aren't going to survive much longer—they don't even have eyes, most of them are missing limbs. And who knows what else the Mumblers have done? More twisted things than even Harry can fathom in his most paralyzing nightmares.

He walks back into the room with feigned calm, takes out his handgun, and shoots each of them in what remains of their heads. The screams die.

The hallway is quiet when he returns. The Mumblers are dead in their own filth, the survivors have fled. And Veronica Lewis is gone.

He pauses in the center of the corridor. A chill settles over him.

She is gone.

He has to find his brothers. They're alive, they have to be, he can't imagine a world where they aren't. Howard would have taken care of Henry, he'd know how to hide from the Mumblers, he'd know how to not end up dead in a pit somewhere with his brains pulled out through his eye sockets.

Harry slams the door behind him. He can't catch his breath.

He has to kill Veronica. He has to get them out. Then he'll go someplace and destroy Benedict Lewis' work, because he doesn't have to give it to X anymore, he doesn't have to risk exposure, he can just burn it and be done once and for all. *Fuck them. Fuck them all to hell.* If X took them to BEESWAX or ARC, Harry will find them. He'll pick X apart one shred at a time. He'll find them.

Harry steps over the Mumblers and makes his way towards the stairwell. He pauses in the center of the corridor.

The door is open. He didn't leave it open. She must have come up this way, she must have left this way.

His mind twists in a million different directions. *Why? Why is she here? How?* His rage is simmering; his thoughts come in screams that rip through his skull. He glances over his shoulder. He reaches absently for the notebook tucked inside his trench coat.

For the second time today, he reaches for something and realizes it is not there.

I flew, she'd said, before falling against him and disappearing once more. Harry stumbles.

Lewis. He crashes into the stairwell and hurdles up the stairs.

34

"Are you going to shoot a blind man?"

X laughs softly. It's a wheezing sound. "Is that how you survived the Myrmen for so long? Did it work on them? I know you're not helpless. I know who you are."

Myrmen. Henry stiffens at the name. He doesn't recognize this voice, but he can picture the scene clearly—a smoky breeze blowing in through the jammed-open doors of the lobby entrance, and a figure silhouetted against the thin light. A man with a gun.

Footsteps echo through the hall. Henry stands rigid. "You are the third brother," the man says softly. "You were supposed to be the greatest."

All the heat rushes from Henry's body. His ears ring. This information belongs in another place, to another time.

"But you don't look like much, do you? You don't look so much like the other two." The man is close now, and his voice has careened from amiable to cruel mockery. Henry's skin crawls. "Why would *you* be the chosen one? Why not your eldest brother?"

Of course, why not Harry? It was the question everyone had asked. Everyone but their parents. *Why you?*

"Who are you?" he breathes.

The man tuts. "Names are currency, Henrik. Now, be quiet, please—I have to find your brother, and I'd rather not attract the Mumblers' attention."

Henry doesn't move. "My brother."

"Oooh. You don't know? He's here!" At this the man seems positively delighted, but still his voice hovers just above a whisper. *He doesn't know where the Mumblers are. He's also afraid of them. Harry is here.* "Agent Markus is tucked away somewhere within this adder's nest of Myrmen. And he has something I need, which I'd prefer to pry out of *his* hands rather than theirs." His steps grow closer. He breathes loudly into the silence.

The rusty pipe still rests on Henry's shoulder, cool on his neck. *Don't move. Not a bit.* He thinks of a snake coiled in the grass, of an animal encircled by hunters. *Harry is here. Harry came back.* A thrill. And then: fear. What is he doing here? He can't fight the entire Mumbler race. Harry thinks he can control the elements and raze entire armies with a sweep of his mighty arm, but he cannot, and Henry has witnessed this firsthand.

"I don't think you should kill me," he says. He can feel the man's breath on his face, stale coffee mingling with the evergreen of the outdoors.

"Why not? Do tell." His voice drips with amusement.

"The gunshot will alert the Mumblers. And," Henry smiles a thin, unnerving smile, "my brother will gut you alive." The man is silent. Henry notes, with grim satisfaction, that he's stopped breathing. "If you know us as well as you say you do," he says, "then you know he will."

Howard stands in a darkened room. The flashlight is frail and flickering in his hand. A chill settles over his heart.

It's a mess. It's hardly a room, it's a maintenance closet, it's a cold concrete chamber ringed with plumbing and random electrical maintenance panels. It stinks of piss. His torch beam finds a scattering of circuit boards and wires on the paint-stripped desk. The room tilts, flickers, stabilizes, and Howard feels like he's existing outside his own body.

Henry was here. He knows his brother's smell—the dusty moth-eaten sweaters he wears in the chilly basement, the weird rye and flax toast he prefers. *Henry was here.* He is no longer here.

A radio in the corner of the room plays a soft stream of classical music. Henry loves classical music. He likes the cellos, with all their intensity, their rich, deep drones. He says it sounds like the wind in the mountains.

Howard listens for a moment, frozen in place.

He backs out of the room. He shuts the door behind him. He leans against it and gazes at the opposite wall. He traces the lines between cinderblocks, numb and confused.

He was here. He is gone. I've killed him.

Howard should have stayed behind. He should have fought his way through the Mumblers descending on the compound, he should have fought his way to his brother, because he's positive that's what Harry would have done. Harry wouldn't have left Henry behind. But Howard had.

He pushes off the door and moves back through the basement in a daze. The music fades out behind him, fades to a low hum in the corner of his mind. His footfalls scuff the concrete. The flashlight flickers. The hum swells to a fluctuating wave, rising and falling, until it is no longer in his mind, and Howard's steps falter.

It's in the walls. His skin prickles and crawls.

In the dirt we mumble, in the dirt we mumble, in the dirt...

He can see the stairs, but there's another floor of basement above that. *Where are they?*

There are doors ahead, lining the corridor between him and his escape. Doors to boiler rooms and the like, places Henry didn't frequent, so Howard hadn't bothered checking them earlier. He becomes suddenly convinced that there are Mumblers behind those doors.

He takes a shallow breath and holds it as he passes by, light on his feet. He doesn't breathe again until he's past the corridor and up the stairs, into the next shell of the compound.

This is below the south entrance. Dust and paint shaken loose from the ceiling speckle the floor with flecks of white. It's quieter here, the chants left behind and below. Howard rubs the chill from his arms, checks behind wide-open doors as he makes his way to the next staircase. These are maintenance and IT offices, all left deserted in the mad rush to escape—sandwiches half-eaten on desks—a newspaper, a novel, an instruction manual with its spine split from lying open so long on a swivel chair. It's a ghost town, like one of those radioactive Soviet cities he's read about.

He needs to find Harry. If he finds Harry, he'll find Veronica Lewis. And he needs to find both without disturbing the Mumblers.

Veronica moves through the dark. She holds the notebook tight against her ribs.

The smoke is thick. She shouldn't smell it anymore, she knows she shouldn't—it's caught in the wind, it's miles away, and she's buried within an intricate maze of concrete and corridor. Her footfalls pound up the stairwell. She stumbles on a landing, slams into a door. She recoils at the crash and resounding echo. Her heart is wedged in her throat as she launches herself up the next flight.

A gentle wind whistles in her ears. It carries with it phantom screams and the chanting of a thousand guttural voices.

Are you lost, Veronica?

No, she's not. No. She's going exactly where she needs to be: away from the Mumblers. Away from Harry Markus.

What is Benedict to you, Veronica? How much are you willing to sacrifice?

Everything. This is everything. *He* is everything.

The next landing is the last. Veronica crashes through the door and into a corridor that feels like something out of a dream: dust motes filling the air, and gray light from vast windows; doors hung half open to reveal empty seats at empty desks. Her footsteps slow to a walk as she crosses through a lobby. She moves around low sofas and a sliver of glass-topped reception desk where someone upset a paper cup of coffee in their haste to evacuate. The coffee has dried to a stain on the white tile floor. There's an open magazine face-down on a sofa. An enormous black-and-white canvas of a pelican oversees the room, caught in a moment in time.

Veronica pauses at the edge of the lobby. She stares down the next stretch of corridor. In the distance, flickering neon green: *EXIT*. Behind her, through the still hellscape of post-apocalyptic business suites, dust motes drift through pale panes of mid-afternoon light.

There's a crash in the stairwell.

Veronica takes a step forward. She can feel Harry Markus breathing down her neck. She can feel his freakish eyes drilling into the back of her skull. A shiver skitters across her shoulders.

She takes another step. She starts running.

And as she moves, she leaves the light behind, she pushes into the shadows. She collides with the door, slams it open.

She stumbles into daylight. She trips up one step—two—falls and catches herself on her hands and knees atop the third step. She scoops the notebook back up and presses it to her chest. She scrambles to her feet.

Veronica stands atop a sea of glaring-white rooftop. The space is dotted with satellite dish umbrellas and shields of solar panels, an empty landing pad, spools of wire and cables. Beyond, against a darkening sky, mountains cup the valley in tender hands. The forest bristles black and ominous in the chill breeze, like a demented audience leering down at the compound from towering coliseum stands. She's exposed to the sky. She's surrounded by open air.

Veronica takes a step forward. She crosses the rooftop and moves slowly to the ledge. There is no fire escape, no ladder, no emergency exit from the rooftop. Tarmac below, and beyond, curlicues of evil barbed wire glinting in the light.

She gazes out at the mountains. They remind her of the mountains back home, the hills she calls home. Her and Ben's home. *Stargazing* is what they call it, and that RV nestled into the hills feels more like home than the trailer in the West End ever did. She isn't scared of the wild animals and the wild weather, the inclines and reaching branches. She isn't afraid of the dark.

The world is deathly still.

Her breath rattles in her chest. Her skin is sticky with sweat. There's blood on her hands, and now there's blood on her father's notebook. Slowly, movements halting, she peels off her backpack. It slouches by her feet. She hums to herself to fill the silence; vibrations travel up her jaw and into her ears. She hums low and off-key as she unzips the top of the backpack and reaches inside. She finds a snatch of lyrics as she finds the missing pages. *If I could make days last forever, if words could make wishes come true....* She kneels on the rooftop beside the bag. She tucks the pages into the front cover of the notebook. She loses the melody; she leaves the song unfinished.

Here it is. Cursed and perfect and destructive. The key to Benedict Lewis.

"Veronica."

She doesn't move. Her fingers tighten on the notebook. *The key. This is what you wanted, you selfish bitch. This is why Creed and Ted are fleeing through the desert, this is why there's a trail of blood across the country.*

"Look at me, Veronica."

She closes her eyes. She lets the wind sweep her away from this moment, to a time when her father held her hands and looked her in the face and said *It will be okay. You're safe. It's a secret.* She imagines his arms squeezing her safe against him. *It was worth it.*

The image slips away. She's falling into a dark place. And she's growing feathers.

"No." Her eyes fly open.

Grant stands at her shoulder. He's tired—thinner, paler, the scar on his jaw startling and bold, as if freshly formed. "You've done your best," he says.

"I did it," she says through her teeth. The words are lost on the wind, but he hears them. He always does. "I did it. Just let me be happy. This is my moment. I did it."

"Veronica—"

"I did it, I found it. I got it back." Her voice rises. "That's what he wanted. It's what he asked me to do."

"Did he?"

"Shut up. Shut the fuck up." She's never wanted to hurt him more. "I'm going to get him back. It's happening now. Can you feel it?" She can. She feels it in her throat. Her eyes burn. The wind sears her face. "Can you feel it? It's coming."

Grant tilts his head. He reaches out and brushes her cheek with his thumb. She didn't even realize she was crying. "You'll lose yourself," he whispers.

Her blood runs cold.

It's coming. It's coming. His hand on her shoulder. And a crumpled chips bag bouncing off his chest. And the realization that

she's never before been able to touch him. Until. Until. *Until.*
It's coming.
She's a canary on the floor of a coal mine, buried deep within the vaults of abandoned tunnels and black-chalked tombs, buried beneath Dane's Chapel. She's a canary pinned down in a cage. The fumes are growing thick and she's singing, singing—screaming—singing—and the voices are growing so loud even as poison descends over her world. There is no room for silence, no room for the end of the universe.
Until.

This is where Harry Markus finds her: silhouetted against a darkening silver sky, bloodied hair snaking across her face, black eyes snapping wildly.
And those pages, in that notebook, held tight to her chest like it's grown from her flesh.
The wind is strong. For an instant, standing in the doorway, gazing at the figure by the roof's edge, Harry can almost imagine that he's in a place that is seared into his soul, a moment he remembers never having lived. Clouds gather and billow beyond the mountains, trees lash against the black slopes, the wind tears across the rooftop and rattles the solar panels, and a golden-yellow feather somersaults over the toes of his boots.
He could kill her right now. Cleanly, quickly. He could just...put a bullet through her head. Take the notebook and leave.
"None of us are gonna get out of this," she says.
Her voice catches in the wind, but Harry Markus hears it like she's right in front of him. "I am," he says. The steps are laid out before him, he'll tick items off the list, he'll move one space forward and remove each obstacle keeping him from his brothers. *Kill her. Take the notebook. Find X. Kill him. Find Howard and Henry.*
"No," she says, "you're not. It's too late." Her tone is flat. "I guess it all happened...just a bit too late. Too late before we noticed. You've done your damage. And I've done mine."
Heat flares in his throat. His hand flexes against his gun. The wind snaps in his trench coat.
She turns to him. Her back is to the sky and the writhing forest. She looks sick and hollowed and hauntingly complacent. "You told

me you didn't work for North Enterprises."

"I lied."

"And I believed you." She shrugs, a jerk of her shoulders. The notebook's loose pages flutter in her arms. He'll grab the notebook and push her off the roof. If it falls from here it'll be scattered on the wind. He must take it *before he kills her*. It won't be so bad, will it? She's monstrous, she's irritating, she's easy for a remorseless death. He'll destroy her and get his brothers back. He'll destroy the world without a second thought.

As if she can read his mind, a smile touches her lips. "Were you going to tell me you're an alien?"

If he closes his eyes, he can picture the ice-spiked mountains and inky black of the sky. The peaks and falls of a city skyline so unlike any he's seen since. The drumbeat of wind in his eardrums, setting the pace of his pulse, a wind so harsh and unforgiving that he craves its abuse. The deep-seated ache does not budge. His heart is nailed to its altar.

"I guess it makes sense." Veronica Lewis' eyes wander, trailing above his head, gazing off into the mountains. "The tear in the universe. It is sort of a wormhole." Her fingers tap the notebook in her grip, drumming the cover. "My dad knew, sort of. He saw it widen. What, five years ago? When you three arrived. The rip is there, and with every passage and every year, it only widens."

Harry does not breathe.

"And I feel it." Her voice is a whisper now. "I feel every stitch tearing loose." Her eyes lock onto his. "Did you know that? My dad knew."

Harry shakes his head. His chest is tight. "You are not...a prophet." She can't know this. No one can know.

But...the notes. But the missing pages of her father's manuscripts. But the strange things the Webber girl said, the streak of white lightning lighting up the Tulsa sky, the Mumblers falling dead in a circle around her as if laying themselves down for sacrifice. Benedict Lewis knew. Harry can't let anyone else know. The Mumblers found their way to his home, and he saw it fall in flames. He cannot let anyone else find the way. He cannot let Veronica Lewis live.

"No." She looks at the notebook, chin to her chest. "Not a prophet. I'm just the canary."

"You're going to come with me." The man's voice is low, but it echoes through the lobby. "You'll come along nicely, and we'll find your brother. And I'll return you to him. And I'll get what I want as well."

Return you to him. A muscle spasms in Henry's jaw.

"Turn around," says the man. "Walk. And please, don't make any trouble—we're in enough as it is."

He's very close. It might be enough. Henry turns, slowly, to face the corridor.

"Now. And be quiet."

Henry drops to the floor.

He chokes up on the rusty pipe at his shoulder. He visualizes where the man stands behind him, just a pace away. As he brings the pipe around, the man lets out a startled cry.

Metal connects with flesh. The impact yanks the pipe from his hand. It clangs across the floor.

The man spits a curse. Empty-handed, Henry rolls away and rises into a crouch. He listens for the man's next move. A gentle thrill surges through him: he is fighting without Harry's help. He's reclaiming someone he used to be. He isn't a damaged relic from a glorious past.

He doesn't hear the approach, but he feels the air move as something slams into his face and his head snaps back. Heat explodes across his forehead. Fireworks erupt in the black of his vision. Pain radiates through his jaw.

He catches himself on an elbow before he can fall flat on his back, before the air is knocked from his lungs. His mouth is numb, hanging open, gasping.

He tries to roll again. A foot pins his chest. The man's voice is a hiss. "I do not *want* to spill the blood of Markus." Spittle flecks Henry's face. "But if one of you is to be sacrificed for this cause...you are certainly the least of the three."

Henry is positive there's a gun in his face.

He grabs the man's foot and twists, snaps it like a twig.

The man screams. The pressure disappears from Henry's chest.

And a gun fires.

The shot rips through Henry's world. He gasps, waits for the numb throbbing and then the slow-creeping searing pain, because he knows what it is to have a bullet tear through his body. He knows the agony of digging it out again.

But the pain does not come. His skull aches and either tears or blood burn down his face, but his body does not buck against a bullet.

There is a dull thud. A choking, gurgled gasp—blood in a throat, blood in the lungs.

And then a cool, familiar hand gripping his arm. "Henry. Henry, I'm here. Can you hear me? You're not dead, are you?"

He shudders. He is not dead. He will not die. "Howard."

"Look, I'm sorry, I didn't want to leave, I didn't know what to do—"

Henry sits up. Howard helps him to his unsteady feet. Howard has the permanent smell of the hangar about him, as do all the pilots; sawdust and something faintly metallic, sweat and adrenaline. He inhales deeply, releases the breath, hopes his injury doesn't look as desperate as it feels. "Harry is here," he says.

"I know. We have to find him."

"You don't know where he is?"

"I only followed him here. I thought he might have found *you*."

Henry kneels again, feels around on the floor for the pipe. "I thought you went to get him. When you left."

"Well, I did, but I was too late, and—what are you looking for? What is it?"

"The pipe."

"Look, here's his gun. Here, take it." Howard pulls Henry back to his feet. He presses the gun into his brother's hand.

Henry wraps his fingers around it. *Not dead.* "Howard," he says, softly.

Howard hears it in his voice. "What? What's wrong?"

"You shot him."

"Yes! He was going to kill you."

Silence falls between them. The blood rushes in Henry's ears and his pulse is loud, but he makes out the quick breath of his brother standing before him, and the death rattle in the old man's chest, and the wind whistling outside the compound.

And a low, terrible hum coming from the floor beneath his feet. It is rising. It is growing.

In the dirt we mumble, in the dirt we mumble....

"Oh," says Howard. "Oh. Well. Damn."

35

A radio buzzes in the deathly silence. A voice breaks through, choked with static. Howard looks at his brother, and Henry furrows his brow.

"Listen, man—the BEESWAX forces are closing in and—I don't think they know you're in there, you should probably—pick you up outside? Over."

Howard nudges the dead man with his boot. The radio blinks on his belt. "Must be his pilot," he murmurs.

"Howard."

"I know. I know. I don't know—" He glances at the entryway. The wind is growing, shaking the doors in their frames, and evening is creeping in, as is a bank of ominous-looking clouds. BEESWAX is on its way. The Mumblers are awake. "I have to find Harry." His voice is desperate.

"You flew here."

"Yes."

"You have the *Medusa*."

"Yes!"

Henry nods. His fingers flex and tighten on the handgun. "So bring it around."

Howard's brain stutters. "I—what? Henry—"

"I know what I said. Bring the helicopter around. I'll find Harry."

The silence between them is no longer silent, because the hum in the floor is growing and spreading through the walls, because the Mumblers are moving through the compound.

Howard can't leave Henry again. He can't. He won't. "I'll find Harry," says Howard. "We'll get out together, run for the hills."

"Before BEESWAX gets here? Before the Myrmen?"

"Shhh." Howard winces. "Don't call them that. I can't do this, I won't make it back in time. I'll be too late." His voice breaks.

"Then get to the hangar. You don't need your access card anymore, everything's dead. Get to the hangar and find something that flies. If you go now you'll make it back in time."

Howard looks at his brother. The blood and sweat streaked across his face. The heavy eyelids that sometimes hang half-open, revealing the startling blue-green of his eyes, but right now are squeezed tight as if in intense concentration. He thinks about the Mumblers climbing closer and dragging Henry back into the shadows, back into their infinite darkness. He just got him back, he can't let him go again. "What if I don't?"

Henry's jaw is set. "*Every fight is a good fight.* Right?"

A battle cry. "*And this one is better than most.*" Howard's heart hurts. He can't believe he's doing this. *Don't leave him! Not again!* "If you haven't found him by the time the Mumblers make it up here, get out."

"I can take care of myself."

"I know you can." Howard takes a step back towards the door, still hesitant. "I know." *But I'm scared.*

Henry makes the choice for him; he turns his back to Howard and limps off into the compound.

Howard is left with the dead body pooling with blood, and the rising echo of the Mumblers creeping towards the surface, and the wind howling through the mountains.

Veronica sees it now.

The wind is screaming in her ears and it's ripped her soul away.

Rising in the darkening sky above the compound, above Harry Markus, above the rise of the mountain slope and the bending treetops, a great dark planet hangs in the sky. It mocks her.

She blinks, tries to focus on Harry. She doesn't recall him moving closer.

Impermanence. A circle of time. It unravels slowly....

"Give it to me," he says.

Veronica tilts her head at him. Her gaze wanders away, back to the hills. Back to the stream of armored vehicles snaking their way down the narrow mountain road to the compound. North Enterprises has come back to claim their property. They will not claim hers.

I need him back.

Perhaps Benedict's breadcrumb trail was in her head after all. He never wanted anyone to find his and Peter Webber's work, because he knew it would spell chaos. He knew it would put Veronica in danger. *He wouldn't have wanted this.* It chokes her, the knowing. *He didn't want this at all. He'd never ask you to do this. He never intended to come home, and he never intended to be found.*

Did he think it would slow the unravelling, if he hid the notebook from her? She doesn't care anymore. She doesn't care what Benedict might have wanted.

Harry Markus stands before her. The vehicles creep closer. And deep in the building beneath her feet, Veronica feels evil things stirring from their sleep.

She pinches the pages in the front of the notebook. She tears them free.

She releases them into the wind.

Harry's eyes widen. He snatches at the papers. They're caught in the breeze, they are swift as birds. He lunges after them, hands reaching, clawing at the air.

Veronica tears across the rooftop.

She only makes it halfway to the exit before he slams into her. For a moment, she is airborne. She is a bird. Then her body smashes into a pole. The wind is knocked clean out of her lungs. She gasps like a fish on a hook. She struggles to sit up. *Get up. Get up, bitch. Stand up, freak.*

Harry Markus, teeth bared, face swimming in her vision, bends and wrenches the notebook from her arms. Two of the loose pages are crumpled in his fist.

No. In her chest, canary wings flutter. Feathers and fragile bones crash against her rib cage. No.

Harry Markus stumbles. Surprise flashes across his face.

Veronica rises to her feet. The wind tears at her hair. She imagines spreading her wings and being caught up into the sky.

He stumbles again. The panels and dishes on the rooftop rattle, but it's not from the wind. The roof is shaking. The building is shaking.

Veronica snatches the notebook from his grip. She drives her fist into his belly.

"Fuck!" She almost breaks her hand.

Harry Markus does not flinch. He grabs her wrist, pins her to the spot, grips the notebooks.

She snakes her ankle around the back of his calf and tries to yank his leg out from under him. He trips—the rooftop bucks beneath him—and he can't keep his feet—and he pulls Veronica down with him.

They both lose hold of the notebook at the same instant.

The cover flies open. Pages rip free, desperate for escape. They're caught in the furious rising wind, they somersault across the roof and scatter across the gray skyline.

No. She snatches at what remains of the notebook, grips it tight, pins it beneath her body. She curls around it. But Harry Markus is already back on his feet.

He lifts her like a rag doll. His eyes shine through the gathering clouds, the sudden darkness, apocalyptic in speed. He lifts her by her arm and slams her down again—she yells, she makes some pained animal sound as her back hits the roof and the air again empties from her lungs—but not hard enough to dislodge the notebook from her fingers; she clutches it to her chest, desperate to keep more pages from tearing free, desperate to keep it together.

Henry hears them coming. He feels the compound trembling around him, and he doesn't know what is causing it, but he knows it is not like the earlier explosion. This feels like an earthquake. If he's honest with himself, the quaking—the thunderous wind screaming through the mountains—the overlapping rise of horrible Mumbler voices—heralds something less indicative of natural disaster, and more of end-times.

He holds the wall to steady himself.

He will not find Harry in time. Not before the Mumblers climb to the surface. Not before BEESWAX descends or the building comes down.

Howard came back for him. His brothers came back. And here he is alone again, alone, alone in the darkness.

Darkness is the word that catches him.

Of course the lights are out. He's positive the Mumblers doused the lights within moments of taking the compound—they cannot abide the artificial electrical lights, nor daylight, nor anything that has been lost to their senses since their evolution in the terrible caverns they call home.

Henry pauses for a moment. He retraces his steps.

He knows where to find the electrical boxes; he's spent years learning the switches and wires that run this place. He passes through the entrance hall, holding his breath as he steps over the body and the growing stench of death. He presses through the doors and into the south entryway.

Night is creeping upon the mountains; the temperature has dropped. The wind howls in his ears. It rips through his hair, tears at his clothes. And it is the most beautiful wind Henry has felt in years—he feels something breaking loose inside himself—memories and fear and bile building in his throat.

He skirts the outside of the compound, he feels along the walls. He knows where he's going, his feet carry him surely, but his mind is lightweight and tumultuous as a leaf blowing in the wind—he gulps breaths of fresh air, he smells ozone, he senses something massive looming.

They are coming.

He finds the electrical boxes as the Mumblers break through from the basement. Inside the compound, they flow up the stairs like a plague of terrible insects.

Henry hears them. He waits for them to crash through the entryway doors and flood into the grounds. He steels himself; he waits to be overrun.

But the Mumblers bypass the ground floor.
They rush towards the rooftop.

When Harry Markus was young, he thought the worst thing to happen to him would be death. But he's learned that there are worse things: being picked apart by Mumblers, watching your home crumble and burn to the ground, the sick sense of helplessness as the people you love are brutally destroyed before your eyes.

"I need him back!" The scream shakes loose from Veronica's chest. She hugs the notebook to her body.

He can hardly breathe on the rooftop—the wind steals breath from his lungs, the growing dark presses against his back—and his vision swims with distorted images.

Kill her. Find your brothers. The list shrinks. The list is falling apart. *Kill her.*

And then what?

Something is coming. It's coming.

Veronica's eyes are black. The whites, the irises, all of it, black like the void. He blinks, or she blinks—or the world flickers, anyway—and they're back to normal. He smells smoke on the wind. The scent of charred flesh fills his nostrils. Bile fills his throat, a shiver crawls under his skin.

It's her. She's doing this. He takes a step back. "They can't have it," he says over the wind.

She laboriously climbs to her feet. She stumbles away from him. Blood trickles from the corner of her mouth. She reminds him of a hunted animal by the way she moves, slunk and wary, ready to pounce and scratch. Her lip curls. Her teeth are red.

He lost his gun. Where's his gun? He doesn't dare look away. He takes another step away from her. They're both stepping back.

"We'll destroy it," he says. *We?*

She laughs.

Oh, yes. He is afraid. He's making deals with the devil. He sees something powerful and nameless and he wants to destroy it, he wants it, he tastes the wind and he *wants it. This. The smoke, the storm, the fear, the fire.*

"We'll get rid of it. We'll get your father back. We'll destroy them."

She tilts her head. Her eyes are black again, and they do not go back to normal when she blinks, and Harry's jaw loosens. He gapes at her as she stands, a dark figure against a pewter sky—hair torn by the wind, the wind, the unnatural wind that did not exist in this world until Veronica Lewis appeared in his narrative. The wind she creates. And the notebook in her arms.

Her voice is calm, carried across the rooftop.

"I don't think I believe you," she says.

When Henry throws the switch and the power surges, overhead lights flash and flare throughout the North Enterprises compound. The Mumblers, nearly to the roof, stop and cower and hold their arms over their heads, trying in vain to block the brilliant light. It burns them to blindness. Their incessant song falters and turns to a low wail.

Henry hears it from his post outside, through the corridors and the windows and the walls. He feels the thrum of energy come alive under his fingertips. He knows it worked.

He doesn't know that it only worked halfway.

The Mumblers closest to the rooftop exit press forward through their blindness.

They know the name Markus, and they hate it. They know the girl has something valuable, and they want it.

They crash onto the roof.

The world is cloaked in sheets of stillness. It all slows around her—the wind gusting in curling tendrils, Harry Markus turning to the stairs, the door slamming open, the wave of Mumblers scrambling from the compound's depths.

There is a helicopter in the distance; she hears it. There are men in armored vehicles along the mountainside. There are monsters lunging across the rooftop, there are cold, lifeless hands grasping for her, there's a taste like metal in the wind.

So slow, yet it still seems too fast. It's too much.

Benedict. With his quiet eyes and his scratchy handwriting, his smell of smoke and evergreen, hikes into the mountains and nights charting the galaxies.

Stargazing. That's what they'd called it.

The world is dark to Veronica now. She's fallen into some deeper version of herself. She is not a bird, not a girl—her arms hug her father's words, but feathers prick through her flesh and wings tug at her shoulder blades. A nightmarish hybrid. A freak. Her heart is a staccato drumbeat in her ears.

The pale boy is there, war-torn and scarred. He stands and blocks Harry Markus. She does not hear the wind. The world slows to stillness. Time means nothing.

"Veronica," says Grant. "Do you trust me?"

He smiles. His silver eyes are bright in the everlasting darkness of the labyrinth. She could drown in his eyes.

He holds his hand out to her.

She looks at it. She doesn't want to let go of the notebook. She can't. She holds the words, she holds Ben, she holds the last scraps of herself.

"What will I see?" she whispers.

But she holds out her hand, and his cold fingers drape along her wrist.

He tugs her into the shadows, into the deepest part of her labyrinth, where white lightning cracks the shell of creation.

"Everything," he says.

The electrical surge dies with a crack. Black clouds douse the sunset and turn the world to night.

The BEESWAX teams on the grounds far below tilt back their faces to the sky. They watch lightning strike the compound.

The rooftop buckles and bends. The Mumblers are sent hurtling along the ledge. They are pinned to the concrete as the building slowly crumbles in upon itself.

The wind screams. Cracking concrete thunders in Harry's skull. Veronica Lewis is standing still in the chaos, unaffected by the wind, unaware of the roof collapsing beneath their feet. Her eyes are wholly black.

Harry makes a choice.

As the North Enterprises compound caves from the top down, he dives towards Veronica, wraps his arm around her waist—smells ozone, smoke, ash—and hurdles the buckling concrete slabs rising up and overturning around them. He stands on the edge of the roof and looks into the abyss, and weighs his odds of survival, and realizes that they've never been so good after all.

He leaps.

36

There is darkness. And darkness. And nothing.
 The impact never comes. He does not know who he is, or what he is. But he does not think that he should be alive.
 He's in a crypt. He's lost in a maze. Fear and despair wrestle for a chokehold in his throat. He's weightless. His bones ache to shatter. He lungs stretch into the shape of a scream. He spins in a circle and waits for the world to materialize, for the darkness to lift, for reality to become concrete and make sense and stop unwinding in his fingers.
 He does not belong here.
 Veronica is no longer in his arms. She stands beside him.
 I should have killed you, he thinks, desperately, furiously. But he understands power and he understands rage, and he knows the darkness in her eyes, the darkness that surrounds them both. When a day of reckoning comes and he destroys every last trace of his enemies, he will need her. He does not need anyone. But he needs *her.*
 He finds stillness.
 She points to something above his head. He looks up.

The nothingness is split into spiderweb cracks of...everything.

All Veronica knows is that she is falling. And then she is not. And Harry Markus is standing in her labyrinth like a wolf in a baby's nursery, like a storm unleashed in a peaceful space.

And then he is gone. And she is gone.

And there's just a canary with wings fluttering against the darkness, singing, singing, its voice shrill and desperate in the eternal silence. Fear and fear and anticipation build in its chest, its small chest, its golden breast, its aching lungs—

Until a pale boy catches it in his fingers. He cups its body in his hands. He presses his lips to its head, and its heartbeat slows.

"I told you I wouldn't lose you," he says.

She's alone again in the darkness. She's alone. And all she can think about is how awfully, terribly silent her labyrinth has become.

37

Howard finds them. He doesn't understand how they are alive, but for the moment he doesn't care.

He found the hangar, and he found a helicopter, and then he found Henry right before BEESWAX descended into the valley.

He has his brother hold the chopper low and steady while he climbs down the swaying ladder, drops the last few feet to the ground, shakes his brother's shoulder and rouses Harry from his stupor.

The world is powdered in dust and sediment. The complex is still crumbling. Neither of them has time to ask questions. Harry's eyes are glazed, confused. Still, he stands and drags Veronica Lewis' body over his shoulder. He spins in a circle, scans the ground.

"The notebook," he says. "The notebook."

They don't have time to search.

Howard climbs up ahead of his brother and helps reel up the ladder. The wind has died. Harry hooks an arm over the side of the chopper and heaves Veronica Lewis off his shoulder, dumps her on the floor. Howard lifts him in, and Harry rolls clear of the door.

Howard seals it. He scrambles back into the pilot's seat and takes control from Henry.

The back of the helicopter is a holding area for crates, with a bench that unfolds for extra passengers. Harry doesn't bother getting up; his head lolls against the back wall. He absorbs the pulse of the chopper until the sound has drilled too deeply into his skull and his head throbs, then he finds hearing protection. He doesn't really want to touch Veronica Lewis, so he just throws his trench coat over her head.

He should be dead. They should both be dead. There is a fissure in the universe, and he has seen it, and he wishes he hadn't.

He opens his eyes and stares at the front seat. "Hello, Henry. Glad you're alive."

"Oh, are you?" Henry's voice is dull through the speaker. He doesn't turn around. "Wouldn't have known. From the way you brutally abandoned us."

"*I* abandoned you," Howard murmurs. And, louder: "I'm sorry, Harry, I didn't know what to do—when the Mumblers showed up I wanted to get Henry out and go find you, but I couldn't find him in time, and I thought—"

Harry is already exhausted. "You did fine."

Henry leans over to the pilot's seat. "You don't need his approval. Harry's already a self-important ass."

Harry stretches his legs, feet flat against the backs of their seats. "We're all alive. Don't be dramatic, Henry."

Henry swivels and finally faces Harry, although it makes no difference—his eyes are shut, he cannot see, he'll never see again. He just wants Harry to see his face. His skin is streaked with blood and sweat. There's an open wound at his temple. "Oh, I'm sorry. I forgot feelings only matter when they're your own."

"It wasn't a feeling," says Howard, "it was just kind of mean, Henry. Would you both calm down? Just...sit down. We're all alive, alright? It's going to be fine. No one should have left anyone, but that's all behind us now."

"Is it? Or is Harry going to leap out of the helicopter and run off on some insane hero mission?"

"That's rich—"

"Stop!" Howard slams his palm on the console, and the

helicopter wavers, forcing a silence in the cabin. He takes a deep breath. "Stop. Not right now. You can duel or whatever later. Let me concentrate on getting us out of here."

He doesn't need silence to concentrate. They all know that. But they do not argue, and Henry settles back in his seat, and Harry sinks down and presses his shoulder blades against the floor and tries to ground his mind. But every time he closes his eyes, he sees a seam of white light streaking across his vision. He doesn't know if it will ever go away.

She knows.

He should have killed her. He still could. He won't.

38

Veronica opens her eyes. Her mind is quiet. She reaches a hand into the darkness, but Grant does not reach back.

Then she feels the vibrations. And the thrumming. And there's something on her head. She sits up and kicks it off. She's in the back of a helicopter.

Harry Markus is sprawled on the floor nearby. He looks like shit. He holds out a headset without looking at her. She snatches it and kicks the trench coat away, scoots to the opposite end of the chopper. She glares at him, and Howard, and whoever the third guy is sitting in front, glares as she puts on the hearing protection, adjusts the microphone, and says, "I'll kill all of you."

Howard jerks in his seat. "Harry! You didn't say she was awake."

"I'll fuck ya'll up," Veronica says, finding comfort in the threats. "You know I can."

"I could have left you to die," says Harry, apparently unimpressed, "but I didn't."

"Well, that was *your* mistake."

"Please settle down," says Howard, "please."

She looks at Harry. There's something wary in his gaze, aside from the usual distaste. "Where is it?" she says.

"Gone."

"I bet you're real happy about that." She can't bring herself to feel anything other than mild disgust.

His face says, *do I look happy?* "I said *gone*, Lewis. I didn't say destroyed. I'd rather it was destroyed."

"You shouldn't have taken it. It wasn't yours." It sounds stupid coming out of her mouth, but she can't hold back the words any longer. She wants to be petty. She deserves a bit of pettiness.

Harry shrugs, glances towards the front seat of the chopper. "You fell asleep."

"Well, I've got to sleep sometime. What, was I supposed to stay awake all the time so you couldn't stab me in the back? Maybe ya'll don't have to sleep, because you're fucking *aliens*, but I'm getting real tired of this game where we try to get each other killed and have to track one another across the country, and then we're taking each other's stuff and pretending *we* killed the Mumblers in Tulsa, as if that was all *us.*"

"I assume she's talking about Harry," says Henry. "I don't even know who she is. It's just, that all sounds like something Harry would do."

Howard shifts in his seat. Harry casts a brief glare towards the back of Henry's head. "You had your father to save," he says. "I have my brothers. Your cause isn't noble, it's just in your own self-interest."

"So is yours," she says.

"I know. And," he adds, somewhat agitated, "I wasn't *trying* anything. If I wanted to kill you, you'd be killed."

"Fucking hell," says Henry.

"Bullshit," says Veronica.

"Please." Howard's voice is strained. "I'll put down soon and you can fight about it then. But for now no one is killing anyone just yet. Please shut up, all of you. Just wait."

Veronica does shut up, but not because he told her to. She curls her legs up to her chest and pins them there, narrows her eyes and glares across at Harry Markus, who glares back until he remembers to be cool and distant, at which point he reclines against the door and shuts his eyes. They're both covered with chalk and dust. The inside of her mouth is coated with the distinctive tang of blood and bile.

She thinks Harry Markus saved her in some way, but she doesn't quite recall how, and she hesitates to feel indebted to him. She had something to do with the saving as well. The longer she lingers on the memory, the more sure she becomes that he's seen something he shouldn't have, that he somehow violated her inner sanctum. Didn't he? Didn't she see him there? Like something that didn't belong. *Like a wolf in a nursery.*

What have I done? She shuts her eyes and wills the pale boy into existence. *Come on. Come back to me.*

But Grant does not respond. The quiet is frightening. She grips her legs tighter, but her fingers ache for the notebook, the notebook with its pages fluttering like insect wings in a storm, the notebook that smells of her father and has his hand scrawled across its graphite-smeared pages.

"*There would be a spell of silence.*" That's what Benedict said. Or someone had said it, anyway.

"*Before what?*"

"*Before it falls apart.*"

Howard puts down in a field in the middle of nowhere. No city lights are visible beyond the acres of waist-high grass, no cars on the distant winding stretch of highway barely perceptible from the air. Harry takes a duffel bag of supplies from the back of the helicopter. Howard kills the lights.

As the blades slow and the synthetic wind dies, silence claims a hold on the scene and persists for the next while as they hike soundlessly through the fields. The grass eventually gives way to some crunchy cover crop which then gives way to mud, and then to moss and soft underbrush as they skirt the edge of a wood.

It finally occurs to Veronica that these three likely have stamina she does not possess, and they might be walking all night. "Where are we even going?"

Her voice startles Henry, who walks closest to her. She can't make out his features in the dark, but he's somewhat taller and slimmer than the other two. "Wherever Harry fancies taking us, I suppose," he murmurs.

"Like hell. Markus! Where are we going?"

"Lewis," Harry returns, without slowing his pace or looking back. "We're going to find your father."

She stops. The others do not. She follows slowly behind Henry and watches the shape of Harry's trench-coated back up ahead. *What is he up to?* "Why?" she says.

"Because while they have him, they have all the knowledge they want. They just haven't tapped into it yet."

She squints. *They don't have everything. They don't have me.* The idea of becoming a potential bartering piece doesn't feel as special as she might have thought. "You know where he is?"

"If they took him where they put all their prisoners, he's at ARC."

Veronica simmers and waits, but Harry refuses to elaborate.

"Aeacus Retention Center," Howard says at last. "ARC. It's where they put all the…troublemakers."

"Hmm." Veronica's fingers want to curl into fists, but she forces her knuckles to loosen, soothes her rage into a dangerous sense of calm–a glassy sea hiding innumerable horrors of the deep. "You knew he was there the whole time."

The air smells charred. The underbrush turns brittle, twigs snapping underfoot. There was a controlled burn through here. Veronica has always wondered at the overwhelming hubris of mankind to think they can control a wildfire.

"In my place, would you have told me?" Harry says.

She wouldn't. "Maybe," she says. "But why do you want to get him out *now*? What's changed?"

"Forcing him to talk will be their only option now. They'll get it out of him, eventually. I don't want to wait for that to happen."

She considers asking how they'll make Ben talk, but ultimately decides against it. "And then?" she says.

"We get him out," says Harry, like it's simple. *He's making lists. He's simplifying everything so he can cope.* "Then we take down the X-System"

"Harry," says Howard.

"What's the X-System?" says Veronica.

"ARC," says Howard. "North Enterprises. BEESWAX. Possibly

some others we don't even know about yet. Everything. It's all under the X-System. And Harry is being—sorry, Harry, that's insane. Have you been to ARC? It'll be hard enough getting someone out of there, where would we even start trying to *destroy* the entire system?"

"If they're onto Peter Webber and Benedict Lewis, that means they're onto us. With the Mumblers now involved, it's only a matter of time before they…" He hesitates.

"Oh, go on, Harry," says Veronica. "Who am I gonna tell? I don't have any friends."

Her tone is condescending enough that he holds the silence for another moment before continuing. "We can't let them find the way home."

There's a dilapidated barn on the edge of the wood, half overtaken with grass, a tree climbing in through the back end. The ceiling is partly caved from water damage and wood termites. Harry finally produces a flashlight from the duffel bag and checks the interior while the others wait outside.

If it's still in use, the barn's purpose is evidently to house disused equipment and moldering hay bales. The floor sports a thick coat of dust that shows no signs of disturbance. Birds rustle in the hayloft and tumble out the window in panic at the first sign of intruders.

A breeze wraps around the barn and squeezes. Timbers groan.

Veronica kicks around a pile of moldering hay to check for snakes before lowering herself–gently, sorely–to her butt. She stretches her legs on the dirt floor. She thinks of all the times she took hot showers for granted as she watches Howard wander around the edges of the barn. He kneels in the center of the floor and builds a small tower of kindling with dry bits of straw at the base. He glances over to where Harry dropped the duffel bag. "Is there a lighter in there?"

Harry crouches beside the duffel bag and rummages around with the flashlight. He tosses something underhand across the barn and Howard snatches it out of the air. A few seconds later, a flame snaps and flickers.

Harry glances over to where Henry stands by the barn doors.

"Sit down," he says. His voice low. "I'll fix your face."

"Right," Henry drawls. "Because you fix everything, right, Harry?"

"Henry, for once, can you just—"

"I don't need you to—"

"What, you're going to do it yourself?"

"I might."

The straw catches. Howard's eyes flick to his brothers.

She doesn't understand the caution in his gaze; she can't unravel the dynamic between Harry and Henry as the younger of the two finally relents and perches on the edge of a hay bale, and Harry holds his brother at literal arm's length to tend to his face. But she finds it vaguely fascinating.

Howard meets her gaze. She watches his shields go up. "What?" he says.

There's a screech from the hayloft. Veronica's heart leaps into her throat and Howard jolts.

Harry's flashlight beam snaps to the ceiling. A stupid ugly chicken-looking head peers down from the loft. Veronica utters a breathless *"fuck"*. "They're guineas."

"Sorry?"

His politeness makes her more uncomfortable than Harry's overwhelming stupidity. "Guinea hens. The birds."

"Oh. I thought they were chickens."

"They're not. They're guineas."

Veronica moves closer to the fire and pulls off her boots. Her heels are bloody and raw, and apparently she twisted her ankle at some point; it's bruised in spectacular shades of blue and green. Howard catches a guinea and snaps its neck. He cleans the bird with startling speed and efficiency before spitting it over the fire.

A cold breeze slips in through the barn doors and calms the heat in Veronica's skin. She picks the blood out from her fingernails, examines the ugly bruising on her knuckles by the light of the fire. *We're going to find Dad. We're going to get him out.* It sounds too good to be true, too clean-cut for this crew. She can't beat the suspicion that Harry has some vindictive purpose in store for her.

If Grant were here, he'd chastise her. He'd say something like "Since when have you gone around just killing people for the sheer convenience?" And she'd say something witty like "Fuck off, Grant." And he'd click his tongue and say she'd better be careful, she doesn't understand what she's getting herself into, *remember January, remember you aren't immortal and your actions have consequences.*

She turns over her hands and inspects her calloused palms. Her breath catches in her throat.

Her veins are dark. Too dark. They're black, tracing spiderwebs under the fleshy skin of her palms, fading past her wrists. Veronica quickly sits on her hands and blinks away the image. Panic surges in her chest.

She can't deal with this right now, whatever *this* is. She feels dirty. She wants to peel off her skin. She wants to take Grant's hand and descend into her labyrinth where there are no thoughts, only fluttering wings and smoke and screams, pressing dark, wandering feet.

Harry is gone. Henry joins Howard at the fireside and warms his hands. Underlit, his face is gaunt. He's narrower than his brothers, and there's something vaguely elegant in the lines of his nose and cheekbones, the length of his fingers, like a concert pianist poised to perform. His brows are high and arching. His hair curls just below his ears. If he weren't a Markus, he might be beautiful.

Veronica stands and wanders over to the barn doors, where the heat from the fire cannot reach her.

She's numb again. She'd like to summon wind and blow herself away, but it doesn't work like that, and she doesn't think she can really control whatever it is that causes the wind and quaking and flashing lights. She's a vessel for something she doesn't understand. She's a loaded gun.

The moon has emerged, just a sliver in the sky. The stars are gappy behind clouds. Way in the distance she thinks she can make out a road, a tiny speck of light from a moving vehicle inching along as a snail's pace.

Harry Markus leans against the side of the barn, arms crossed. His trench coat sways around his legs; his collar is popped against the chill. His silhouette is a mask.

"I saw you," he says. He glances at her. "I saw it."

It's hollowness or desperation or resignation in his voice, she cannot tell which, but Veronica recognizes all three; it's this frustrating trio of emotions and a healthy dose of fury she wrestles with on a daily basis, a lethal cocktail. She settles herself in the grass a ways off, presses her back against the warped barn panels. Splinters rub her neck. The old wood groans. "Oh. That."

"Is it real?"

She doesn't like being observed. She shrugs. "Of course. How do you think you got here?" The question lingers. "How *did* you get here?"

He tilts back his face to the sky, stretches his neck. The silence pans out. For a moment she thinks he might not answer. "Mumbler ship. They attacked our home. We snuck back on one of their ships."

"They visited your alien planet and you decided to fly off into space with them?"

His brow furrows, and he's his old condescending self again. "You can't understand."

"No, I guess not. I'm too logical and grounded in reality. I have a scientific mind." Within the pocket of the hoodie, she slides her hands into her sleeves. She imagines she can feel something dark trickling through her veins. Does he have X-Ray vision? Can he see in the dark? Does he have, perhaps, hidden antennae or a tail? "What's it like? Your planet?"

"It…" Harry clears his throat. "It's. Uh. Cold. Dark, most of the time; the nights are long. It storms in the mountains and—in the city, there is wind. Like the wind on the rooftop." His voice drops as if, if he's quiet, she won't hear the emotion in his voice, the longing. "There are two moons. One is red."

"Always?"

"Yes."

"I don't think that's possible." Harry Markus stares at her. She smiles. "The Mumblers know how to get to your alien planet. Why aren't you more concerned about *that*?"

"They can't get back."

"Why not?"

"Howard and I…in your own words, we *fucked them up*. Quite seriously." She wishes he'd look away. "When we arrived, it was to their caverns in the north. We inflicted some damage on our way out. I believe we incapacitated their ability to locate our home or launch any further expeditions in the future."

Veronica wonders, if she holds his gaze long enough, whether he'll look away. Like a cat, unnerved by her audacity. "Did you make things go boom?" she says.

He blinks. He looks away. "I suppose we did."

"Why did you jump?" she says.

Harry thinks on it. "I thought it was better than being buried alive."

"Why did you jump with *me?*"

"Are you complaining?"

"I'm not gonna thank you. I was the one who saved us, after all."

"I guess that answers your question. We both want to get Benedict Lewis out of ARC. We both want the X-System destroyed."

"I can't control it," she says.

"What is it?"

"Oh, wouldn't I like to know, Space Boy." She pauses, feeling she's overstepped, then decides that she doesn't care. "But I don't understand how it works. I can't control it. I'm not a weapon."

"Well," says Harry. "Maybe you should work on that."

Voices drift through the walls of the barn, the low current of murmured conversation around the fire. Does it bother the other two brothers that Harry seems to be in charge? How was the hierarchy decided? And is sibling loyalty really unconditional? Veronica would follow Benedict Lewis to the gates of Hell. In a way, she already has. And—a chill settles over her, a deep ache in her chest—like Orpheus glancing behind for Eurydice, she found, in the end, that she stood alone. What did Ben ever want? For her to sit like a duck in a pond, floating stupidly, waiting for the hunters to return? Her lungs squeeze. What will she say to him? She's always known love to be conditional. And just now she's not so sure she's ever known love.

"Are you going to apologize for stealing the notebook and trying to kill me?" she says at last.

Harry snorts. "No. Are you sorry for nearly handing over your father's research and endangering all our lives?"

Veronica smiles. "No." She digs in her fingers, finds some

leverage, and shoots her shot. "You don't tell anyone what's going on with me, I won't tell anyone ya'll are extraterrestrials. Neither of us gets thrown in a lab and vivisected."

Harry Markus looks to the sky again. "I'll think about it."

"Is there really anything to think about? No vivisection sounds good to me."

"A deal requires trust," says Harry.

"No," says Veronica, "we have an even playing field. It's all strategy. This has nothing to do with trust."

Later in the night, they sit awkwardly around the fire and rip apart tough guinea. Henry eats like someone who hasn't seen food in a week. The brothers hardly speak, but Veronica watches Harry and Howard communicate with their eyes. She senses that an entire unspoken conversation is taking place.

She drops a bone into the fire, watches the gristle pop and hiss. "Where's ARC?" Howard glances at Harry, as if waiting for permission.

Harry wipes his hands on his trousers. He doesn't look at her when he speaks. "East coast."

"That's all you got?"

"Maine," says Howard. "I think it's Maine."

"Maine's pretty small," says Veronica. "How do they hide a secret prison in New England?"

Harry shakes his head. "It's underwater. Off the coast. They have an underground compound with a disguised entry point. I've been there before, Cage wanted an escort for a prisoner."

"How do we get in?" The barn door rattles in the wind. Veronica crosses her arms and sinks back into the hay.

"I tapped into their radios," says Howard, "a couple days ago. All the North Enterprises staff are being housed at ARC, so the place is in chaos right now. We can probably get in disguised as refugees."

"We'll have to avoid X," says Harry.

"Oh. No, you won't." Howard clears his throat. "He's dead."

"Dead." Harry raises his eyebrows, and a ghost of a smile touches his lips. "Really."

"The old guy?" Veronica looks between Howard and Harry.

"The guy from the funeral?"

Harry nods. "He worked for North Enterprises for years. Neither Cage nor Billings liked him much."

"Andre Billings?" Howard says. "The BEESWAX guy?"

"Yeah." Harry turns a bone over in his fingers. "He was with X on the mission I sabotaged. BEESWAX and North Enterprises working together—although I'd hardly call it cooperation, what I witnessed between the two of them. If you hadn't killed him, Howard, I reckon Billings might have."

"I don't care for Billings," says Howard, carefully. "I don't care for the idea of BEESWAX, either."

"Why not?" says Veronica. "Ominous acronymed societies don't fill you with happy feelings?"

Howard gazes across the fire at her, troubled. After a moment he continues. "I've just...heard things. That's all. People talk about what goes on at BEESWAX. They call them the 'freaks'. The BEESWAX Freaks. And they're not talking about the people who run the place."

39

Benedict thinks they were drugging him before.

In the shuffle from cell to cell, they've left any IVs and lab equipment far behind. He goes from a room the size of a closet, to a space the size of his lab, which he shares with two drowsing men in hospital gowns; all three of them are left on the floor with hands shackled in front, a bin of piss in one corner and a bin of questionable drinking water opposite.

By the third move, the drugs have worn out of Ben's system. For the first time in weeks, his head is clear. He remembers where he was when they took him: on a steep bit of road coming down from the East End in Dane's Chapel. Hands in the dark, quick and quiet. He was returning home from the lab, where he had sat in silence and done nothing but wait. It was a waiting game, those final days. People always say there are restless spirits and wandering things in the Appalachians, and Benedict believes he might be one of them—sitting in the dead of night with the wind caressing the walls of the ancient RV, moonlight painting weird white shadows across the floor, moans and hisses from the woods that might come from trees and breeze and nocturnal animals, and perhaps from something else.

He was gone so often, those last few nights. He hadn't wanted to be in the West End when it happened; he didn't want Veronica there. He didn't want them to see her and he didn't want her to see. But now he thinks about the long nights he spent sitting alone in the hills, and he thinks that she must have spent similar nights sitting alone in their home in the West End doing God-knows-what. He wishes, during the waiting, that he'd been able to do it with her. And he's fairly certain that he is a terrible person and a worse father.

He never asks himself if it's worth it; he isn't intelligent enough to foresee all the possible outcomes and gauge their value. When the drugs ooze into his system, he wishes he were dead. When his head is clear, he'd do anything to not die.

When he hears the key in the lock and the footsteps coming close, Ben slows his breath. He shuts his eyes. He feels the thud of their boots through his cheekbone as they approach.

"We can't keep doing this," says one man.

"Told you we'll be putting more under soon. They'll clean out the cryochambers soon enough. Stuff this place full again and repeat. It's how it goes."

"It's never been like this. Too many."

They take Ben under his arms and heave him off the floor. He hangs between them; his legs drag as they pull him into the hall. His head lolls forward. The other men in the cell do not stir.

"The North Enterprises guys will be gone soon enough," says the first. He shifts his grip on Ben to lock the cell door. "Gone and we'll have more space. Don't know why we don't just hold out a bit longer instead of…all this."

"Where are they going?"

"Heard they're being relocated to that empty facility in Canada."

"The abandoned one?"

"Yeah."

"Wasn't there a reason why they cleared everyone out? I remember–"

"I don't know why they shut it down. But it's open again. Cage better hope everyone stays on after what's happened, that would be my biggest worry."

"I don't even really know what's happened."

"Yeah, me neither. You hear what they're saying upstairs? *Monsters*. Aliens. Tell me why *aliens* is easier to believe than *monsters*, huh? They're bringing them here. Cadavers and the living and all. I say, leave that shit for BEESWAX. We're not a burial ground, we're not a biohazard lab to pick apart monster carcasses."

"I don't like that. Don't like that they're bringing those things here. Feels like spreading a virus, doesn't it? Like what happened to North Enterprises might happen here."

"Halleck won't allow that."

"You trust Halleck?"

"I trust Halleck when Andre Billings is in the house. He's got too much riding on him just now to slip up. All eyes on ARC."

Ben's eyes flutter open a crack. A paved concrete floor and cinderblock walls slide past. The legs to his right are gray-clad and thick with muscle. There's a keyring clipped to his belt and a gun strapped to his side.

He forces a retch. The groan comes from his belly, cracked and wheezing.

The steps halt. "Oh, no."

Ben twitches and becomes a deadweight.

"Oh, God." They lower him to his belly. His cheek presses into the cold floor. The thicker one bends over him and peels back Ben's fluttering eyelids. "Aww, man. I think he's dying."

"He can't die. They don't want him to die."

"Yeah, yeah. I know. Where's James?"

"Oh, he's way up top, I think."

"Well, go get him!"

"Radio him. Just radio."

"The radios don't work down here. Just go get James. Now. And a medic. Hurry!"

The thin man takes off running.

Come on, Benedict. He digs deep. He clenches his abdomen and forces another retch—pees down his leg—*dammit*—and then the bile comes. He gags. He can't remember the last time he ate, his stomach has nothing to empty but water. *This is a bad idea. Bad idea. Bad idea.*

"Fuck. God*dammit*." The guard heaves him up, drapes Ben's

limp body over his knee so he doesn't choke on his own vomit.

He has one crack at this. One. He lets the bile drain out of his throat, coughs with a cracking chest.

He lurches upright. His elbow smashes into the guard's nose. "Fuck!"

Something crunches. Something bleeds. The man's head snaps back. He wheels backwards.

Ben loses his balance and falls on his stomach. He gasps for air, throws himself forward, crawls towards the guard.

The man covers his face. He rolls to his side. He props himself up on one arm. "Fuck!" His voice is thick.

Ben throws his shackled arms around the man's neck. He slides behind him. He hooks his forearm under the guard's chin and crushes it close to his chest, pins it there. He won't let go until one of them is dead. He won't let go. His vision is red and swarming black dots. His ears, his skull, it's blood and gasps and a high-pitched buzz that won't quit.

The guard bucks against him. A gurgle crawls up his throat. He attempts to stand and falls instead to his knees. He reaches around and grabs at Ben, who ducks his head. The guard finds a fistful of Ben's hair and he yanks.

The hair comes out. There is blood. Ben does not let go.

The guard scrabbles at his throat, tries to stand again, and collapses onto his elbows this time.

Ben does not loosen his hold until the man twitches and is still. He still doesn't let go. He holds him there against the floor, arms shaking, muscles spasming.

The man's body relaxes. He deflates. He is still.

Ben holds him for a moment more. He releases. He finds his feet.

The corridor spins. *What's the plan?* He doesn't have one. He's taking this a step at a time. His hands don't feel like his hands. His body is disjointed, random pieces and part, defective and unsteady. *What's the next step?*

The doors along the corridor are of steel frames and fogged glass panes. Ahead, the hall fades into the distance in a haze of fluorescence and dust motes drifting from ventilation ducts. The way back to his cell is intermittently blocked by sealed doors. He seems to recall a freight elevator, some days ago. How long will it take the second guard to make it through, find a medic, and return?

Ben takes a deep breath. He unclips the man's keyring from his belt. He wrestles with his shackles and, when freed, stuffs them into the man's pocket.

He drags the dead guard down the hall. He's panting by the time he reaches the nearest door. He extends the man's keycard from his belt and swipes it. He drags the guard over the threshold and pulls the door shut behind them.

The room is frigid. Conditioned air billows across the floor. The overhead lights cast a strange blue tint, painting his hands ghostly white. Ben drops the man just inside the doorway.

The chamber is long and high-ceilinged; it curves out of sight past the rows of equipment. Cords and tubing snake along the walls, down to ventilators and flickering machines plugged into the coffins.

Not coffins. Ben knows what they are. This is the cryochamber. Both walls are lined with fogged caskets, their toes pointed out towards the narrow walkway between, like some army infirmary from a science fiction nightmare.

Ben's mouth is dry. He shivers in the thin gown. He steadies himself against the wall, fills his lungs with freezing, sterile, manufactured air. Then he undresses the dead man.

He leaves the gown tossed over the body and pulls on the guard's clothes, which are too big yet somehow preferable to a paper dress. He pulls down the gray cap over his bleeding scalp. The boots pinch his toes, but he can barely feel his feet anyway.

He holsters the gun, pockets the keys and card, and drags the body behind a bank of equipment.

Ben stands and gazes down the chamber. He steps towards the nearest casket. He can't tell whether the glass is fogged from vapor trapped inside, or to obscure what lies within. A strip of tape near the bottom of the curved lid reads *Adhya, Anil.* He continues to the next one, and then the next. *Amberley, Aprils, Awan.* And more.

He isn't walking anymore—he's jogging along the silent hall, his breath loud, his footfalls uneven. *Declan, Duoreske, Eaton, Ester....*

He comes to the curve in the hall. He slows, but does not stop. The corridor grows darker as he leaves the entrance far behind; the lights dim to a dark blue, energy-saving, because who needs light in here anyway? Who is there to see? And who visits the long-forgotten dead?

Not dead. Sleeping. Decades of people too valuable to kill, to dangerous to leave on their own. *Like me.* And then: *Like Veronica.*

Vabe, Veyatte, Waddaford...

Ben stops. He feels frozen in place, standing at the foot of this casket, cast half in eerie blue shadow. A forbidden secret tucked far away from the world, as if everyone might forget. As if Ben would ever forget. The tape is old and faded, but the name is still legible.

Webber, Peter.

"Hawk. It's Billings."

Andre adjusts the radio settings and rests his elbows on the desk. He leans forward, turns away from Cage, who sits in the corner of the room with a headset and a pallid complexion.

Adrien Hawk's voice cuts through the static: brusque, robotic. "We've secured the property. Secured the survivors. A dozen sedated, twice as many in what Keeling perceives to be critical condition. Hundreds dead."

Reliably, painfully professional. Andre appreciates that about him, though oftentimes it feels like a competition: which of them will exhibit signs of humanity first? "And X?"

"No sign yet. We're still sorting through the rubble. On site, with this level of destruction, his survival is unlikely. I won't make an official report yet. But he's dead."

Billings glances up at Cage, who is visibly aghast at the news, as if he can't process the idea of his own people dying in response to his poor decisions and lack of action. Billings really hopes they get rid of Cage in a satisfying manner. But also, justly. Justice is important. "I have Lawrence Cage here. Give him the brief."

Hawk rattles it off like he's numb to the event already. So admirably disconnected. "Seismic reports haven't come in yet, but the first team that arrived in the vicinity of the North Enterprises compound witnessed earthquake activity of considerable magnitude. The surrounding hills and forest are clear of damage aside from a section in the south, where there appears to have been a detonation of some kind. There's nothing there. I have forensics looking into it. Any other evidence is buried beneath fifty-thousand tons of concrete."

"Fifty...?" Cage's face twitches. Billings has never had less respect for the man.

"The compound evidently imploded," says Billings.

"It *what?*"

"Who is that? Is that Cage? Tell him his border security is abysmal. Tell him to do better with the next one."

They both know there won't be a "next one". Cage end up in one of those ARC cryochambers downstairs if he doesn't play his cards right with Westmore.

"And the team?" says Billings.

"Competent. Messy. Somewhat underwhelming. If I were an optimist, I'd say there's a grain of potential. I'll issue a full report when I return to headquarters. We've just done a headcount and we're about to ship them back to the facility, but I'm staying in the field for a bit longer. Westmore is sending in a team to clean up and cover the site."

"Halleck has received the first wave," says Billings. "We're struggling to secure everyone here. Running out of space. We need to get the North Enterprises staff out of here."

"I'll talk to Jorgen, see if he wants some cadavers for his lab. Poke around in there."

"They're ugly," says Billings.

"Yes, they are. I have a channel open to Westmore, I'll see if we can get Cage's people out of ARC. I think you should come out here, Andre. If you make it out before noon, Westmore's people won't be here yet to tear it all down. There are some things you might want to take a look at. Some items we found."

"I'll see if I can get away," says Billings. "Once Halleck's people have everything secured—"

The office door crashes open and slams against the wall. Cage reels back in his chair. Billings is halfway out of his seat.

Halleck stands in the doorway, eyes wide. "Sorry! Sorry. Is that Hawk? Tell him they found him, the Raccoon. The Raccoon found them."

Billings settles. He can only handle so much more of his supposed peers' hysterics. "Take a breath." He nods at the chair beside Cage. "Sit."

Halleck perches on the edge of the seat. He grips his knees. He does take a breath—several breaths—until his words come out slow enough so as to be discernible. "It's...the Raccoon. He found them."

Adrien Hawk switches off the radio and crosses his arms.

He surveys the carnage: a sea of jagged beams and concrete cliffs, failed supports and cavernous mouths peering into the layers of basement hiding beneath what was once North Enterprises. The air is still thick with settling chalk, and each breeze twisting through the mountains and black-rattling trees only spreads the dust farther. There will be one hell of a cleanup in store for Westmore's people.

The floodlights on the BEESWAX vehicles and tents turn the valley into a giant crime scene. Or a midnight carnival. In some ways, he supposes, it's a bit of both.

Hawk rests his hands in his pockets. He walks the perimeter of the grounds, through the scurrying recovery crew, the soldiers hunting through mountains of stone and drywall for any lingering survivors. He walks in and out of the shouts and babbling voices, walks until he reaches the outer corner of the floodlights' reach, and the sounds of the . He stops beside a demolished shack—maintenance supplies or a guard's post, he can no longer be sure—and watches a red-haired man with a clipboard approach from the ruined structure.

Newt extends the clipboard. "They found more caught up in the fence."

Over the man's shoulder, Hawk takes in the compound in its enormity, the flashlights clambering across its crevices like sharks circling a shipwreck. There's a sick sense of satisfaction in something so hubristic and manmade brought low. "Billings is coming. He'll want to see as much of this as we can salvage. Keep the search going until we're forced to clear out."

"Yessir."

"Tell Circe to round up a team and get on Halleck's channel. He has coordinates for her. I want Delta Squadron with the exception of Brianna Kelly, I want them off the ground within the hour."

When Newt retreats to the tents, Hawk stays in the shadows. In the deep stillness of the valley he thinks again of underwater beasts circling. He thinks of a whale fall. It hits him over and over again these days: none of them are ready for this. It's too big and it's happening too quickly and there are days he feels that himself and Billings are the only people in charge who really understand the gravity of what they're trying to accomplish. Throwing Westmore into the mix, that's three. That is simply too few.

Hawk stays in the shadows. He pages through the clipboard's contents, page after burnt and torn and smeared page. At the bottom of the clipboard is a single piece of charred black leather—a notebook cover, worn by time and disaster.

40

Veronica only dreams when she's half-asleep—turbulent dreams, rapid and bizarre—dreams like falling and dying and drowning. Dreams where she scares herself awake. And when she bolts upright in bed and kicks off her sheets and feels the tickle of sweat break on her skin, Grant is always there. He sits and stares. He holds her gaze. Then he holds out his hand.

She's dreaming about Ben now. She doesn't remember the last time she told him she loved him. She doesn't remember the last time he told her he loved *her*, but she wishes she'd said it all the same. If she walks backward through her memories, she thinks it was evening when she last saw him. Late evening. Dozing on the couch, a book on her stomach. Maybe she was dreaming. Maybe she was watching Grant pace or flop on the sofa or lay on the floor and smile up at her. Or maybe she was sitting in numb silence, feeling the weight of the world crowd in closer, tightening her lungs.

And he left. And she didn't know she wouldn't see him after that.

And she wants to scream at him to come home. She sees it over and over and over again: his retreating back, the screen door snicking shut, his footfalls on the squeaky steps, and the crunch of gravel growing fainter as he walks away and doesn't come back.

Slam. Crunch. There he goes.

He won't come back. But when she sees him again he'll be too relieved to be angry, she'll be too relieved to feel betrayed, they'll laugh. When was the last time they laughed together? She'll spin her pistol. Holster it. *Yeehaw.* Like the Westerns. *Dad, I dealt with it. Dad, I did my best.*

There he goes. *Slam.*

Grant should be here. Grant should hold out his hand and smile through eyes like rainclouds. *Don't you trust me?*

Where are you? Where? Why did you leave?

There is no one to lead her down into the labyrinth, but she falls anyway. Her soul leaves her body behind and finds wings and golden feathers. She does not fly. She sits in the bottom of the darkness like a bird on the floor of a mine, because there is no labyrinth. Not anymore. No corridors branch off for her choosing. She gazes up at the splintering crack, the tear in the universe, unveiled and terrible before her eyes.

She's come to the end.

There is no longer a labyrinth. It is this: a gaping wound in reality, and a bird. The rip grows wider. Through the blinding light, there are shapes and figures. There are things waiting on the other side. She does not think she wants them let loose.

A tendril of darkness whispers through her feathers.

"One. Two. Three."

There's a pulse, the echoing vibrations of ticking clock hands counting up to something terrible. *"One. Two. Three."*

Slam. Crunch.

"*Primus. Secundus. Tertia.*" There's a voice at the end of the labyrinth. The voice is not Grant's.

He won't come back. *Slam. Crunch.*

"One. Two. Three."

No. Stop. But Ben won't stop leaving and the fissure won't stop growing and she shrinks beside its expanse, and she shrinks into the sofa, and she reaches out but no one is there to lead her to the light.

Stop!

She lurches off the sofa. She lurches upright. A hand claps over her mouth.

Veronica tastes cold flesh and sees scuttling forms behind her eyelids. She lashes out in the dark. She scrambles upright.

Harry Markus pins her back down. He doesn't remove his hand. In the light of the dying fire, he puts a finger to his lips. "Someone's here," he hisses.

Veronica drags his hand away and spits out the taste. She shoves him off with her elbow. "Get off me." Her heart hammers into her ribcage, but the Mumblers aren't here, the Mumblers are dead, they should really be terrified of her and stay far away. "Get off."

He intensifies the finger-to-lips gesture and rises to his feet. Howard and Henry are already awake.

The barn is quiet, the midnight breeze has died. Veronica tastes chalk and dust. Her spine crawls.

Harry looks at his brothers and motions to the creaking barn doors. *I'm going out.* Howard shakes his head.

"I'm going too," Veronica whispers.

Harry shrugs. He reaches inside his coat as they inch forward; he holds out a gun to Veronica and switches off the safety. She takes it as he pulls a knife from his boot.

Clouds have swallowed up the moonlight again. Through the gaping doorway, the night is like something from a horror film: still, silent, full of awful potential. Veronica shrinks into herself. The door creaks and sways. She can barely make out Harry beside her, putting out his foot to stop the door from shutting. She can barely make out the swaying grass right in front of her.

The silence.

The night explodes into daylight. Brutal light. White light. A dozen floodlights and flashlights burning in her face. Something electric and radiant like a sun.

Veronica stumbles back. She crashes against the barn doors. She raises the gun and fires blindly into the grass.

The gunshot has not faded from her ears when the shouts reach her, and it sounds like a dozen voices screaming from megaphones, overlapping, all at once, pouring in from all directions: "We have weapons trained on both of you! Drop your weapons! Drop your weapons now or we'll open fire!"

Her mouth tastes like dust. The smoke is thick.

"Tell the others to come out with their hands up! Drop your weapons!"

She can hardly see Harry through the smoke–*is there smoke?* He's looking at her. For once she's glad she can see his eyes, bright, inhuman. He shakes his head. She blinks, eyes streaming, and says, "There aren't anymore. It's just us."

Then Harry is moving.

Veronica drops to a crouch as a great wind rips through the field. It flattens the grass; it reveals the armored figures bearing the lights, weapons propped in the soft soil, legs in cargos and combats. She can't catch her breath. She grips handfuls of soil.

One of the figures wheels back and collapses into the grass, a knife buried handle-deep in their chest. Harry Markus hooks the leg of another and drops them. He has their firearm. He has a knee in their face. Over the roar of the wind, Veronica hears bones crunch.

A shout from a greater distance: *"We found them. They were climbing out the back."*

He has a gun. He disarms another soldier, blade to the neck, holds him there and begins firing into the field. The megaphones are screaming. The wind is screaming. Harry uses the man as a shield as he backs towards the barn.

They won't kill me. They won't kill me. They won't kill me. Veronica rises from her crouch. She raises her gun again. She thinks of little mason jars and milk bottles balanced on a sawhorse, she aims at a floodlight, she fires.

Glass shatters. The light goes out. Headtorch beams redirect into her face, the wind floods her ears, suddenly her senses are overrun and Veronica stumbles, she finds her knees, she loses the gun. Her eyes crowd with tears. *Fuck.* She can't see anything. She can't feel anything. Blood rushes, pulse hammers, the soil is damp on her knuckles. Her skin is burning. *Fuck.*

The lights advance. Somewhere nearby, vehicles creep through the field.

The wind hitches.

And Veronica feels that curl of smoky air wrap around her neck, feels the wings in her ribcage. Her skin cools. The roaring wind dulls in her ears, dulls to a hum. She shivers and leans into it, the darkness and lightning and pulsing gash in the fabric of reality, letting in all the wrongness, the otherness. She hums.

—*'til eternity passes away, just to spend them with you*—

Harry Markus shouts, as if from a great distance.

One, two, three, she thinks. *One. Two. Three. Click, crunch, slam. The screen door slamming over and over and over and over again in the wind, the lightbulb flickering, switchblades snapping open. Click, boom.*

The world unravels around her, one thread at a time.

Good. More.

Veronica finds her feet. The ground is shaking. The barn is shaking around her, behind her. The lights come crashing down. Hands grasp at her, drag her down to her knees in the cold soil. She twists and screams, she kicks at the men closing in around her.

The wind howls. The barn doors slam and groan. Electricity pulses through her body. *Snap. Crack. Boom.* Her limbs jolt. Her mind spasms and quiets.

She can't drag herself out of the dark. She can't.

Veronica falls back into her familiar darkness, into a place where restless feathers and pulsing energy wait. A place where Grant can no longer reach her.

41

Through the winding blue corridors, Benedict Lewis hears voices.

He crouches behind Peter's casket and holds his breath. He listens through the ringing in his ears. He is not a religious man, but he prays. *Dear God. I'm so close. So close.*

He cannot make out what they're saying. Their voices are not raised in alarm, so they haven't found the body yet. After a moment, when they do not come closer, Benedict slips out from behind the casket and creeps down the hall. He pauses every few steps, listening for their approach.

"How many?" It's a woman's voice. It carries; this doesn't feel like the sort of place to speak at full volume.

"Ten is enough for now," says a man with a thick midwestern accent. "That's what Halleck said."

"Oh, if Halleck said it—"

"Don't."

"This is not his area. He's never been down here, has he? He hasn't seen them. He wants us to kill people in their sleep, but he cannot stomach to watch. How is that right? Tell me how that is right."

"He doesn't *have* to. That's what it means to be the big boss man."

She mumbles something. The man does not respond.

Ben looks back at Peter's casket. He imagines the body within—long limbs splayed out like a frog pinned to a dissection board, his face slack with years-long sleep.

He needs to get him out. He needs to get them both out.

He moves towards the bend in the corridor. He slides the gun from its holster. He switches off the safety. He's already killed one man—why not another? Why not anyone else who gets in his way? He's always struggled with subjective morality.

Ben catches the woman in the chest, and the man in the side. A stray shot buries itself in the wall, and he prays he has not set off any alarms. He's praying more and more often these days, it seems. Perhaps he's religious after all.

He finishes off the man when he gets closer, a clean shot to the head. Their puffy yellow HAZMAT suits catch a lot of the blood, but there's more with every passing moment. He thinks there must be a better way to do this, a way with less blood. It gets all over his hands as he heaves the bodies into the corner where he left the guard. It leaves stains on the clean white floor. The puddles are already skimmed over.

A cart waits in the corridor beyond the cryochamber. It's a miniature truck bed for the bodies, a tarp to conceal them. The executioners' biohazard masks rest on the tailgate. He pictures the two of them in their plastic yellow suits trundling back through the many layers of the compound with a heap of ten dead humans piled in the back of their cart, arms dangling loose from the tarp, killed in gentle sleep. Maybe Peter was meant to be one of them. Inside the truck cab he finds a couple vacuum-sealed parcels with the same disposable biohazard suits. He takes one back into the cryochamber.

Peter's casket rests on a trolley. The wheels are stiff from disuse; Ben has to use his full weight to shove it along the blue-lit hall. It's a strange, desperate procession—a lone pallbearer, abandoning all the other in their sleep. *I'm sorry. I'm not a hero. I'm just a man.* He's a murderer now. Sweat stings his eyes.

He's out of breath by the time he wedges the trolley through the doorway into the corridor. How much time does he have? Not enough. Even if he somehow misses the second guard returning with the medic, it's only a matter of minutes before they realize he's on the loose. The moments run together, liquid memory; he has no idea how much longer he might have.

His limbs are shaky. His lungs are weak; he's never had good lungs, the smoking made it worse, the panic does nothing to help. It takes all his strength to heave the bottom of the fogged case onto the truck bed, and even more to push it all the way onto the platform.

He kicks the trolley back into the cryochamber. He drags the bodies out one by one, piles them on the cart around the casket. He secures the tarp over the truck bed.

Benedict climbs into the cart. He starts the engine. He doesn't allow himself a sigh of relief; he hardly breathes at all.

There is nothing to be relieved about. Not yet.

ARC is in a state of chaos like Halleck has never witnessed. Although, to be fair, he hasn't been in the job long. He inherited his position from a string of aging ex-military psychos, the first of which was fired for trying to put all the prisoners into a cryosleep (he was "tired of listening to them crying") and the second of which became claustrophobic and hopelessly lost in the lower levels of the compound, eventually giving up entirely; they found him hanged in a deserted office deep in the belly of ARC. Halleck's direct predecessor was a quiet German man who played chess with his officers while prisoners starved to death in their cells. He'd leave the bodies for weeks; he said he wanted to send a message to nearby captives.

Westmore eventually decided to switch up tactics by putting the thirty-two-year-old Anthony Halleck in the role of ARC's Director, the idea being to employ someone young and ambitious. He'd been at ARC for five years before that, but he's still quite confident that he has no idea what he's doing and has no business working alongside people like Andre Billings and Agent X.

"Was it ever like this before?" he says. He stands on the catwalk above the cavernous entry chamber to the compound. The freight elevator to the surface grinds open to reveal yet another truckload of sedated monsters. ARC security swarms the vehicle as it rolls into the hall and screeches to a stop.

Danica Danilovskaya clips her chirping radio back to her belt. "No. I won't lie. No."

Halleck rubs his temple. He feels like she's mad at him. But she's always like this, he reminds himself: brusque, unreadable. Today she's just extra switched-on, and Halleck finds it hard to talk to her like this. With every new garbled report of refugees acting out and complaints about relocating prisoners, her jaw seems to get tighter, her sentences more clipped.

She looks at him. Her features are small and fierce on her broad face; her eyes are chips of ice. "Someone needs to take over refugees. It cannot be me. I am too busy. Fix this."

"Okay," he says. He turns back to the floor. The truck rolls off into the next room, where the creatures will be unpacked into labs and cells. Halleck foresees dissections and a lot of visiting biologists. And medical people. He doesn't like medical people, ever since he cracked open his knee in high school and spent too many days trapped in a hospital. And then rehab. He'd prefer that they immediately transfer the creatures to Jorgen's lab over at BEESWAX, but Halleck has surprisingly little power over current ARC operations. "Sofia Kovala."

"Tell her."

"I will."

"I cannot handle the detainees if I am also handling Lawrence Cage's staff members. They are trouble. Sofia will deal with it."

Danica has always referred to the prisoners as detainees. Halleck thinks this a strange, transitional designation, suggesting that the ARC inhabitants will someday be released. "I know," he says. "You won't handle them anymore. We just don't have anywhere to send them yet. Westmore hasn't cleared the transfer to the Canada facility. I...don't know why."

Danica crosses her arms. "You are moving detainees to the lower levels to make room for aliens and refugees. They are all moving around the same area. Too close. Too much contact. I don't know where the detainees are being kept now, I don't know which cells. This is happening too fast. No one is trained."

Well, I wasn't either, Halleck thinks. Then he realizes maybe it's him she's referring to. "I'm not comfortable with it either," he says. He hasn't been comfortable in days. He isn't sure he's been comfortable in his entire life.

"Where is Andre Billings?"

"He's gone to meet Hawk at the compound."

Danica points with her chin. "What is that?" A lumpy tarped flatbed creeps into the entry chamber. Its driver is clad in a biohazard suit. The truck pulls to a stop before the freight doors.

Halleck recognizes that cart, and the yellow plastic suit. He swallows. "We're clearing out space."

"Space."

"In the cryochambers."

Danica has a much higher tolerance for this sort of thing than Halleck does, but even she looks vaguely uneasy. "Does anyone know?"

"I've gathered no one here likes to acknowledge the cryochambers or what we do to maintain them." Halleck sighs. He unclips the radio from his belt and raises it to his lips. "This is Anthony Halleck." Across the chamber, the guard at the freight doors tilts his head to the radio on his shoulder. "Let the truck through. And tell the guys up top."

The guard waves the truck through. The elevator doors slide open to accommodate the flatbed.

Halleck turns to Danica, who has schooled her features back to impassive. "There's...a cremation center in the countryside," he says.

"Oh," she says. "That's decent."

On a fine ocean-sprayed morning on the coast of Maine, hidden doors snick open in an overgrown levee. A tarp-covered flatbed rolls out of the shadows and crunches down a pebbled path. Beyond, a man in a guard's post flips a switch. The security gate grinds open; he waves the truck on through.

When he's out of sight, Benedict Lewis pulls off his mask. He breathes great gulps of salty air, he blinks—eyes streaming—into the light of day. He never thought he'd see daylight again. He never believed he'd really get out. Now he has bodies in the back of his truck, now he has a casket with something breathing inside, and inside his gloves, there is blood on his hands.

He doesn't stop driving. He doesn't slow down. He sobs until he's raw and empty, he sobs himself to numbness.

Above him, the sun is rising.

42

The hours and days bleed together into one endless stream of motion, of opening eyes and catching breaths and sinking once more into evil darkness.

In the brief windows between blinding wakefulness and deep unconsciousness, Harry Markus catches bits of past and present—footfalls thundering down dark streets running with fresh blood and stony sediment, fingers twitching towards a weapon that is always just slightly out of reach, while blows strike the back of his head, and his brothers' brains are blown out in strings of pale tissue—they fall at his feet and he begs to be stricken down beside them. But he will not die.

"Three brothers," says Billings. His voice weaves its way through the shadows, caressing Harry's consciousness. He claws his way to the surface. "Three different stories. A slew of impressive allegations against each of you, from meddling to outright treachery."

Harry's arms throb. His cheek presses into a cold tabletop, and he tastes rust. His vision is still blurred when he peels himself upright. He feels the shackles before his eyes clear; cuffs linked to the table, chains around his ankles, a figure seated opposite him in a very white room, the blankness of which makes him question whether he's still unconscious. His mind and body are disjointed. It's too bright. His shoulders are light without the familiar weight of his coat.

"It begs the question," says Billings, "where *do* your loyalties lie?"

The fog clears. Andre Billings' face betrays only the slightest tinge of disapproval, but Harry doubts the man is terribly shocked by the turn of events. Billings never really trusts anybody, does he? His uniform is perfectly wrinkle-free, his hair ever within regs. He clasps a brown leather folder on his lap. He sits ramrod straight, yet manages to exude a sort of inscrutable ease.

"Where do you think my loyalties lie?" says Harry.

"Honestly," says Billings, "I don't know. I'm not sure that you even know."

This is a man, Harry thinks, that he may have admired in another lifetime, if his own experience had not taught him to despise authority figures. As it is, he wishes Billings would drop dead.

Billings flicks open the folder, but maintains eye contact. "You joined North Enterprises three years ago, and have since completed over thirty missions, saved the lives of twelve of your fellow agents, and have proven yourself 'dependable yet volatile', according to your superiors. Yet, when asked, the men whose lives you saved refuse to vouch for your integrity. You are not only universally disliked but, it seems, feared."

When the silence lingers and it becomes clear that Billings will not continue, Harry fishes for words that will betray nothing.

"Perhaps they should stop being afraid," he says.

Billings' jaw tightens. He flicks the folder shut; it seems more of a prop than anything. "You were never meant to be involved in the Benedict Lewis operation. All information was classified. You not only violated that classification, but you deserted your assignment and interfered with a highly-sensitive operation." Billings tilts his head slightly. "Your brother Howard claims that this behavior is most unlike you. He says you wouldn't have knowingly deserted an assigned team. He says you couldn't possibly care enough to meddle in something that doesn't concern you." He pauses, perhaps for dramatic effect, perhaps to elicit a response. "Your brother Henry says, I quote: 'Harry does whatever he wants'."

Fuck you too, Henry.

Billings sets the folder on the edge of the table and crosses his arms, finally sitting back and relaxing a bit. It's calculated, this change in demeanor. "What do you know about the creatures who overran North Enterprises?"

"I know that Henry and Howard tried to warn Cage about them. They were ignored."

Billings does not blink. "Anything else?"

They ruined my life. Although perhaps it had been ruined from the start. It's easier to blame the Mumblers than it is every other element that has shaped Harry's identity.

"Your brother Howard called them Mumblers," says Billings.

And Harry thinks, *fuck you, Howard.*

"Why did he call them that? It seems you three are more familiar with these creatures than anyone realized."

Why would you say that, Howard? Why wouldn't you keep your mouth shut? Harry stares at Billings. The words are all caught up in his mouth, his mind is still bleary—*make a plan, make a plan, you can save this.* "Do you know what X called them?"

Billings' gaze is level.

"Myrmen." The word cuts through the silence of the chamber, foreign and frightening, a purr through gritted teeth. A muscle twitches in Billings' cheek. *Go on, Harry. Salvage this. Drive the blade home.* "Did you know he had an agreement with them? He was corresponding with them. They had an agreement. They cornered me in St. Louis. He called them off like trained animals. He intervened on the condition that I deliver Benedict Lewis' work and his daughter directly to him. "

"To him?"

"Him. Not North Enterprises. Not BEESWAX."

Billings' face betrays nothing. "You refer to him in the past tense. Is that an admission of murder?"

Harry's stomach is clenched in knots. Rage like magma trickles through his veins, warming his joints, loosening his muscles. He's clinging to composure by his raw fingertips. He could raze cities.

"Allowing him to return to North Enterprises was his death sentence," says Harry. "But you don't really care about that. You didn't want to work with him from the start. Not since the funeral."

A glint of understanding flickers in Billings' eyes. His lips narrow. "You've known Veronica Lewis since Dane's Chapel. Tell me about her."

This is a battle of wills, of underlying threats. Setting aside weapons for later use. "She's simple and she's mad."

"And her father's research?"

Those precious pages, caught up in the otherworldly wind. Flittering across the imploding rooftop like leaves, like feathers, ripped free of his fingers. Flames lick his ribcage. "She never found it," says Harry.

One. Two. Three.

The fabric of time and space stretches and separates. The edges of reality soften, the fine lines blur. Poison fumes billow in the scentless breeze. You're in a mineshaft. There's no way out.

You're a bird in a cage. Count your dying breaths. One. Two. Three. You're already dead.

"*Get ready.*"

For what?

"*For the end.*"

Veronica is in a place she does not know. It might be a coffin.

The world is cold and clean, nothing like the blood-tinged air of North Enterprises, nothing like the sweet-smelling mountain breezes of Dane's Chapel. She's come to the end. Man abhors nature and enters into the ruthless embrace of sterile modernity.

"She's awake." The voice comes from a great distance, but with each syllable it grows closer.

"Careful with the sedatives. Don't put her back under."

Veronica's eyes grind open. She blinks away the blur.

"I know you can hear me, Miss Lewis. You've led us on quite the chase."

She's reclined in a hospital bed—no, a cot. A stretcher. Whatever it is, it isn't meant for sleeping, because it's impossibly hard and digs into her spine. She tries to move, but her limbs are weighted down, aching dully, just painful enough that Veronica knows they're still there. She blinks and a face comes into focus, hovering bedside. She recognizes that face. It puts the taste of stale store-bought cookies in her dry mouth; she'd almost prefer the nitrous oxide.

"Oh, the PI." Her tongue is stiff and shriveled.

"You may call me Andre," he says, "if you'd like."

Oh, he's trying to be nice. How sweet. How lovely it would be to gouge out his fucking eyes with my fingernails. Veronica's eyebrows pinch together. "What am I–how did we get here? Where are we?"

"You're safe," says Billings. "We can speak freely here, just the two of us. What do you remember from the past few days?"

Days? It's been days? A thread of desperation corkscrews around her vocal cords. Veronica strangles the rage into innocent confusion, which is a lot more difficult than it might seem. She's surprised to find tears warming her eyes. "Not much. Nothing. Am I in...New Mexico?"

Billings quirks an eyebrow. "What is the last thing you can remember?"

"I think...I was in Tulsa. I was going to New Mexico. Are we in New Mexico?" Her eyes flick behind him, take in the steel door and windowless walls. Billings catches her eye. She lowers her voice, lets it crack. "He isn't here, is he?"

"Who?"

He isn't taking the bait. She lets a tear spill down her cheek. *God, what a fucking brilliant actress.* "Harry Markus."

"Harry Markus," says Billings.

Veronica flinches. She drops her voice to a conspiratorial whisper, as if Harry might be listening, as if that's a terrifying notion. "I got away from him in St. Louis. And then in Tulsa he–I don't remember after that." She lets the tears flow freely–exhausted tears, stressed tears, tears because her eyeballs are dry as fuck. "I don't know. I don't remember. He doesn't know where I am, does he?"

Billings gazes down at her. If he feels any pity, it's fleeting and indiscernible. His tone is flat. "Do you really expect me to believe that you *lost* Harry Markus, and he only found you again in *Tulsa?*"

Veronica's run out of tears, and she doesn't feel up to begging.

Perhaps her performance was overkill. "Okay, fine," she snaps. "Am I not allowed to go on a cathartic cross-country road trip following my father's suicide?"

Billings raises his eyebrows.

"Okay, you got me," she says. "I brought along the cute guy from the funeral—"

Billings reaches into the breast pocket of his immaculately pressed uniform. He holds up a polaroid.

Veronica falls silent.

"Miss Lewis," says Billings, "I underestimated you once before, and was forced to escape the local county police. It was, to say the least, annoying. We have all suffered for your actions. My partner is dead, murdered by one of your accomplices. Let's put a stop to the lies now. I'll speak plainly with you. Be honest. We can come to a conclusion less-devastating for both parties."

Oh, so many masks to choose from. It's all crumbling down around her now. Shall she become weepy and distressed? A belligerent teenager? Something with horns and long teeth? *One, two, three.* She's ticking down to something inevitable. It's coming whether she plants her feet or not.

"Devastation." Veronica smiles. "I don't know, it's been coming up all sunshine and lollipops for me."

"Miss Lewis—"

"Why don't you just leave us alone? How about that?" She drops the smile as quickly as it was conjured. "Leave me and my dad alone. It's all over, anyway. None of it matters. Just let us be and move on with your life. Retire and get a beach house in Florida."

There's a moment of silence, and Veronica fantasizes that her words might have hit a chord. *Retirement. Beach house.* Who doesn't love to hear that depressing elderly-people shit?

"You know why you're here," says Billings.

"I can't help you."

"You already have." He opens a folder across his lap. He pulls out a scattering of black-and-white scans—blurry and speckled with pixels, crumpled with near-illegible writing. He pinches one between thumb and forefinger, holds it up for her to see. Star-charts and scrawled formulas. "Recognize it?"

Gone, Harry Markus had said. Gone. Not destroyed. Just…gone.

But it isn't. She can't breathe.

He isn't here to interrogate her. He's here to gloat.

Billings takes her silence for obstinance. He places the scans back into their folder, shuts it gently, and bands it shut. He speaks to someone outside of Veronica's vision. "Put her back under."

"No." But the word is scarcely out of her mouth when she feels herself slipping—slipping—slipping back into that shadowy space within her, empty, quiet, apocalyptic. She clings to wakefulness by her fingertips.

She slips. She falls.

43

"It was the wind."

"It was a terrible wind, but it was more than that. I haven't felt anything of the sort in years. It was as if–"

"I said. It was only the wind."

"It didn't feel like the wind, Harry...not in the slightest. It felt like the end of the world. It wasn't natural. Could the Mumblers do such a thing?"

"Oh, say it again, Harry. Say 'it was only the wind'. I'm sure if you say anything often enough we're bound to believe it."

"Henry–"

"Say it again. You do love the taste of secrets and lies. Nothing much ever changes, does it? Only the scope of these things."

In her dream, Veronica is running. Her feet carry her through a collapsing city. On either side, great walls of black stone dissolve into landslides of rubble. She can't see her own legs for the dust. Smoke fills her lungs.

She is a bird. She skims over the top of the destruction, hurtles through the darkness while the world caves in around her. This road is a ravine, an underwater trench. Things twist and swirl in the eddy. Her heartbeat is thunderous.

There's someone waiting at the end of the ravine, on the edge of the city. There's someone standing with their back facing her, a silhouette, a shimmering outline of humanity. A finishing line. If she can make it, she's free.

The avalanche stirs the bird's feathers. The city breathes down its neck.

This is it. This is escape. Crawl your way out of the mines. Somewhere, the sun is rising.

The figure is a girl with black fingertips and demons crawling under her skin. It's a man with eyes full of stars and blood on his hands, gulping lungfuls of fresh air. For a mere instant, it's a pale boy with a terrible scar.

Then the bird plummets towards a faceless figure. Something stitched of shadows.

This is not an escape. This is a threat, this is eternity, this is a trap.

Let me go!

Her wings stop working. Her feathers are on fire. The city seethes at her back. The creature holds out its hands to her.

Let me go!

She is a broken bird at the base of a mineshaft. *You were never meant to escape.* Something faceless and formless looms above her. Three wolves prowl through the shadows.

"At the barn, Harry, something happened–you can't deny that. It smelled like lightning. The whole barn was shaking. Do you suppose it was BEESWAX that did it?"

"Howard, leave it."

A wolf in a nursery.

Veronica opens her eyes with some difficulty. The cell is cinderblock. There's a worn steel door of rust-red to her right, a foul-smelling plastic bin to her left. Damp cold leeches through her leggings and the worn fabric of the Harley Gharials shirt; she feels it in each of her vertebrae from where she slumps in the corner of the cell, her head tilted at a stiff angle against the adjacent wall, her forearms pale and bare. Goosebumps prick her flesh. Her hairs stands on end.

She raises her eyes. Harry stands above his brothers, shoulders pressed into the wall, arms crossed. His trench coat is missing. He has a human form and she finds this unsettling.

Howard sits cross-legged nearby, fingers tapping on his knees, head tilted back to look up at Harry. He's been stripped of his flight suit and reduced to black joggers and an undershirt. Henry sits in the corner diagonal from Veronica, head resting against the wall, one knee pulled to his chest. His eyes are shut. His posture does not suggest sleep.

Veronica's gaze drifts back to Harry. He's watching her. There is nothing approachable about this version of Harry Markus, with his bare arms and his cold sea-glass eyes. He's a cornered animal liable to bite.

Howard follows his brother's gaze. "Do you know what happened at the barn?" he asks Veronica.

Harry does not look away. Veronica tilts her head. "Probably tectonic plates."

"What plates?"

"It happens in the midwest." She doesn't know shit about fault lines. She looks at Harry Markus and she sees a wolf, and there is something in her chest that wants to explode into a fury of feathers and screams. *So close to escape. So close to something like freedom.* Her body seizes up in a shiver.

One, two, three. Primus, Secundus, Tertia.

"They're sending Westmore." Henry doesn't sit up when he speaks. He drops the information like a bomb, like it has power.

Westmore. Veronica eases upright so her spine aligns with the wall; joints quietly pop and crack, and a chill settles across her back. "Who's Westmore?"

"She heads up the X-System," says Howard. He glances sidelong at Harry, as if expecting his brother to weigh in "We've...never met her. I suppose most people haven't. She's a bit of a phantom."

The silence that follows is ominous—an unknown threat, a stunning catalyst obscured by sheets of secrecy, and it's breathing down their necks. A haunting.

Something vast and faceless is descending upon the world. Her world. In a rush, she misses the close and familiar cage of Dane's

Chapel, with its fresh air and all the bad blood and bad kids and fresh hell and the predictable threats of weather and wildlife. She thinks burning her dad's trailer was the final *man versus nature* move in her narrative. "Is that where we are? The X-System? Where is that?"

"Billings is here," says Harry. "That suggests BEESWAX."

"But we don't really know where we are," Howard tells her.

"It's probably BEESWAX," says Harry, with perfectly feigned confidence that makes her want to rip off his face skin.

"So what does that mean?" she says. "Bringing in Westmore? What's that mean for us?"

Howard ducks his head to his chest and rubs his hands through his hair in a slow, anxious gesture. "It means...something big is happening." He speaks to the floor.

"Big like Mumblers and a compound imploding?" says Veronica.

"Big like us," says Henry, his tone altogether unextraordinary. His voice is low and he still hasn't bothered to raise his head.

Veronica shifts; her tailbone is sore. "You saw Andre Billings?"

"*He* did," says Henry.

He. Him. Everyone knows who he's talking about, because everything is about Harry Markus. His brothers orbit around him, and Veronica's existence in their strange circle poses a thrilling challenge to the delicate gravitational balance.

"Did he tell you?" she says.

Silence. A low exhale. "Tell me what?"

"They found it."

She was waiting for this, for the spark of understanding, for the muscles to tense around his shoulders and his head to whip around. Henry opens his eyes to gaze at the ceiling as Harry pushes off the wall and faces her.

How satisfying to see her own dull horror reflected in his face; perhaps that makes her a bad person. She doesn't feel like a particularly good person. She feels like a daughter who has betrayed her father. She feels like the villain in her own story.

"They found it," she repeats. "So I don't know what happens now."

Ben only stopped once, and that was to get rid of the bodies.

He rolled them off the flatbed and onto the rocky Maine shoreline. They floated stiff and gray in the shallow water, like horrible buoys. He stood shins-deep in the water with the bodies floating around him. He prayed they'd be swept out by the tide. Part of him wished he'd be devoured by the waves, dragged under and suffocated in a cool, dark embrace. *I killed them.*

Then he trudged back up to the shore and started the truck again.

The breeze pulls him back to life. He can feel the air on his skin again—cold and salty and savory with the smell of growing things and damp soil—and occasionally, as he bumps down narrow back roads, his heart fractures and deep relief floods his body. *I'm alive. I'm free. I found Peter. I'll find Veronica and I'll find Grant.*

He is in an empty warehouse behind an abandoned gas station, at the edge of some town. He propped the rolling door open with a rusty paint can, and a narrow streak of red evening light cuts through the garage. There's barely room for him and the flatbed. He isn't sure what state this is, how many miles lie between him and Maine, but he keeps expecting someone to break through the door and drag him back into the shadowy compound. He still can't shake the chill from his skin. The light seeping under the door stains his hands red.

I'm alive. This is life. I'm breathing and the air is rich with minerals and green things and a world that still belongs to me. I can get this back.

He'd like to get farther away, but he doesn't know how much fuel the truck's got left, and he doesn't want to risk breaking down on the side of a road. He needs to do this now.

Benedict Lewis draws the tarp from the flatbed. The casket's windows are still fogged. He walks a slow circle around the truck, inspecting the vessel from every angle—bundles of wire and bulky battery packs, blank screens and inserts for plugs and tubes. There's a pressurized tank at one end, with a dial set to two. He rests a knee on the flatbed and leans forward to press his ear to the tank; a soft hiss fills the silence.

He doesn't know what he's doing. This is BEESWAX technology. He draws back and takes a deep breath. He sets the dial to zero.

The garage goes quiet. Ben hadn't even noticed the gentle hum emitting from the casket, but now that the flow of gas has died, he's aware of how heavy his breathing is, and how the walls creak and groan in the coastal breeze.

He runs a hand along the side of the case. He searches for hinges.

In a rusting garage on the edge of a desolate town, a fog-filmed casket creaks open with a pop of released pressure. Benedict Lewis covers his face and steps away, but not quickly enough to escape the taste of something bitter and sweet.

He waits for the gas to empty. He waits for the air to clear. A night breeze snakes from under the garage door and carries away the final tendrils of vapor.

The tank emits a final sputtering hiss. Benedict hesitates before putting out his hand. His palm hovers over the body, the chest. And he slowly lowers his hand. He holds his breath, shuts his eyes, listens through the thunder of blood in his ears. He flexes his fingers.

There. The soft beating of a heart, rising, quickening. *Awakening. Drums welcoming the troops to war.* The body nestled within the casket is not hollow. There is still life in its flesh.

His vision blurs through a mist of tears. Ben touches the familiar face, the hair tipped with synthetic frost, and once again feels the heartbeat growing stronger and stronger and stronger, and with each beat and moment and breath in his lungs, Ben's body floods with warmth.

Sometime later—he is not sure how much time passes, time does not matter, time cannot touch this sacred scene—eyelids flicker. A snap of silver-gray, ice on pale lashes. A gaze that wanders, distant, until settling on Benedict. Recognition dawns.

A flicker of a smile touches Peter Webber's face. The fog clears. His eyes come alive.

"Hi, Benny."

44

Two sets of footsteps echo down the gray corridor. Two pairs of crisp leather boots clip-clop over tiles, two distorted figures slide across the charcoal marble panels lining the hall. Intermittent steel-framed windows spill panels of silver light against the walls; they reveal a skyline split between a billowing gray morning and a seething forest of black firs. More gray marble. The overhead light twitches like a muscle.

It's a gray sort of day.

Andre Billings always feels a bit gray. He's come to believe that he simply does not possess the capacity to feel things the way he should, the way other people seem to. He's made peace with that. Rarely does he allow himself to mourn the lukewarm temperament and pitiless gaze he's grown into, though there are days when he thinks he's drowning on all the things he's incapable of feeling, choking on a thick pool of silence and unspoken screams. This is before he settles back into the cold, stable embrace of duty and protocol.

A cloud of gray carries him from one task to the next, a buffer between input and what might be his conscience. He feels it now, carrying him aloft with his chin raised, straining against the anchor tugging in the pit of his stomach.

The second figure moving down the corridor, matching his pace with short legs and heeled boots, is a swatch of scarlet.

Later, when Westmore closes the conference room door behind her and stands looking at Billings with that cautious intelligence in her pale eyes, no light or life or flush in her porcelain complexion, he feels that she is also gray, but she hides it beneath garnet pantsuits and purplish lipgloss, as if painting life into the face of a corpse. *Morticians do that,* he thinks.

She does not smile, but tilts her head knowingly. A careful arch of her eyebrows, the artful way her hair tucks behind one ear, set and arranged like a staged home. Or an open coffin.

She knows about the grayness, he thinks, nodding back to Westmore, the anchor weighing in his gut. *She knows about duty and emptiness. And what does that make me?*

There was a brief period of time, buried deep in the bowels of her chaotic childhood, wherein Veronica taught herself to make traps from twigs and thread. She'd sit cross-legged in the woods and construct tiny contraptions, leave cobwebby nets of fishing twine under an arranged bed of leaves, make baskets and cages from pine straw. She feels she'd been caught in one of those webs.

She's a restless creature sitting in the belly of the conference chamber, under a cavernous auditorium ceiling and gold-tinted lights, synthetic-wood table spread out like a sea before her, her arms wrapped around the back of a sticky leather seat. Waiting for the prodding and poking to begin. She believes, in a way, that she has helped set this trap for herself.

Her shoulders strain in their sockets. If she can manage to get to her feet, she can slip her shackled wrists above the back of the seat. But the chair is one of those swivelly types she has always envied —which, admittedly, has a certain irony to it—and she doesn't trust her sense of balance.

She never even caught anything in those traps. She just enjoyed making them. She thought she'd be like Billy from *Where the Red Fern Grows* and trap for furs, but when it came down to it, she reclined in a throne of moss and roots, her spine pressed into the damp wood of a tree older than her grandparents, watching birds hop along the creek-bank and bushy-tailed critters twist around tree branches overhead. She didn't want to trap anything. She just wanted to know that she could. She wanted splinters to prove that she could.

The world is disorienting and nightmarish. She can't block out Harry's deep, measured breaths from beside her, nor the sweaty dusty scent of him, both of which are real and looming and grounding her to this moment. She isn't sure *she* is breathing. She feels full of something foreign that she does not understand. *I am a vessel.*

One.

Harry stares down the length of the table, watches the door through his eyelashes, his gaze clear and cold and predatory. A coiled spring, a snake, a wolf in a nursery—he's everything and he's nothing. He's an angry boy. He's a furious god.

Two.

Howard is curled into himself, chin resting on his shoulder, body angled towards his older brother. He's poised and posed like a statue, something freezing and molded from marble, veins in his scarred arms, eyes downcast. Waiting for the killing blow.

Three.

Knees spread and feet planted flat on the floor, rooted and growing independently. Henry's chin is on his chest but he is not sleeping. His skin is so translucent that she can map the green web of veins in the side of his neck.

One, two, three. A bird with a broken wing.

The door opens.

Harry Markus raises his head.

Claire Westmore rests her elbows on the back of the nearest chair and leans into it. She gazes down the length of the table and inspects the collection of strange creatures gathered before her.

She looks a bit like Creed, only sharper. A blunt bob of hair paler than the pale boy's, a sharp jawline parallel to the crisp collar of her ruby-red jumpsuit. Her frame is small and delicate. Her boots sound clicky and heeled. Her eyes are faded and makeup-less, but her lips are painted a glossy blue-red so jarring that Veronica thinks it must be a strategic choice, drawing attention away from her shifting gaze. Veronica won't be distracted by the vampire lips. Westmore looks at her like Veronica's her next meal.

"Which one of you killed my Agent X?"

Her voice is mild and thin, and Veronica reckons Westmore couldn't shout if she wanted to; her narrow chest wouldn't have the capacity.

"Your Agent X was conspiring with the Mumblers against you," says Harry.

He thinks he can maintain some control. He thinks he can intimidate her. But he can't. Westmore doesn't look at Harry Markus like he's an intriguing specimen or even an interesting meal–she looks at him as if he's nothing at all. She tilts her head. Her slinky film of hair casts a strip of shadow across her face. "Xander Schwarztnimble was operating under my orders. He was a loyal participant in the X-System, and now he is dead. One of you four is responsible."

She looks at each of them in turn. *She's a vampire. She's dangerous.* And then: *She took my dad.* Anger clambers into Veronica's throat, strangling her vocal cords; she might combust. She might dissolve. She might burn the world to ashes. The canary is silent but it is not dead.

A light flickers in her periphery. Veronica's eyes snap to the corner of the room. No one else seems to have noticed. Perhaps she is simply hoping.

"And we call them *Myrmen*, Harry," Westmore says. "Mumblers is slang, and quite unprofessional."

While Harry stiffens at the use of his name, something about the word *unprofessional* seals it for Veronica. Professionals kicked Benedict Lewis out of Florida. Professionals kidnapped her dad and left a burnt-out pickup in Lake Tan. Professionals drove Creed and Ted Webber out of their home.

"Myrmen," Veronica says, "are the male mermaids. They're *guy mermaids*. Do you understand how fucking *stupid* you sound?" Under the weight of Westmore's gaze she's a rodent pinned by a bird of prey, just one of those roadkill squirrels with a vulture bearing down from above. She speaks through her teeth. "Where is my dad?"

"We're not here to talk about Benedict Lewis," says Westmore.

"Well, I am." She knows she didn't make it up this time, the light flickering. Still, no one else seems to have seen it: the stutter in the electricity flowing through the room; her rage slicing through the atmosphere like a razor.

Westmore returns her focus to Harry. "To preface the main agenda of this meeting"—as if it is a business meeting, as if all of them but one isn't in shackles—"X and I were the only personnel aware of his unique position in the X-System, which is why he worked with Andre Billings on the mission—"

"Where is my dad?" says Veronica.

Westmore continues as though Veronica didn't interrupt. "X understood that there is a higher purpose. None of you seem to realize the enormity of the damage you have caused to hinder our progress with your unprofessional—"

Veronica imagines that night at the bus station in Tulsa, wills a gruesome streak of white lightning upon Westmore, and finds nothing but the void inside herself, like the pit of a mineshaft. "You didn't hire them because they're fucking professionals," Veronica says. "And you don't get to decide—"

"She didn't hire us at all," says Henry, and even Veronica falls silent. He raises his half-lidded eyes to where Westmore stands. "Lawrence Cage hired us. He doesn't consult with the X-System for recruitment. She didn't even know we existed until Harry went rogue."

Howard turns several shades paler at that, but Harry just grows still—so terribly still. The room temperature drops to absolute zero. And then atoms stop moving.

Westmore raises a perfect eyebrow. "That is true. But I am terribly glad he did recruit you. It's turned out to be awfully convenient. Although something you'll learn about our operation, if you haven't suspected already, is that I have the unorthodox approach of balancing the concepts of fate and strategy. I admit that even I could not have orchestrated this meeting so perfectly. Destiny," she says, to her quiet captive audience, "is an intriguing variable to consider, when you're wrestling with the fate of worlds."

Worlds, Veronica thinks, blandly, running the word over and over in her head. *Oh, she said* worlds. *Worlds.* Such a round world, so precise, so particular. An ominous weight lifts off her shoulders —*a secret. We won't tell anyone.*

But someone always tells the secret, in the end. Fathers say they won't leave as they're walking out the door. Lies are smoother than oil, slicker than blood. Secrets don't stick, they slip out from between Veronica's fingers as she stands on an imploding rooftop and breathes a vicious wind out of the mountains. They flutter away like canary feathers. Nothing is made to last.

"Where is my dad?" Veronica whispers.

"I'm sending you away," says Westmore.

Harry straightens. Howard leans forward, straining against his cuffs. Veronica cannot breathe.

"It is not without due consideration," says Westmore, "that I am sending the four of you somewhere you will not longer be a hindrance and may be of some use to this operation."

"What operation?" says Howard, his voice low.

Veronica knows, she has always known, she's known since that dark planet rose in the night sky above Dane's Chapel, since dreams of smoke and cities of rubble imprinted themselves in her bloodstream.

Westmore straightens and clasps her arms behind her back.

I want my dad, Veronica thinks, desperately, as her heart shatters.

"In approximately three months' time, the four of you will be aboard a spacecraft," says Westmore, "and bound for an off-world mission."

He can't look at his brothers, can't even look at Westmore.

He hears the words over and over and over again. Her voice fades to static like a dying radio, and his mouth is open, but he cannot speak. There is lead in the pit of his stomach. It feels an awful lot like being shot in the gut, like having something sharp slipped in between his ribs, like swallowing poison and waiting to die.

She can't know. *She can't. Know.* There's something so sick and wrong about her, Harry is suddenly gripped with the idea that she must be a Mumbler, some form of a Mumbler, somehow connected to the most hideous creatures he can fathom in this moment.

"What the hell are you on about?" says Henry.

Shut up, Henry. Just shut up.

Harry speaks before he can fully construct the thought. "You sent them," he spits. Westmore raises an eyebrow. "You sent the Mumblers to Markusheim."

Veronica Lewis makes a choking sound. Howard flinches at the name, shuts his eyes and sinks into himself as if Harry has made them vulnerable. But they're all stripped to the bone. There's nothing to hide behind now.

"No," says Westmore, "what happened five years ago was outside of my knowledge and control. X and I wouldn't have let that happen, but unfortunately by the time we realized what the Myrmen were planning, it was too late to stop them. And, until quite recently, I was not in possession of the coordinates needed to find the…well." Her gaze slides to Veronica Lewis. "Your father refers to it as the *entry point*."

"Wait," Veronica leans forward against her bonds. She reminds Harry of a dog pulling tight against its leash, feral, foaming. "Wait. Markusheim? Is that a joke? Are you fucking joking? I'm not going to space."

"You are," says Westmore.

"I'll show you the trailer I burnt down," says Veronica, as if anticipating this response. "I'll show you the Webber house if you let him go."

"You are in no place to make bargains." For the first time, an amused smile touches Westmore's purple lips. "How about this instead? How about you do exactly as I tell you, and I won't kill Benedict Lewis. After all, that's the deal we currently have arranged with your father."

"There's nothing there," says Harry, but his own words sound desperate and muffled in his ears. "They destroyed everything. You're just going to send your people to an empty planet. Why? All to send us home?" He wasn't fast enough. He wasn't strong enough. In the end, the hopelessness always catches up to him. He takes it like a bullet to the chest.

"I'm under the impression that quite a bit of the planet's population survived the Myrmens' invasion," says Westmore, no longer smiling. "As for my intentions, those are my own. If I were you, I'd accept the situation and adjust as soon as possible.

Benedict Lewis will die if his daughter steps out of line, and I'm certain I don't need all three Markus brothers to survive the journey. Certainly, some of you are more important than others."

The walls contract. Is this worse than a death sentence? Right now, his body cannot distinguish the difference.

Westmore speaks and Veronica does not hear her. The woman's voice distorts. One by one, the lights in the room flicker and go dead, and still no one notices, no one but Veronica.

There is a foreign presence waiting for her within herself. There's something more alien than the pale boy, more ominous than the low hum of the Mumblers, more ancient than the widening fracture waiting for her when she closes her eyes. Something she suppresses with every fiber of her will. Something that fights for a voice.

Darkness creeps into the corners of the room.

"Consequences," says Westmore, but it isn't Westmore anymore. "Consequences for your own actions. Don't be so surprised, Veronica. Didn't you know this was coming? Didn't you know?"

Shadows writhe in the edges of her vision.

"Canary girl," Westmore croons. "The mad daughter of a mad father. Legacy. There were three and then there were more, Veronica Lewis, did you know that? Of course you do. Look a bit deeper. *Primus, Secundus, Tertia.*"

The shadows encroach—they slither towards Westmore. They eat away at the scene until there is nothing, there is something wearing Westmore's' skin and there is nothing else.

"Of course there were more, Veronica. You thought you were the only one? You thought you were a bird. You thought you were a symbol."

She can see Westmore's teeth. She can't tell if she's smiling.

"You're a loaded gun," says Westmore. "And you're the finger pulling the trigger."

Bang. It slams through her skull—it knocks the breath out of her.

Veronica jerks upright. The lights flicker back to life, and Westmore pauses in her monologue to glance at the ceiling. Other sounds crawl back into Veronica's ears: Harry breathing beside her, the tick of a clock out of view, the hum of air conditioning in the walls, a ragged breath in her throat.

We broke something. A voice hisses past her ear.

Veronica jerks her neck like she's been bit, she swivels and checks over her shoulder. She can't get used to the empty space beside her, the absence in her head, it's going to drive her mad. She can't do this alone, she can't do this without him, she doesn't know who Veronica Lewis is without Grant Webber.

We broke something, says the voice, which is not Westmore and not the pale boy, which might be a *something* and not a *someone.*

It's time to put it back together.

Grant is gone. She imagines Benedict with a gun barrel pressed to the back of his head, the horrible potential in the slightest twitch of the trigger. Her hand is on that gun. She moves, and the bullet moves with her. She takes a wrong step, and her dad is dead.

She can't breathe. *Gone. Not destroyed.* The room tilts at a nauseating angle and she shuts her eyes to block it out.

"*Can we stop it?*" she'd asked Ben.

"*We?*" he said in return. "*I certainly cannot.*"

It's time to put it back together.

She should have burned the notebook when she'd had the chance.

She smells smoke now. She smells Harry Markus and an apocalyptic wind and a street full of fire. Her wings unfurl. Her heart beats against a fragile ribcage. There is a slow groaning like an old god on its deathbed; the sound of an expanding universe surrounds the canary. She's a bird hurtling through a ravine of twisting shadows—alone, buffeted by the wind, buffeted to places she should not go, witness to things she should not see.

It's all wrong. Ben was *wrong.* When he and Peter gazed up into the cosmos and pried those secrets from their forbidden places, they should have put them right back again. They should have padlocked the door and burned down the labs. She might have known Grant Webber. She might have known the real Benedict Lewis.

Instead, she knows too much. This is a spell of silence. Harbinger of Doomsday, canary in a coal mine. The song is over. It is the end.

Some things belong in the shadows.

Epilogue

Somewhere, a girl bursts into flame but is not harmed.

Somewhere, a young man's dreams tell him of a cruel future.

Somewhere, a boy closes his eyes and sees a desert like a blue-gray sea, and moonlight painting the dunes in crescent shadows, and blood staining the sand. The colors bleed together, a ruinous painting.

It still matters, he thinks.

Time slips away like sand in an hourglass. It won't be stopped.

Footsteps pound down the corridor. Rubber treads squeal on tile, catch, scramble. Loose laces snap and crack. Here he comes: shuffling and skipping along the low-lit corridor, an awkward skidding slide that turns into a stumble, arms grooving, eyes blissfully shut. A cassette player bangs at his hip.

The tinny wail of a whistle drifts from his headphones, a boppy guitar riff, and he's off—arms punching, legs kicking, kung fu fighting his way down the hall, oblivious to the world.

These corridors were not made for dancing. Regrettably, none of the BEESWAX HQ was made with boogying in mind: these halls were built for jogging four-abreast and marching in an orderly fashion—which has yet to actually be accomplished—and not for groovy acoustics; his steps make an unsatisfying patting sound. Regardless, he kicks it from the hip.

He whistles (or tries to whistle, but he can't be sure what sort of sound is actually coming out) and claps his hands with the beat drop. He executes a little hop-spin and lurches forward.

His legs pinwheel. He erupts into a sprint.

He ricochets off a wall and launches himself around a corner. Overhead, a light flickers. This particular light has been flickering for seven months, and at this point he has a personal vendetta against the spasmodic fluorescents. He skips backwards to stare it down. Then he wheels around and pounds down the corridor towards a set of steel double doors.

He slams his shoulder into the doors at full speed.

The impact knocks him sprawling. He lands on his butt, out of breath. The headphones fall around his neck, the song cut short.

He blinks up at the doors. They're a gruesome shade of mauve. His tailbone stings. A vague sense of betrayal settles over his heart as he slowly, sorely, hauls himself back to his feet and clicks the cassette player off.

He uses the handle this time.

Down another corridor—walking this time—he bangs on an office door.

"Enter."

He knows he's expected, he knows he's late, he knows etiquette demands a gentle rap on the doorframe and nothing more. But he knocks away in a jaunty rhythm until Andre Billings loses his will to live and opens the door himself.

The lanky young man on the other side is grinning just a bit too widely, a bit too friendly, a fake light behind his gray eyes. He leans into the doorjamb and folds his arms across his chest.

"Oh, hi, Billings," says Grant Webber.

"Sit."

But Grant has already taken a seat in the armchair before Billings' desk. He crosses his legs. His foot jogs side-to-side, up-and-down.

The office is sparse; it barely deserves to be called an office. Grant has never seen Billings do any actual work within this space, only hold conference from behind the desk. He has a straight-backed swivel chair that looks like it came discounted from Office Depot. The walls are white—not eggshell, not even gray—and the floor is the sort of green scruffy carpet that would be well-suited to a mini-golf course, but not an office. Nothing is particularly ergonomic. None of this does anything to alter the perception that Andre Billings is a robot masquerading as human.

When Grant first laid eyes on Billings, it was at his father's funeral. Grant had a napkinful of pigs-in-blankets that he'd pulled bare-handed from a hot tray, and his memories of that day include oil burns on his fingertips. And across the room, a man who looked like he wasn't used to dressing himself outside of a uniform.

Billings stood with his back against a wall, watching the room stiffly without moving his head. He had a plate of store-bought cookies balanced in one hand—the gross type, with an aftertaste like Play-Dough—but Grant never saw him eat one. They didn't speak that day, but Grant remembers thinking: *This man doesn't know how to act human.*

Good to know people don't change.

Billings does not sit behind his desk. He takes the seat beside Grant. This has suddenly become an intimate discussion between friends or colleagues. Grant is neither, and he finds this stupendously entertaining. Andre Billings does not like to be so close to the BEESWAX kids.

"How is your training progressing?"

Grant cups his kneecap with knitted fingers and leans toward Billings. Billings leans away. "Outstanding, Andre. Thank you for taking an interest in my education. Would you like to sign off on my report card?"

Billings narrows his eyes. A brief, intensely-uncomfortable silence lapses between them.

"I can do three pull-ups now," says Grant.

"Okay, enough." Billings breaks. He drags a folder off the desk and flips it open in his lap. He still does that thing where he won't move his head, but he watches Grant out of the corner of his eye. *What is that? Some intimidation tactic?* "What we discuss today will not leave this room. That means you are not permitted to share with Obrien nor Kelly."

"Sharing is caring," says Grant.

Billings has to pause a moment for recovery. Grant smiles pleasantly and the clock on the wall ticks just loudly enough to send spikes of pain through Andre's skull. He takes a deep breath before progressing. "You are familiar with Benedict Lewis."

Grant's foot quits bouncing. "I...guess I am. Yes. Sorta, kinda. Why."

Billings takes his time. He flips through the folder. "Are you familiar with his daughter?"

Veronica Lewis is the sort of person who has spiraled into childhood lore within Grant's memory, like the trip to Disney World they'd taken when he was four, or the mean lady at the post office who refused him a lollipop because he'd been disruptive while waiting in line. (Creed had gotten a lollipop. Life is cruel.) Veronica is a little dark-haired girl who takes his plastic cowboy pistol out of his hands and refuses to give it back. She hangs on her father's leg, gripping his khakis, standing on Benedict's shoes and glaring at Grant like she wants to skin him. He thinks he hit her once. He recalls getting in trouble for that.

Grant clears his throat. He leans back and crosses his arms. "Not really."

"She will be present on the mission."

A chill crawls around on Grant's back. He squirms a little. "Oh. Why?"

"Because she and her father both possess knowledge valuable to the expedition."

"Wait, you're sending Veronica? Why not Ben?" Benedict Lewis in BEESWAX HQ....if he had Ben here, Grant would have closed this case and found his dad years ago.

"We've found that Benedict Lewis is more useful to us here during this time. These are Westmore's orders."

"Uh-huh." What does Ben's *daughter* know?

"Veronica has been assigned to Commander Hawk's squadron. Full assignments will be given after launch, but I'm telling you now because it's pertinent. You are also in Hawk's squad. This is purposeful."

Grant nods. "Because Hawk likes me so much," he says, but there's somewhat less humor behind the words. He finds that he's gnawing the inside of his cheek. He forces himself to stop.

"We want you to keep an eye on her." Billings reaches into the folder flap and extracts three mugshots of an angry-looking young man. No—three different men, all alike, who all seem they are willing the camera to shatter.

Grant leans forward. After a moment of intense inspection, he says, "Which one is she?"

Billings is visibly shaken. He takes a measured breath. "Veronica is one of four new passengers on the mission. There are three brothers she was traveling with. She will likely spend most of her time with them, and we won't stop her. Your job is to establish a connection and gain her trust."

Grant reaches for the photographs, but Billings puts them away. "Am I a spy, Andre?"

"I don't care what you call yourself."

"You want me to become buddy-buddy with Benny Lewis' daughter and extract all her secrets. I assume that means she isn't here of her own volition? No? How terribly unlike this organization to hold people against their will."

Billings snaps the folder shut. "Is this going to be a problem, Webber?"

Is it, Webber?

There was a time not long after his father's funeral when Grant had been pulled out of class to speak to an army recruiter—ridiculous, since he'd had a P.E. waiver for severe asthma since eighth grade. The robot man from the funeral was waiting in the hall. The two of them had taken a long walk around the football field. Grant walked along the bleachers, and his footfalls echoed across the empty lot.

"Where's my dad?" he'd asked.

This was the most honest Billings had ever been with him. They both knew Peter Webber wasn't dead. "He has information vital to world security. His research concerns BEESWAX. He works for us now." *Like he had a choice.* "What did he tell you about us?"

Grant was unconsciously running a thumb along his scar. It had been months, but it still felt fresh. Sometimes his head ached. He stuck his hands in his pockets. "He told me to stay away. Everyone told me to stay away."

"You don't remember what happened that night in the desert."

"No." *It's easier to lie when the lie is fed to you.*

"There's a revolution, young man. A scientific revolution, and it's happening right now. You and your father and his colleagues are caught in the thick of it. Nothing will be the same until the dust settles over this war."

Grant stopped walking, then. "When will that be?"

"That depends on your cooperation. And your father's. You're aware that your story made the state news?"

The conversation was giving him whiplash. "My—?"

"The incident outside the cinema. With the car."

That's what this is about. Grant ducked his head and continued walking. Again he felt the urge to touch his scar, but he kept his hands firmly by his sides. *Think smart thoughts, Grant.* "Yeah. That was wild. Lucky to be alive."

"That's not what the medical report said."

"Man, are you guys stalking me, or something?" Nervous laughter.

That had been the first day he'd brushed off Billings. Sometimes, he feels he gave in too early. Maybe there were other options, and he only would have seen that if he'd stuck it out a bit longer. Other times he feels as if he's crawling closer and closer to the truth about Peter Webber, gaining inches at a time. And most times, he wonders if that's the whole point; he wonders if Billings and Hawk and the rest are doing it on purpose, this game of cat and mouse.

And then sometimes, he feels they are unwittingly handing him a shiny new weapon to stab them in their backs.

"Not a problem at all," says Grant. He grins widely. "When do we start?"

ACKNOWLEDGEMENTS

Unending thanks and praise to my big sister Claudia Edwards, to whom I have dedicated two novels, and not without good reason. She is always my first reader and my chief editor. I'd be remiss if I failed to mention that the world of BEESWAX—including the Webbers, Billings, X, and Hawk—are all Claudia's creations; she handed over the world of Grant Webber and the X System for the sake of this story. *Canary Girl,* from its earliest conception, would not exist without her. She also created Harry Markus.

My parents, Chris and Jeanette, have read endless drafts of this dumpster fire of a novel. My dad in particular would ask to read back-to-back drafts in quick succession, and offered invaluable feedback each time. If they hadn't put books in my hands and stories in my ears from a young, young age, I never would have gotten to the point where I am, impossibly, publishing my third novel.

And as always, thanks to the amazing team of beta readers who swooped in and offered feedback: Dallas Anne Duncan and Elena Arredondo—both women with very busy lives, who generously donated their time and talents to the improvement of this project.

The essence of *Canary Girl* is 14-year-old Abby trapped in a moment in time. This story began its life as a jumbled stew of contributions from three homeschooled teenagers. The memory is static in my mind: my perch on a mattress by the bedroom window, the others sprawled on cushions and cold bamboo floor. It's an image trapped in a snow globe: laughter, shrieks, the liberty of mindless, meaningless creativity that would pave the way through my tumultuous teenage years. I am eternally thankful for this moment. Thnks fr th mmrs.

Abigail C. Edwards was born and raised in North Florida. She graduated from Florida State University in 2022 with a BS in Hospitality & Tourism Management, and in 2023 she earned her Advanced Baking Diploma from the School of Artisan Food in Nottinghamshire, UK. She is the author of *And We All Bled Oil* (2021) and *The Time Walker* (2023). She currently resides in Edinburgh, Scotland.

Printed in Great Britain
by Amazon